THE HUMBLER CREATION

Pamela Hansford Johnson

THE HUMBLER CREATION

HARCOURT, BRACE AND COMPANY, NEW YORK

THE HUMBLER CREATION

Chapter One

'THE last rowers of summer.' The younger man looked pointedly towards the lake, flirtatious eyes slanting the joke.

The other did not see it.

In the middle of the field, in the middle of the autumn park, in deck-chairs, remote from the nice children, the duck-feeding, the boats on the Serpentine, the two men enjoyed the mugginess of the afternoon. There was not much wind. When it did blow, the brittle leaves came towards them over bright grass like a mild tide scuttling in. There seemed to be no sun, but over the trees a spire caught a shine from somewhere. The men wore clerical collars, both were smoking cigarettes. David Beattie, twenty-six years old, had a pipe but it had gone out. It was a concession to his curacy, no pleasure.

It was Saturday, late enough in the year for a few lights to glimmer along Kensington Gore, promising softness, plush, a fire, and something special for tea. A child by the water's edge, having spent the last of his bread upon the ducks, was alarmed to find himself encircled by pink-nosed geese debouching from the west; he backed and ran. The skiffs split the grey fabric of the water. Along the far bank cars were drawn up, bumper to bumper, and people sat in them. Maurice Fisher looked at his watch.

'I shouldn't mind if this went on for ever. For ever at precisely twenty-seven minutes past four.'

He was a big man in his middle forties. He had once had a fine figure, but it was thickening now around stomach and hips. He had the ugly, prideful, green-eyed face of a ginger cat; back from his high knotty forehead fair hair curled close and intricate, like undergrowth. If his expression had not been open and sweet he would have looked dangerous, like a broken boxer.

To-night he felt peace upon him like some delectable, healing ointment, smoothed from shoulder-blades to wrists, from thighs to ankles, relaxing muscle and nerve. To-night, again, the house would be empty and he would be getting his own supper.

He looked forward to his empty house. Since his marriage nineteen years ago he had never, apart from the week now drawing to a close, spent an hour alone in it. Now, however, his wife Libby, overstrained, her mother, less well than usual (though she was never well), and Kate, his sister-in-law, had after long debate gone off on holiday, in the hope that a week in late September might do them all good. So last Monday he had seen them off, with Kate's boys, to the sea. The day after to-morrow they would be home again.

He thought of to-night. He had a new detective story waiting for him. He would read it by the fire, and this time he would get to the end without interruption. There would be silence like sea filling the house, and light only in his study. He would indulge himself. He would smoke five more cigarettes, leaving another five for the morning. Remember: to get an extra ten on the way back.

'Mrs. Fisher is being admired as usual, I expect,' David said brightly.

Maurice had long discovered that David, for all his brightness, was very kind; but had about as little idea of what one didn't want to hear as anyone on earth. He had needed to keep thoughts of Libby out of his mind: now that David had spoken, back they came.

He stirred, picked up a twig from the grass and stuck it up the side of his shoe. Moving his foot, he admired the effect. It distracted him from the old, irritable, dishonourable reflection that Libby's beauty did her no good. She could never believe that it was not important to him, never understand that this was the only thing about her that could not matter, that could

2

never spell love. It was not for that that he had wanted her. It irked him when she pushed it at him, when she sat in favourable lights, when she stopped for effective seconds in doorways, ran a rapid hand up the nape of her neck and rested it, fingers splayed, upon her smooth, coiled plait of oatmeal-coloured hair. Other people noticed her doing it, and he believed they laughed at her, that they thought her vain. And so she was: but for him only.

'You must miss her awfully,' said David.

Maurice said it seemed extraordinary to be without her.

'I don't know why you haven't been having your meals with me, it would have saved you bothering. My Martha is always willing to oblige.'

'I don't want much. I have it on my knee and read at the same time.'

David said it sounded a bit desolate.

'Does it? And you a bachelor?'

'I may miss that sort of thing when I'm not a bachelor.' David gave his betrothal smile, comfortable and shy. 'Still, at the moment I'm a lonely man. You might have taken pity on me.'

'Oh, you're all right.' Maurice knew he sounded offhand, but he had not meant to be. 'Thank you, though.'

The air smelled sweet, of leaves, of deep, wet earth.

'If they're having weather like this——' David began.

'The boys could bathe.'

Maurice imagined them in the motionless, opaque sea of a dream, under a violet sky. He could not picture any of them at the seaside except in the context of a dream. He had spent holidays with Libby, of course: but to imagine her on holiday without him could only be done by fantastication of the possible reality. It was too dark to sit upon this beach. These were the last few minutes before night fell. He could see Libby's white, wedge-shaped face looking outwards to the muffled horizon: she was a sentinel while the others slept, the old woman and Kate lying huddled on the sands like soldiers sleeping at the tomb, lying so still that the water might flow over them when

3

the time came and still they would not stir. Yet of course neither Kate nor her mother would ever *lie* upon a beach; one was too active and one too old. There would have to be chairs against a breakwater, knitting-bags, newspapers, cigarettes and sweets.

'Mrs. Fisher must have been lovely as a girl,' said David.

Maurice was startled: he had not realised that to his curate she would seem not a girl, but a woman on the edge of middle age. She was thirty-eight. He answered, though he did not mean it, 'I think she's better-looking now than she was then.'

'*La fille aux cheveux de lin*,' David said romantically, and whistled a few bars. The florid notes rested, round and white, upon the air and dropped into invisible staves.

'That reminds me.' Maurice removed the twig, snapped it, and flicked the pieces over the grass. 'We'll have to talk to Plym about the music again. It's painful, but it must be done. People are getting restive.'

'I was inclined to back him at first. I thought he'd get us known for our adventurousness, and people would come flocking in. But it seems otherwise.' David took on a portentous air, an air of heavy responsibility. 'What they want is Handel's *Largo*.'

'Somehow we aren't quite the right church for Plym. I have always thought so.'

'So has he. He wanted a cathedral. We're a bit of a comedown.'

'He isn't good enough?' Maurice enquired.

David, something of a musicologist, shook his head. '*Just* not good enough. He'd have been happier if he'd been worse. Not so many hopes.'

'You have a word with him,' Maurice suggested, like a coward, 'you know about music.'

David shook his head. 'He'd never take it from me.' He began to whistle again, drawing the notes around the line of admiration that was still in his head: and he brought Libby's beauty into the park. I do miss her, Maurice said to himself. When she comes back I must help her more.

4

'I suppose we'd better go.'

Reluctantly he heaved himself up out of the chair, and stood a head taller than David. The lake was empty of boats now, the cars were thinning from the further shore. A red and a green star drew a slow ellipse across the sky and the sound of the plane trembled under their feet. They walked together over the grass to Albert Gate. There were still people clambering around the Memorial where the Prince Consort sat with his dull book, and down the steps a party of black nuns in a hurry swooped like a flock of ravens.

Maurice was suddenly exhilarated. The transparent sky, its greenness brushed about with the charred fragments of sunset cloud, gave him a feeling of thirst, not for a drink but for some livelier pleasure than the fire and the book; he would like to be in Cambridge again, at a party, in his old rooms, permeated by the comfortable, *angst*-ridding smell of parchment and wine and dry-rot, to be among people laughing, talking college-shop, and making a noise. His capacity for enjoyment, so long battened down, soared up again. Yet, he thought, it was no use hoping for that, except on the rare occasions when he was invited for the Commemoration of Benefactors. The book and the fire were pleasures enough, and it was absurd to feel like a schoolboy clamouring for a special treat to mark the last day of the holidays. Peace returned to him. 'This is the best kind of sky,' he remarked to David.

They strolled back slowly eastwards, down Exhibition Road where the Science Museum disgorged a crowd of adolescents to scrap all over the pavement; along the canyon of Cromwell Road where lemon light shone high in flats and rooming-houses, and variegated Asians and Africans with pocked or handsome faces and beautiful bodies waving like palm leaves were going back to their lodgings for tea; through half a mile of shabby squares and misty, padlocked gardens; to the square where St. Lawrence's was, a big, mud-coloured, wide-hipped church, the spire still lopped as a precaution against bombing, a precaution taken fifteen years ago.

'What it looks like,' said Maurice, pausing, 'is a camel in

5

skirts, curtseying. How I envy East Anglian parsons with their wool churches!'

'Yes, but we do have a congregation.' David, feeling himself more evangelistic than his superior, was a little shocked.

'True.'

The church stood on the east side of Vernon Square. It had an asphalt forecourt, and shrubs on either side. In front were the square gardens, for residents only. They were kept up in a ramshackle way: the grass was unkempt, and trees straggled down over the iron railings, but the dahlias were handsome, roaring away like fires in the dusk. The smell of the swept wet leaves was pungent. In the nineteen-thirties the houses had been well kept; huge as they were, at least half of them had been owned by single families. People in evening dress had walked their dogs at night. There had been lavish elderly parties. Some of the party-givers still remained in what they could retain of their houses; the rest had long since gone away, and the hostels, the boarding-houses, the lodging-houses, had burgeoned here as elsewhere.

The vicarage had once stood next to the church. Shortly before Maurice's induction, under pressure from incumbents who could not bear the cost of keeping it up, it had been sold, and a slightly smaller house in the next street had been acquired. 'Here's where we part company,' Maurice said. David lived in a comfortable basement flat in the square itself — two big rooms with bathroom and service. They stood looking down through the area railings. The curtains were undrawn, the lights were on: the housekeeper was laying tea.

'Come on, do. You can have something with me. Why not?'

Maurice shook his head. 'I want to read my book.'

He watched David bolt down the steps, swinging on the banister as on the rail of a bus: then he walked on.

The sense of peace was so deep now that he seemed to move without breathing. Such wind as there was had died.

He turned the corner of the square into the street where he lived, and stopped dead.

The house was blazing with light.

6

Chapter Two

His first impression was of utter disappointment. He was drenched by it, as by a booby-trap.

It was only momentary; almost at once fear dried it up. Something was wrong with Libby. As he fumbled with his key, the sweat broke out all over his face.

But it could not be Libby, for he saw her shape through the frosted panel of the door, coming to meet him. They collided. 'Sorry,' said Maurice.

'Where have you been?'

She sounded accusing. Her large eyes flared. She had a smudge on her forehead.

'Only for a walk with David. What's the matter?'

She flung up her arms, crashed them to her sides. 'Oh, nothing, *now*! Nothing. But this morning was awful.'

'Hullo,' Kate called, as she went upstairs with a tray. Her voice was dry. She disappeared round the bend of the landing.

Libby put her head on Maurice's shoulder. He raised it and kissed her. 'Now then.'

'Well, we can't stand in the passage all night. Come on, for Heaven's sake.'

It was into his study that she led him. The fire was still glowing, the detective story was ready on the arm of the chair. The coffee table was drawn up where he had left it.

'You can't imagine!' Libby said, beating her arms up and down. 'It was such a business! We're all home.'

'So I gather.'

In the drawing-room next door, the boys were playing jazz on the gramophone.

'What happened?'

She began to tell him. Mother had been taken so ill that morning, so giddy, she had looked terrible. Libby had been scared out of her wits. She couldn't have her being ill in an hotel, among strangers. She had had no thought but to get her home. They had driven back, and the boys had followed by train.

'How is she now?'

'She's perfectly all right. That's just it, *perfectly* — we needn't have come. But if you had the faintest idea what she looked like this morning, if you could conceive it——'

Kate came in. 'Bad pennies, Maurice. There was not the slightest need for us to cut our holiday short. The boys are sulking like mad. But Libby got frantic.'

She was dark, thinner than her sister, and five years older. Both of them had light olive eyes, but Kate's were sharper. She stood against the doorpost, arms folded, cigarette in her mouth.

Libby turned on her. 'And so would you have been frantic, if you'd seen Mother as I did! Of course, by the time I fetched you she was looking brighter.'

'Certainly. So we needn't have come.'

'The whole of the responsibility rests on me,' Libby said tightly. '*I* have to make the decisions. *I* can't take risks. I have the *whole* family to think of.'

'Why?' Kate went out again, closing the door with a jolt.

'Now let me just be quiet,' Libby said in a small tight voice, 'let me be very quiet and hold your hand for a minute, and not lose my temper. There, dear. Hold me.'

She sat on the arm of his chair, as she did so knocking the book off on to the rug. He stood in front of her. She put out her hand and he took it, as if they were being introduced. Her back straightened, her shoulders went hard back, her face flushed. She was like a child holding its breath to scare its parents.

'Very, very quiet, just say nothing. Not for a second. I intend to keep perfectly quiet.'

8

The trumpet screamed up in crescendo and stuck in a groove. One of the boys lifted the needle and started the record again at the beginning.

Libby exhaled violently, shivered, rose, and threw herself into Maurice's arms. He had a moment's hope, too swift to be consciously developed, that she might save something for him out of this wreck by letting him sleep with her tonight. He began to fondle her, but she pulled away.

'No, honestly, Kate is intolerable! It is all very well for her to talk, but I *am* the head of this house — that is, except for you, and you're too busy — and everything does devolve on me. No one but me ever takes action. Mother looked terrible, terrible——'

'I'd better go up and see her,' Maurice said.

As he went, he heard Libby rush into the drawing-room and shout at the boys. Louis Armstrong ceased.

Mrs. Marsden was not in bed, but in a chair by the gas fire, drinking cocoa. She looked tired, but perfectly well.

'Ah, Maurice, it wasn't any fault of mine!'

'Fault? What fault could there be?' And indeed he could not see that there had been one.

'I do get giddy turns, as you know, but after breakfast I really felt dreadful. I wouldn't have spoiled things for the others, though. "You just leave me," I said to Libby. "I'll be all right. Anyway," I said, "I don't think I ought to be moved." But she would do it. And now,' she began to weep a little, 'the boys will blame me! It's Grannie's fault, they'll say, wretched old woman. *Damn* the old woman, they'll say!' She raised her chin. 'Yes, they will! And I shan't blame them.'

'Oh, a couple of days,' said Maurice impatiently, 'what's that? What can it possibly matter?'

'And Kate's cross because of them. She thought of them first, of course — which is only right. So she should. But she can be so sharp.'

'Kate is my refuge and my strength,' said Maurice.

The old woman looked at him, half in amusement, half in reproof. She had forgotten to cry.

9

Maurice went down again and into the drawing-room. The boys greeted him with silent movements of their lips. Simon, aged fifteen, was expressing outrage in his usual manner: which was to sit slightly out into the middle of a room, his feet in the way, entirely unoccupied. Dick, who was two years younger, had unscrewed the arm from the gramophone and was doing something or other to it.

'I'm sorry about this.'

Simon shrugged.

'Aunt Lib got in one of her flaps,' said Dick.

Both boys, like Kate, were dark-haired. Simon was tall and inclined to be thin; the skin of his face was fine and transparent, his feet and hands were large. Dick was short for his age, short-necked, square-shouldered, long-bodied.

Simon spoke. He said deliberately, but not loudly, spacing his words. 'There was nothing wrong with Grannie. You know how she is. Anyway, there was no reason to lug *us* back. We could have stayed on.'

'You couldn't very well stay by yourselves,' said Maurice, instantly wondering why not.

'*Oh*,' said Simon, with heavy sarcasm. He said nothing else. Dick had replaced the arm of the gramophone. He wedged his handkerchief into the soundbox and started the record again.

'Oh, stuff it,' Simon said, 'there will only be a flap.'

Maurice said, 'Look here, you've just got to take this with a good grace. There's nothing else for it.'

Simon said, 'Quite.' He swung round on the back legs of his chair and faced the other way.

Maurice waited for a second, then left them. He went into the dining-room, where Kate was getting a meal.

'It will have to be high tea or low supper,' she said. 'We're all starved. I hope you've been looking after yourself properly.' She smiled at him. 'But I don't suppose you have.'

Libby came in. She had washed her face, changed her suit for a dress. It was a new one, of some olive-green stuff, the top of it draped like a chiton. She stood against the fireplace, one arm disposed along the shelf. 'I bought it while we were away. Do you like it? I know we can't afford it. But I was tempted and fell.'

'Oh, I expect we can. It's very nice.'

'Come here.'

She raised both arms into the air, contemplated him, and allowed her hands to sink on to his shoulders. She was pushing her beauty at him again: he wished she would not do it in front of Kate, who always looked away and smiled at nothing. Whether it was a smile of contempt or a smile for lovers, he had never been sure. Certainly she always spoke as if she still thought they were lovers, but it was not always easy to match Kate's words to her thoughts.

'Now,' said Libby reasonably, with the calm air which gave such confidence to people who did not know her, 'I am well aware that I got into a state. But I did act for the best. Mother *might* have been really ill. And, when all's said and done, aren't you just a little glad to have me home again?'

He told her how glad he was.

'And of course to have me,' said Kate from the sideboard, 'and Mother, and the boys, mad as wet hens. So nice for you. I suspect you've been having a wonderful time on your own.'

'He's been lonely,' Libby said confidently, 'and he looks thin. We are simply never going to desert him again, not all of us at the same time, because he hates it, though he's been awfully unselfish in letting us go.' She put her arm round his waist and swung him back and forth a little, as in some very decorous dance.

She looked so proud of discovering that everything had turned out for the best, that he was swept with tenderness for her. When Kate went out to the kitchen, he kissed her and told her once more how much he liked her dress.

'Oh, you're a dear!' She yawned. 'A dear, a dear. What should I do without you? Or,' she added with firm quaintness, 'you without me?' She paused, and yawned again. 'I'm dog-tired. And the boys will be beastly to me at supper. I do wish you'd talk to them. After all, they haven't got a father, and it *is* your place.'

'Kate doesn't think so,' said Maurice.

'They're both heathens. And she doesn't care. So is she.' Libby smiled.

'They're not so bad.'

'No, I know. And after all, they are,' she added, with a nod, 'one's own flesh and blood.'

They went up early to bed. She undressed, as she always did, in the bathroom, and returned to brush her hair before the glass. She did this slowly, ritually, stroking rather than brushing, from the pale crown to the straight, darker ends, first over the left shoulder, then over the right: she never took her gaze from the gaze of her own reflected eyes. 'I know I have been silly,' she said at last, in a meek voice. 'I do get upset.'

She put down the brush. Head hanging, she sat there. Her hair was arranged now in plaits over her back. If she could have made it speak to him, it would have said, Look! look! look!

The faint hope revived. It was a long time since they had been parted for more than a night or so. She might even be feeling differently about him, after so much absence. He came to her and set his hand in the small of her back. She turned on it, as on a swivel, and looked up at him. There is something silly about Libby's face, he thought, and the shock of the thought made him drop his hand. He beat it down by spurring his own desire. He lifted her, almost roughly. 'Come to bed.'

'Well, of course,' she said, laughing like a good-natured, badgered housewife. 'Well, of course, of course! I told you, I was worn out!'

She dropped gracefully on to her knees in prayer. He hesitated, then knelt beside her, and when he had finished, waited patiently. Her prayers were always much longer than his. He knew that to-night she was praying as a defence against him (well, she needn't worry, she was safe now), and wondered, as often before, whether she had always prayed so. He was a sensual man: his body had been a nuisance to him. He had married Libby because she had seemed, beneath her smilingness and her calm, to match his own sensuality; for years he had, on the whole, believed this was true. Yet he had never made love to her with an innocent heart. As a boy, he had been frightened by his desires; as a student at Cambridge he had yielded to them for the first time, and had found he could be perfectly happy provided he pushed all thought of his vocation out of the way. Sex was too like sin to be comfortable. He had talked the problem over with older and wiser men, laymen and priests: had accepted intellectually all they said to him, but could not feel the reassurance in himself. When he married he could worship God and enjoy Libby: but not, somehow, do both at the same time. He was disconcerted when she had insisted that they should pray together before getting into bed. She was right, he knew, and he was wrong: all the same, it spoiled joy for him. She was smudging with — with what? — some kind of falsehood, of *theatricality*, something that could have been more innocent for him, laying less of a weight upon his conscience. She made him feel guilty — why, he did not know. No well-adjusted man, priest or no priest, should feel so with his own wife. He had felt worse when he realised one night that Libby's desires were faked. If she prayed, it was for the power to submit cheerfully. He was bitterly humiliated; humiliation crept like sour water under his tongue.

A year ago, her prayers in this respect had mysteriously ceased to be effective. Without the slightest warning, she had informed him solemnly one night that she thought she was 'past all that sort of thing'. It was physiological, she explained. It did sometimes happen to women early. She was very grave, sweet and reasonable. She recognized the strain she might put on him. 'But,' she said, 'you *are* forty-four. And you have enormous strength of character.'

For some time after that, he had found his strength of character hardly equal to her conviction; he had desired her, and he had taken her. She had behaved cheerfully. But slowly, without a further word or gesture, she had managed to discourage him.

He was becoming used to deprivation. Enforced celibacy did, at least, lessen the strain of his own peculiar dichotomy. She wanted love without desire and he tried his best to give it to her. He only wished that she would not 'push her beauty' by way of compensating him. That, on its own, was nothing. It never had been. He did not care at all whether others envied him or not.

She rose up abruptly, flung back the sheet and hopped like a schoolgirl into bed.

'So nice,' she said, 'so nice to be with you again. And you have forgiven me for, well, not losing my head, exactly, but getting just a bit too worked up? It's the responsibility, you see, and I do have that, don't I?'

He said, 'Oh yes, I forgive you, all right.'

Chapter Three

THE Pelhams, Humphrey and Georgina, were getting ready for church. The bells were tolling through the soft rain, the streets had some of that exhilaration which is often felt on Sunday mornings, collapsing totally later in the day.

Humphrey and Georgina were the last people in Vernon Square to retain entire possession of their own house, and this was because the top two floors had been beyond any effective repair by the War Damage Commission. Twenty years ago they had been great party-givers, givers of decent, quiet parties for relations and academic associates — Humphrey was then principal of a university college in London. They had kept a cook and a houseman, and two women of miscellaneous capacities came in by the day. Now, Georgina made do with one woman three hours a morning and had learned not to see shabbiness. It is true that they would have been less shabby — in fact, not shabby at all — in a small modern flat: but the past was eating them away, they knew it, they did not care. They would rather be destroyed by its gentle cannibalism than by a plunge into the cold and grubby river of a world they felt it unlikely that they would understand.

They had always gone to St. Lawrence's: they remembered Maurice's induction, in the last year of the war, in the week the rocket fell, carrying away part of the tube station. They did not know him well, since they had not cared to know anybody new for the past twenty years, but they thought him a nice man and a reasonably good preacher. The life of the church, though they stood just beyond it like spectators at a football match, interested them very much; they were both sermon-fanciers, and at the moment were a little downcast because David Beattie would be preaching.

'So inhumanly bright,' said Humphrey, 'so damned intimate. He hangs farther and farther over the edge of the pulpit till you expect him to come down the side head first, like Dracula.'

'He's young,' Georgina said tolerantly, 'he'll learn.'

'Oh no, he won't. When they start bright, they get brighter. I don't know that Fisher's improving. Far too much exegesis, lately. I think a man only goes in for exegesis when he's taken his eye off the ball.'

She said she loved him, but did not approve his metaphor.

'I love you, my dear,' he said mechanically, but meaning it as much as he meant his prayers, which he said mechanically also.

'And very nice too.' Georgina smiled at her reflection: she did not think many people would guess that she was seventy. She looked, in fact, so young for her age that she would sometimes take the opportunity of disclosing it to shop assistants or bus conductors, just to see their jolt of surprise. She had that look which is peculiarly English, the keen, sharp look of an aged girl. 'By the way, did you know the family was back?'

'Whose?'

'The vicar's. I meant to tell you. When I came back from the post last night the house was lit up as if they were giving a dance.'

'I hope nothing's wrong,' said Humphrey. 'They weren't due till Monday.'

'Well, I expect we shall find out.'

As they went to their pew, Plymmer was thundering out Reger's Introduction and Passacaglia in F minor. 'What on earth is he playing?' Humphrey whispered. 'What a very noisy man he is.'

As usual at Mattins, St. Lawrence's was about half-full. It was pleasanter inside than out, the light softened by the clear, pale green glass with which Maurice had replaced some lurid windows shattered by blast, and warmed by the new red matting in chancel and nave. It had two treasures: a fine brass lectern of Flemish design in the shape of a spread eagle, and a reredos donated by an Episcopalian soldier from Long Island who, having wandered by sheer chance into the church ten minutes before the small bomb struck the east wall, and having escaped with nothing more than a cut on the cheek, had expressed his gratitude in this way. Otherwise, it was a typical church of the early nineteen-hundreds, bleak, draughty and without style.

The Pelhams had their pew just behind Mrs. Fisher's. The first few rows were usually filled with immediate neighbours, and by the more active participants in church activities. Peter Betts and Louis Waterer sat right up in front, on the right of the nave. People from farther afield tended to sit farther back, leaving an empty space in the middle where, in fact, the acoustics were poor. Right at the back sat the churchwardens. Members of the Youth Club shuffled, lunged at each other, whispered, and occasionally conducted flirtations at the back of the gallery, where Maurice was only just audible, and David not at all.

Libby came hurrying in, bareheaded. Advanced in her views, she had made a point of wearing no hat since women had been permitted to come without them to church. Behind her wandered the two stony boys, dragging their feet.

'It's either Mrs. Morley or the old lady who's ill then,' Georgina muttered, 'if anyone is. Poor Mrs. Fisher.' They were sorry for Libby, who always looked so burdened.

They watched her as she bent her neck, graceful, giraffe-like, the coiled plaits rising up it, watched the boys bump their foreheads down on the back of the pew in front of them. All three rose again; they sat in order of height, Simon, Libby, and Dick.

Plymmer stopped playing, then plunged in a rather perfunctory manner into the processional hymn. The congregation rose. The choir streamed in, headed by Derek, who was the son of the Pelhams' grocer, and looked a different boy on Sundays, remote, almost lunar, infinitely good. He was the youngest singer in the choir, which had men and women, but no children. The cross bobbed along towards the chancel, throwing off lemony gleams of light, for the rain had stopped and the sun had come out. As Maurice passed the pew where Libby sat she turned her face full upon him, uplifted, unashamed, and smiling: just perceptibly, with one corner of his mouth, he smiled in return. The Pelhams, moved, remembering the facts if not the emotions of old pleasures, smiled at each other and touched forefingers under cover of their respective prayer books.

An English Sunday, Humphrey thought, may not be flashy, but there is nothing like it. He made a mental note to say this to Georgina.

She was thinking that the vicar looked tired: but then, poor man, he would. They did too much, all of them did. She thought he rushed the service a little.

'Funny old girl,' Humphrey murmured, under cover of the lesson, jerking his head in the direction of Miss Falls, whose only eccentricity — but it was enough — was to wear the skirt of a perfectly ordinary suit down to her ankles. In the eyes of some parishioners, but not of the Pelhams, she had another eccentricity: she turned up unfailingly to the service at 8 a.m. Georgina nodded to show that she had heard. Miss Falls was funny every Sunday.

'"Grant that this day,"' Maurice was saying in his clear, rather dull voice, '"we fall into no sin, neither run into any kind of danger——"' He twitched his head towards the gallery, where there had been some faint sound of giggle and scuffle — '"but that all our doings may be ordered by Thy governance, to do always that is righteous in Thy sight. . . ."'

'"In Quires and Places where they sing,"' said Humphrey, quoting in a whisper, '"here followeth the Anthem." Heaven help us.'

This was Plymmer's moment, this was where he came into his own. Where he got his anthems from, the Pelhams did not know; nor why the vicar did not restrain him. Humphrey, though uninterested in music, had a good ear; he had recognised that Plymmer's anthems were not infrequently too much for the choir.

The performance that morning was ambitious and ragged; also it was long. Only Peter Betts and Louis Waterer, in their front pew, maintained an attitude of enthusiasm, even of excitement. Peter sat rigid, with parted lips, his first and second fingers to the knot of his tie. Louis, much smaller, much younger, much darker, glanced at him now and then, beaming and sharing. David Beattie, in his stall, carefully pleated his surplice.

During the hymn which preceded the sermon, the time at which mothers with young children took them out, Libby Fisher rose very quietly, and with a small, strained smile upon her face, left also. The boys stared after her and shrugged at each other. Maurice made as if to get up, sank back again. He looked bewildered.

'Oh dear,' said Georgina, 'now what is it? Ought someone to go after her?'

'Well, not us,' said Humphrey, 'it's not as if we really know them.'

Georgina could not resist looking round. She saw Mrs. Walkeley, who ran the Mothers' Union, lean out of her pew and speak anxiously to Libby, who shook her head, smiled and tiptoed out of the church. The hymn came to an end; David took his place in the pulpit. The ledge was high, David was short. Ignoring the pulpit-rest, he came round to the side of it and leaned companionably upon his elbow.

'Like a dance-band leader,' Humphrey whispered, 'poor man, he can't help his looks.'

'It occurs to me,' David began, 'that it must strike some of you how seldom the church appears to give guidance from the pulpit on the practical problems of life, how often it may seem, as it were, "off the beam". This morning, on my way across the square, I happened to notice two young people——'

'Fudge,' said Georgina.

'— not, I may say——' David raised a playful finger, 'of this congregation — who were having one dickens of a row. I

couldn't help hearing what it was all about. Shall I tell you?'
He leaned in what seemed to be a dangerous fashion over the
pulpit. 'It was about that old, green-eyed monster, jealousy.
She was pitching into him — yes, pitching in! — about another
girl he had been dancing with the night before. And he wasn't
liking it one bit: on this beautiful Sunday morning, they were
making each other perfectly miserable. And I said to myself,
"What would God think about it? What does *he* think about
jealousy?"'

His gaze rested tenderly upon the head of Lucy Simnett,
just below. He was in love: he needed to talk about love.

'— suffereth long and is *kind*,' he said; '*kind*: that's it.
Now between these two young people there was unkindness.
The most — the most——' Like Henry James he seemed to
descend into the depths of his spirit for the right word. He
floated up again, smiling; he had found it: '— sickening unkindness. Yes, quite honestly sickening. Here was this delightful
autumn day, with all the leaves changing into their gold and
russet robes——' He went off into a descriptive passage.

Georgina, liking him rather better than Humphrey did (she
thought him silly, but could feel his gentleness), patted her
husband's knee. It occurred to her often, uneasily, that it
might be a sin to despise sermons not of the highest intellectual
content. The worst, like the best, was an offering to God: and
if God had wanted to listen to something on a loftier plane,
then he would have put it into the preacher's mouth. She
decided, to atone for this sin of cerebral pride, that she would
say something agreeable about David's sermon to the vicar,
when she shook hands with him after the service.

Maurice, however, did not appear: did not, as usual, pull off
his surplice and race round by the back door in time to greet
the first person to leave the church.

There was only David, chatting away as at a cocktail party;
and because he talked too much and would keep her too long,
Georgina decided not to offer her compliments. She slipped
behind him, and walked home with Humphrey through the
mild weather.

Chapter Four

MAURICE said sharply, 'What's the matter?'

He had found Libby in the dining-room, laying the meal like a conscientious sleep-walker, pretending not to hear him as he came in. She pushed the hair back from her forehead and stared at him, as if awakened. 'Oh, that. Nothing to worry about, darling. I just felt a bit faint. It passed.'

She went on talking. There might be a germ going round; it was so like that odd thing which had happened to Mother, in fact, extraordinarily like. The giddiness, then the quick recovery. But for the moment it had been most unpleasant. She really had wondered what was going to happen.

'Poor dear,' he said. He put his arm round her. He had understood her perfectly. She was feeling guilty because she had denied him, last night, what he should never have asked. This was her excuse, the excuse of some vague illness 'coming on'.

'I really am all right now,' she said, looking brave, 'it was only for the moment.'

'You caused excitement,' said Maurice.

'Now be fair,' she protested at once, 'I got out as quietly as I could. I didn't disturb a soul.'

He asked her how Kate was. Normally she came to church with Libby, but to-day had been forced by one of her migraines to go to bed. Maurice dreaded them, not only for her sake but his own, and was ashamed of his dread; they were so horrible for her that he had no right to feel the petty misery of inconvenience on his own account. Since her husband died in the war, he had made a home for her and the boys; in return,

21

she ran his home for him — but that was an unspoken secret between them. Kate did the house-keeping. Everyone pretended that Libby did, Libby included.

'She ought to be down soon. I feel better now. Sure I didn't frighten you? I'm so dreadfully sorry.'

'You couldn't help it.'

He went to the window and looked out. It was raining again, this time heavily, and the few parked cars in the street were gummed all over by falling leaves. It was a sad day, and hope was done with. He had hoped, he now thought, up to yesterday's homecoming; which had shaken things into place. Yet he was filled with tenderness for Libby, something only a little short of love, but utterly unlike love. They were on their own now, he and she: and no amount of prayer would help, for prayer would not come indoors with him. He had fallen into the habit of leaving his faith on the doorstep and making do without it: relying on himself and his own endeavours.

'You couldn't help it,' he repeated.

'Well,' said Libby briskly, 'so long as you do realise that. By the way, Kate took a message from Mrs. Fraser. I said you could see her at three.'

'I can't, I've got a churching at three and a baptism at three-thirty. She needs time.'

'If only you'd trust me, I could talk to her. I *want* to help you in your pastoral work,' Libby urged, 'if only you'd let me. A woman might be able to help her better than a man could.'

'You're not going to talk to Mrs. Fraser,' Maurice said flatly, 'she's my business.'

Mrs. Fraser was the mother of a boy of fourteen who stole, and who interfered sexually with other children. She dared not leave him alone with his young brother and sister. She had gone to the police, who had told her they were powerless until he was actually caught committing an offence. She was only one of Maurice's worries. He said he would telephone David, and ask him to go round to the Frasers' house, putting her off till five.

'I shouldn't have bought it,' Libby said, energetically

22

straightening the knives and forks, 'I knew I shouldn't have. That's why you're angry with me.'

'Bought what?' He was bewildered.

The dress, she told him: he had been nice about it, but angry: and quite right that he should be. It was true that they couldn't afford it. She knew what a burden her family was on him, even with Kate's army pension, her mother's contribution.

'Oh my poor dear.' He assured her he had not been angry, he had not thought about the dress.

'But you are. I saw it yesterday.'

He kissed her — 'You're being silly.'

Kate came downstairs. She was still ravaged by the pain; he could see the swelling of her eyelids, the tic in her left temple.

'You'd better go back again, hadn't you?'

'I think I'm a bit better. It may be passing.'

'It's not passing, you know.'

'Well, just let me pretend it is.' She went by him, to help Libby. The boys came in, banging the front door. She screamed out — 'Don't! Don't! Don't!'

Simon looked in at her. 'What is it, one of your heads?'

Kate said, trembling, 'I am very, *very* sorry to shout at you like that. But a loud noise is an actual pain. I really mean, it isn't just an annoyance, it makes a pain.'

'Hard luck.' He went on up to his room, Dick behind him.

'There's not the slightest point in trying to help if in fact you can't,' said Libby, in a good-natured, bluff voice, 'it only makes things worse. We'd prefer your room to your company.'

Kate laid down the spoons she was holding, very gently, so as to make no sound at all. She turned and went back upstairs.

'I think,' Libby said, 'that she ought to go on seeing doctors till she finds one who can help, not just give in like that. Did you know old Imber was in church this morning? Alice Imber was with him, too. I wonder when she got back?'

She began to talk of church matters until Mrs. Marsden appeared, hungry.

23

'Maurice, my dear, I would have come this morning but the girls wouldn't let me. No, they said, it wouldn't be wise, not after yesterday, so I thought I had to bow to public opinion. The trouble with people of my age, they so often won't, and that makes trouble all round. Who was at early service?'

'David took it. I expect Miss Falls was there.'

'I used to go once. Yes, when I was younger and stronger, I used to go.'

'You thank your stars you're not younger and stronger, Mother,' Libby said tartly. 'That's my worst cross. All my other parish work — yes; but——'

'Don't call it a "cross",' the old lady said, very gently indeed. They looked at each other, old, affectionate enemies.

When the meal was over, Maurice went upstairs to see Kate.

'I'll be better soon,' she said, out of the darkened room. 'I've started to cry.'

It was true that, for her, the end of an attack was marked by involuntary weeping. These were tears she was quite powerless, with all her iron will, to check; tears scarcely of pain or of exhaustion, but of disappointment that this thing, which had tormented her for years, was never going either to leave her alone, or to shorten its course by half an hour.

'Then you had it yesterday,' said Maurice, sitting down on the edge of the bed.

'Under control yesterday, even through that awful drive back. But I couldn't handle it this morning.'

Kate had suffered from migraine headaches as a young woman, had virtually lost them during the whole of her happy marriage, had found them again a year after her husband's death. Unlike her sister, she had never been a Christian: once she had tried to be, as a resort against pain, but had found it no good. She felt some resentment towards the God in whom she did not believe because he could not, or would not, check these agonies. She had spoken to Maurice about them often, as if clinical discussion helped. The day before an attack occurred, she often felt unnaturally well: she had come almost

24

to dread the sense of well-being. The moment she began to see, in the air, tiny dot-and-tail phantoms like germs or tadpoles, constantly dropping down out of the range of her vision and soaring up into it again, she knew that nothing could help her, that she must go through with it: but she could never keep from hoping that, just this once, she would escape. She had confessed to Maurice, in a final weakening moment, that, for her, migraine was sometimes associated with violent sexual excitement: that was the worst thing of all. Once or twice she had attempted to ease it, only to find the attack prolonged and herself sickened by self-disgust. Indeed, there was something totally disgusting underlying this misery, something obscene in the remorseless clenching of the blood vessels, the hot blood tumescent in the vein, the triumphant conquest of will by agony.

'So silly, you see,' said Kate, her words blurring a little. 'Nobody worries about it, because it is quite innocuous. It doesn't hurt us at all. It must be the only form of torture that doesn't do us the least bit of harm.'

'One of these days I shall pray hard enough to help you.' He felt, at that moment, as though he might even be able to succeed.

'Don't kid yourself,' said Kate. 'Such an expense of spirit, poor old Maurice. You'll only give yourself a headache if you try that.'

But she had spoken more easily. As his eyes grew accustomed to the gloom, he saw that she was smiling a little.

Then she said, in a relaxed luxurious voice, 'Poor old boy. I often ask myself, why *do* you stick it?'

'Your headaches? You have to stick them, don't you?'

'I didn't mean that. I meant everything.'

'I really do not understand one single word you're saying,' Maurice said, in a sudden bluff, parsonical manner. 'What you need now is a nice drop of sleep.'

'Oh no. I saw your face when we all came tumbling home again. And you simply couldn't bear it.'

25

Chapter Five

MAURICE listened, as he did once a quarter, to the
treasurer, George Kitson, explaining that the Parochial
Church Council was under no obligation to pay the
vicar's rates, couldn't afford to do so, but nevertheless would.
This Scrooge-like conduct arose not out of any meanness in
Kitson's nature, but out of a fanatical desire to have every
technical point perfectly comprehended. If any one had
suggested to him that since the rates always had been paid
and always would be, it was a waste of time to debate them
for twenty minutes four times a year, he would have been
outraged. The money was not the point: the important point
was that people should always know just where they stood.
Broad-shouldered, short-necked, his skin lined and muddied
by almost forgotten suns, stubby-nosed, his eyes blue and
bright, his grey-ginger moustache squeezed into a short upper
lip, Kitson looked like a retired Colonial administrator: which
he was. Johnson-Black, the Vicar's Warden, made a parade of
sinking lower and lower in his chair. His look was steady and
unhopeful; his long, blueish chin sank into his collar. He is,
Maurice thought, Vicar's Warden in more than a formal sense.
He is my man; he would like to save me the rag-chewing.

Jeremy Fawcett, the People's Warden, clasped his beautiful
hands together on the ginger-coloured table, and awaited his
turn. He was the youngest member of the Church Council,
a highly-active churchman of impenetrable conceit. He was
rather handsome; he had one of those countenances which are
reminiscent of Roman heroes in profile, a little silly full-face.
A trickle of sun from the vestry window caught his strawberry

blond head, and sparked off spectral colours from individual hairs. Feeling the sun, he lifted his profile into it: David, at the far end of the table, sent an azure gleam of amusement in Maurice's direction, which was not returned.

Maurice was remembering, not so much what Kate had said, but his own blurred response and quick exit. He knew how much Kate saw, had always seen; but had never suspected she might put it into words.

'. . . after all,' Kitson was saying, 'we've got the dilapidations ahead of us: we have to take that into account. Seven years up next year, and believe me, we're pretty well in the red.'

Fawcett seized his opportunity. 'My dear George, when weren't we? We just stagger on. Nothing else we can do.'

'And the roof——'

'Now look, I've been up there. It is by no means bad. I had one of my own surveyors with me, and he thought we could safely leave it for six months.'

'That being so,' said Johnson-Black, heaving himself up again to take command, 'I suggest we pass on. Fawcett's the expert, and if he can bring us the slightest good news, let's thank God for it. Could we settle the matter of the sidesmen, Vicar?'

At this, there was a run of laughter around the table: this was light relief. Even Plymmer, little and bald, his fair skin wrinkled by concentrated scowling, briefly grinned.

'Well, it's an unfortunate vacancy,' said Maurice. 'I was hoping we could have muddled through to the Easter Church meeting.'

'We can't,' said Johnson-Black. 'Scott will be in hospital for at least six months. We must make a temporary appointment now, if we don't want gaps in our duty list.'

Maurice said uncharitably, 'Neither Peter nor Lou is going to prance round with the plate in any church of mine.'

'They are enthusiastic candidates.'

'There can surely be no question of Lou,' said David, 'can there?'

'Betts, then,' said Fawcett. He smiled. 'He is really most

faithful. And I hardly think a man's personality ought to matter.'

'Certain members of the Youth Club,' said Maurice, 'are in a perpetual state of hysteria — no fault of yours, David, it astonishes me that you do so well with them. But the sight of Peter in any official capacity would just about touch them off. I cannot have an explosive atmosphere in the gallery.'

Plymmer straightened his narrow back, grotesquely broadened by the corduroy coat. He said, in his heaviest North Country accent, 'I don't know why we can't all say what we mean. If those two cissies want to come to God in some demonstrative and official manner, who are we to stop them?'

'You're jarring us, Plym,' said Maurice mildly, 'don't do it.'

Plymmer shrugged. He could never accept rebuke, or train himself not to court it.

'One could hardly pretend,' said Johnson-Black, 'that Betts and Waterer set an example by their lives.'

'How do you know, Colonel?' Plymmer sat up. 'Have you ever so much as been inside their front door, let alone any other door of theirs? We all make too many assumptions of this kind.'

'I don't think the appointment of Betts would be continued when it came to a show of hands next Easter,' said Maurice.

'And what would *they* know about it?'

Kitson said, in his soft, heavy voice, 'Mr. Garrett has volunteered to serve for the time being. I think that should meet the case.'

'Assumptions, assumptions,' Plymmer muttered, 'always believe the worst.'

'I think we should accept,' Maurice said, 'if everyone agrees.'

Nobody said he did not, and the meeting went on. Sometimes Maurice found it almost unbearably tedious: to-day its very tedium was a relief to him. In his own church he felt safe, he even felt guided: danger lay outside. He thought of his home with dread since Kate had exposed it to him, ripping up the fabric of tolerable and decent self-deception as she might have ripped up a sheet of tissue paper with her fingernail. He came out of his dream to hear Fawcett paying the usual tribute to Libby as the usual preamble to suggesting that she take on some more work. Maurice wondered how she had managed to convince them, all these years, that she did any work at all. Delegation was her gift. Nobody was so good as Libby at delegating. She was supposed to run the Working Party and the Young Wives, to take round the parish magazines, to be responsible for the flowers and do her share of visiting. It occurred to him that she made her effects by dropping in briskly at three functions in turn, and apologising at each for being unable to stay on the grounds that she had been called urgently away to one of the other two. As for the flowers, she had what she called 'a corps of willing helpers'. As for the visiting — well, she still did some. She was good with some of the male chronics in St. Mary's, who were pleased by her beauty and her gentle smile. He supposed she did them as much good as anyone could hope to.

'Mrs. Walkeley is finding the Mothers' Union terribly tough,' Fawcett said, kneading his hair. 'She'd loathe to admit it openly, but she did hint as much to me. She's a nice creature: she's always confidential if she trusts one. I wondered if Mrs. Fisher could bear to take over? She could give up the Young People, couldn't she? Lucy could do that. Then she wouldn't feel it was too much.'

Maurice put up immediate resistance to the idea that all would be well if Libby gave up a trivial job in exchange for an extremely exacting one. Not that she really does the one, or would do the other, he thought; but, like Kitson, I'm fond of illuminating a principle. He said she was busy enough already.

Fawcett persisted. The women adored her; to some of them she was a sort of ideal. She could do splendid work. 'It cheers them up to see a parson's wife looking so attractive. It means something to drab lives.'

'Condescend, go on, condescend,' Plymmer said under his breath: and to pay him out for this, Fawcett, as soon as he had badgered Maurice into saying he would at least put the idea of the Mothers to Libby, began to attack him about the music.

Melvyn Hannaway, the secretary, came in late, just in time to hear the familiar, sub-hysteric run of Plymmer's protests.

'Vicar, my dear fellow, do forgive me; I have a host of excuses, all valid, I'm sure you don't want to hear them. What's up? Are they complaining about Plym again? Now that's where I'm on his side, yes, slap-down on his side.'

Hatchet-faced, dark-complexioned, eyes dark, eloquent and dramatic, his grey hair wandering and soft like wild clematis, Hannaway reminded Maurice of Father Time. He spread himself at the table, put out his right hand to catch and wag Plymmer's left. 'Tremendously stimulating, the stuff Plym gives us. Must move with the times.'

'Bloody well resign if I have any more of it.'

'Now, now, Plym! Do remember where you are——'

'Not likely to forget it!'

'Oh, but you do, you *do!* You're a wild person, dear boy——'

'Forty-four.'

'I didn't catch?'

'I said I was forty-four, Mr. Hannaway,' said Plymmer in a shout, 'not a boy.'

'Well, you're a boy to me. Bless you, when you're getting on for seventy——'

'I'm just about fed up with it.'

Kitson interjected, with his odd, dry humour, 'Question of organist raised and not dealt with as usual. Excellent. I move we pass on to the next business.'

They dealt with Maurice's coal and telephone bills, with the Savings and Old People's Committees, with the magazine. The meeting petered away as it usually did, into desultory snackings and exchanges of fellowship. The night came down and the room got cold.

When they rose to go, Maurice noticed that Johnson-Black was lingering.

'Just a word with you?'

Maurice nodded. He waited till Plymmer, the last, had huddled slowly into his mackintosh, had slowly hunted for, and found, a lost score, had spoken slowly of the philistinism of his colleagues, and had gone off to the organ loft.

Johnson-Black said, 'I ran into the Archdeacon yesterday.'

The Archdeacon was priest of a very prosperous church not a mile away: to Maurice he had always seemed much too near.

'He asked me about your marrying Rogers and Mrs. Stevenson.'

Johnson-Black hitched himself on to the edge of the table and frowned down at his swinging foot. Maurice said nothing.

'I think he's unlikely to make an issue of it.'

'He can't.'

'You'll upset the bishop again.'

'Nonsense,' said Maurice. 'At worst it means that the bishop must pretend to be upset again. He's a liberal chap. And I'll tell you this — I'll marry any other divorced persons if they're as decent as those two.'

'A vow's a vow. It's hard to get round it.'

'I didn't. I went right through it.' Maurice looked up at the dull and dusty glass globe, through which the light filtered greenly. 'Stevenson was a drunk and a brute. She married him at eighteen, before he showed any sign of being either.'

'I only thought I'd tell you.'

'Well, thanks.' He felt tiredness hanging on his shoulders like a coat sodden with rain.

'I should support you, of course,' said Johnson-Black, in a soldierly voice, 'in anything. Whatever my personal views.'

'I knew you would.'

They went out together into the chilly night. The stars were spinning in the sky: it would be frosty next day.

'Whatever my personal views are.' The Vicar's Warden snapped off a sprig of privet. 'Sometimes I can't be as sure of them as I'd like.' He tossed the sprig away. 'If there is anything I can do to help——'

'The bishop?' Maurice said irritably. 'There's not going to be a fuss.'

'I didn't mean him. I just thought you were looking under the weather. If things are hard, I wish you'd let me know.'

Maurice hesitated. Then he said, 'We rub along. It's easier for Libby since we got an extra cleaner.'

He pretended not to understand what his warden had meant: pretended that it had been simply a reference to his hard work and poverty — old stories, both, though Libby could not realize that they were too old for further retailing and debate. They were the hard-luck stories of all parsons whose luck would never get any better.

When Johnson-Black had gone, he turned and went back into the church. Plym was practising, and the stones rumbled underfoot.

Maurice went and sat in a back pew, trying to think before he prayed. It surprised him to find himself near to tears; not for years had he felt the prickling at the back of his eyes. He took his own pulse, which was steady enough: he had not the excuse that he was going to be ill.

He thought with longing of a walk somewhere between hedges, alone. He looked towards the modest cross, standing on Mrs. Walkeley's crochet-work. I have not been a bad man, he thought, I don't think so. I have tried to do things right.

He longed for some sort of confirmation, for the inner voice, the pat on the back. He was becoming afraid that it might desert him. For too long now, he had felt that God was with him only in places of his, Maurice's, own choosing; he was beginning to make God private, to enjoy him in solitude. At home he could no longer, in the clutter of life with Libby, Kate, the old woman, the children, hear him at all: so he did not try to. He felt he had invented a new heresy, and at the bottom of his imagination he had an image of black earth split open, like the crack of a chilblain. He was afraid for himself, and for the people who depended upon him.

He tried, in the noisy, reverberating church, to pull himself back to Libby by remembering the early days. For him, they had been silly and exalted, high-riding days, the richest, wildest part of his love concealed even from her. All that first month

32

of their marriage he had had Crashaw on the brain, almost
convincing himself that Libby, too, stood on the same giddy
heights.

> *Boundless and infinite, bottomless treasures*
> *Of pure unbridling pleasures.*
> *Happy proof! she shall discover*
> *What joy, what bliss,*
> *How many heavens at once it is,*
> *To have her God become her lover.*

A devotional poem, but not, then, for him. He had hoped to
be Libby's god, to soar above her, and to be accepted with the
same incredulous, incandescent joy with which he took her, with
which he looked down, as from a mountain, upon the open
plain of her beauty. 'Oh my America——' and all that: it
shamed him to think about it. Yet if it had been so, he might
have turned out a better man and a better priest.

He knelt. 'Almighty and most merciful Father, shut my
mind to all those things that should not be in it. Let me still
feel thee; O God, let me behave myself.' He waited for the
responding voice: he was strong with anxiety. Usually it
spoke to him in the semi-archaic language with which his
imagination clothed it — 'I will be thy strength', or 'Lean hard
upon me', or 'Who am I that thou wilt not trust me?' Sometimes he had heard it say, quite simply, 'It will be all right.'

All these voices he himself made: yet he knew they were
outside of himself. They would not come at once: he had to
be quite silent, quietening his breath, even, and listen.
Occasionally they did not come, they deserted him: then he had
to pretend not to care, to switch his thoughts to practical
matters, to go about his business. But on the worst of his
days they came; and then he knew he had invented them
wholly, that they were not of God.

They were silent to-day. He believed they would answer
if only he could pray the truth: but he could not form the truth
in his mind.

His knee slipped from the hassock, bumped on stone. He

had better make an appeal to the women to do some mending, there would be no money for new hassocks yet awhile. The damp smell from the flags was like tainted flower-water; it was all right for Fawcett to say they didn't need a new damp-course, but the place struck chilly.

He said painfully, 'Let it not be as it is now, let it be only passing, let me wake to-morrow and find I can still endure.'

His mind strayed off again. It was odd that he should choose words like 'endure', phrases like 'let it not' when talking to God, as if God could only understand a kind of religious pidgin-English. He wondered if all parsons did it, if all people who prayed did it.

The organ reared into a fury of sound; sound hacked and slashed the fabric of the atmosphere until it hung floating in tatters under the inverted flower-heads of the white glass lamps. Invaded by Plymmer's row, infuriated by it, grateful for it, Maurice rose to his feet. If he could hear no answer it was because nothing could penetrate this, no still small voice enter into competition.

He looked at his watch. Tea. Confirmation class. Two couples to prepare for marriage, one first, one second session. Look in at the Youth Club to see how David was coping with the rowdier elements. Prayers afterwards, his eye like a lion-tamer's upon them, just holding them in check. After supper, finish magazine-letter.

Work was all right. He could steady himself with that. His mind, blessedly, switched to it. Libby would certainly jib at taking the Mothers: he would have to make excuses for her. Who might take it on? Alice Imber was back, someone had told him so: Kate? Libby? — someone. She might do it. He hadn't seen her for five years. She used to do a certain amount of church work before that, more or less to please her mother: he had never been sure whether or not Alice was a believer. But he might try her. He had rather liked Alice.

Plymmer stopped playing. So as not to have to stop and talk to him, Maurice went home.

Chapter Six

H E WOULD have been surprised to discover how very
little he knew about his curate. In everything he did
know about him, he was correct: David was in fact
kind, gentle-natured, in outward behaviour a bit of an ass,
and utterly insensitive to what should be said and what should
not. This insensitivity, however, arose not out of dullness of
perception but out of sheer miscalculation. David knew a
great deal about people: but made the mistake of thinking he
was the only one who did. Besides Maurice, there were only
three persons in the circle close to the church who realised
the full extent of Libby's uselessness, and David was one of
them. But he was devoted to his vicar and passionately eager
to spare him all painful things, even the discovery of the
inadequacy of his own wife. When he had broken Maurice's
dream of solitude in the park, he had done so deliberately
out of a mistaken belief in his powers of psychological pressure.
By speaking of Libby's looks and the admiration in which she
was held, he had hoped to confirm Maurice's belief in both:
had hoped to instil into his mind the idea — or, more correctly
to strengthen the idea — that the homecoming must be an
occasion of great pleasure.

David was a fervent believer in fruitful seeds dropped
quietly into receptive minds. He could scarcely have intended
better, or done worse.

He owed Maurice much. A young man, somewhat bizarre
in appearance for one of his calling, he had come straight to
St. Lawrence's from Lampeter after only a year at a theological college meant primarily for non-graduates; he had been

35

inexperienced, ardent and shy; and Maurice had made a friend of him. In his modesty, David could never accept the friendship fully. He had been invited to call both Maurice and Libby by their Christian names: he had never managed to get his tongue round them. Nevertheless, the relaxation of not having to feel subordinate except by his own choice was precious to him. He knew Maurice enjoyed his cheek: he did not know exactly how far he could go, but did know how far he wanted to go, and knew that, thus far, cheek was acceptable.

He was an ambitious man — this, too, would have surprised Maurice. In the same way in which, in infancy, David had hoped to become a bus driver he now hoped some day to become a bishop, if his lack of inches did not militate against him. He did not at all realize that both bus driving and bishopric were unattainable ideals — that he was as little fitted for the one as for the other. He was working steadily towards his end by attempting to cut a figure both in his pastoral work and in his preaching. Maurice was content to let him cut one, if he could; David was grateful for that, among other things.

If he knew a good deal about other people, he was nevertheless shaky on the subject of himself. He was convinced that it would be to the glory of God if he did become a bishop: he would be a far better one, he thought, than most, less worldly and more prophetic. He never saw his ambition in terms of power-politics, and was surprised by the lack of it in his vicar. It never occurred to him that he had chosen Lucy Simnett not only because he loved her, but because she had all the potentialities for developing into the perfect bishop's wife. He was a reader, he knew his Trollope: he thought he knew what to avoid.

Yet there was another thing Maurice did not know about David, which would have stupefied him had he learned it: that once or twice, pulled too violently by mutual attraction, he and Lucy had slept together. Their love-making had been done rapidly, fearfully, with shame, either in Richmond Park or Wimbledon Common, in the high bracken or beneath the thickly-knotted may trees. David, at any rate, had been ashamed; he was not so sure of Lucy, whose lapses did not seem to fret her too much. She combined a lively almost aggressive faith with a vestigial, but still adhesive belief, acquired in a co-educational school, that sexual expression should be free, bright and natural. Certainly she had prayed, as he had, for forgiveness and the strength not to do it again; but somehow she seemed to take the sin rather lightly. Like Maurice, both she and David were persons of high sexual energy, and at times life was hard for them. It would be a long while before they could marry.

They were on their way home from Kew, where, although it was late in the year, they had been spending David's day off. They could not go about much together in the neighbourhood of the church, because they inevitably became the target of comment. Either they were considered improperly affectionate towards each other in public, or not affectionate enough: like Maurice, they suffered from the limelight of a parish. Lucy was a tall girl, small-headed, of athletic build. She had grey eyes, rather too sharp, slanted downwards at the outer corners: an inquisitive nose: a small, thick, pincushion mouth of fine natural pinkness. She was something of a schoolgirl, something of a prig. She believed implicitly in David's future and sometimes, in secret, looked at the back of the dictionary to exult over the correct ceremonial form of address for a bishop.

To-night, happy to be with each other and lighthearted because they had resisted temptation, they were to have supper with Plym, who lived with his big wife and his two big, ugly, musical girls in a top-floor flat near Earls Court station. At the moment Mrs. Plymmer and the children were away, the girls at boarding-school, she with her mother in Sheffield.

Welcoming them with the festive air of one who is off the chain, Plym showed them into his littered sitting-room. 'You know Alice Imber, don't you? — No, you don't, David hadn't come here and Lucy was a brat. Turn that off, Alice, there's a good girl.' They had been listening to Messiaen, on the record-player.

'Of course I remember Lucy. She was the Angel Gabriel in the Christmas play. She had wonderful golden wings.'

'Gosh!' said Lucy, who became more schoolgirlish than usual when she was unexpectedly pleased, 'they had a hinge that dug into my back.' She rubbed herself reminiscently.

'I've heard all about you, Mrs. Imber,' David said. His meaningless twinkle gave the impression that what he had heard was amusingly to her discredit. 'The vicar is on your track already.'

'But he was on it on Tuesday,' she said, 'and no, I will not accept the Mothers' Union. Because I wouldn't be any good at it and because I don't want to.'

'You'd be a hundred per cent honest instead of merely ninety-five,' said Plym, 'if you simply said you didn't want to and left it at that. Qualifications — people can't do without them.'

She smiled at him, her face broadening out. 'No more they should. What a beastly world you want! Everyone making short, raw statements of impeccable truth.'

'I'm all for truth.'

'Mr. Beattie,' she said, 'you've done nothing to fatten Plym up since I went away. How impossible it is to trust anyone!'

She and Plym had been at Cambridge together; he had been a music scholar, she had read modern languages. She was two years younger than he and looked much less. It was her father-in-law, with whom she now lived, who had recommended him to St. Lawrence's.

'You can't argue with him,' David said. 'If Mrs. Plym can't, I don't know what hope there is for the vicar and me.'

Plymmer brought in two extra glasses and poured beer. 'Not for me,' said Lucy, 'it's so gassy.'

Alice looked around her, as if she found the room aesthetically delightful. She seemed relaxed and happy. 'It is nice to be back, you can't think! I want to celebrate it. And we could celebrate your engagement, Lucy, couldn't we? Plym told me.'

'It's rather an old engagement now,' Lucy said, with a touch of resentment.

'Well, break it off and get engaged again. Plym has some burgundy.'

David liked Alice Imber, her long body, her small, rosy face. He liked her bright eyes, her high cheekbones and the way the flesh tightened beneath them; he liked her short, fine hair, of no particular colour, lightly streaked with grey, that fell into commas over her brow and the tops of her ears. He thought she was a nice woman. His feminine eye appreciated her clothes, which were smart, and the easy way in which she wore them, as if, like other clothes, they were just coverings. Some clothes were red, some were blue, some smart, some dowdy (hers seemed to say); there was nothing more to it than that. He found her high spirits infectious: he too wanted, as she did, to turn this evening into a party, a secular party, miles away from the familiar 'social'. She did not, he saw, wear her widowhood as Kate did, like a brand on a sheep, and he wondered that it had not seemed to touch her. What had her marriage been like? So disagreeable that she was glad to see the back of it, or so happy that she was still illuminated by remembering it? He had heard of something like that, though he was unable to take it into his imaginative experience. If Lucy died——

' — I do *wish* you'd take on the Mothers,' Lucy was saying earnestly, in her gentlest and most badgering manner.

— if Lucy died he would be miserable for the rest of his life.

'Not on your life,' said Alice, 'because, as I said, I don't want to, and because I'm not a believer. But anything like delivering the magazines, or a little purely practical visiting — I'll do what I can.'

'I don't know what it can be like not to be a believer,' Lucy mused, putting her head on one side, parting her lips. 'It seems quite extraordinary to me.'

David guessed that having at first liked Alice, she did not like her now. She was given to violent veerings of affection.

He mentally applauded her for her demonstration of faith, and at the same time wished she did not sound so priggish.

'Oh, can it, Lucy,' said Plym, 'you know I'm not, either.'

'I've never understood how you can sit up in the loft Sunday after Sunday——'

'Oh come, live and let live!' Alice said. She gave Lucy her friendly smile. 'If you want to rebuke heathens like Plym and me, Lucy, you shouldn't wear such an attractive frock. Most worldly.'

'Oh, do you think so?' Lucy was appeased. David thought she had been jealous, and hoped he would one day be able to afford nice clothes for her, and a little unobtrusive jewellery.

'Can't all starve,' said Plymmer, 'we must eat. Take up my beer and walk.'

At this Lucy showed signs of breaking out into fresh admonishment, but Alice shook her head.

'You can't change him, none of us ever could. Let me help, Plym, will you?'

He would not let her. Alone he set the bright, grubby check cloth, a reminder of one of Mrs. Plymmer's holidays among Middle European peasants, put out cold meat and salad, french bread, butter, cheese and wine. Having guests all to himself gave him an air of importance.

When they were seated, they drank to Alice: she drank to Lucy and David. 'And you,' she asked David, 'are you run off your feet?'

He told her that all curates were, and half-starved.

She asked him if he did not prefer to be called an assistant priest. She had a penetrating eager air, as if she wanted to know all at once about the world in which she found herself after so long an absence, as if she wanted to catch up with it.

'Too High for us,' David said. 'We keep well in the middle——'

'Like castor oil between two lots of orange juice,' Plym put in.

'The vicar doesn't like people who call him Father. We calculate the length of surplice to the last centimetre. And no lace trimmings.'

Lucy said loudly and firmly that David was wretchedly underpaid. 'Four hundred a year, that's all. It's an outrage.'

He flapped his hand at her in little, down-beating movements. When Lucy took up these vain cudgels on his behalf she was more like Mrs. Proudie than he cared to contemplate.

Plymmer grinned. 'Yes, yes, sit on her. Mustn't talk money. Nasty vulgar stuff. I keep all my gold in thin sheets under the wallpaper, so as not to be ostentatious.' He pointed to a damp stain on the ceiling. 'We paint that in, to put people at their ease.'

In fact, he was not badly off: he had a small private income: but he rather liked a tinge of squalor in his surroundings and his wife did not notice hers at all.

'Some churches have a Whitsun offering for the curate,' Lucy persisted. 'I don't know why we——'

Plym howled like a dog.

'Now what?' she said.

'Boring.'

'Boring,' David agreed. He caressed her, moving his hand in the small of her back, irritating her by awakening pleasure as he had awakened it in himself.

She looked baffled and angry. Then she gave her sudden, girlish smile. 'Oh, all right. Sorry.'

Alice had been looking at them, silent, amused; she seemed to contain within herself some intention, to be moving steadily towards it. When she did speak, she took David aback.

She said abruptly, 'I am rather rich.'

It was the sort of remark to which no reply seemed possible: he could not understand why she had made it.

'Well, we knew that,' said Plym.

'So long as you knew.'

There was a silence, not resentful, but puzzled. He broke it by asking her what it was like to be back in England.

She said at once, relaxing in her chair, lighting a cigarette, 'Like getting out of a smart coat into a scruffy old comfortable dressing-gown.'

41

'Rough on us,' David said.

She replied, no: her image had been a silly one because it was too feminine, but it was accurate. Living in Canada, she had been exhilarated by the feeling of newness, of progress, of pressure; it was extraordinary to be in a country that was getting richer and more sure of itself with every day that passed. Yet she had felt the weight of her own country hanging on her, it had corrupted her judgment. She had found herself contemptuous of new cars, new highways, lavish food, an infinity of gadgets: had found herself valuing the concept of poverty and decay for its own sake as if, because it was at least the poverty and decay of an older and richer culture, it was something to be proud of. 'That's where we're so false,' she said; 'because the broken-down is all we've got, we treat it as if it were the only excellence. Miles settled down more easily than I did.'

'I'm sorry,' Lucy said maddeningly, 'but I'm afraid I think we're a great country. We still are. I can imagine,' she added, 'what my Guides would say if they'd heard you.'

'I wouldn't have said it to your Guides,' Alice said, 'or I'd have said it differently. Yes, of course, we're a great country. But not a great power. And I've been living next door to one, in something that looks just like one.'

'Material things aren't so important.' Lucy said it in a pleasant, matter-of-fact way, as though expecting automatic agreement.

'Tell that to peasants in India,' said Plym rudely.

'Or to curates,' said David.

'Well,' said Lucy, evading the renewed caress he could not resist giving her, 'you all know what I *mean*.'

Alice said gently, 'Of course they know. And I do too. But I've expressed myself badly. I only meant that it was silly of me to resist the "new world" as I did, just because it had so much. It's just the same as when the middle-classes used to round on the poor for buying pianos. They simply felt they weren't qualified to play them.'

David asked her if she had never been happy in Canada.

42

Only in the last year, she replied, when she had suddenly taken to it: and then she had had to come home. The shadow of a death touched her: for a moment she had left them. Then she said, returning, 'But I like it here. I fall just inside the generation that hankers after the sweet smell of the tumble-down. One of these days I shall find myself passionately defending Vernon Square as a work of art — a work of art, mind — when somebody wants to pull it down and put up Gropius flats. Which will be dead wrong of me.'

David had an uncomfortable feeling that she was too far ahead of him. He himself found it hard to disentangle sentimental from intrinsic value: because a place was as he had always remembered it, he, too, was in danger of thinking it beautiful. Yet, he thought, St. Lawrence's *is* like a camel in skirts: Maurice is right, only I like it like that.

He had a feeling of panic that Alice, and people like her, would by their building up, by their determination (even against their instincts) to make new, obliterate all the things he understood; that beneath their energy the Church itself might at last go down, to be nothing more than a residual mumble beneath the racket of a new day. It was no good her saying that her emotions were upon his side; somehow, mysteriously, she had come to destroy. For no reason that he could understand, even though she attracted him, even though he felt that she was good, she threatened to make a crack in the familiar, comfortable and shabby wall of their lives.

'Dead wrong of you,' Plym agreed, who alone was sure of himself.

Alice looked at the table. She rose abruptly, said, 'I won't be ten minutes,' and went out.

'I wonder where on earth she's gone?' Lucy demanded.

'Probably to the little girls' room,' said Plym in accents of savage refinement.

'No, she hasn't. She's gone out. I heard the front door.'

'She's a law unto herself.' He put on a record.

Alice came back with a bottle of wine.

'Where did you get that?'

43

'The pub. I told you I was rather rich. Surely you can't possibly mind? Not even Lucy, who is so cross with me?'

'I'm not!' Lucy exclaimed. She coloured.

'We don't mind,' Plym said. 'Catch us minding.'

The evening passed back into an atmosphere of celebration. David felt very happy, among friends, able to put his arm openly around Lucy's waist, drinking a little more than he was used to. He felt almost as though he had been caught out when, just as they were getting up to go, the door bell rang: and Plym, who answered it, came back with Maurice.

'I'm sorry to spoil your day off, David,' Maurice said. He looked flushed and upset. 'But there's trouble. The police have caught the Fraser boy, and I'm on my way to the station now. Libby's with Mrs. Fraser, and she can't cope.'

Chapter Seven

OBEYING instructions, the first thing David did was to try to make Libby go home. She appeared not to hear him. Bundled into her clothes, her hair pinned up as best she could, she looked to him like some pre-Raphaelite figure mourning at right angles over a tomb. She was, in fact, leaning over the sofa on which Mrs. Fraser lay, head dangling over a tin bowl, repeating over and over that if she could be sick she would be better.

The Fraser house, one of the last few prefabricated boxes in the neighbourhood, had something of that awful neatness which comes as the result of a struggle against odds. It had even a sort of prettiness. The frill pinned with drawing-pins to the mantelpiece was of the same fabric as the curtains; the Queen, tacked to the wall above, had on a dress of the same yellow as Mrs. Fraser's cushions. There was a pitiful touch of taste about the room, of a baffled artistic sense. At the core of it all was an incomprehensible horror, as if a tarantula had been packed into a chocolate box.

Alice stood by the door waiting to take over, but plainly doubtful whether she would be allowed to do so. Libby had barely acknowledged her. It was ten minutes past twelve.

Mrs. Fraser reared up and leaned on her elbows. 'I don't know why he should! His Dad was never like that.'

David, on a spur of unaccustomed cynicism engendered by the excitement, by the lateness of the hour, and by the sudden severance of some dangerous fantasies about Lucy, felt that this was just as well. The Fraser boy had criminally assaulted a child of nine on Putney Heath.

'No,' said Libby, weeping, 'and you're not like that, and Derek isn't really, not deep down.'

'Yes, he is,' said Mrs. Fraser. 'What do you know about it?' She grabbed at the basin and this time she did vomit.

'I do know. You must listen to me if you want to be helped. *Do* you want to be helped?'

She pushed the basin away, laid hold of the woman under the armpits and rolled her onto her back. 'If you want to be helped, you must help yourself.'

'Go away.'

'I'm here to help you. We all are. Now pull yourself together!'

'I think her doctor ought to be called,' said Alice. 'He might give her a sedative.' She approached Mrs. Fraser gingerly. 'Who is your doctor?'

'What good's he?'

David took up the basin to empty it.

'You put that back!'

'I want to know who your doctor is,' Alice said.

Libby looked up, steely through tears. Under her strong hands, Mrs. Fraser thrashed about.

'Can't you see she's not fit to be badgered? It's very kind of you, but I'm trying to look after her.'

'Look,' said David, 'the vicar said he wanted you to go back home. Mrs. Imber and I will stay.'

'Doctor Harper,' said Mrs. Fraser. She reared away from Libby and was sick again. Somewhere in the house a child started to cry. 'Oh God, that's Michael. I must go to him.'

She tried to rise, but Libby pushed her back. 'You stay there. Mr. Beattie will see to the children.'

'They don't know him, they'll be scared silly.'

'Let her go,' Alice said. 'Of course she must see to the children herself.' She laid a hand on Libby's arm. 'Mr. Beattie will fetch the doctor.'

'I am in charge here,' Libby began, and at that moment Mrs. Fraser slid from the sofa and walked unsteadily off into the bedroom. David picked up the sour bowl, found the lavatory, and cleaned it up. When he came back he said, 'I'll go now. I won't be five minutes.'

As he went, he heard Libby saying to Alice, 'Can't you see, it is most important that she should help herself *now*, at this early stage? She must make an effort. She's letting herself go to pieces.'

But when he came back with the doctor Libby had gone, and Mrs. Fraser was back on her sofa, eyes closed. The child too was quiet.

He said softly to Alice, 'How did you do it?'

'I shan't be popular. Mrs. Fraser ordered her out, and I backed her up.'

The doctor said he would give the woman something to quieten her and asked if there was anybody who could stay the night.

Alice said she would, suggesting that David should drop a note in at her house, to stop her father-in-law from worrying.

The doctor said, 'Can you get her to bed?'

'I'll try.'

When he had gone, David lingered. 'You can't do this alone.'

Mrs. Fraser was crying. 'What are they going to do with him? What will they do? He's only a child.'

'Yes, I can. Don't worry about me.'

Alice remembered to take her coat off. She hung it over a chair, took out her cigarettes.

'Mrs. Fraser, I want to smoke. May I? Do you smoke too?'

A violent shaking of the head. Mrs. Fraser had pretty, pinched, wan features, an irresolute mouth.

'May I, then?'

A violent nodding.

'I'm going to put you to bed. Have you got a hot water bottle?'

'I don't want to be touched. What are they going to do with him?' She grasped Alice by the knees. 'I want to die. I want to die.'

'Go along,' Alice said to David.

47

When he returned from his second errand she was sitting by the fire, alone in the room.

'How did you manage it?'

She smiled faintly. Libby's error, so far as she had been able to judge, had been to insist that Mrs. Fraser should make an effort. Alice had simply insisted that she should not. 'She was glad to be in bed. She's asleep, or nearly.'

They let Maurice in. He stared at them for a moment as if he did not know them, then went and knelt by the fire.

He said, 'Since it happened, he's become a child again. He is sitting there crying for his mother.'

'What will they do?' asked Alice. Her eyes filled; David was surprised to see her vulnerable.

'Well, the boy's mad as a hatter. They'll see that. It won't be a matter of punishment.' Maurice passed his knuckles over his forehead, kneading it. 'He went on crying for his mother. There was a child — Oscar Wilde wrote about it — who came into Reading Jail, and they couldn't find a prison suit small enough to fit him.'

Mrs. Fraser cried out suddenly in a hoarse, mannish voice, 'God made him! It was all God's fault!'

Alice went to the bedroom, looked in. 'You don't want to wake Michael and Jean, do you? We've only just got them off.'

Silence fell again, full of the echoes of that unnatural roar: it lingered in their ears.

'I'll talk to her,' Maurice said; but she would not have him. Alice went to her instead.

Maurice asked about Libby. She had done her best, David replied, but it had been beyond her. She had not wanted to go home.

'I don't suppose so. Especially as it was Alice. They didn't see much of each other in the old days, but Libby never took to her.'

An idleness, a peace, seemed to fall upon them. There was nothing for them to do, in such a lull, but to talk as they might have talked in Kensington Gardens, on a muggy afternoon with the leaves falling.

48

'She must find the old man pretty heavy in the hand. I suppose she had no one else to live with.'

David asked about her husband.

'Miles? He was a sober, young-old type, good-looking, a bit of a stick. But he did well for himself. He's changed her. She was rather dowdy all those years ago.' Maurice saw Alice's cigarettes and took one. His hands were still shaking.

When she came out at last he said to her, 'You can't stay here alone all night.'

'Of course I can. I'll sleep on the sofa. When can she see the boy?'

'Any time after eight. I'll be here about half-past, and take her along.'

'Good night, then,' Alice said. 'You look all in, and there's nothing more you can do.'

'I'll stay for half an hour. You cut along, David. You'll have to take the eight o'clock: either Kate or Libby will be there. I'll just finish my cigarette.'

As he went along the street, David looked back. There was only one lighted window among the stubble of concrete huts. Every other house was asleep. Two children, the insulted and the injured, lay far out, one in prison, one in a hospital ward. A long cat slit the shadows of the gutter, scurried in wet leaves. A late walker went by singing, in a throaty, pseudo-American voice, a popular song. His happiness, his unawareness, made David feel that the world had suddenly come afloat from its moorings. In the black stubble the tragic window glowed on, like the butt of a cigar.

Chapter Eight

IN THE pretty, finicky, little poor room, in the crack of the wound, they sheltered behind small talk.

They had drawn their chairs to the fire, were trying to forget about the shut door. Maurice forced to the back of his mind the misery of the crying boy, so far lost, so far out. The image of Alice that also contained himself was strange and yet strangely domestic; they might have belonged there, at that fireside, it might have been any hour of any evening. He hardly knew her at all; their previous acquaintance had been sketchy. They had used each other's first names, but that was only because her mother had been near to the church, and was his friend. Alice, as he remembered her, had been a clever, amusing girl, always a little detached. It had been his recollection of her general competence which had given him the impulse, that night, to ask for her help: and she had proved competent. But what made him feel now that he did not know her was this: she was as shaken, almost, as he. She was the kind of woman unwary people think would make good nurses, when they would not at all, not with imagination running all the time at full current.

As she spoke unsentimentally of a dullish life with her father-in-law, of a busy one with her husband, she was lit with affection; for a moment it eased her, taking the strain away from her eyes. He thought how odd it was to see her so unobtrusively elegant, an attractive woman, sufficiently assured not to think about herself very often; his gaze was caught by her high instep, arching down into the expensive shoe, the bone polished inside the thin stocking. Alice Forbes, as she used to be, had never seemed to him like this.

'Can we put any parish work on to you?' he asked her. 'Say no, if you don't want to.' He added loyally, 'Libby's pretty overburdened.'

'That clock has a loud tick. I wonder Mrs. Fraser can stand it. I'll do what I can, if it's hack work only.' She paused, then said: 'Have one more cigarette? You can't stay all night, I know, but don't go for ten minutes. I'll be all right then.'

'For as long as you like.'

'No. Libby will be worrying, I expect.'

'She was tired to-night.' He explained carefully how much fell upon her, the burden of her mother's delicate health, care of the boys when Kate was busy with other things.

'I saw the older boy,' Alice said, 'Simon. He's growing up.'

'He's a difficult child.'

A coal fell into the grate. 'I shouldn't make it up, really,' said Alice, 'not if I'm going to bed. I can't use all Mrs. Fraser's coal.'

They watched the glow rusting down, the papery ash settle.

'Listen,' she said, 'it isn't relevant, but I should like to tell you. Miles had a younger brother, he died of TB. When he was fifteen he got into a bad set, he held up an old woman for a dare, she shouted, he got panicky, and he bashed her. Miles was in the juvenile court, his mother was too ill to go. He was a nice-looking boy, tall, he had a fresh colour, his voice was gentle. He wouldn't speak up for himself, he just looked proud, as if he despised everyone. He was very smartly dressed that morning, new sports coat, new flannels. It maddened them. They sentenced him to be birched. Miles told me how he walked away, very dignified, quite stony. He put one hand in his pocket and tried to swagger. The back of his neck was scarlet, he had a very fair, delicate-looking neck, like a child's. Everyone seemed to stare at his buttocks as if they couldn't help it. It was more shame than he could bear, but he deserved it, didn't he? And it cured him. He never misbehaved again. Only, he died. That was fifteen years ago. What can we do in this filthy, sickening world, Maurice? What is there for us to do?'

She put her head in her hands and wept.

She said: 'Miles was very graphic. It helped him to lay the ghost, passing it on to me.'

'We can believe in the purposes of God and do what we can ourselves.'

'I haven't a ha'porth of that sort of belief. To me, you're just talking.'

'What are you raging at, if not God? There's no point in denouncing nobody at all.'

'Perhaps no point,' she said, 'but raging helps.' She leaned her head back against the chair and closed her eyes.

'We can't live with some things,' Maurice said, 'we have to try not to, or we're no use to other people.'

'I don't live with them most of the time. It was only to-night.' She added, 'We didn't have children. Sometimes I'm glad.' She looked sideways at him as if there might be something else, but she added nothing.

'Nor did Libby and I.'

'And are you sometimes glad?'

'No.'

Mrs. Fraser, waking from her drugged sleep, called out: Alice started up and went to her, Maurice following. The light from the sitting-room fell on her, making the thin night-gown on the thin body look like the drippings of candlewax. She was sitting upright.

'It was only yesterday I could hold him in my one hand, he was a tiny baby, only five pounds. He was such a pretty baby, all the nurses used to say so. "Mrs. Fraser," they used to say, "that baby's going to be a heart-throb." '

Alice sat down on the bed beside her, and put her arms round her. She cuddled her, cheek to the crown of Mrs. Fraser's thin, frizzled hair.

'What will they do to him?'

'They won't hurt him, darling, they won't punish him, they'll take him away and try and cure him. And they will cure him.'

Mrs. Fraser whispered, 'They can't. He's dirty, you see. All dirty inside.'

52

'I promise you they will cure him. Try to sleep.'

'They'll treat him as though he is ill,' Maurice said.

She pushed out of Alice's arms. 'Is that the vicar? You oughtn't to be here. You don't know how these people talk.'

For the moment, out of sheer prudery, she had forgotten what they would really talk about. 'They're a low-class lot,' she said.

As he left her with Alice, wondering what sort of night lay ahead of them both, he could think only of one thing, the kind of unimportance that grips after the exhaustions of too long a day. He thought of Alice's word of endearment to Mrs. Fraser, the unselfconscious way in which she had brought it out from an impulse of pity and exasperation combined. For some reason that he was unable to analyse, he had felt a stirring of hostility towards both women in the moment after it had been spoken: they had locked him out. He was, he believed, so shut in himself that he had begun to practise Libby's vice: the vice of delegation. It was to Alice that he had delegated work which must fall hard on her since, for all her willingness, she would take it harder than a man whose profession it was to cope, and to console.

In a cell of his mind, he saw the small weak face of the child crying for his mother.

St. Lawrence's blunted spire rose up against the washy sky.

Maurice thought how sharply personal tragedy set one back on one's heels: even in his job, where he saw so much of it, to meet it face to face was still as nonplussing as it would be to meet a diplodocus in a country lane. The vast majority of people were ill-used to the violences of life: even he was. One was lost with them, as at a social occasion among utter strangers whose lives and interests were miles away. It was even possible to detect, in one's jibbing at tragedy, something like a social embarrassment. The wrong words came so readily. The wrong references. But Alice had not felt this, not she, with her endearment: she had known what to do.

'Where did you get to?' Libby demanded, out of the dark. 'I thought you'd never come in. Darling, I know I mustn't quarrel with parishioners, even *you* couldn't but admit that I am church-trained, but I do think Mrs. Imber is quite intolerable. I would have stayed on, only I thought poor Mrs. Fraser would only get more upset if we were both there, positively wrangling. So I withdrew, and prayed that I'd done the right thing. Did I do the right thing? You know I'd never have left unless I'd felt it was the right thing to do.'

He began to undress. He was desperately tired.

'I wanted you to leave her,' he said.

Libby's voice ran on. 'I can't get that poor woman out of my mind. I do hope Mrs. Imber didn't encourage her to give way completely. If people won't face life, they have to be made to.'

He got into bed, put his arm round her. She rested her head on his breast, as she always did, for a few minutes before sleeping. She had washed her hair earlier that evening: it blew up into his nose, it smelled of lemons.

'And that poor little girl! I got the feeling no one but me remembered her. They were all worrying about that beastly boy. Say what you like, one has to be charitable, but strictly between you and me and I wouldn't say it to anyone else, wouldn't he be better off dead?'

'Possibly,' said Maurice.

'There ought to be some very *kind* way of putting these people out. Not to hurt them or frighten them, just eliminate them.'

She lay quiet for a moment. Then — 'I used to think Alice Imber was rather a nice girl. But now she's so full of her own importance. I wonder she still wants to live around here. I know we're not a slum parish, but she looks as though she ought to be living in Knightsbridge, in a service flat or something like that.'

Maurice saw the coloured whorls of approaching sleep at the back of his eyelids. 'I'm going to turn over now.'

Libby turned over first. Her rope of hair slapped at him.

She said something.

'What?'

He could not hear her.

She made a half-turn back. 'I'm sure it couldn't have been necessary for you to stay all that time, darling. You let people exhaust you.'

'I don't think so.'

'Ought I to ask Mrs. Imber to take a stall at the bazaar? There's nothing for her but the books, really, and Mrs. Walkeley might want to do that.'

'It must be nearly two,' he said.

She went on talking for a few moments, but he did not answer her, pretending to be asleep. Within moments she slept, announcing her fall into the dream with the curious bucking motion of her body, half a heave, half a kick, familiar to him over the years.

He tried to make himself more comfortable, apart from her, on the cool edge of the bed; but the mattress and springs were old and he had to balance carefully, hands stretched out and gripping before him, not to slide into the hot trough, packed against her. Her breathing ran musically up and down like an animal's purring: for ten minutes or so after falling asleep she made a little trilling sound that was not a snore, but a substitute for one. She sighed, and heaved over towards him.

And then he was wide awake, the colours gone from his darkness, his head open and roomy for the thoughts to rush in, especially one thought: before this night, from the night of her sudden return from holiday, he had ceased to love Libby: but on this night he knew it was worse, that he could not endure her.

Pressing himself away from the hot trap, he levered himself out of bed and sat with his feet to the floor, his head in his hands. He prayed for the panic to pass, for his life to become bearable again. Around him the house was heavy with people; Kate, the old woman, the boys, all pressing in upon him, needing him, thinking about him, perhaps watching him. He went on praying, his lips steadily moving, but could get no pressure behind his prayer. She was good, she needed him, she was his charge: somehow he must come to need her also. For here they were, he and she, together; in this shabby room, in this hot and sterile bed, for ever.

He lay down again beside her, putting as wide a space as he could between them. In sleep, or perhaps she was not asleep, she lifted her hand and laid it on his thigh. He laid his over it. Somehow, they had to manage. Somehow, it would be better in the morning. For he had, not to love, but to be fond of her. Whatever happened, he must drag himself to that.

Chapter Nine

THE Christmas bazaar was always held towards the end of November. 'We must get people before they've started their serious shopping,' George Kitson had said, 'it's no use when they've only fourpence left.'

At bazaars, Libby glowed. Here she could shuttle about, busy in the eyes of all, beautiful, almost flirtatious. She was a leading lady: all the others were in the chorus. This year the event opened much as usual, with the hall empty, except for stallholders, for the first ten minutes after the advertised opening. The decorations were not as successful as usual, since it had been Libby's idea to leave them to Simon and Dick. It would draw the boys in, she had explained, to have something in which they could co-operate together, without interference from others. Simon had the artistic touch, Dick was practically and mechanically minded. She expected their efforts to stupefy everyone.

'People may well be stupefied,' Kate had said wearily, 'but I doubt whether they'll be pleased.'

In fact the boys, dragged away from their own favourite employments or lack of them, had sulked through the job in a perfunctory way, and the hall, its khaki paint and pitch-pine relieved only by a few ill-hung paper chains, did not look festive.

'You are little beasts,' Kate stormed at her sons, as they loafed behind the bran-tub which Libby had also put in their charge, 'especially you, Dick, because you can be decent if you choose.'

'Oh, so I can't,' said Simon.

'Perhaps you could be, but you don't choose.'

'We *are* going to have a nice time,' he observed, heavily sarcastic. He went to start up the gramophone. Dick had not, as he had promised to do, mended the loud-speaker: the noise came through with an echoing rasp.

Maurice asked Kate if she was all right. He knew what a morning she had had; both the cleaners had been away with colds. 'No headache, anyway.' She touched wood. She smiled. 'Libby looks far too attractive for a parson's wife.'

Libby was wearing her green dress and had done her hair a new way. She went from stall to stall, giving a little touch to each. As soon as she had passed by the china stall, run by Lucy Simnett and three of her Guides, David unobtrusively put things back where they had been before.

Mrs. Walkeley was running the bookstall, with Alice assisting. It was a more attractive feature than usual, since Alice had enlivened the usual collection of dog-eared novels by a donation of Penguin books in bright and decent condition. 'Don't we look smart!' Libby exclaimed, looking at Alice as she said so. She took a volume from the top of the centre-piece, a tower of those books with the most colourful jackets, and placed it sideways. 'There! Isn't that better?'

'Yes, I think it is,' Alice agreed.

Joan Johnson-Black, on the largest stall, which was for household goods, shared her husband's opinion of Libby. Before her display could receive a little touch, she said heartily, 'Now, hands off, Mrs. Fisher! I must stand or fall by my own efforts.'

Libby went into the back room, where helpers were getting tea under the direction of Mrs. Kitson. Among them was Mrs. Fraser, creeping brokenly around, her eyes on the ground. Libby had insisted that she come, being convinced that it was good for her not to hide away from people. 'After all,' she had said, 'it isn't your fault. It's all a question of genes, and we can't tell where poor Derek got his.'

Derek had been put into a County Council home, with the promise of psychiatric treatment. Mrs. Fraser was still receiving abusive letters from maniacs, who felt it would have been more helpful to the protection of the community if her son had been flogged.

People were trickling in now: in twenty minutes the hall would be full, and Maurice would ask Mrs. Hannaway to perform the opening ceremony. It was his practice not to invite semi-celebrated outsiders, but to bestow the honours of official opening upon the wives of particularly praiseworthy parishioners. It made Libby cross that, because of her office, she could not do it herself. When she was a girl, she had been captain of the school debating society. She knew she had a pretty, carrying voice, good diction, and could speak to the point. She would have felt better if she had had to give way to some television figure, but it irked her to have to listen to Mrs. Hannaway. She heard enough of her as it was.

George Kitson, though for another reason, deplored Maurice's policy. 'If you want to lose money, lose it. But we need a draw of some sort.'

'I have absolutely no other way in which to reward people who work like dogs,' Maurice replied obstinately.

Jeremy Fawcett had moved to Alice's side. 'I say, what a wreck those boys have made of the place!'

'Nobody will notice.'

'I notice. It hurts *me*.'

Peter Betts and Lou Waterer, running some harmless gamble, had been stowed away by Maurice in a dark corner behind the platform, for he could not help feeling that their bizarreness would otherwise be noticed. He recognized his own lack of charity: yet they were thorns in his flesh. Hardly a month passed by without their coming to consult him privately either about their theological difficulties — they delighted in the tortuous — or, worse, about the difficulties of their own position in society. He found it hard to regard them as religious men, believing they were interested only in obtaining petty office in the church. He thought he knew why they wanted it, too: they had a passionate belief that it would get them accepted as respectable persons. It would be a score for their side.

'I say, Vicar,' Peter called out, 'would you mind too ferociously if I asked one of those nice nephews of yours to rig up something, say an arrow, in our direction? Otherwise people simply won't know we're here.' He was a middle-aged man, tall, with a grey fur-cap of hair; Lou was in his early thirties, small, dark as a Spaniard.

'I could try,' Maurice said, rather ungraciously.

He spoke to the boys.

'Nothing to make an arrow with,' said Simon.

Dick had brightened a little, encouraged by the influx of people, by the festive noise. 'Oh, I don't know. We could cut one out of cardboard and string it across those lights.'

They pottered about with cardboard, crepe paper, gum and wire.

'You can't use that colour,' Simon said, with an air of maidenly repugnance, 'it will scream at the chains. It will be bloody sickening.'

Dick said they hadn't got another colour, it would have to do.

'Well then, don't expect me to help. I won't have anything to do with making the place look ghastly.'

His brother picked up a string of crepe paper, looked at it, let it concertina between his hands. 'All right,' he said acquiescently, and together they kicked the materials for the arrow under the novelties stand.

Mrs. Hannaway, after a pleasant little inaudible speech, was presented with flowers by Mary, the sacristan's youngest.

'And now,' said Kate, sardonic yet faintly hopeful, 'this is where we put up the crush barriers.'

But buying was not too sharp. The household stall was quickly diminished, the handwork and books, as usual, hung fire.

Maurice came to stand by Alice. He had not spoken to her alone since the night Derek Fraser was arrested.

'So much noise,' she said, 'for so few sales.'

'If we make less than two hundred, Kitson will refuse to pay my rates again.'

'I'll pay your rates if he does.'

He smiled at her. 'I believe you would.'

'But of course I would. Tell Kitson to jump in the Serpentine.'

Plym came up to them. 'What have you got here? I can't afford more than five bob. Oh, my God, Longfellow in diamond type!'

Alice told him he had not got to buy it: there were other books.

'I hate books,' said Plym. 'Here you are, here's the five bob. Put it in the kitty.'

'But you must have something——'

'Don't use that bazaar-voice to me, it doesn't suit you. Colonel's looking for you, Vicar, he's got someone in tow. He's over by the door.'

It was typical of Plym not to have recognized the Archdeacon. Maurice did, and his heart sank. He was conscious of his own bluff, parsonical bearing as he went towards him; a parson is first of all a man, he thought, but not at bazaars and not to Sandeman.

The Venerable Alfred Sandeman was a very tall, fat man with a thin man's long, shrewd eyes. He was a dazzling preacher, who drew full churches and not infrequent newspaper publicity. He had the trick of expressing his reactionary opinions in so honest, humorous and daring a tone that he sounded like a liberal churchman and was, indeed, often taken for one by persons not in the habit of listening very carefully. Success, and the prospect of greater success, lay on him like a powdering of gold dust; Maurice, who could not stand the sight of him, suspected that he would emit a faint phosphorescent glow if shut in a dark room. He guessed Johnson-Black would not have brought him along had he had any choice in the matter. Not that they had ever discussed the Archdeacon between them; but Maurice and his warden knew each other's hearts.

'Well,' he said, 'this is an unexpected honour,' and despite himself, his voice fell at the end of the sentence.

'Not a bit of it! A chance meeting, in Harrod's, as a matter of fact. James told me you'd got your "do" on, and I said, "Well, I'll come along with you, high time I knew a bit more about my Archdeaconry." '

He knew too much already.

'Have some tea?' Maurice suggested.

'Yes, I think I will; wet my whistle, as they say. Fisher, you're looking well: and this is a jolly affair, isn't it? Ah, behold your good lady!'

'My dear Archdeacon!' Libby cried. 'How very, very nice! And such a stranger, alas.'

'Now, now, now, now!' He bent a comical frown upon her. 'Are you rebuking me?'

She looked at him under her lashes. 'You know I wouldn't dare.'

'Wouldn't she, Fisher, eh? Now, I've never had time to know your lady very well, but as something of a judge of men *and* women, I'd say there was nothing she didn't dare.'

'Do I dare tempt you to inspect our modest display, then?' said Libby.

'If you reward me with a cup of your excellent tea afterwards and something home-made. I bet my bottom dollar the buns of St. Lawrence's are the best in six parishes.'

As Libby led him triumphantly off, Maurice heard Plym at his elbow. 'The *whats* of St. Lawrence's?'

'Go away, Plym.'

'I must have heard wrong.'

Maurice whispered to his warden, 'What does he want?'

Johnson-Black said unhappily, 'I don't know. It wasn't my fault. I'll get him away again if I can.'

'Who is that, making the party go?' Alice said to Maurice later.

The Archdeacon was the centre of a laughing group. His head thrown back, his eyes wide, he was recounting some serio-comic anecdote.

Maurice told her.

'Why are you so worried?' she asked him. 'You can't have been doing wrong.'

'Should you say I couldn't?'

'I should say you couldn't.'

He felt the sudden wash of an emotion he was unable to analyse. Standing at his side, she seemed to be one with him; he could almost imagine the physical touch of shoulder and thigh. He was conscious, too, of a draining tiredness. He sat down on the edge of her stall, jumped up again as it tilted. 'Sorry. Well, I suppose I'd better go and seek Mahomet, rather than wait for him to come to me.'

As he approached the group, the Archdeacon left it. 'Ah, Fisher! We should get together more often, I must arrange it. Things crop up, one lets them slide: a weak lot we are. Everything all right?'

'Perfectly.'

'That business about, what's his name, Rogers; not the right time to go into it, but do *think*, my dear fellow — that's all I ask, just *think*. You know the first principles. Whatever our sentiments may be — and mine tempt me often enough, I assure you—we have to stand firm. Otherwise the whole fabric crumbles. Cruel to be kind, that's what it has to be, eh? A word to the wise: I don't need to rub it in.'

Maurice said, with that bravery which is worse than cowardice because it sounds like cowardice, that there were special circumstances.

The Archdeacon, younger than he, looked at him fondly. 'No. There are none. We have to get that clear, Heaven help us: you and me, and the most generous-hearted.' He swung round to greet Libby again. 'Do you know, much as I'd like to stay, I really must be running along? I'm sure you'll have a great success, Mrs. Fisher, I can hear the money rolling merrily in.' He lowered his voice to a jocular whisper. 'It is most improper for me to say so, but I suspect you are the chief attraction.'

Johnson-Black came up to ask if he could drive him anywhere.

'No, no, no! A bus is the ticket for me — I say, that's a bit clumsy, a bus-ticket! No, no, James, you stay here and keep the ball rolling. No, I simply refuse to disturb you.'

Johnson-Black said he wasn't disturbed and took him away, casting at Maurice, as he went, a blank, gloomy look which only Maurice could interpret as friendship.

'"A darlin' man!"' Libby quoted, in a brogue. 'Well, that was a surprise! "A darlin' man!" I wish he could have stayed for the entertainment.'

Later, Alice took an opportunity to whisper, 'Was it all right?'

Maurice stared at her. For a second he was faintly ruffled that she should feel she had the right to ask him. Then he said, recognizing her right, though he could not understand it, 'More or less.'

She said uncomfortably, 'Libby has asked me to come back to you for supper. I should like to, of course.'

'Of course, come. But it will be scraps, I'm afraid.'

He found Libby. 'Why on earth did you ask Alice back to-night of all nights? Kate will be about dead after all this.'

She tucked her arm companionably through his. 'Well, darling, you know what a gossip-shop this place can be. I thought it would look better.'

'Why on earth should it look better? Better than what?'

She replied that (by sheer accident, she knew) he had seemed to spend a lot of time with Alice Imber. 'You know, and I know, how ridiculous it is, but people here will seize on anything. You've been talking to her on and off the best part of the afternoon — it doesn't mean *anything*, but these old tabbies will talk.'

'This seems mad to me,' Maurice said.

The bazaar was dying down: he was hungry: it was nearly closing time. The floor was littered with sweet-papers, crumbs, trampled cigarette-butts. A paper chain had come loose at one end and was trailing over the platform. Peter and Lou, from their corner, were still spiritedly crying 'Walk up, walk up,' at the few lingerers. In the back room, George Kitson was counting the takings. He looked up as Maurice came in. 'Not bad. One hundred and seventy-four pounds eight shillings and threepence to date. But not good.'

'Who guessed the cake?'

'The Archdeacon,' said Kitson. 'There is no justice in this world.'

'He would guess cakes,' said Maurice, with bitterness.

Mrs. Fraser came through with a tray of dirty cups. 'If this is all, sir, I shall have to be getting back.'

Surprised, he told her she might go whenever she pleased.

'Mrs. Fisher said she wanted me to finish.' She added softly, looking at him with what might have been a gleam of despairing amusement, 'She said it would take me out of myself.'

Melvyn Hannaway came rushing in, breathless. 'Last come, last served! I tried to get here before, but not a hope, not a hope. Is there a cup of tea left, however wet and warm? Did Dolly open the affair in style?'

Maurice assured him of his wife's success, but broke the news that there was no more tea.

'How much, Kitson, dear boy? One seventy-four, eight and three? That's — let me see — eleven and eight, no, eleven and nine, to make a hundred and seventy-five, a good round sum: let's see if I've got it. Ten shillings — one shilling — sixpence — *and* a threepenny bit. And another quid, the married man's mite. Is this our grand total?'

'One seventy-six,' said Kitson. 'With some oddments to come.'

Peter and Lou, who had taken over the last hour of the bran-tub from Kate's missing sons, brought in nine pounds seventeen shillings and sixpence. The greater part of this was represented by a five-pound note, and Maurice felt an unreasoning anger.

'Mrs. Imber?'

'Just this last five minutes,' said Peter, 'it was so sweet of her. And all she drew was the most repulsive little pocket-comb, pink, with diamanté.'

It was just on eight o'clock. Plym came back to play 'God Save the Queen' on the piano to the last half-dozen visitors, Youth Club members who were jostling each other all over the littered floor. Soon they went away. Soon most of the lights were out. The cleaners would be round on Monday morning, Mrs. Fraser among them. Stall holders packed up their remaining goods. Melvyn Hannaway had calculated that half a crown would bring the takings up to a good, round one hundred and eighty-six and had made up the difference himself. The street echoed with good-nights.

Supper had that air of festivity often achieved by exhausted people who would rather go to bed. Kate, apprised of a guest at the last moment, had managed a hot meal of sorts. Dick was upstairs asleep, but Simon, in one of his manic phases, was helping with the dishes, smiling all the while to himself in a mysterious way as if he had discovered the whole secret of existence and was contemplating the shock it was going to be to the others when they found out. Mrs. Marsden, who had known the Imbers but not Alice, since she had not come to live with Maurice and Libby until Alice had gone to Canada, was full of reminiscence. 'I remember when this was a prosperous parish, my dear. Vernon Square on Sundays had a regular church parade, there was nothing less than a half-crown in the plate, except for what the children gave.'

'There's never much less than a half-crown now,' said Kate, 'only it buys about as much as sixpence would in your day.'

'Oh, that I wouldn't know,' said the old woman, nodding her head, 'I've lost touch with things. I say to my girls, sixpence for an *egg*? And they laugh at me. Mother, they say, you just don't know.'

Libby, who had left the table to lie upon the couch, saying that if she did not put her feet up she would drop, looked long and gently at Alice, as if computing her measurements, and, like Simon, smiled a good deal to herself. 'Forgive me if I don't talk much, Mrs. Imber,' she explained, 'but I've been going the social rounds till my throat's dry.'

'Yes,' said her mother, 'I don't know how you do it. I don't know how you have the patience. Such quarrelsomeness among all the old dears, who has which stall, whose is the best cake — I should never have made a parson's wife. I used to say to Libby, You marry a lawyer like your father, but never a doctor and never a parson. Your life won't be your own. But there was only one who would do for her.'

'Only one,' said Libby. She looked intimately across at Maurice.

Alice asked if she might smoke.

'If you're not afraid,' Libby answered. 'We're cowards here, except Maurice and Kate. And I'm always nagging him to give it up.'

'Too true, too true,' said Simon in a comic whisper, just loud enough to be heard. He walked out with the pudding plates.

'He is such a brat,' Libby told Alice, 'and such a dear, really. It's lucky we do all get on so well, because Heaven help us if we didn't.'

'We have been known to have our occasional spats,' Kate put in, her eyes brightened by sarcasm. 'Families do.' A din came from the next room; Simon, tired of company, was playing the gramophone. She rose. 'You will probably hear one of them in a minute.' She left the table. They heard her shouting at him above the uproar.

Mrs. Marsden told Alice that now she was home, she must never go a-roaming again. St. Lawrence's had so few nice people left, Alice would know what she meant; she was not a snob, but the people in the requisitioned houses on the south side of the square were very rough. Sometimes they tied string to the railings.

'Now, Mother,' said Libby, judiciously, 'there are a few very decent people among them, though I do tell Maurice he ought not to countenance the things some of them do.'

He said sharply, 'I don't. I don't even know what they do.'

She looked at him. He saw her surprise. He had spoken too sharply, out of his tiredness, his irritation with her that she should have invited anybody home, to lay more work upon Kate. He must be careful not to speak like that again.

She seemed to hesitate before speaking. Then she said,

'But you should, shouldn't you? After all, we had that Fraser business right in our midst——'

'Sh,' said Kate, returning, 'not with Simon still on the prowl.' She lit another cigarette, let it hang from her lips. She turned to Alice. 'Mrs. Imber, did anyone but Maurice properly thank you for looking after her that night? We're rather poor thankers, and it was right outside your line of country.'

Libby flashed, 'I'm sure she knew how much we appreciated it!' She had a wild look, as if her mind was upon something quite different.

'You had had the worst part of it,' Alice said, 'before I came. And you have a parish to look after.'

'People don't always understand,' said Libby, 'but I knew by instinct that you did.'

Chapter Ten

WHEN a single remark made Libby realise that Maurice was lost to her, she thought she would faint. All her life the idea of fainting had fascinated her, but she had never done it. In crises she had sometimes shut her eyes, swayed from her ankles and tried to feel earth falling away; when she was in her teens, these demonstrations had succeeded to the point of being known as 'Libby's turns', and they had got her out of some tight corners. But that night at supper, though it was only for a moment, she had felt the sick drop of her heart, the swamping wave of heat, and then the bitter cold. She had not moved. She had just sat there, on the sofa, with all of them around her, she had made some comment, and time had moved on.

She had known, ever since they came back from the sea, that something was wrong with him, that he was not pleased with her. At first she thought he was angry because she would not sleep with him — though it had been a mad request to make of her, after the long, anxious, exhausting day she had had with her mother, Kate and the boys. Then it had struck her that it was not this at all: though he would not show it, he had been upset because she had spent money on a new dress. This had upset her. She was not extravagant, she was used to making-do. It was the first dress she had bought for herself in two years. She had, in fact, been planning to re-open the matter with him that night, to make him admit that she had never been selfish, never wasteful.

Then this blow had fallen. It was not a matter of words. She had made some comment about not countenancing the behaviour of certain people in the parish, and he had replied,

'I don't. I don't know what they do.' Nothing more than that. But for the first time he had not spoken *to her*. He had spoken with a remote and bitter sharpness to someone who had talked to him, to a mere voice. She might have been a nagging stranger at his elbow whom he had pushed away with no more concern than he would have shown to a piece of furniture obstructing his path. Now, shut for privacy in the bathroom, she pressed the flannel to her hot eyes, rinsed her face again and again to distract herself by physical sensation from hearing the words a second time. She turned on all the taps and let them run. 'It is not true,' she said to herself in a loud, reasonable voice, 'you are imagining things.' Clinging to the towel rail, she swayed back and forth, touching her forehead to the wall, bringing it away again. A glimpse of her face in the glass before it steamed over showed her that she had not become ugly: she had not cried yet and she would not cry.

There was, she knew, no question of 'somebody else'. A priest could not do that, and anyway, Maurice had never looked at other women. It was just that she was no longer there for him. She had been pushed outside his love and, worse, outside his interest. I shall 'win him back', she said to her dimmed reflection, and her thoughts scurried towards the advice pages in the magazines she sometimes read when Kate was not there to jeer at her.

Still: what had she done? It could not be the dress, she must have been wrong there. The worm of real guilt stirred and she was, for a moment, sickened by that too. But she was not going to give way over love-making. It was no fault of hers that her body had revolted from the interminable years of pretence. She *could* not do it, even as a loathing child cannot swallow a morsel of fat, but gags, and holds it in his mouth. It was her age, she was thirty-eight, her mother had told her that some women began early. The repugnance was connected, she knew, with the approach of menopause; it was the herald, the first sign.

'Aunt Libby! Are you in there? Are you going to be all night?' And then, jocularly, 'El-ee-zabeth, open up!'

'Go away, Simon,' she shouted, 'you ought to be in bed.'

He pounded on the door. 'I can't hear you.'

She turned off the taps. 'I'm having a bath. I said, go to bed!'

He grumbled; she heard his footsteps retreating.

She sat down on the edge of the bath; she was trembling. She must go to him soon, as if nothing had happened. He would be wondering now why she didn't come.

I love him, she said to herself.

I have been a good wife, I've done my best. Nobody could say I haven't.

As the steam cleared, she looked at herself again and thought, with detached interest, I am in a state of shock.

Slowly, as an excuse for having kept him waiting, she undressed, took her hair down and put on Simon's dressing-gown which was hanging behind the door. When she got back to their room, Maurice was in bed.

'Hullo,' he said, smiling, 'what have you been up to?'

It seemed like a relief. She wanted to run to him, to tell him all she had imagined, how awful it had been. But she did not.

'I had a bath. I forgot my dressing-gown.'

He said, 'I'm dead to the world.'

She said slowly, 'So am I. When do we ever feel anything else?'

He made room for her, put his arm round her.

Now, Libby thought, I shall have to be brave. Putting her head up, she kissed his throat. He did not stir or speak. 'Maurice,' she said.

'What?'

'Love me?'

He patted her, squeezed her shoulders. Still he was silent. She stretched herself against him, as if she were climbing a wall. Her toes and her knees touched his. He shot away from her and sat up. 'You've left a tap running.'

'I don't think I have.'

'I can hear it. I'll go and turn it off.'

71

When he came back he kissed her briskly, said, 'A hundred and eighty-six wasn't bad, even Kitson couldn't conceal a degree of sober satisfaction,' and turned over onto his side, away from her.

I won't cry, she said to herself, I will not make myself ugly. It isn't true, anyway. I have been imagining things. Relief at his rejection, at least, quietened her. She lay awake for a long time, savouring it.

Chapter Eleven

THE Pelhams had known Jeremy Fawcett since he was a child. They were entertaining him and his wife Louisa, a tall, good-looking girl who always seemed to be embarrassed by her husband's sprightliness. They had been married seven years and had one son, but Fawcett still behaved, Georgina considered, in the showy and rather selfish manner of a bridegroom. It was ten days to Christmas.

'Poor Kate Morley's coming in later,' she said to him, 'I thought it would be a change for her.'

'Poor dear Kate!' Jeremy exclaimed. 'I wouldn't say this to anyone but you, darling Georgina, but she gets more and more wan about the vicar. It's frightfully tragic for her.'

'Scandalmonger,' said Louisa heavily. 'You're absolutely unsafe. You ought to be gagged.'

'The back of a hairbrush for you,' Fawcett said luxuriantly, 'if I have any more nonsense.'

'He means it.' She appealed to Humphrey. 'He honestly does.'

Humphrey smiled on her as on all young women, but Georgina was cross.

'Your wife's right, Jeremy. A church is quite a bad enough place for gossip without tittle-tattle from churchwardens.'

'I am a bad boy,' he said smugly, raising up very slightly so he could just see himself in the pier-glass.

'And I'm sure it is untrue about Mrs. Morley. I have never heard it suggested,' Georgina added.

He told her that it never had been suggested except by himself, and he tucked into crumpets boyishly, somehow giving the appearance that he was sitting cross-legged to do so. The gone-to-seed drawing-room looked handsome in the glow of fire and lamplight. Georgina had already put holly over the pictures. 'You two are quite above the struggle,' he said, 'which is why I gossip only to you. I know you have no one you could possibly repeat it to.'

She replied that it was not a question of having no one; if she had a circle of the most avid listeners she would not say a word.

Humphrey asked how Fawcett's own work was going.

'Oh, busy, busy enough. What with that and my parish labours, I hardly have time to take Louisa to a flick.'

'It's true. I'm alone night after night.'

'Any more slander,' Fawcett said, pinching her just above the ankle so that she gave a little squeal, 'and you'll pay for it when I get you home.'

'You know it's true! Where have I been lately? Only to sherry at the Johnson-Blacks'——'

'Now he can only just about keep going, poor old boy,' Fawcett said to Humphrey. 'His army pension's worth less and less. He's worried about keeping up his clubs.'

'And what else?' Georgina asked tartly. 'What other distresses don't we know about?'

'Well,' he grinned, 'Kitson's son only got three subjects in "O" level. The poor lad is almost moronic — not that George is clever, but he does have a kind of *tang*. Louisa looks at Adrian while she's bathing him, and prays for him to be as bright as I am.'

'She should pray for him to be less conceited,' said Georgina.

She went to open the door to Kate, who came in with her long, tired stride, hat on the back of her head. She greeted Humphrey with some deference, shook hands slackly with the Fawcetts and refused everything but a cup of tea. Not knowing the Pelhams very well, surprised at their invitation, she was at first rather stilted. It occurred to Georgina that she was not very good at concealing her feelings; obviously she had not much use for Jeremy, and, as obviously, Humphrey impressed her. She felt the former must be wrong about her. If Kate Morley had been at all attracted to her brother-in-law, half the parish would have known about it. Yet, as she was aware, Jeremy was shrewd. He was shallow and lightweight, he had stretched his rather slender talents to the full: but he had always been a sharp boy. Ashamed of herself, she asked Kate about the vicar.

'Exactly and precisely as usual,' Kate said. 'What else can he be? If you're run off your feet, you can't afford to be variable. Christmas, of course, makes it worse for all of us.'

'But it is a lovely season,' Georgina suggested.

'So my mother says.' Kate grinned suddenly. 'She sings "I saw three ships" to herself from the first of December onwards. And she makes it "*Chrissimas* day in the morning". The boys just cannot bear "*Chrissimas*". It makes them rush to the gramophone and play jazz with loud needles. Our household is the scene of contention at this time of the year.'

Humphrey, unexpectedly, said he entirely understood. Christmas was getting increasingly commercialised and he doubted if some of the hobbledehoys he saw streaming out of the hall on Youth Club nights would be able, if requested, to make any significant proposition as to its meaning. He and Georgina were content to go to church twice that day, instead of once, and to drink a little of his remaining port. They neither of them cared for Christmas food. This year they were to buy themselves a little foie gras and a pork chop.

'Still,' said Georgina, 'there is the spirit of the thing.'

'When Adrian's older,' said Louisa, 'we shall have all that fag with a tree.'

The curtains were undrawn. Outside in the square the church tree, with its sparse lights, twinkled through the drizzle. Some unofficial carol singers were making their rounds, slurring in an ugly and perfunctory manner through a verse of 'Hark, the Herald Angels' and then rushing to bang on doors.

'I am not going to give again,' said Georgina firmly. 'This is the ninth lot since Monday.'

They waited till the bangers were tired and went away, trailing their carol after them through the slush.

'And yet,' said Kate, 'when the Sunday School give their carol concert, I daresay I shall cry my eyes out. Certainly Libby will.'

'Hasn't that nice Mrs. Imber been producing their little play for them?' Georgina asked.

Kate replied that she had, and for her pains had merely got accused of pushing herself forward. She had paid for half the costumes, too, which had only seemed to make her offence worse.

'But why does she do it?' Fawcett wondered. 'She's always been an agnostic, and she does look a fish out of water in our rather, let us say, compressed community.'

'To get herself out of the house, I expect,' said Louisa, 'which I'd do myself if I had half the chance. Looking after one old man can't take up much of her time.'

'On my word,' Humphrey observed, 'you really do seem to be an uncharitable lot. Can't you simply be grateful for the poor girl's help and leave it at that?'

'Did _I_ sound ungrateful?' Kate said slowly. 'I didn't mean to be. And don't reprove me, Mr. Pelham, because I can't stand an awful lot of anything these days.'

To their consternation they saw her eyes fill with tears. She turned her head away. They were stricken with embarrassment. She sat in silence, a good-looking, bony woman who might once have been good at games, staring at the window.

'My dear, I didn't mean that,' Humphrey said at last.

'He was rebuking me,' Louisa said, 'people always do. I'm utterly used to it. Jeremy is rebuking me from morn till night.'

Kate said she must soon be going. It had been nice of them to ask her, it made a break in the trivial round, the common task. Her voice was light and sarcastic, her smile warm.

In the hall, Georgina put a hand upon her arm. 'Mrs. Morley, you seem so overstrained. Is there nothing we can do to help? Humphrey and I are broken reeds, I know, but anything we could do. . . . And you mustn't think Humphrey meant anything at all, he never does. He is the most harmless of men, which is why I love him so much.'

'I know he is,' said Kate. 'I'm so sorry. But I don't go out socially very much, so I forget how to behave. Also, I've had a heavy couple of days. There was the Youth Club last night, I have to look in now and then——' She stopped.

'Yes?' Georgina prompted.

'I have to look in now and then.' Again she hesitated. 'Don't tell Maurice.'

'— tell?' Georgina was bewildered.

'I must go before I get any sillier.' Kate picked up her loaded shopping-basket, her bag, mackintosh, umbrella, books in a library sling. 'I miss my car. I used to have a little one, when I was living in the country.' She insisted incongruously, 'You must come and see us soon.'

'Extraordinary woman,' Georgina pondered aloud, returning to the drawing-room. 'Is she always like that, Jeremy? It is really most extraordinary.'

Humphrey said, 'But whatever did I do?'

'I don't think you did anything,' Louisa intervened. 'She was just in a general state. All the Fishers are, except Mrs. F., and she just seems to float through things.'

Humphrey said he would hate to upset her, he was really most upset.

Chapter Twelve

HE WAS in the small room of the church hall, where Alice's children were preparing their play. In the hall itself the Youth Club was in full session, the noise deafening. Kate said he ought to look in there later on, and had been insistent: though it was not his night for it.

Alice, in sweater and trousers, was helping to sketch out sheets of cardboard with Noah's Ark trees, cottages and clouds. A gaggle of smaller children were stamping away in a country dance, their faces intent. One little girl with a gap in her teeth was sliding wildly up and down, crying 'Whee-ee-ee!' each time as she went. Maurice caught her and lifted her up. He asked her if she were in the play.

'I'm the star,' she said coldly. 'They don't give me nothing to say, though.'

He pulled her plaits and returned her to her game. He went over to Alice. 'Perhaps it's as well she's got nothing to say. What's her part?'

'She's the Virgin Mary in the mime section,' Alice told him. She stood upright, panting a little. Her colour was high, her hair untidy. She looked young, happy and absorbed, and Maurice felt the infection of her pleasure.

'It's very good of you to do all this.'

She denied it. She had nothing else to do, she was enjoying herself. They had almost finished the costumes; Libby had seen them that afternoon and had been complimentary, though, Alice added, she had thought the colours rather violent.

Maurice looked at her sharply, but saw nothing in her face. In a way, he would have liked to catch her out in a touch of malice, however small; he could then have said to himself that she was no better than Libby, and no more likeable.

'Have a cup of tea,' she said, 'it will stiffen you for the rowdies. Now that is a job I would not take on. I can't manage not to bridle when they giggle at me. Is it my trousers, do you suppose? Do they think them inappropriate to my age?'

'Mrs. Imber,' shouted one of the children, 'Joyce has got a sore throat, she says she feels sick. If she gets ill, can I play Joseph?'

'I had better cope,' said Alice. She went away.

Maurice watched her for a few minutes. He would have liked to stay, to have had the cup of tea, to have talked to someone for whom, on the surface level, life seemed so easy. He thought Miles Imber must have been fortunate; she was a bringer of rest. Yet he fancied she would bring a man more than that. He liked the way she steered the sore throat under a light and peered at it: asked questions, reassured, extracted the admission that Joseph did not feel so sick after all — 'I get my nerves from my mum,' the child complacently explained.

But he had to get on. Calling good-night to Alice, he went into the cacophony next door. On the platform, two of the older boys were playing ping-pong in an inept but savage manner, using bad language when the balls rolled off into the body of the hall. Behind the platform, a few of the more earnest and mechanically-minded were working on some sort of lighting scheme. At the far end, the rowdier elements were playing jazz on the old gramophone; boys and girls clustered with dead faces round the music, slapping their hands together on the off-beat. Two girls were jiving together, performing their violent evolutions without any facial signs of pleasure or excitement; yet, as Maurice knew, they never missed a club night, and they never varied their activities. He was puzzled and worried by the phenomenon of that inverted pride which scorned to show happiness; he had a suspicion that more than a few of these sullen children were, in fact, as happy as he had been as a child, and he believed the real danger lay in the ugly pose. In the middle of the floor, David and Lucy were dancing

79

stiffly and decorously together, partly in the hope of encouraging others to join them, and partly because it was an excuse to hold each other without undue remark. They got, of course, a certain amount of remark; a derisive boy shouted out to Lucy that she was a 'cool cat', and made sucking noises at David. Neither of them reacted to this stimulus, and Maurice admired them because they did not. David, odd-looking as he was, a natural butt for boys of aggressive virility, had nevertheless made himself popular: he did not mind if people laughed at him, he was perfectly content to offer himself as part of the entertainment.

Maurice called up to the platform that if he heard any more of that dirty language he would throw them out. They responded, he knew, to this hard and simple phraseology: also, he was more or less confident that he had the physical strength to make a good try at it, if his bluff were ever called.

'Oh, Cor, Vicar,' one of them protested, 'it don't mean nothing. It's only for something to say.'

He told him there were other things to say, and started across to the jazz group. They turned bovine faces upon him, one or two negligently raised a hand in salute: but that was all. That was customary. He stood for a few minutes and listened to what was, to him, an appalling monotony of noise, while he took notice of three of David's worst thorns in the side, two boys of seventeen and a girl of sixteen, all three distinguished in the past by terms in approved schools or detention centres. They were quiet enough to-night: there would be no trouble until the music was over, the gramophone was locked. As snakes were supposed to be hypnotised by music, so were they.

Then, at the back of him, he heard another sucking noise. It struck him that he would have to stop it: however indifferent David and Lucy might be, there was no reason for tolerating the more repellent forms of bad manners. He turned: and saw that the boy was grinning at himself. The record had come to an end. Somebody in the group tittered; a subdued wave of tittering broke out, like the noise of small birds in a tree over a river.

'You might as well let me share the joke,' he said. 'I could do with it, at the end of a long day.'

The faces, momentarily animated, shut up again. No one spoke. Someone put on another record, and the slow, sodden clapping went on.

Lucy and David had retired to sit on wooden chairs against the wall. Maurice joined them. The boy who had sucked at him grinned, stuck out his behind, put a hand on his hip and made a maidenly twirl. Then he ran off behind the platform, and a row broke out between him and the electricians.

'What's all that about?' Maurice asked.

David said, 'I don't know. They've been a bit odd all the evening. Something's amusing them.'

'Apparently I am.'

'Oh, I'm sure it's not you!' said Lucy in a hasty, social voice. 'You know what they are.'

Maurice looked at David and saw his unease. He was silent. He wished so hard for Lucy to go away that after a second she did, making some excuse about one of the girls.

'Well?'

David said, 'I swear I haven't any idea. They laugh at me, too.'

'They always laugh at you. But why should I have become hilarious, all of a sudden?'

'I don't think it was meant for you particularly.'

For no reason except some mysterious operation of the herd instinct, the floor began to fill with couples. At first, the girls usually danced together, and a few of the boys also, disagreeably clowning. Then, gradually, the sexes mingled. Two girls dancing past the chairs where Maurice and his curate sat were overcome with silent mirth. Breasts pressed together, they leaned their heads on each other's shoulders.

'No,' said Maurice, 'it's definitely for me. Do I look peculiar? Or has someone stuck "Kick me" on my back? That has happened before.'

'A simple joke,' said David, with the same unease, 'but unfailingly pleasing. Only to give the maximum of pleasure one must object. I have to pretend to, sometimes, or it would spoil things for them. I don't mean just that joke. Any joke.'

Maurice said he thought he had better take prayers. If that went off all right, there was nothing to worry about.

It went off extremely quietly, but was not all right. They sat before him with bulging faces, the joke swelling in all of them now. Some of them were innocent, some good, some generous, some would make successes of their lives: but they were all potential witnesses, titillated and charmed, of a ceremony of torture. In Nuremberg, twenty years ago, they would have stood by grinning while Jews scrubbed the pavements with acid-soaked rags, while the guards swamped their buckets over the fur coats the women had not been allowed to remove. They would have laughed, not because they were essentially cruel, but because they could not feel at all for others, could barely feel for themselves. After all, a clown swamped with whitewash in a circus was offered up for the amusement of children: what was the difference between that and Mrs. Steinbaum in her slimy squirrel, her fat bottom in the air?

A sense of proportion, Maurice thought, is something I tend to lack. This is nothing to do with Nuremberg. This is some harmless private joke, and if I'm the victim what is it to me?

He heard himself saying, rather brusquely, 'The almighty and merciful Lord, the Father, the Son, and the Holy Ghost, bless and preserve us. Amen.'

It seemed to him that they cleared out rather more quickly than usual: well, that was all to the good. If a private joke could do that, then a private joke was an admirable thing.

He did not think about it any more, or so he thought.

He was surprised to hear himself say next morning to Kate, as she went through the washing-up in her efficient, windmill style, 'What's wrong at the Youth Club?'

She turned, hand uplifted, the steaming swab depending from it. 'Wrong? Is there? How should I know?'

He reminded her that she had seemed anxious enough for him to look in there. His ears were pricked. Libby was moving around in the next room, Mrs. Marsden was humming 'Chrissi-mas Day'. He did not want anyone to come in, so he stood with his back to the door.

'My dear boy,' said Kate, 'I don't know what you're talking about.'

She had urged him twice to go, he said: he had not forgotten. 'Oh, all right.' She let the swab slide into the bowl. The hot water splashed up at her and she swore. 'When I looked in myself, I caught one or two of them laughing about you. There's some sort of talk going on.'

'There can't be. What on earth have I done?'

'I don't know. And I shouldn't have brought it up, only I was upset last night.'

He asked her why.

She asked him rather violently what that had to do with it. The point was, there was some sort of talk.

He pressed her. She must have heard more than that.

'I didn't. I heard that thug Harry Clark say something about the dee-ah vicar, and then they all tittered.'

Though he could not imagine what sort of gossip was in circulation, it struck him that Kate had her own ideas. Her eyes were always honest and direct, but when her mouth tightened it had secrets.

He took a cloth and started to dry up. She thanked him.

'What can't be cured,' he said at last, 'has to be put up with.'

Simon, whose school had broken up early, came in and asked for the kitchen scissors.

'No,' said Kate, 'you've blunted them enough already.'

'I like that! It's Dick who's always taking them, but of course all he does is perfect.'

'Now look here,' she said, 'I can stand a lot, but not asinine bogus displays of utterly baseless jealousy over your brother. You're not jealous of Dick, and you know it, you read things like that up in books.'

'Oh, I am a great reader,' he returned sarcastically, 'but I still want the kitchen scissors.'

She spun them at him and he caught them. 'Many thanks, O gracious one.' He went out, banging the door.

'Fool,' said Kate. 'He really is. I don't know why I like Simon. If I weren't his mother I wouldn't.'

Tenderness gave her a heavy, ageing look. She went on staring at the closed door.

'If you liked me,' said Maurice, 'you'd come out with what's worrying you. Don't you really know?'

She turned on him in a flash. 'No, I don't! And if I didn't like you, I can't imagine why I should be sweating away here. I could put the boys in a nice, cheap boarding-school and become companion to one old lady.'

'All right,' he said, 'all right.' He knew his tone was grudging. Kate should know he was fully aware of all she did, and aware that she did too much. She should know that between them acknowledgement was no longer possible. 'You would poleaxe an old lady in no time.'

'Ah, no,' she said, 'I would hold wool for her and she would say to her relations, "Kate is a treasure, what would my life be without her?"'

'Kate is a treasure,' Maurice repeated.

'Don't dry the big ones, stick them in the rack.' She snatched the cloth from him. 'Don't rise to me, you ass! You should know when I'm fishing for compliments. And I might remind you, you've got religious instruction at the school at eleven. It's nearly ten to.'

She was also his secretary, his memory. He was wholly reliant upon her.

'As for the titters,' she said, 'I expect we shall be the last to know the reason why.'

Normally, Maurice would have fretted on to the bottom of the matter since it was in his nature to hate and even to fear mysteries, even of the most trivial kind: as a child he had been ambivalent towards his birthday since, as well as meaning pleasures, it had meant "surprises"; and a surprise, if it were only the springing upon him of some long-prepared treat, had held a quality of terror and humiliation. Surprises made a

84

fool of him. His attention was distracted, however, by the coming of Christmas: of the annual Social, of Alice's play, which had a touch of professionalism — a touch which seemed to be regarded by some with a good deal of suspicion. One or two of the churchwomen had made derogatory comments. (The gap-toothed child had been a great success in her part, since it had not called for smiling. Disappointed parents of other children had referred to her performance as 'rather actressy'.) Then there had been the carol service, the services of the day itself, and the usual strung-up celebrations at home, with Simon manic, Dick in bed with a bilious attack, Kate with a migraine aura and Libby and her mother gently snacking at each other in tones of excessive goodwill. Had it always been like this? he wondered. He was unable to remember other years. He tried to be specially tender towards Libby, who had bought him some shirts neither she nor he could afford, and he fancied her day had been a happy one. At night she clung to him as she had not done for a long while and in bed took his hand and fell asleep holding it.

One evening a few days later, however, he received a note from Johnson-Black asking him if he could look in for a drink: any time would do. This was so unusual a circumstance that he recognised it in the light of a command. The two men, though they were close, met little socially and had no friends in common outside the church. Also, the Archdeacon was the warden's first cousin; and though Maurice knew that Johnson-Black did not like him and saw as little of him as possible, he could never rid himself of the feeling that the two were physically inseparable, nor enter the warden's house without a feeling that Sandeman was concealed behind a door, ready to bear out, beaming, upon him.

Libby, recognising the handwriting, said, 'What does he want?'

Maurice told her.

'Am I to come?'

He said, no: he supposed it was church business.

'But surely he could do that before or after church! Not

to ask your wife if it's just a drink does seem odd — not that I could go. I'm far too busy for festivities.'

Maurice laughed at her.

'What have I said?' She lifted her hand in a gesture of classic amazement, stood motionless, lips parted. She looked sleek as a marble by Canova.

'Can you imagine poor old J.B. having such a thing as a festivity? With Japanese lanterns and punch,' Maurice added imaginatively.

'You know perfectly well what I mean,' said Libby. She assumed her frank and confiding look. 'Honestly, darling, Joan Black is *very* odd; she just seems not to like other women.' (She did not believe that people with hyphenated names deserved to have them used. 'It nearly always indicates colour,' she had said, 'Gold Coast Negroes take names with hyphens.') 'I think it's one of these strange forms of jealousy, though how anyone could be jealous of the poor Colonel I don't know! Still, I certainly won't give her cause to worry about *me*. Do you know, I'd do almost anything rather than give another woman the least cause for jealousy? I'd run a mile. It's the way I'm made.'

'You're my dear good girl,' Maurice said, and kissed her. Through hard praying, through strenuously remembering the habits of love, he had lost the actual repugnance he had felt towards her flesh on the night of the Fraser child's arrest; now he felt nothing towards her but gentleness, and he was grateful to God that it was all. He had been desperately afraid that she would have sensed the physical withdrawal, and that he should have made her ashamed and wretched. Now, he felt, it was even possible that, thinking about her as little as he could, he might keep her moderately content. He was surprised to find, having lost love for her, that he could sometimes look with detached pleasure upon her beauty, that it did not irritate him so much when she displayed it, that he could feel a touch not only of irony but of pride when he thought that other men might envy him.

Chapter Thirteen

JOHNSON-BLACK was alone when Maurice went to see him. He led the way into the high, brown, leathery drawing-room that looked like a men's club, turned on the second bar of the electric fire and put out half a bottle of whisky. It was odd, Maurice thought, how much older he looked in his own home than in the vestry, authoritatively concerned with church affairs. Here he seemed, like his cold sofa and chairs, leathery; the network of wrinkles in the tight, dry skin might have been scratched on a saddle. He wore black coat, striped trousers, a stiff collar; his hair was parted, like a boy's, on one side, a short, slashed flap of it falling over his forehead. He told Maurice it was a pleasure to see him out of shop-hours, as it were; and then seemed at a loss.

'One eighty-six at the bazaar,' he said, 'not bad.'

Maurice agreed.

'Carol Service packed them in, too. That last thing of Plymmer's, though, Lord knows where he got it. Anyhow, nobody could sing it.'

Maurice agreed to that, also.

Silence fell, not uncomfortably, though plainly there was much behind it.

He thought how disproportionately pleasurable to a priest any half hour was, when spent away from duty, from the familiar ambience. His gaze rested peaceably on his warden's books, the tooled volumes of Scott and Thackeray, the Merediths, Surtees, W. W. Jacobs, the bound collections of *The Illustrated London News; Crockfords, Who's Who,* and, a little sadly, *Who Was Who.* He was not anticipating any serious trouble.

Johnson-Black said, 'I think we ought to find Mrs. Fraser another job.'

'Isn't she any good?'

The warden looked at his shoes, which had been shone to a colour between olive and chestnut, a military colour achieved by forty years of practice with expert hands and a detached mind.

'She's a trouble-maker.'

Maurice asked him how. Johnson-Black blinked unhappily. 'A bit mad, it's the only charitable thought. Mind you, I'd have known nothing if her next-door neighbour didn't do a bit of charring for Dolly Hannaway. She told Joan, and Joan told me. It's a lot of bosh, but I think you ought to know.'

Into the peace of the room a niggling unpleasantness intruded, like a sour smell from some alien kitchen. Maurice felt it. 'Come on, James, out with it.'

His warden stiffened up. He said in a rough, dull voice as if giving evidence at a courtmartial, 'Put it like this. She's going around pretending you and Mrs. Imber were behaving improperly in her sitting-room the night they took the boy away. She says she was drugged at the time.'

'Alice? Drugged?' Maurice could not help laughing; after amazement, laughter was his first impulse.

'Mrs. Fraser says *she* was drugged, not Mrs. Imber,' Johnson-Black returned humourlessly.

Maurice went on laughing: he could not stop. This seemed to him the funniest thing he had heard for years, life's lightening bonus.

'Look here,' said his warden, 'she's got to go. This damned rot is all over the Youth Club, and it's going to percolate. It seems to have percolated.' He was shocked by Maurice's merriment; he could not understand it. He went on, 'It's absurd to repeat it all. In fact, I draw the line.'

'But you mustn't draw any line,' Maurice said, steadying his voice. He was sober again now, remembering the sucking noise, the titters, the girls embraced. 'What else is there?'

'Well, nothing *else*.' It sounded as if Johnson-Black thought it was quite enough. 'So far as I can make it out, Mrs. Fraser says the doctor gave her drugs, and she went to sleep, and then she woke up in the small hours and you and Mrs. Imber were there.'

'I went home at about a quarter past one, feeling extraordinarily guilty at leaving Alice to it.'

He accepted another whisky, another cigarette.

'I thought you should know,' his warden said painfully, 'bunkum though it is, in case it gets to your wife.'

'Libby would think it quite insane,' said Maurice, then stopped. He had remembered the pet of jealousy which had made her force Alice upon Kate as a guest on the most inconvenient of all nights. 'I think I should go straight to the fountain-head. What do you think?'

'To Mrs. F.?' Johnson-Black considered the idea, then nodded: direct action was dear to him, it savoured of honour and open spaces, voices unafraid to shout and to be echoed and re-echoed. 'Yes, I think perhaps that's the best way. Though it will hardly be pleasant for you.'

Maurice said that a good deal of his work was far removed from pleasure. He thanked his warden for the information; as he did so Joan Johnson-Black came in, as if at a signal, to turn the remaining twenty minutes of his visit into a social occasion.

When he left, he was not laughing at all. He was angry less on his own account than Alice's: he hoped this rubbish would somehow be kept from her. He did not want to watch every step of this inoffensive friendship, to stumble at a word, to have an eye for the eyes of others, to be self-conscious about some ordinary exchange and to make her so. As he walked through the December night that anger grew, and with it his impetuosity. It would be wise, he knew, to go quietly home, spend a couple of days thinking out what he had to say, and then warn the woman that he wished to speak to her. In fact he went steadily across the square, down a small rich street of people who did not attend his church, and into the little wasteland where the concrete boxes were, the windows glowing low in tomato reds, lemon yellows and pallid greens, little windows in the houses of dwarfs. It was only ten past seven now: he had nothing to do till nine, when he had to take an adult confirmation class.

He found her in. She had been sitting by the fire, looking at the small screen of her television set, the remains of supper on a tray at her side, some mending on the arm of her chair. She greeted him without any appearance of surprise and pulled a chair forward for him; she did not turn off the set, though she reduced the volume.

'Well, this is a pleasure, Vicar,' she said, in a genteel tone he had not heard her use before. The paper chains were still up, and a shank of holly was stuck above the overmantel. It was not yet Twelfth Night. On top of the set was a tinted photograph of Derek, pink and yellow, black pupils painted into starch-blue eyes. She offered him a cup of cocoa. She didn't drink much tea; Derek had liked it, but not she; she thought tea was insipid.

Maurice refused. He did not speak at once, since it occurred to him now that he had made no plans for approaching his subject. One eye on the screen, where a comedian with a coarse, swollen face was killing himself with laughter over his own inaudible jokes, Mrs. Fraser brought him up to date about Derek: she had had two letters, they didn't seem unhappy.

He thought the approach of certainty was best. He told her he knew that she had been putting rumours about: he had come to ask her to stop.

Slowly and painfully, she coloured; she seemed to sweat. Yet still she went on looking at the comedian, and as he put a woman's wig on his head she laughed aloud. His act over, and superseded by a row of dancers, she half-turned back to Maurice. 'I'm sure I don't know what you're talking about.'

He insisted that his information was exact; from no one but herself could such a story have got round. 'I know you've been through a rough time and I couldn't be sorrier. It's enough to make anyone behave out of character. But you must stop it.'

'I don't know what you mean about my character,' said Mrs. Fraser, 'no one's ever criticized.'

He told her rather irritably, aware that this was not the best line for her but at a loss for another, that such rumours, absurd though they were, could do harm to a church. He and his wife had done their best to help her: surely she didn't want to injure them?

'Mrs. Fisher,' she burst out, ' "Pull yourself together," she said, "don't give way." She went on and on till I thought I'd go daffy.'

The dancers had made way for another comedian, this time a woman, very tall and garrulous. Mrs. Fraser turned up the volume control slightly, so that she could just manage to hear.

Maurice, who had to raise his voice, told her that she must not only stop the rumours but contradict them, otherwise they could not keep her on as a church cleaner.

'Don't make me laugh,' she said, 'I only do it to oblige. It's sixpence below the ordinary rates as it is. I can get a dozen better jobs and less dirty.'

He appealed to her: why should she have said what was not true? Why did she want to hurt him? He had tried to help her and Derek.

'I don't say what's not true,' she retorted, smiling not at him but at the woman on the screen, who had tripped over a bucket. 'Ha! She's daft, she is, I always like her, she's always on on Tuesdays.' Her prettyish, wan face was appeased, her eyes glittered.

He said, 'You know it's not true.'

In a sudden fury at his interruption she switched off the set and confronted him.

'Who says I know it's not?'

He felt this cross-talk might go on for ever. 'I say it's not. You should know that Mrs. Imber went out of her way to stay with you that night, she stayed all night, and I had to leave her to it.'

'They drugged me. They thought they'd put me right out, but I woke up in the early morning and there you two were. Do you think I couldn't see what had been going on?'

91

'I left your house about a quarter past one. Mrs. Imber stayed with you alone.'

'The *time* doesn't matter.' Her lips were tight and colourless, she meant to fight.

He felt himself caught in the silliness of a nightmare. Rage swarmed up in him; he wanted to seize and shake her. 'If this goes on, I shall sue you for slander. I mean it.'

For a moment she paused, considering. Then she said, smiling and temperate, 'You wouldn't get anything out of it. I've nothing but my pension.'

He tried something else. 'You go to church. Don't the Commandments mean anything to you?'

'Whatever Derek may have been, I've always kept myself respectable.'

'Bearing false witness against a neighbour isn't respectable, and it's a sin.'

'Oh sin this, sin the other! Anyway, I haven't been saying anything.'

He could not bear to go back again to the beginning of the horrible and ridiculous round. He said, 'Why did you do it?'

'Now look! Mrs. Fisher kept on and on at me, "Keep your end up," she said. So I'm not taking things even from you, Vicar. Some people think you *are* God, but I know you're not, you're only another man, and I know what men are, all of them. Derek used to say, "Oh, this God tripe, it makes me puke." And I used to go on at him, but he was right. If there had been a God, he wouldn't have made Derek like he is, he wouldn't have left me alone, not like this, with everyone pointing the finger at me.' Furiously she flicked at the knob: in a moment or so the sound returned; it was a sports commentator, hoarse with enthusiasm over Wolverhampton Wanderers.

'Turn that thing off!' Maurice said. He was shocked to hear himself shouting.

Surlily, she obeyed. He was not to think she had anything against him, she said; he'd tried to do his best, such as it was, but what she knew she knew, she had seen them kissing. No —

92

she stopped him — she wasn't going to be put upon, that was what she'd seen, not that she blamed him, he was a man, they were all the same whatever silly collars they wore.

He felt quite helpless in the face of her mania. 'I assure you, I shall see a lawyer if you don't stop it.'

'I wonder what Mrs. Fisher would have to say about that?'

'My wife will know all about it when I go home to-night. I'd have told her at once what you were saying, if I'd known it earlier.'

He remembered Alice holding her in her arms, trying to give her comfort.

'I hardly know Mrs. Imber,' he said; 'apart from the night she spent with you, I have never seen her outside the church. I can only think you really believe what you're saying. You must take it from me that it is not true.'

'I was drugged.'

'The doctor gave you a sedative. Did you think he was in my pay?' He was instantly ashamed of arguing with her; he resented the smile she gave him, full of complicity.

'That's a good one,' she said, and then was silent.

Getting up, he walked about the room, looked down into the earth of her little plantpots, filled with ivy, coleus, tradescantia.

He said at last, 'If a stop isn't put to these rumours, I shall raise them, and your part in them, publicly, at the next parish meeting.'

'That wouldn't do no good, really it wouldn't. Louder you say no, the less people believe you.' She sounded surprisingly sympathetic, as if she had nothing but his good at heart. 'Besides, it would upset Mrs. Fisher something awful.'

Maurice said, 'I shall do it.' He knew that he would not. He paused. 'I'm going to pray with you. I want you to join me: or at least to listen.'

'You go ahead,' she told him indifferently. Surreptitiously her hand moved to the knob.

'No,' he said.

'This is all the time I get for a rest with my feet up! I've suffered enough, haven't I? Do you want to take even that away?'

Still he could see nothing but black earth, the delicate tributaries of a root, the pin-like bright blade of a weed. 'You can spare five minutes for God.'

'What does he spare for me?'

'The hope of Derek getting well,' Maurice said. 'And you have the other children to love.'

She told him Derek was rotten, only she knew how much. He might fool them into thinking he was cured, but he'd soon be up to his filthy tricks again, quick as lightning. 'If I'd told them the half of what I know!'

A worm, minute, terracotta-coloured, moved in the soil. Maurice said, 'O Lord, we speak of the devices and desires of our own hearts, but often we don't understand those devices at all, nor why we do such evil. Help us to know ourselves, so that we may watch our tongues and keep them from hurting others. The best of us enjoy talking about our fellow men: nothing is so interesting to us as thy creation, Man, and it is our vanity that we are always trying to understand his heart as thou only canst. And so we often speak in malice, invent a story when there is none. When, in the monotony of our lives, we crave the excitement of evil-speaking, look with thy mercy on that vanity which shows itself in malice and invention. Forgive us, O Father, help us to carry only truth upon our tongues, so that we may live in friendship with all men and with thee, in the love of thy Son, Jesus Christ our Lord. Amen.'

'Amen,' said Mrs. Fraser mechanically. She got up, steering him towards the door. 'But I'm sure I don't know what all the fuss and commotion's about. I haven't done anything.'

Again he asked her to promise, not only to keep quiet, but to deny what she had said.

'I'm sure I've better things to do than go on gossiping all day. Careful as you go out — the step's broken.'

With that he had to be content. He was no sooner over the

threshold than he heard the door close behind him. He did not know what he wanted to do, pray, rage or laugh. The sky was brilliant with wheeling stars. There was frost in the air. He walked quickly, swinging his arms, ringing his heels on the pavement. He wanted to defer the moment when repulsion would rise in him, when he would feel greased all over with the woman's slander, would feel his hair rank, his breath disgusting. It was bad enough for him: he could not bear that she should have touched Alice. He had a vision of Alice and himself as Mrs. Fraser had imagined them; his heart raced. He drove his thoughts down, he walked faster, he was sweating, he could not get his breath.

Chapter Fourteen

NEXT day he told Libby. She stared at him incredulously, then said, 'Oh, but what drivel! Alice Imber, of all people! My darling, you couldn't possibly worry yourself about *such* stuff as that.'

'Well,' he said lightly, 'I should have been surprised not to find you loyal in my troubles.'

She expanded upon the absurdity of it all, her eyes shining, her voice loud. It was ludicrous enough to accuse anyone like him, happily married for years, of that sort of thing, but to couple his name with Alice's was just about the limit. 'Maurice and Alice' — why, with those names they simply couldn't misbehave! It sounded like a music-hall turn. And Alice, nice woman though she was, was no beauty, she wouldn't have that sort of appeal for men at all. Of course she was smart and wore all the latest things, but they couldn't make her attractive, well, not in any film-star sense. She, Libby, found no difficulty at all in being loyal — really, it wasn't putting much strain upon her.

Kate was moving about in the next room, ironing shirts. Libby ran to the door and called to her, 'Katey! You must come in and hear this! It's absolutely wonderful!'

He could not stop her. She told Kate everything he had told her, from beginning to end. She could hardly speak for laughing, until she found that Kate seemed unable to speak at all.

'Well? Well? Isn't it rich?'

Kate looked pale. She stared at Libby as though she were not quite sure who she was. 'Rich?'

'Yes. Of course it would be awful if people believed it, but it's so — so——'

'Maurice,' Kate said, 'don't let Libby tell that to Mother or to anybody. You must not let her.'

Libby said, more loudly than ever, that if she minded telling it, it would mean she thought there was something in it. What harm could it do, just mentioning it inside the family——

'You should not even have told *me*.'

'Well!' said Libby. 'Well, well!'

Kate went out.

'What do you suppose she meant? Sometimes I think Kate's quite crazy. My own sister, and I shouldn't have told her!'

Maurice said the real trouble was that Kate did not think the affair funny. That sort of rumour could spread like a drop of ink in a glass of water, and even though nobody believed it, a good many people would like to, merely to discover an added interest in their lives. A good many people might even pretend to. Smoothing her arm as he spoke, since she was still excited, he remembered his second, senior curacy in Leeds, where he had been in charge of a daughter-church. Shortly after his induction, the vicar's marriage had been annulled on the grounds of non-consummation. Maurice remembered the unholy interest the case had aroused, how the congregation would stir as the poor chap mounted the pulpit, regarding him throughout his sermon as though he were some mythological freak, half-fish, half-man, or the creation of Hermaphroditus and the fountain-nymph. Many of the less sophisticated had been persuaded that he must be physically quite different from themselves, and had found it hard to raise their eyes from round about the area of his navel. It had taken a great deal of living-down.

'Well, at least they'll think you're doing something ordinary,' said Libby, still obstinately flippant. 'Don't you think Mrs. Imber should be warned? I could do it quite tactfully myself, I think, if that would be better. Isn't that an idea?'

He instructed her sharply that nobody was to warn Alice: with luck she might never hear the rumours, she might escape them. In any case, to repeat them would be an insult. He felt himself prickling with horror at the thought of Libby being tactful. As it was, something had been spoiled: he would find it hard to speak naturally with Alice again.

'I think the three of us should be seen together,' Libby insisted, 'that would be the best thing. We must make a point of it at the very next social.'

He told her that they were going to make a point of nothing: that the subject was to be dropped.

'What a silly old thing you are!' she said affectionately. 'I honestly believe it's quite upset you. I can't understand people being upset by absolute nonsense — I'm like that. It is quite beyond me.'

Maurice was not unperceptive: he had seen the strain lying at the back of her bright eyes, and something warned him to be careful. But of what? Of upsetting her? He would give anything rather than do that, his state of lovelessness strengthening his sense of obligation. Years ago, when he had been passionately in love with her, he had often upset her quite deliberately, to give his sadistic, her masochistic instinct, rein: he had been ashamed of himself afterwards, of course, had known that what he had done was wrong and could not be otherwise: yet they had had pleasure, being in love, in tormenting each other, it had sometimes spurred the kind of desire that even Libby had failed to check by prayer. These had been the sensual histrionics of love, and he could not look back at them now without remorse: yet they could not have been so bad, for in those days he had thanked God as trustfully and enthusiastically for Libby as, in childhood, he had thanked his uncles for their Christmas presents.

He made up his mind that he would confide Mrs. Fraser's gossip only to one person more; but when he did so he found, of course, that David had been aware of it from the beginning.

'You could have tipped me off,' Maurice said.

'I couldn't,' David replied simply.

They sat on the edge of the table. It was very cold in the vestry, but it was private.

'All right.'

David said, after a moment, that the less anyone talked the better. Nine days' wonders died down, especially in a church, and one mustn't exaggerate the harm one woman could do. Lucy, for instance, had heard nothing and was still puzzled. With any luck another wonder might supervene: Kitson was ripe for a row with Hannaway, who had forgotten to pass on receipts without which he could not get the books straight. 'People will not be diverted from me by Kitson and his accounts,' Maurice said realistically.

The following night, just as he was sitting down to a meal, the telephone rang. When he heard Alice's voice his heart jumped: he believed she, also, must have heard. But she told him that her father-in-law was ill, the doctor thought he was dying. She would like Maurice to come.

Old Imber had been remote from the church for a good many years now, and indeed had only attended it to please his wife, dropping the practice when she died. He had been one of those men comfortable without faith, finding one world enough to cope with, and observing, when he felt tired, that to go out like a candle was the luckiest fate that could befall a man. Most of his life luck had been with him, and this was the luck he looked for in the end. He had been successful in his work and in his investments, his marriage had been happy, his old age cared for: somehow, though he had not believed it could be possible, he had survived the death of two sons and had pushed them into the stained-glass windows of his mind where they stood serene and still, and were nice to look at. He had loved his daughter-in-law, and she had been fond of him.

Maurice found him in the extreme terror of death.

'Help him if you can,' Alice said, 'I can't.'

The room was light and cheerful, bright paint, Swedish wood, flowers, a fire. The nurse sat outside, waiting. The old man had had a stroke, he might last twenty-four hours, a week, a fortnight. Nobody expected more.

Maurice had seen this terror before, the terror that dresses up the living man as a corpse; but he had not expected to find it here.

His face yellow and smooth as macaroni, his eyes protruding, his mouth a hole, Imber looked at him. He could not speak.

'Shall I stay?' Alice asked. His fear had infected her. She looked sick.

He shook his head and she went away.

Maurice said, 'Hullo. You've had a bad time.'

The old man stuck a foot out of bed, began to grope.

'What is it?'

He said, out of his slipped mouth, 'Got to go to the rear. Feel better then. Feel better.' He tried to move, sank back again. Water stood on his forehead. He grunted and strained.

'You can't move,' Maurice said, 'don't try. Nothing matters.' He put his hands on the thin arms; it was like gripping stretched ropes, they were so rough and taut. Old Imber jerked his body up, bringing his face into Maurice's as if he would kiss him on the mouth. Then he relaxed, slumping back upon the stacked pillows.

'What will happen to me?'

It was the cry of Mrs. Fraser, of Derek, of the dying, of half mankind.

'You will go to God.'

Again the grunting, the straining, the struggle to speak. Then, in a slur, 'Not me.'

'You. I am sure.'

The old man squeaked, 'Alice! Alice!'

Maurice fetched her.

'What is it, dear?' she said, bending over the bed.

'Tell the nurse, I've got to get up. Got to go along the passage.'

'No, you haven't. Stay still. Maurice is here.'

'Hullo, Fisher,' said the old man, as if he had just noticed his visitor. He found fascination in the sheets, he pleated them like a needlewoman.

'You will go to God,' Maurice said, 'I promise you. You've lived a decent life.'

'Not me.'

'Listen.' He paraphrased the text. 'If you were always willing to turn yourself inside out for your children, to forgive them anything, do anything on earth to please them, do you imagine God, who is your father, would do less for you?'

In the hole of the mouth, words moved. Maurice bent his ear to it.

'What if he isn't there?'

'He is.'

'How do you know?'

'By experience: like the experience of heat or cold.'

Imber mouthed, 'I am afraid.'

Alice leaned on her elbows upon the mantelshelf. Her back was turned to the room. For something to do she turned on another of the lamps, a globe of bottle-glass with a shade striped pink and green. In the prettiness of the room, the moneyed brightness, life slid away.

Maurice said, 'There's nothing to be afraid of. . . . What?' He added desperately to Alice, 'I can't hear what he's saying!'

She came to the bed and listened at the mouth's black receiver. She nodded and tried to smile; and in her smile was a flash of delight and hope, because something of her friend, characteristic and racy, was still left. 'He says there must be, if you're here.'

'I'm here as a friend. Do you want me as a parson?'

There was conflict in the shell, then a nod. Maurice sat down on the bed, took a hand and held it. He said: 'God the Father who created thee; God the Son who suffered and died for thee; God the Holy Spirit who strengthened thee, bless thee, O Christian soul, on thy last journey; God of his great mercy forgive thee thine offences, and may thy portion be peace and life eternal. Amen.'

When the nurse came in the old man was quiet. He had stopped tweaking at the sheets and his gaze was straying over the ceiling, on which the lamps had printed interlocking roses of light and shadow. She sent Maurice away, and Alice too.

In the hall they looked at each other.

'Shall I stay?'

'No. The doctor's due again any minute. You've done all you can.'

He made her promise to telephone him at once, should he be needed; but when she did so, early next morning, it was to tell him that her father-in-law was dead. She did not say how he had died, if he had died comforted. And he dared not ask her.

Chapter Fifteen

'THAT stony sort of behaviour, with no expression at all, doesn't mean that people aren't feeling terrible,' said Libby after the funeral, which she had attended; 'the old man must have been a burden and she'll be freer now, but I'm sure she must feel grief, deep down. Don't you think so?'

On the next night, Alice called at the vicarage and was shown by Libby, with hushed politeness, into the study.

'I have a problem,' she said.

He waited.

'It is just to clear my conscience, that is, if anyone can.'

She told him that, an hour before he died, her father-in-law had suddenly turned to her with a demand that she herself should reassure him of everlasting life. She had tried to, in vague terms: but he had not wanted that, he had wanted a blueprint for Heaven, he had needed her to tell him, *ex cathedra*, that he would at once see his wife and the boys again, that they would all sit and talk together. She could not. She had tried to evade his eyes, she had said, 'We can't be sure, but millions of people *are* sure.' He had not spoken again.

'So you see,' she said, as if chatting over a tea-cup, 'what I have done. Because *I* couldn't say what I didn't believe, because I stuck up my piffling, disgusting honesty before his need, because I couldn't tell a lie that would have meant nothing, he died afraid. What punishment shall we get for the sin of intellectual pride, Maurice? Shall we wear dunce's caps for ever on burning stools in hell?'

'But you don't believe in hell.'

Still lightly, she said she was in it at that moment. She had loved the old man, he was her last tie with the past, and she had let him——

'Don't say it again.' Maurice looked at her, and saw the light of tears flickering along her lids. 'You'll have to live with this, like anything else. And you mustn't add to it the vanity of thinking any small harm that you can do weighs so much as a milligram against the good of God. It is all right with him now; he's with God as he hoped to be. I am quite certain that all he longed for he has now. And furthermore, you can go away not thinking of the pain you might have given him for a moment——'

'That's a prissy word, "pain",' she interrupted, stretching her mouth in the effect of a smile.

'— but of all the care you gave him, and the pleasure he had from being with you.'

She said she envied him his own faith, and she wiped her eyes.

He asked her if she felt any better.

'No,' she said, rising, 'but I have a faint hope that I may do, later on.'

She talked a little of her future. There was no point in her staying on in the house alone. She would sell it, as soon as she could think of doing anything practical, and rent a flat. She did not mean to stay in the neighbourhood, there was nothing to keep her.

He had a piercing sensation of loss. All he could say was, 'We shall miss you.'

When she had gone he sat thinking about it. After all, he could not even claim that she was somebody he liked to talk to, since he had talked to her so little. He could not even call her a friend: only an acquaintance.

It struck him that the room was chilly. Libby, who had sporadic bursts of belief in fresh air, had opened the window too wide; the curtains bellied out in the draught. One of the cape gooseberries, stuck with grasses in a jar on his desk, fell off the stem and rattled over the wood. He stretched up to close the window, and as he pushed at the frame the physical effort jerked open a window in his secret mind and the thought blew in like wind: you are in love with her.

With a bang he shut out the cold. The curtains hung motionless. The flames of the fire, which had been fluttering about, burned steadily.

Libby came in and asked him how he could bear to be so stuffy; he was simply asking for germs to hang about. 'What did she want?'

He said he could not tell her; Alice had come to him in his capacity as a priest.

'Well, then of course you can't!' Libby exclaimed, laughing and staring. 'But — do forgive me, in confidence, just between ourselves and I know I'm being dreadful — I find it hard to see Alice Imber getting religion.'

Chapter Sixteen

To David, the death of old Imber appeared to have checked the gossip. Even the Youth Club crowd, he felt, had thought it decent to hold their tongues for the moment: and when the moment was over, found they had forgotten what subject it was that they had meant to resume. This cheered him up: he had been miserable about the whole thing, and had not even had the comfort of confiding in Lucy, who remained obtuse. The New Year opened in a humdrum fashion. George Kitson's quarrel with Hannaway had not materialised and nobody had taken steps about Plym, despite criticism of certain items in the Carol Service. As for David himself, he had abandoned his Christmas dream of marrying Lucy whether or not they had twopence between them to rub together. As a married curate, his hopes of a better job would not be obviously improved; and he was by no means sure that, at the moment, he wanted one. As with many men of sanguine temperament, the thought of a minor pleasure or triumph to come next week would give him the heart to contemplate next year with enthusiasm. He was not farsighted; he lacked the imagination for it, and was happier than many people because of that lack.

He had triumphed, temporarily at least, over his body's itch, and though in unworthier moments he fancied that this triumph had disappointed Lucy, he was sure she would be grateful to him later on. His sole anxiety was Maurice, his sole aggravation Libby. David knew there was something wrong between them, but his instinct told him that it had not been openly acknowledged. She still went busily and uselessly about the parish, always in transit to something more urgent than anything she had contracted to do: her eyes were bright and her attitude towards her husband almost too demonstrative for a vicar's wife. As for Maurice, he was living a surface life to such an extent that David was afraid others besides himself would find him out. And David knew something that was like the sour nudge of jealousy; it was not that Maurice was any less friendly to him, encouraged intimacy less: but he encouraged it with a straying gaze, he spoke, as it were, out of the side of his mind.

Alice had seldom attended church services; now she had almost drifted away altogether, except that she still went round with the parish magazines. Her house was up for sale; there was a board outside it. She seemed to be having a good time. David, whose way home from hospital visiting lay along her street, had once seen her emerge with a man, and be driven away; she had been wearing a dance dress of bright pink papery silk, and was laughing as if she had not a care in the world.

Well, he thought, so much the better: and he took the practical step of urging Libby to accept for the first time a part in the dramatic society play: he wanted her to glow in Maurice's eye.

To his surprise, after a good deal of protest, she agreed. She couldn't act, she said, she had never been much good at it at school: but after all, it was only for fun, only for charity. People wouldn't be critical.

The play was a simple drawing-room comedy on a very old theme: a beautiful, but middle-aged and highly respectable woman became the object of a young man's passion, and by a kind deception disillusioned him, so that he was set free to marry the girl who had been waiting patiently in the background.

'What bloody awful rot,' Maurice said when he had read it, 'can't they really do better than that?'

For him to swear was such a rarity that David was not only shocked but thoroughly startled. 'Oh, it's not that bad,' he said. 'Mrs. Fisher will be absolutely right.'

'It will keep her busy,' Maurice began; then was silent. For a moment, David realised, he had forgotten that she was supposed to be busy enough already.

After a week of rehearsal Lucy, who was playing the young girl, began to complain. She was a surprisingly good actress, not a thoughtful one and not, so far as David could judge, particularly intuitive: but she had a knack of transforming herself quietly into somebody else. Though he loved her, he was realistic; he had never thought her clever, had gone so far as to think, at times, that she was empty-headed. (It was true that he did not mind. Like many simple and honest men he was a little conceited, and he believed he had enough in his own head to serve them both.) Nevertheless, he believed she could have been a professional actress if she had chosen, and was often puzzled that at no time had such an idea ever occurred to her.

'Mrs. Fisher is a most awful stick,' Lucy said. 'One might as well say one's lines to the kitchen stove.'

'She'll look wonderful.'

'Oh, that's all right for the first act. But by the time the second comes, people will be pretty bored. She has the same sort of smile on her face all the time.'

'It's all right for amateurs.'

'It's not all right for me!' said Lucy, in a flare of temper. 'She doesn't *give* anything. I must say I wish you hadn't thought of her!'

Plymmer, also, wished he had not. It was his annual duty to produce the play, though not to choose it nor to allot the parts. This, for the sake of harmony, was done in committee. David knew he disliked the job, knew he raged at the gulf between what he was able to make of actors and play, and what he could make if he were able to choose both.

Plym walked miserably up and down in the body of the hall, the big corduroy jacket hanging with the weight of armour on his narrow frame, his delicate nose twitching, his lips moving over words of silent abuse. Sometimes he stopped to bellow, 'I can't hear a word. Speak up!' Sometimes he shouted at old Hannaway, who didn't mind, since he was used to producers, and did not respect them unless they were rude. As a younger man, he had played with the Stock Exchange Amateur Dramatic Society: character parts.

'Melvyn!' Plym shouted. 'Stop guying it. You're not Father Christmas. You're a wise old jaw-bacon full of the milk of human kindness. You're urbane, see? Urbane. And don't come in with a hop, how often have I told you?'

Hannaway came anxiously to the edge of the platform. 'Do I hop, dear boy? I don't think so. I'm only trying to give my entrance a touch of lightness.'

'Hopping like a bloody flea on the beach,' Plym muttered, but only for David's ears. Aloud he said, 'Well, don't. Go back and try it again.'

It was the penultimate rehearsal. Maurice was there, in the front row, with the Pelhams, who had been privileged to come and watch, since they would be away over the time of the dress rehearsal and the two performances. There were no other visitors.

Plym was quiet while Hannaway went through his scene with Lucy, a smug consolation scene, which Lucy played as if she meant every word of it.

Maurice rose and went quietly to the back. Libby came on next.

She came through the centre door back, shutting it behind her with such force that the whole set, of canvas and thin wood, quivered as beneath an avalanche.

She began, '*Why, Uncle, darling, I thought you'd gone!*'

Plym shot up his hand.

'Mrs. Fisher,' he said in a quiet, steady, carrying voice, 'will you please go back and make that entrance again, or you'll bring the house down in more senses than one.'

She looked astonishingly beautiful under the bright lights. David glanced backwards at Maurice, hoping he thought so too.

'Oh, Reginald,' she said pettishly (she was the only person Plym knew, except his mother, who persisted in calling him by his hated first name), 'it isn't my fault! If you just *touch* the handle everything rattles. It's all so frightfully badly made.'

He told her it was the most they could afford.

'In that case I don't see how I'm to help it.'

He was thunderously silent for a minute. Then he suggested that she should simply come in, and Hannaway should step back to close the door behind her. 'It will look daft,' he said, 'but it's better than a ruddy earthquake.'

Libby squatted on her ankles and looked at him with gentle reasonableness. 'My dear, if it won't shut quietly, I don't see how Melvyn can do it any better than I can.'

'Melvyn is going to have a good try.'

'But, Reginald, there is no dramatic *reason* why he should shut the door. Now look.' She sprang up lightly and left the stage. In a moment she entered again, stretched her right hand gracefully behind her, and swung the door to. This time a picture fell down. She flushed. 'You see, it can't be done!'

David saw Maurice grip his hands together on his knees.

'She really does look wonderful,' Georgina whispered, 'it's almost improper!'

Humphrey whispered in return, 'Do you remember Mrs. Rose, who lived in Chaucer Road? The resemblance is quite striking.'

'In Chaucer Road, dear? I thought it was Cherry Hinton.'

Plym said in a loud voice, 'If people would keep quiet in the body of the hall, we could get on a bit faster!'

'I am so sorry,' said Humphrey immediately, 'I do beg your pardon.'

Plym, nonplussed, muttered something of a conciliatory nature. Then he sat down and for a moment or two said nothing at all, while Libby experimented with the door.

At last he said, 'Let's take it that you're inside. Melvyn, go on from, '*I lingered, my dear*——'

'*I lingered, my dear*,' said Hannaway, '*just for a word with this young lady*.'

'*Don't call me your young lady!*' Lucy retorted, in such a fiery burst that she seemed quite incongruous, like a real person intruding grief upon a game of charades. '*Words aren't any good, any more*.' It was her exit line; hands to her eyes, she ran off.

'*Well*,' said Libby, '*what was that all about? I don't*

think I shall ever understand these girls of to-day.' She gave to every word precisely the same stress, not varying a single one by so much as a quarter of a tone.

'Stop.' Plym moved forward at a tortoise pace, dragging his legs. 'Mrs. Fisher, I want that again. Say it as if you meant it. You're completely puzzled. You're very fond of Stella, and you can't imagine why she tears out just as you come in. Go on. Take that speech again.'

Libby took it, precisely as before.

'Have you really no idea,' Hannaway went on cosily, *'not even a very faint one?'*

'Stop,' Plym said again. 'Mrs. Fisher, it's still not right.'

'Then perhaps you could show me what you mean,' Libby said. She had coloured, her eyes were angry. Maurice was moving up from the back; he stood half-way down the wall. leaning against it.

'Oh, Jerusalem,' said Plym. With surprising agility he hopped up on to the platform, brushing Libby aside. He thought for a minute. Then he became Libby: he had her pleased smile, her tilt of the head, he took a step as light as hers. He had not meant to caricature, or even to imitate her, and David knew it; but he saw her flush deepen, her lips press hard upon each other.

'Well!' Plym repeated, on a high, feminine note, *'What was that all about?'* He swung round on his toe, to regard the door through which Lucy had made her exit. With a confiding smile, he laid his hand on Hannaway's arm. He continued musically, *'I don't think I shall ever understand these girls of to-day!'* — and he gave a sigh of amused bewilderment. 'Something like that,' he said to Libby.

She laughed out loud. Her eyes filled with tears, she could not check herself. There was quiet in the hall while she laughed it out, till she came to an abrupt and gasping stop. 'Oh, Reginald, you'd make a marvellous girl, you really would!'

He said to her quietly, 'I know I look damn' funny. And now we've all had a good laugh, we can get on with the job. I expect we'll all feel the better for it.'

The tears of rage and strain and miserable laughter were still on her cheeks. She brushed them away.

Hannaway began quickly, '*I lingered, my dear——*'

Then Libby started to laugh again. Peal after peal broke from her; she was beside herself.

Plym, smiling nervously, waited.

'I must say, I thought it was rather *well* done,' Georgina whispered to Humphrey.

Again Libby came to a halt.

Plym jumped down from the platform. 'All right, go ahead.'

'But I can't do it like that,' she cried in despair, 'I'd look ridiculous! I have to do things my own way.'

He asked her what she thought was the function of a producer.

'Oh, there's no need for us to pretend we're the Old Vic!' she shot at him. 'It's just for fun, it's for charity,' she added, 'so there's no need to talk like that.'

Maurice had come to the foot of the platform. 'Come on, dear, try again. Plym's within his rights.'

They stared at each other as if they were alone together. David stirred unhappily: he hated tension. He blamed himself for all this. He should have realised what might happen.

'I can't see it's a question of "rights" when we're all giving our time to it just for fun.'

'I'm out,' said Plym. 'This play can produce itself.' He started towards the door.

Maurice called, 'No! Come back. We can't do it without you — can we, Libby?'

He held her eye like a tamer of animals.

'I suppose there always is this sort of thing with amateurs?' Humphrey muttered hopefully to Georgina. 'Only natural, I expect.'

Libby said at last, 'No. All right, Reginald, I'll do my best, though I still think it's silly.'

He came back. He was not looking triumphant, as one who had forced a surrender. He looked a sad and tired little man who would far rather be doing something else. 'Better have a coffee-break. Then we can get down to it again.'

He went off towards the back room. Libby and Hannaway left the stage. Maurice made no move to join them.

'Can I get you a cup?' David addressed himself to Humphrey and Georgina. They said awkwardly that it would be very nice, if it was not a trouble, if they were not drinking up the comfort intended for the actors.

When he returned, Humphrey was sitting beside Maurice, talking to him earnestly.

'If you'll be my guest,' he was saying, 'I shall be very pleased. Why not? I'm sure you can be spared just for one night. I can book you a room in college.' His face was anxious and kind.

Maurice thanked him, but said he would have to find out whether he could manage it. The lines in his face were heavy; he was finding concentration hard.

'You look into it, Vicar, and then you let me know. Let me know, of course, that you will come, not that you won't.'

When Humphrey came back to sit by his wife, David saw her hand move over his. So they also know, he thought, they have seen.

Libby burst out into the hall, her arm round Lucy's shoulders. 'David, isn't she a wonderful little girl? She's so terribly good. She's a real "pro", too; she doesn't get all agitated like me. I'm afraid I was rather naughty, but I did so want to do well, and I just couldn't get the hang of it.'

Lucy looked at her now with the admiration of a loving subordinate, having forgotten, under this glow of generosity, what a shocking actress Libby was. She, David thought, had not seen: and he marvelled at it. But he was glad.

He was badly shaken, however, when, the rehearsal having started again in a peaceful if flaccid manner, Maurice said to him quietly, 'This wasn't a good idea.'

It was an open admission of something wrong, it was the one admission he had passionately not desired. This was not a new intimacy to bring them together: he believed it was one that must finally separate them.

Chapter Seventeen

'ALL right,' said Libby, 'say it.'

'I haven't anything to say.'

She was standing beside his chair. Putting out his arm he clasped her around the thighs and drew her to him. It was all he could do.

It was nearly midnight. She had just come in from the rehearsal, which he had left an hour before. The household had gone up to bed. There was no sound but the rush of water from an overflow pipe; Simon took baths at eccentric hours and Kate had long since given up trying to stop him.

'You see,' said Libby patiently, 'it is my time of life. You don't know anything about medicine, darling, you admit you don't. But I do know a bit. I've missed three times in the past year, and that is always the beginning. I know it's hard on you to be specially patient, but you do have to be. And I *am* patient with you. I'm not going to reproach you for butting in on the rehearsal, though you shouldn't have done it. I'm sure Plym didn't thank you for it, not really.'

He did not speak. He was going through a bad spell that week, and he knew he must keep a check on his tongue. After twelve months, the habit of continence still refused to come easily. For weeks it might be all right: and then, perhaps for three or four days at a stretch, he would find it almost intolerable. At such times he thought (trying to laugh away an ill as adhesive to his whole nature as a cancer) that he understood the temptation of Saint Anthony. It would begin with some innocent image; Libby and himself on Midsummer Common, one evening in Cambridge at the bluest hour of a warm evening, turning to kiss after a quarrel; a slack afternoon in Leeds before a winter fire, when she had stretched out, with firelight on her arms, to pick up beads from a broken necklace. But it would spark off the demon, he would be sick with love for the past, to make love to her not as she was now, but then. The hot rods of pain would begin to throb, in his loins, his spine, down from his shoulders; he could feel the vibration of desire in his wrists. And as there was nothing to be done for it, he would be racked with irritation; it was hard for him to speak gently to anyone with this misery caged inside him. A sharp word could be something of a release: an expression of an old grudge, spat out like a broken tooth, almost a complete check to the tumult. Yet he knew he did not dare to take this way out. At such times he believed he had no right to be a priest, and he was tempted to envy those without faith. For his was steady enough; he had always felt God, as he had said to old Imber, like heat or cold; but he had always known that at times it was impossible to reach him. God was there, all right, as a king might be inside a palace: but there was no way of breaching the walls to him, of making passage through the armies of court officials, the secretaries, equerries, chamberlains, whom Maurice had made in the image of his own sins and weaknesses.

'What you lack,' said Libby, 'is any capacity to understand how other people feel. It's called empathy, isn't it? You haven't got it. You're turning away from me because of something I can't help, something physiological.' She gave him a strained, brave stare: she was tense in his embrace.

'Look,' he said, 'we can't quarrel any more: the time for that has passed. Don't you see? We can't, because we can no longer make anything good of quarrelling. It can't end in the way it should if it isn't to go sour, not any longer.'

'Sex?' She snipped it off as she might have snipped a tape with scissors. He felt the quiver of her contempt.

'If you like.'

'It's not what I like, it's what you like.' Pulling away from him, she made a turn to the fireplace more dramatic and more graceful than anything she had been able to achieve for Plymmer. She faced him, beseeching, spreading her arms, somehow contriving to give the impression that she wore draperies, that her hair was flowing. 'Dear, I didn't mean that. Only, can't you be patient? You're not young, neither of us are——'

'Bosh,' said Maurice uncontrollably.

'Don't you dare!'

This time he apologised, and Libby said, 'It sounds mean of me to say it, I know, but . . . Well, I should think so!'

'I can't say more.'

She said, 'You don't love me. You haven't for some time. I *know*,' and her face was innocent with misery.

He got up and cuddled her to him, rocked her to and fro; he was full of a remorse that was somehow like rage. 'I do. Of course I do.'

She told him he did not. He was miles away from her; he criticised her; he had spoken to her sharply in front of strangers.

'To-night? Lib, I didn't!'

'I didn't mean to-night.'

'When, then?'

'Never mind.'

'But when? You must tell me!'

She would not. She said, 'Let it go.'

Exhausted, they fell into something that was like the silence of amity.

'Better go up,' he said. He started clearing up his desk and she helped him efficiently.

That night she offered herself to him. He tried to take her and failed.

Through her tired and muffled weeping, he could detect her satisfaction. Hadn't she been right, after all? She was convinced that his desire was on the decrease, that soon everything would be all right, the way she wished it to be, without any crudity, indignity, or silliness.

He knew he would never touch her again.

Chapter Eighteen

THERE was a large attendance on the first night, the seats close-packed. 'Jam to-day,' David said to Maurice, 'and jam to-morrow, I hope.'

The hall was hot; the boiler had been stoked too vigorously, and the energy of some of the Youth Club boys had been diverted by Kitson into trying to get a few more windows open.

Maurice sat with Kate in the front row. Mrs. Marsden would bring the boys on the following evening. As he leaned across to speak to a young reporter who had attended St. Lawrence's social events for years, and who never seemed to grow any older or more eminent, he was accosted by a tall man whose face he did not know. He was, he said, a new recruit to one of the local papers. 'My name's Westlake. We ought to meet often, Vicar, if all your shows are as popular as this one.' He looked for a spare seat: there was one on Kate's left, so Maurice introduced them.

Westlake was a handsome, skull-faced man who, although his clothes were good, looked seedy. His skin was large-pored, there were pouches below his intelligent, pewter-coloured eyes. He was about fifty. His grey hair was still thick, and he had been to an expensive barber. He bore with him a whiff of after-shaving lotion; he had shaved that evening. He and Kate began to talk.

Joan Johnson-Black sat down at the piano in front of the platform to play a selection from a musical comedy. This set the Youth Club singing, and David said, 'I knew Plym was wrong about that. She wanted the *Liebestraum*, but he said the mood wasn't right. Silly ass. One should always start these shows with a powerful depressant.'

Maurice smiled faintly. He had left Libby in a furious state of nervousness, her lips twitching uncontrollably, tears just held in check. He had tried to buoy her up, but she had not wanted to talk to him.

Kitson went to the back to reprove two couples who had begun to dance. There was an altercation at the doors about some tickets issued for the wrong night. The noise rose, and Plymmer, sticking his head out briefly between the curtains, was greeted with a howl of mirth. Apparently he had an idea, for he came down into the hall and whispered to Joan. She banged at once into God Save the Queen, which meant that everyone had to stand up and keep quiet.

'That's very good Old Vic,' David whispered approvingly. 'I like that.'

When the curtain rose, Libby was discovered arranging paper flowers in a bowl. There was a murmur and a ripple of applause, for she looked calm and most beautiful, gold dust in her hair, bright blue on her eyelids. She went about humming to herself: and if she walked upon the stage as if she were a little lame, it did not detract from the impact of her presence.

The juvenile lead, a boy of some accomplishment who had recently taken over the Scouts, slipped in across the sill of the open window. '*I say, what luck finding you alone for once!*'

Libby responded, '*My - dear - Dennis - must - you - enter - houses-like-a-burglar-what-a-child-you-are.*'

It was as flat, as dead, as it had been in rehearsals; yet Maurice knew she was not nervous now. She was enjoying herself. He prayed silently, 'O God, it is a trashy thing to ask, but make Libby a success; it would mean so much to her.'

The juvenile, hitting himself shyly on the calves with a tennis racket, explained that he was not such a child as she thought. He would prove it to her.

Libby, who had forgotten her moves up to now, remembered them. She went stiffly upstage, and started work on another vase. One of the flowers dropped from the sheaf in her hands, and it disconcerted her; instead of leaning down to pick it up, she gave it a surreptitious kick into the wings. Someone tittered, someone shushed.

She recovered herself. '*Now-run-away-you-mystery-maker-or-you'll-be-too-late-to-meet-Stella.*'

This was the clue for Hannaway's entrance, which he made with far more farcicality than Plym had ever tolerated at rehearsals. He got his laugh, and under cover of it, Maurice heard Kate murmur to the reporter 'own sister . . . refuse to be disloyal!'

Her face was bright with secret amusement. Westlake gave her a bold, admiring, undressing look. Maurice could not hear his reply.

The play went on, in an atmosphere of uncritical enjoyment. The audience liked Libby's looks, Hannaway's tomfoolery, but seemed almost embarrassed by Lucy, as if she were committing a breach of taste in making so obvious the charade-level of everyone else.

When the curtain went down on the first act, Maurice was besieged by congratulations upon his wife's appearance, but not her performance: even for his sake, nobody could compliment him upon her acting.

Westlake, passing him with a glass of lemonade which he had bought for Kate, said, 'Lively little show. Mrs. Fisher reminds me of Gladys Cooper in the old days. I shall say as much.'

Kate gave him an odd glance of complicity. She was as a rule remote, by no means easy in social relations, and Maurice was surprised to see her so relaxed. Earlier that evening a headache had threatened, but she had drugged it down. Now she looked undrugged and animated.

'That will give my wife a good deal of pleasure,' said Maurice.

Kitson's voice rose in a shout. 'You, there! Get off that sill!'

Some boys scrambled down with a crash.

At the end of the second act, during one of her two big scenes, Libby forgot her lines. She seemed unable to hear

Plym's clear and bitter prompting. She just stood and smiled, moving her hands very slightly like fins at her sides.

'*What do you know . . .*' said Plym.

'*What do you know about me after all?*' She came out with it in a burst, and was again brought to a halt.

Plym enunciated, in a quiet voice that reached the back of the hall. '*For all you know, I may have been . . .*'

'*For all you know I may have been . . .*' She added, quite audibly, 'I can't.'

Lucy saved her. '*For all we know you may have been a criminal,*' she paraphrased. '*You haven't lived here long; where were you before that?*'

Libby drew a long breath, and carried right on without any further trouble till the end of the act.

'. . . agony,' Kate muttered to Westlake.

Maurice felt a stab of amazed anger that she should be seeming to side against her sister with a stranger. He could feel not only for, but with Libby; he might have been standing inside her shell, as lost, as frantic as she. He was relieved when she won a special round of applause from an audience either in sympathy with her predicament, or impressed by her belated presence of mind. Indeed, it relieved him so much that he remembered to look round to see if Alice had come. It was a pleasure to have forgotten her; with every day that she did not enter his mind, though such days were few, he felt he was winning a battle.

He saw her sitting at the back, not talking to anyone: she was trying to prolong the applause. Her small face was alert, as if she were enjoying herself: she did not glance in his direction.

Westlake said, 'I'll take a rain-check. Be back.'

Maurice, not certain of this idiom which he vaguely knew to be American, watched him go. 'Has he had enough?' he asked Kate, more to make her talk than because the answer interested him.

'I should make a guess that he has to have a drink.'

He asked her why she thought so.

She replied, smiling, that he was very talkative and up to a point very frank: he had once been in Fleet Street, but they had thrown him out. This new job was a come-down for him; he had to bear it with fortitude. 'But I should think the trouble was drink, shouldn't you?'

He thought of the handsome, ironic, porous face. 'It might be.'

Alice came up to them: he found her at his elbow. 'Libby looks wonderful,' she said, 'it's a joy all the time.'

He was defensive. 'She's very nervous.'

'But she overcame it.'

'Poor Libby,' said Kate harshly, still smiling, 'she is no Siddons. But I grant you, she looks nice.' She moved away from them.

'I've sent her flowers,' said Alice. 'I hope it's all right.' She left him, and went back to her seat. The curtain rose on an uneventful third act. At the end, Libby and Lucy received bouquets: Libby three, from Maurice, Alice and Young Wives, Lucy two, from David and Melvyn Hannaway. Westlake, who had come back to his seat half-way through the act, applauded in a manner that made him conspicuous. Maurice heard people wondering who he was.

Libby, embowered in her flowers, held court in the women's dressing-room, a cloakroom converted for the evening to accommodate herself, Lucy, a Youth Club girl who played the maid, and Mrs. Walkeley's niece who was the character woman.

Maurice congratulated her, wondering what kind of reception she would give him: but she cried theatrically, 'Thank you, darling! Such lovely flowers, they must have cost far too much.'

On the way home she said, 'So odd of Mrs. Imber to send a bouquet — far too much of it, but well-meant, of course. People probably thought they were yours, and Kitson worked it out that if you were so well off he could dock the rates. Oh, I was all right, I know: but I'll be better to-morrow. Did you notice me fluff?'

He said he had happened to notice it.

'I think I recovered myself pretty well, though.'

121

She was too excited to go to bed. She had to go over the play, line by line, incident by incident. She had to re-live it. For the moment she was entirely happy. He was glad: he knew that without her happiness he could have none of his own, though what sort of form his was likely to take he could not begin to imagine.

'You aren't saying much, Kate,' Libby teased. 'I believe you're jealous!'

Certainly, Kate replied, she was extremely jealous, eaten up with jealousy.

'Who was that baggy-looking man you were talking to afterwards?'

'Who was Kate talking to?' Mrs. Marsden put in.

'Only one of the reporters.'

'I thought he looked sinister.'

'No,' said Kate, 'not sinister.'

Libby wondered whether it would look like showing-off if she arranged her own flowers on the stage at the next performance instead of the paper ones. 'Funny, Plym wanting bouquets sent up on the first night instead of the last.'

Maurice explained that it was Plym's idea to maintain equal excitement on both evenings. He himself would send up flowers to Libby and to Lucy to-morrow, and so would Johnson-Black.

'Well,' Libby said, 'I do think Plym owes me something. I've worked myself to death for him.'

When it was finally over she seemed at a loose end, with nothing to look forward to. She went with her dream-walk about the house, she forgot her visiting, sometimes she fell into despondency and sat doing nothing at all, neither reading nor sewing, for half an hour at a time. She was not at all pleased that Maurice had accepted Humphrey Pelham's invitation to Cambridge, and was less pleased when he decided to indulge himself by remaining there over the week-end.

'It's far too wearing for you,' she said indignantly, 'with all you've got to do, and if David has to take all the services it means that everything else will go by the board. You ought to consider yourself more.'

Kate, not minding her own business, observed that he was considering himself for once, and a good thing too.

'That's what I said to him,' said Mrs. Marsden, who was getting over a heavy cold which she had transmitted to the boys, 'I said, "You ought to get out more, even a clergyman can manage it if he tries." I told him, "You're looking pasty."'

'Mother, do *not* interfere,' Libby begged her, in a very gentle voice. 'He knows as well as I do that he won't be properly looked after in a beastly damp room in college, and he's just not fit to stack up a whole lot of work to cope with when he gets back.'

'Now, I don't agree with you. He'll be perfectly all right, and a man likes to get away with other men sometimes.'

Kate asked whether 'he' was the cat's mother. 'Do say something, Maurice, or leave the room with dignity. You can't just sit there being talked about.'

'Then I will leave the room with dignity,' he said.

He was looking forward to Cambridge as a boy might look forward to an act of truancy. The weather was bright and, for January, not cold: he looked anxiously every night for the forecasts, to see if it were likely to change. He kept his mind steadily upon his treat; nothing must happen to spoil it. Once or twice he caught himself praying that Humphrey would not be ill: he was an old man and there were colds going about. In the middle of a sermon, he noticed him sneeze. It was all he could do not to beg him, then and there, interrupting a carefully prepared and rather self-indulgent piece of exegesis, to take care of himself.

A few days before the visit he happened to go further afield than usual, to visit a parishioner in the hospital of St. Mary Abbott's. Crossing Cromwell Road on his way back, he saw Alice walking with another woman. She had not, he thought, seen him, and he was flooded with disappointment. He looked after her. Then, at the corner of Collingham Place, both women stopped. They exchanged a few words and parted. Alice turned, and came straight to him.

'Hullo,' she said. 'I spotted you, you know.'

She was wearing no hat, and the breeze blew her short hair about. The sun, flashing from the windscreens of passing cars, made a dazzlement about her. Tall, young-looking, she looked at him, no longer smiling.

He asked her meaninglessly what she was doing so far from home.

She told him she had found a flat at last, that she would be moving within the month. She had sold the house, but not for so much as she had hoped. He and Libby, she said, must come and see her when she had settled in. They must not lose touch with one another.

He could not speak.

'And you,' she asked, 'have you any news? I never see you these days.' As he still looked at her in silence — 'Maurice?'

He made the effort. He talked about Libby, Kate, the boys: Simon had his General Certificate examination coming this summer, he ought to do quite well.

'What is it?' she spoke gently, as if she thought he might be ill.

A lorry bounded thunderously past them, flicking up dust from the gutters. A swaddled Indian woman, middle-aged, with a long silken plait of hair shining like jet in its cleanly oils, waited patiently for them to get out of the way of her perambulator.

He told her about Cambridge: how he was going to dine there, and spend the Sunday by himself.

'I'm glad,' she said, 'it will be nice for you.'

They were enclosed in a capsule of the city's noise and glitter. Clouds raced over the starch-blue sky, behind and above the leafless branches.

He heard the voice that must be his speaking from miles away, the voice for which he could not be responsible. 'Will you be there?'

She looked away from him, down the long wide road. 'Yes.'

'Where?'

She mentioned a small hotel at Trumpington, on the main road. Her mouth was trembling.

Then neither knew what to say. They walked a few yards in silence. It happened that they were passing the bus stop, just as a bus drew up. Alice jumped on to the step. 'I've got to go.'

She did not look back. He saw her running up to the top deck; it was over. She had gone.

He could not believe it had happened; he would have believed it was an hallucination, if he could have accounted for the invasion of shame and excitement that made him lean, as if he were indeed a sick man, against the porch of a house. It was not too late, it was not irrevocable, it could all be undone. It must be undone. Yet how was he going to undo it? Write to her? A letter could go astray; well, he might write a non-committal letter that would mean nothing to anyone but herself. But he knew he could not insult her by a letter containing less than the whole of what he was, and this he would not dare to write. He could not call upon her, not after the rumours. He could, of course, tell Humphrey Pelham that he was not coming to Cambridge: he need not go. There was time to cry off.

It was an ordinary winter's day, Wednesday, three o'clock in the afternoon. Painters were working on a house. On the site of the airport coach station, they were using an electric drill. A covey of nurses in white caps, scarlet and navy-blue capes, came blowing round the corner of Marloes Road, making a noise like young birds. Outside an hotel, removal men were heaving a sofa into a van. A girl in drainpipe trousers and duffle coat waited at the end of a lead for her dog to follow her. A perfectly ordinary day, and this had happened, these words had been spoken, the whole focus of the world had shifted; all things were monstrous, beautiful, naked, and more than he could bear.

He could feel the seed of joy urgent to break out, like the seed cracking the soil, racing into root and stem and leaf and bud and flower, in the speeded nature film; and this terrified him. So long as he could stamp it down he was safe, he was not yet lost. Keep fear, shame, shock in authority and all would be well. He dared not admit joy. He would not admit it.

For apart from anything else: supposing he gave himself up to it and went in search of her: and she did not (she would not, of course) come?

Chapter Nineteen

THE weather had blackened; it was bitterly cold. Beyond the windows the hedges blew stringently in the wind and the grass whistled. Alice sat in the lounge bar before the fire, her hooded coat over the arm of her chair. Horse-brasses, tankards, platters, caught the colour of the flames; it was a comfortable place to be in, and she tried to tell herself that even if he never came it was better for her to be alone, here in this place far out, where no one knew her, and where nobody she knew could find her. It was nearly a quarter to three, and the barman had cleared the last of the regulars away.

'Looks like snow.'

She agreed. There was a reddish stain in the sky, and the wind was keen under the door.

For the past half hour she had tried to ridicule herself by stamping into her mind her own age: forty-two, forty-two, forty-two. She knew what she was doing, and that it was wrong: but she was riddled with love like a disease, she believed that she must have some moment of it for herself or she would be ill. Her thoughts were ecstatic and ugly: the birched boy stood in the back of her mind where he had always stood, the expiator, the one of whom they had 'made an example'. So far she had escaped scot-free, not merely from punishment, but partially from sin. She had learned, through indulgence in immediate pleasures, the revival of old friendships, the party round, to live with her murderous honesty: it had become harder and harder for her to believe (in such a short time, too!) that whatever she said, one way or another, could have harmed the old man dying. Maurice had looked after her, he had talked her out of horror.

The barman had gone. The clock ticked loudly in a silence of heat and red berries. Alice saw herself reflected in the glass, not a pretty woman but a smart and equable one. How little, she thought, I look what I am. There had always been darkness in her mind, obstinate and irrational; in a way Miles had known it, and because of this she had loved him, for a short while at least. People had thought him a dull man. She had stood around at parties, gloating in the thought that they were so mistaken: he had tormented her, in his time, he had tried to prise open the oyster of her thoughts, and she had respected him because he had thought it worth the effort. Her public face was a social one, too round to encourage speculation. She hid behind it, it gave up no secrets.

Now she was in love where no hope lay, and she was to be left alone. The room held no promise; it was a room for one person only. Upstairs she had a narrow bedroom, a slip-room, too small for weeping in, just the right size for sleep. She would get through the hours somehow, there would be a hot water bottle, she would edge herself into sleep by thinking of all the animals beginning with A, with B, with C, etcetera.

This place, this country pub on the featureless main road, with its local life, its mountainous fires, its horse brasses, its comfortable English food, might have been a place on the moon, so far removed was it from anything real to her. She had run out of cigarettes and the barman had gone. The clock struck three. What could she do? Nobody answered the bell. Like a sneak thief she slid round behind the bar and took a packet of twenty Player's. She put the money on top of the till.

Who was Libby Fisher, who was Kate Morley, who were David, Lucy, Plymmer — who was Maurice Fisher, come to that? She didn't know him. She was like the child in the game of hide-and-seek who, by hiding too well, wearies the seekers, and is left to squat in the laundry-basket till he grows tired of it, and sheepishly emerges to find everybody engaged in quite another game.

Around her, Cambridgeshire stretched in the nakedness of the fens. There might be a bird in a thicket, a cat attentive to that bird: nothing else. She started to count in tens: twenty, thirty, forty.

When he came in she rose at once and put on her coat, pulling the hood over her head. They went out into the empty road, where the first few flakes spun along the wind. He tucked his hand under her arm and gripped it. They moved off towards Grantchester together.

'Well, we are here,' he said at last.

It was safe enough, far too cold for people to be out. There was hardly the smallest mathematical chance that they would encounter anyone who knew either of them.

She looked up at him. He was wearing a high-necked sweater that concealed his collar.

'Yes, I know. I look just like other men. It is a disguise.'

His boxer's face was hard and sad. She wanted to say, 'Can't you stop being sad, just for this hour, the only one we have ever had together?'

They walked past fields and box-like houses.

'Not a pretty walk,' she said.

The light was sizing the grass in preparation for the paint-work of snow.

'This is all we have,' said Maurice.

With love swelling in her, hot, selfish, dissociated from conscience, from all other human beings, she thought that it should not be all: neither of them could bear it to be all.

'Are you happy?'

'Both happy and miserable,' he said.

'It was unfair that this should happen to us.'

He said it was not unfair, that they were not without guilt. There was nothing involuntary about falling in love: at a certain and precise moment, there must be a deliberate choice.

'I don't believe that.'

'It's true.'

They had passed a church at the bend of a road, were within sound of water. No one was about. He stopped and bent down to her. She put her hands upon his shoulders. He kissed her in the dark and the warmth of her hood.

'At least we have had this,' he said, when they had moved on in the dream of winter, the mud crackling underfoot, the noise of the weir slotting the silence like the running thought of some abstract intelligence.

'Better turn back.'

'Why?' she asked.

'I must get back to-night. Libby telephoned. David's got flu, so I shall have to take early service to-morrow.'

She said despairingly that he could not leave her: there was so much to talk about, they had not even begun to talk.

'It will do us no good to start.'

She felt anger rising. If he loved her as she loved him, he would be incapable of leaving her: nothing else would matter, the world could rot. Feeling the tension in her body, he pulled her closer to him, as if she were a prisoner and he a warder intent that she should not escape.

Her eyes filled. He would deposit her back in that fiery room, the hot, smug comfort, the nearness of teatime, leave her to be alone, far out, in the little sliproom under the eaves; as much alone as if he had never existed.

She burst out, 'Can you believe that what you have to do really matters? Suppose you didn't take early service, just for two or three people, in such a world as this one? What good do you think you're doing?'

'It does matter.'

'More than this?'

'If it didn't, I should be finished.'

'You're not making me think any better of God,' she said, as if it were a joke, as if this were a time for witticism.

'I can't help that.'

She stopped still. She was raining tears.

'Don't, don't, don't, don't, don't,' he said.

She had an impulse of surrender that was quite new to her, simply because he had the strength to let something be more to him than she was. And she had no doubt, really, just how much she did mean. She apologised stiffly, as at a committee meeting where too personal a note had been intruded.

'Don't, don't.' He put his arm round her, quickly hugged her. 'If there's nothing else for us, doesn't it mean something to you to know that we have this?'

'What am I supposed to do, feed on it, till it tastes like rags?'

He did not reply. They walked, silent, close, back along the road.

She realised that she had hoped, no matter how grotesque the hope had been, that she could somehow have brought him secretly to her narrow room without a soul knowing, and that they would have been together. Now, when he left her, she would not even be sure that he had been anything but a reflection of her own desire: not even the barman had been there when he came, so she could not say 'My friend who called for me . . . did he leave his cigarettes behind?'

Across the glacial fields a light sprang up in a window, self-contained as a ruby. Alice said, 'If only we could be behind there, nobody knowing, for ever.'

'If we could.'

They turned into the long stretch of Trumpington Road. Ahead of them the hotel threw out its hospitable glow. It was nearly at an end now.

He kissed her again, gently, on her cheek. 'Let's make no plans.'

'Why not? Because we are going to make them, or because we're not?'

She was so beside herself with panic and grief, that when he told her he loved her she hardly heard it, casting back her own admission at him casually, like a formal politeness. 'Are we, or not?'

'No. I should never have asked you to come.'

'Yes, you should. You had to. Even if it was only for this, for to-day.'

They were outside the hotel, lit up like figures on a stage.
'But I love you,' Maurice said. He went away out of the ring
of rosy light, into the swallowing dark. She did not try to look
after him. She went across the lounge and straight upstairs,
threw herself face downward upon her bed.

Chapter Twenty

HE FOUND David so ill that for days he had hardly time to think of anything but having him cared for and coping, single-handed, with the work of the parish. This enforced activity seemed to him like a heavenly intervention. Coming home in the train from Cambridge he had not known how he was to carry on; a way of doing so had been found for him. Even in bed at night, he managed to keep the thought of Alice dreamlike and remote; exhaustion sent him to sleep early.

He found he could retain this suspension of private thought even after David was up and about again. It struck him that there was nothing like wrongdoing for producing the conviction that to be good was possible; it was easy to be affectionate towards Libby, since for once she had been really a help to him. She was, she said, 'run off her feet'; and the claim did not seem absurd. He was in the suspension of a false peacefulness, which was sometimes like felicity; he meant to cling to it as long as possible, he would not throw away this unexpected moral reinforcement which had come to him out of nothing but the indisposition of his curate.

He heard from Libby, almost without interest, that Alice had gone away to live on the farther side of the park. She had left her address and telephone number, had apologised for having to give up the odd jobs she had done for the church. Beyond that, there was no message.

Meanwhile Kate, defiantly, without explanation, was going out two or three evenings every week. The moment she had put the last of the dishes in the rack and seen that Dick was in bed, she would run upstairs, make up her face, change her dress and bang out of the house. She usually came in between eleven-thirty and midnight but did not look into the study to see whether Maurice was still up. Libby, annoyed by the secrecy, teased her at mealtimes with strangely old-fashioned terms—'Your beau', or 'Your boy-friend', or, in Gallic style, 'Your *prétendant*'. Mrs. Marsden looked anxious. Kate smiled and changed the subject.

She was handsome and excited these days, but there was little pleasure in her face. At home, she sank into herself. She worked no less hard, but she did so with rapid, angry, impatient movements and with far more noise. Maurice watched her and was worried.

One night he found her alone in the kitchen, reading a newspaper spread out across the table while she waited for a cake to be done.

He sat down. 'Is all this making you happy?'

She raised her eyes. 'Is what?'

'Whatever you're doing.'

'I think I've earned the right to a private life.'

'I know you have.'

'Well, then.' She formed words with her lips, to impress on him that he was interrupting her reading.

'I only want to know that everything is all right, and that you're happy.'

She said: 'My dear old boy, since you've gone away from us, I may as well do what I please.'

He asked her what she meant. She pushed the paper away so that it slid on to the floor and regarded him steadily. 'Oh, you have, you know. Some time ago. But I don't ask you questions.'

She was talking nonsense, he said.

'Oh? But I know you, much better than anyone else does, I know when your thoughts change gear. How unpleasant that must be for you!'

Getting up, she opened the oven door, releasing a gust of scorching air into the kitchen. She stuck a knife in the cake, examined the blade.

Maurice said, 'I'm not prying. But I care about you.

'Very nice. Don't think I'm not grateful.'

He exclaimed, 'Oh, *what* is the matter?'

'Matter? Nothing. I've just taken to going about a bit. I've spent years here without any fun of my own and now I'm having some. Is any of you the worse off?' Her eyes flashed; she was keeping in check some violent resentment.

'None of us is. You hold this place together as you've always done, and there's precious little I can do to thank you.'

She said that he had given her and the boys a home: she was still more in arrears than he where thanks were concerned. 'And do move over, Maurice — you're right where I can't get at the drawer.'

He got out of her way, but did not leave the kitchen.

'Is there any reason why you shouldn't enjoy yourself with Westlake?'

She dropped the knife she had been holding; it fell with a clatter on to a vegetable dish, cracking it in two. 'Now look what you've done! Do stay in your part of the house and leave the kitchen to me. Oh, it's a shame!' She looked ready to cry. 'It's past riveting, and it's the last we've got of that pattern.' She swept the pieces together and thrust them into the pail. Kneeling to retrieve a shard of china she said, not lifting her head, 'Is this all around the parish, too? God, what a life! I'd as soon live in a glass case in Piccadilly Circus.'

'Not so far as I know. But I saw you in a car with him last night, when I was coming back from Kitson's.'

'I see. And do the others know?'

'I don't think so. Does it matter?'

She sprang up nimbly from her ankles, leaned on the edge of the dresser and lit a cigarette. He noticed that her eyes were reddened by the constant stream of smoke.

'Not a bit. Only I have so little all to myself that it's nice not to have to throw everything into the common pot. He likes to take me out, I like to go. And it's my business.'

He said he was sorry: she had every right to a secret, if she wanted one.

'That's right! Throw it back to me indulgently, give me permission to have it. That takes the gilt off, all right!'

'Kate!' He took her hands and held them.

She blinked. 'I shall be like Libby, and put it all down to my time of life. With slightly more excuse. All right, Maurice, I'm horrible, I have a nasty temper and no God. Please make allowances.'

'I haven't gone away from you, you know.'

'Poor old boy. Life's not easy for you, either.' She paused. 'Nothing more from that bloody Mrs. Fraser, I hope and trust. You were right to find her another job.'

'Your glass cage couldn't be worse than mine,' he said. He let her hands fall from his. 'Well, forgive me; I won't ask you questions again. I wouldn't have done it, if I hadn't thought you were worried.'

'He drinks too much. I wouldn't be, but for that.' She added in a changed voice, housewifely, domineering, 'And now, please get back to your sermon before you make me smash up the place again. I'm busy.'

He went on worrying about her. He was pretty sure that she was Westlake's mistress; and though he felt that this was none of his affair, was troubled by the impulse to make it so. If her body was appeased at last, her mind was not; her headaches, if anything, had been worse lately. He wondered if there were any likelihood of her remarrying, and what the boys would say if she did. It was obvious even now that her behaviour had disturbed them, though they had no idea of the cause. Simon would barely talk to her; Dick had formed the habit of making a fuss at bedtime, keeping her with him (in her ferment of impatience) as long as he could. Maurice ached to talk to some-one about it: and thought of Alice, the one person to whom he could have spoken of anything. He tried to put the thought aside.

Kate said loudly and clearly, one night at supper, 'I shall bring my young man back for a cup of coffee this evening.'

'There, I knew there was something!' Mrs. Marsden sparkled with excitement. 'I was saying to Libby, I know

Kate's got a friend, why can't she bring him home? And Libby said——'

'What is all this mystery?' Libby had coloured. The strings tightened in her neck. 'Who is he, anyway?'

'His name is Westlake.'

'I don't know him.'

'That doesn't automatically lower him in my eyes,' said Kate.

Libby told her there was no reason to be rude.

Simon suddenly began to mutter, over and over again,

'"Exton, thy fierce hand; Exton, thy fierce hand——"'

'What on earth are you doing?' Kate demanded.

He looked at her impudently. 'Saying my English prep. Is there any harm in that?'

'You're too old!' cried Dick, finding his voice. 'You can't have a young man, you're too old!' He beat his hands on the table in an access of mirth.

'There's no need for you to do your prep while we're having a meal. Have another chop and be quiet.'

'"Hath with the King's blood, hath with the King's blood——"'

'Now let us hear all about him,' Mrs. Marsden said comfortably, 'we all want to know.'

'He's a reporter on a local rag,' Kate replied shortly.

'"Stained the King's own land, *stained* the King's own land, *stained*——"'

'Shut up, Simon!'

He retorted that it was hard luck to be stopped doing his prep.

'"*Hath* with the King's blood——"'

'You can take your plate into the study and finish your homework there.'

'All right!' He rose furiously, glared at her and stalked out, not slamming the door but shutting it with aggressive precision.

Libby remarked how very odd it was of Kate to have said nothing before.

'Ah, but then I like being odd.'

Mrs. Marsden hoped he was nice.

'Very nice.'

'I shall look forward to meeting him.'

Kate said the reason why she had told them she would be bringing him home was so that they might keep out of the way. She would like the sitting-room to herself if that were possible: parsonages were not in his style, he was not particularly sociable.

'I honestly would have thought,' said Libby, with an air of stately amusement, 'that for a reporter not to be sociable would be a considerable disadvantage to him in his work.' She finished her well-turned sentence with a vocal flick, as if she had tied a bow on it.

'Other things are a disadvantage to him.' Kate got up. 'So may I have the sitting-room?'

'It sounds just like the way we did our courting in my young days.'

'It is not in the least like it, Mother.'

Libby got up too. 'How awfully funny it is! Kate's young man seems to have produced an atmosphere. I can't imagine why. It is entirely her business, isn't it? Can anyone see why there's an atmosphere?'

'No, dear,' Maurice said, 'nobody can. And the sitting-room shall be vacant.'

'Thank you.' Kate stacked the plates and went out.

Libby suddenly said she wondered whether Kate would like to borrow her green necklace; and Maurice, glancing at her, saw that for the moment she was genuinely carried away by the thought of romance, she really longed to be generous, to give pleasure. He wanted Kate to see her while the mood lasted, for she was softened and made young by it. 'Why not go and ask her?'

He was working in his study when Kate came racing, at her new pace, down the stairs. But this time she did not pass the door. She looked in. 'Maurice?'

He turned round.

'It wasn't meant for you. I'd like you to be there, that is, if you're up.'

'All right,' he said, 'if I am. You can bring him in here.'

Libby had gone to bed early: he pretended that he still had work to finish. He wanted to see Westlake, to find out, if he could, what sort of a man he was. He was obsessed by a sense of duty towards Kate, since he had for so long used not only her labour but the secret side of her humour. Hardly a word had passed between them that Libby and her mother could not have heard with equanimity: yet when he had wanted to blow off steam, to slough off the irritation of his days or the pressures in his mind, it was to Kate he had gone; and without a word said between them, she had accepted his need for emotional release and had given it to him. Once Libby, annoyed because he had seemed to side over some trivial matter with Kate rather than herself, had said: 'I wonder you didn't choose her instead of me.' But he could not have married Kate, even if she had been free for the asking. He had never found her physically attractive. Not that he had ever doubted her possible attraction for other men: he could appreciate that, but at a remove, as a brother could see it in a sister. No: Kate was not for him, and Libby had been. Whenever Libby had exhibited some small spurt of jealousy he had felt himself between laughter and outrage: she was absurd, and he was not incestuous.

At a quarter to twelve he heard them come back, heard them speaking low in the hallway. Kate opened his door a little way. 'Still there? May we come in?'

He got up. Westlake followed her into the room; as if unsure of himself he had not removed his top-coat. He smelled of drink, but he was sober.

'You remember my brother-in-law,' said Kate.

They shook hands. Maurice pulled up a chair, suggested he might find the room rather hot.

'I was only looking in for a minute.'

'It will be longer than that,' Kate said. 'I have to make coffee and it has to stand. You want a decent cup, don't you?'

She was speaking to him with a sort of rough, rallying intimacy. Taking his coat from him, she threw it over the back of the sofa. She had something of the awkwardness of an adolescent girl bringing her boy home; it was an awkwardness Westlake's demeanour seemed to match, yet Maurice fancied that, beneath it all, he was at ease. As he looked at him at close quarters, he found he was not so handsome as he had thought, for the classical nose was too big and too pulpy, the upper lip too long, but the total effect of the face was striking, and had once been imperious. The eyes were still splendid, watery but brilliant, neither shifty nor suspiciously frank.

'It's late to intrude upon you,' Westlake said.

Maurice replied that he was used to late visitors and was glad to sit and talk. He had been writing all the evening, his hand was tired.

'We've been to the cinema.' Westlake's voice had a pleasant west-country richness beneath the carefully cultivated standard English. 'I don't suppose you ever get there, do you?'

Maurice said he hadn't set foot in one for more than five years — 'and I used to like the pictures. Did you see anything good?'

'Not for my taste, but Kate liked it. Kate's easy to entertain, it's nice to see her enjoying things.'

This thrust of intimacy, deliberately making itself known, was not lost upon Maurice. He said non-committally, 'She doesn't get entertained very often, I'm afraid. It's good for her to get out.'

'I enjoy taking her. Do you mind?' The question was asked rapidly and lightly, with a smile and watchful eyes.

'Mind?' He was gaining time.

'Well, another intrusion into your *cercle de famille*. A parson's must of necessity be a pretty closed one.'

'On the contrary,' said Maurice, 'the doors bang open and shut all day with the wind of new passings.'

Westlake laughed aloud, throwing his head back. 'Vicar, you should be a pressman, not me.'

'I don't think mine could be described as a racy, journalistic style.' He asked if he were liking his new work.

'Well, it's a bit cramping, being in so small a pond. But the Windermere of Fleet Street, as it were, rejected me.' The eyes sharpened. 'I expect Kate told you.'

Maurice was saved from answering by Kate's entry with the tray. 'I've brought a cup for you, old boy. It won't keep you awake for once.'

He said yes, it would, he would have some milk. He did not like Westlake, partly because he felt his pretentiousness was a double deception, designed not to draw attention away from a genuine fundamental unease, but to make people believe an unease really existed, and to be distracted from the truth by admiration of their own perception: it was a kind of three-card trick. Partly, he disliked him because he had gone down-hill. His duty, he knew, should be with such people, who needed more help than the others: but, just as many men felt their duty was toward the advancement of the coloured races while rejecting the idea that black men should marry their sisters, he did not want any derelict to take love from Kate. Westlake might need love, but he could go and get it elsewhere.

She and Westlake talked about the film, almost quarrelled about it. It seemed to be their accepted way of converse, this half-affectionate sub-snacking. With him she was not so much witty as rude; he seemed to enjoy it, encouraging her by deprecating shrugs, outward flicks of his long fingers, while all the time his eyes were steady upon her face.

'But this is a bore to you, Vicar,' he said. 'It must be like listening to other people's dreams.'

The word 'dream', too, had a double implication; he was trying to convey to Maurice that Kate was his, that he was to be accepted.

Maurice thought: and who am I not to accept him? This is all the fun she has, all the life she has. What does it matter what I think? Her own attitude was harder for him to analyse. He felt she was 'in love' with Westlake, but that she did not love him: she felt no admiration for him, only the excitement his interest in her had stimulated. He sensed an undercurrent of defiance. Yes, she was saying, he is rather a poor thing; but I can't be alone any longer, I have had nothing for myself till now, and I am old enough to do as I please.

He tried to be as friendly as he could. He congratulated Westlake on his criticism of the play, said how extraordinary it seemed to find something of such high professional quality in a local paper.

'Vicar, I am grateful. Such praise makes me feel I am not, even now, altogether shouting down the wind.'

'Don't be soapy, Tom,' Kate said, 'you don't for a moment imagine you are. Even on *The Argus*.'

He replied unexpectedly, 'Soapiness is the badge of all our tribe; the worse your luck, the soapier you have to become.'

'You'll get back, though, won't you?' Maurice asked him.

Westlake smiled. 'Oh, sure, sure, as the Americans say.'

'But you will,' Kate insisted.

'I said, "sure, sure". We must wait and see. Fortunately' — he looked at Maurice — 'I have a small private income, so I shall never be found in the doss-houses.' He looked at his watch, which he wore on an elaborate gilt strap an inch wide. 'Forgive me, I'm keeping you up. So nice of you to let me in, Vicar.'

'You can call him Maurice,' said Kate, 'it sounds more human. We are all human in this house, we are nothing like a stage parsonage.'

When he had gone she said, 'Well?'

'We may be nothing like a stage parsonage,' Maurice said, 'but he is very like a stage down-and-out.'

'So you don't like him.'

'I didn't say so. He's obviously a clever man.'

'What an uncharitable bastard you can be!' She was angry enough, disappointed enough, to want to shock him.

'I'm sorry. After all, nothing matters if you like him.'

'Precisely.'

'Is he married?'

'Ah, I wondered when that would come up! Yes, he is, but

he's been separated from his wife for about ten years. She's R.C., so there's been no divorce. Anyway, he's not interested one way or the other.'

She came to stand beside him, and hung her arm through his. She stared at the carpet.

'Now look, I'm my own mistress.'

'Yes?'

'Oh, stuff, Maurice! Cheap-jack stuff. I'm surprised at you.'

'I'm only asking you to watch your step. Bring Westlake here when you like. This is your home.'

'Lovely. He'd enjoy himself so much with Mother and Lib.'

He was angry: he wanted to help her, he did not know how to do it. He could not have lied about his opinion of Westlake, even to appease her: it would have been as impossible for him to do that as for Alice to give old Imber his blue-print for heaven.

Then she kissed his cheek: she could not have kissed him more than half a dozen times in the years he had known her.

'You do try,' she said, 'I know it. Well, up we go.' She quoted a maddening comic phrase of her mother's: ' "Ain't none of us got no beds?" '

Chapter Twenty-one

THIS was an informal meeting, to make preliminary arrangements for the part of St. Lawrence's in the Missionary Festival some months away. It was February, cold, sludgy, lightless, and Plym had seated himself upon the radiator, the one warm spot in the vestry.

Maurice wished he had postponed discussion for a week or so. The event seemed remote and nobody, except David, was touched by the sort of animation which made discussion fruitful.

'Now if we contribute a stall, we must make it something special. We aren't rolling in wealth like our friends round the corner, but we have got ideas,' David said.

'Excellent,' said Kitson, without any sign of catching fire from this. He added, as an afterthought, 'Have we?'

'*I* have ideas,' said Plym, 'and what do I get for them?'

'Now listen, dear boy,' Hannaway said earnestly, 'the choir is not up to it.'

'Thank you, I can cope with the choir.'

'Ah, the intention is good! Of course you could cope, if coping were all. But the fact is, so many of them can't be coped with. That is, can't sing.'

'I'll make them sing if I have to kick their behinds for them.'

Maurice intervened to say that at the moment all of this was academic: none of them knew what would be proposed in the way of entertainment, or even whether there was to be one.

'The point is,' said Kitson, 'what sort of a stall are we going to have? We shall have to consult the other churches in the Deanery and see what they're doing, but our best move would be to have something up our sleeves that none of them could have thought of.'

'A slave market,' Plym muttered, 'we could sell off the Mothers' Union.'

Johnson-Black gave an unexpected grunt of laughter. He laughed so rarely and so unpredictably that they all stared at him.

Kitson, who would normally, in his tight-lipped fashion, have been amused, was not amused now. He said that jokes were all very well, but they were there to get something settled; if they weren't going to do that, they might as well have stayed at home. The crux of it was, they must opt for their stall being decently placed. It was no good working like blacks if they were going to be stuck away in a corner of the school hall.

'I don't know that one can opt,' Maurice said, 'last time we had a do like this we drew for our pitches.'

He knew he should be taking an interest: but everything was savourless. He had never been sure, in the unanalysed caves of his mind, of the value of the mission field. To-day, in a world alternately crawling with fright and making Zulu noises of optimism, it seemed more vain than ever. His own depression weighed on him, discolouring his normal hopes, narrowing the vision that made such endeavours tolerable.

'Then we'd better find out,' Kitson replied. 'Who would know?'

'I'll make it my job to find out,' said David. He added, 'What a pity Mrs. Imber isn't still around! She was always full of original ideas.'

He had spoken in a careless, buoyant tone, high-pitched. Maurice knew well enough what he was up to: he thought it was a good and healthy thing to break the new convention that the less said about her the better. But he wondered when David would learn when it was well to keep one's mouth shut. The mention of her had sent a thrust of pain through him; had David expected it to be a thrust of joy?

'She made a charming little thing of the children's play,' Hannaway agreed eagerly. 'But there, that's life.'

'What is?' Plym mumbled. 'People always nattering on about life. Bloody silly.'

Kitson raised his head. 'Plymmer, I wish you'd watch your language. Never mind what you do, or any of us do, outside. It's not suited to the building we're in.'

Plym hopped off the radiator. 'What is all this? For Pete's sake, Kitson——'

'Now, George, dear boy,' said Hannaway, 'we all know Plym's mode of speech. It means nothing.'

'It means disrespect for an institution and I don't like it.'

Maurice intervened hastily, before Plym could burst out in one of his gnome-like flurries of rage. 'Have we all got the general timing clear? Short service at two-fifteen, non-liturgical, just hymns, prayers, sermon, and all over to the hall by three-fifteen. Fête at three-thirty.'

'Yes, we've got the general timing, Vicar,' said Plym tightly, 'and what I want to know is, why I am suddenly attacked, on a filthy cold afternoon——'

'All right, all right,' said Kitson.

'Suddenly attacked, for *no* good reason——'

'Let it go,' said Johnson-Black, 'we shall never be through by teatime at this rate. Is Fawcett coming?'

Maurice said he couldn't get there. He suggested that a special appeal should be made to the Mothers' Union and the working parties. The meeting ended with nothing much decided, but three pages of packed notes in Hannaway's book. As David and Maurice left the church, they heard Plym attacking Kitson, Kitson replying with the clear, half-bonhomous, half-contemptuous drawl he might have used to native offenders in fly-ridden, tropical courtrooms many years ago.

'What's the matter with George?' Maurice asked. 'I thought going for Plym like that was a bit on the un-Christian side, I must admit.'

David said he was by no means sure that Kitson was a Christian: but he was becoming more and more a fanatical churchman. 'He believes church is good for people, like compulsory games. We have to think he's right.'

'We do.'

'Somehow it's not enough.'

146

'I like George,' said Maurice.

'Oh, so do I.' David ran his finger along the dripping railings, dislodging a string of water-drops. 'But he doesn't think even you are quite serious.'

Maurice said nothing. David was in one of his revelatory moods, when he spoke in all good faith for the good of others, unaware of the disquiet he caused.

'Not that he hasn't enormous respect for you.' The curate cocked his head, his flowery blue eyes a little anxious.

'It's mutual. He does a good job. The Bishop's Eye has never found a farthing in the books to complain of.'

'He was absolutely staunch over the Mrs. F. business,' David murmured. 'Did you know he ticked her off himself?'

Maurice shook his head.

'Well, he did. Put the fear of God into her.'

They came to the parting-place.

'Well,' David said, still looking anxious. Maurice was sorry for him, but could not help him. It was impossible for them now to be as they had been. 'I'd better be getting back to my labours. Work, for the night is coming.'

Maurice went home. The boys had just come in from school and the gramophone was going strong. They were using the loud needles they liked best. He heard Kate shout out to them, unheeded. Libby came brightly to greet him.

'Have a good meeting, darling?' She kissed him. He pulled her against him with a series of little tugs, comforting and quite automatic.

'I've been to the hospital. I saw Mrs. Jones and poor old Figgis.'

'Good girl.'

'Do you know what Figgis said to me? He said, "When I see you coming along the ward, it's like an angel." Wasn't that charming?'

'Did you see Mrs. Brent too?'

She replied that she hadn't had time: the other two were quite enough for one day. Maurice told her impatiently that both Mrs. Jones and Figgis could have waited: Mrs. Brent was really ill.

Libby looked at him quizzically. Drawing away from him, she leaned against the wall, pretending to scratch her head: 'Isn't it extraordinary?' she said in a detached, good-humoured voice, 'Libby never gets things quite right, does she? Whatever she does is just a tiny bit wrong. But I'm afraid it's the way the poor girl's made.' She patted his cheek. 'Never mind. I'll put Mrs. Brent — such an awful woman, one has to face it — first on the list next week. Libby will be good.' She gave him a kiss of forgiveness and went upstairs.

All through supper he was troubled by the nag of an intention. What it was, he did not know: but there was something he was going to do, the moment the meal was over. The meal crawled. Kate made the mistake of trying to force upon Dick a pudding he detested, which brought them both into the kind of conflict that springs from the deepest and most twisted roots of filial relationship, the kind of conflict parents and children can only hope to pass by in silence. They sat and glared at each other, deep in rage, both determined not to give an inch.

'Now, Dick,' said his grandmother, 'you mustn't look at your mother like that.'

'Please leave this to me,' said Kate tightly.

'But you couldn't see how he was looking at you just then when you'd turned your head away! *I* could see it.'

'Dick! There is nothing wrong with that pudding. I will not put up with your fads and fancies at every meal.'

He gave the plate a push. It spun along the table top and crashed into Simon's. Boiled rice splashed over on to the polished wood.

'You little beast!' Kate cried. 'You did that purposely!'

'So you did,' said Simon, grinning. 'You're a dirty little beast, your manners are nauseating.'

'You shut up!' said Dick. 'She wasn't talking to you.'

Libby said to Simon, 'Two against one isn't fair. You should mind your own business.'

148

'Oh, Aunt El-*ee*-zabeth! I'm only trying to bring him up the way he should go——'

Dick flicked his napkin across his brother's face. They rose simultaneously, Simon with sparkling eyes and the same grin, Dick as white as the spilled pudding.

'Sit down!' Kate got up. '*Will* you sit down when I tell you, and let us get on with our supper in peace?'

Maurice pushed back his chair and went to the study. He locked the door. Carefully he chose a sheet of blank paper and an envelope, tested his pen. It was a ball-point. The ink had run out. He found a refill in a drawer. He wrote, 'My dear,' then stopped. He rose and made up the fire, held out his hands to it. He found he had no cigarettes, so he went out again to the machine on the corner and bought a packet of ten. Even now, with the first words written, he was still unsure what he meant to do. He tried not to think at all until he was back in the study, before the writing paper that had no heading.

The noises of quarrel had ceased, though he thought he could hear Dick crying. Simon was running a bath.

' "My dear, It isn't any use . . ." '

The bell rang. Pushing the paper into his pocket, he waited. He heard voices in the hall. Libby tried the door, called out 'Darling!'

He let her in. She said, in a muffled, hasty voice, 'What on earth are you doing, locking yourself in?'

'Nothing.'

She said aloud, sociably, warningly, 'It's Mr. Betts, dear. He wants to know if you could spare a few minutes——'

Maurice told her despairingly to show him in. He crumpled the letter and tossed it into the fire.

Peter entered, bearing his problems with a presentation air, like a butler a boar's head. For years he had been taking them to Maurice, for years had got only a strained and conscientious sympathy. It did not seem to worry him. He loved to talk about his moral difficulties to a hearer compelled by virtue of his office to give them weight.

'May I have my special seat?' he asked, as he dropped on to

a fireside stool on which nothing was normally put except a book or an ashtray. Doubled up on it, his knees almost to his chin, he looked about him. 'Now, here, I always feel at home. But you must turn me out if you're busy, I couldn't bear to feel you were saying to yourself, "Oh, that Betts! It's him again!"'

Maurice said he had time to spare.

'Well,' said Peter, 'Lou and I have reached a decision, and we thought you ought to know. It hasn't been reached lightly, we've talked till dawn, I assure you.'

Despite himself, Maurice felt his attention caught. He waited for the news of renunciation; and was touched by pity. After all, neither Peter nor Lou could help being what they were, and to condemn them both to a life of solitude could be nothing but brutal. Yet what could he do? He could scarcely urge them to stay together, could scarcely go to the length of encouraging their way of living. He was, he knew, less tolerant than many men of his time, of aberration; because it was incomprehensible to him, because, even in adolescence, he had escaped the ordinary impulses of love towards his own sex, he found it hard to contemplate the homosexual with any sort of imaginative sympathy. He even had to repress the instinct to regard Peter and Lou as farcical; they were not funny to themselves, not within the defensive cocoon of their relationship; even their mannerisms were in part a defence mechanism against laughter, a deliberate invitation of the titter so that it should not catch them unawares. Yet now his sympathies were more nearly stirred by them than ever before. He was touched by the cheerfulness with which Peter came with his sacrifice; it was the kind of bravery Maurice had always admired in others and had hoped to find in himself, if the need for it should ever come to him. Thinking rapidly ahead, he wondered what answer he should make. Perhaps he ought to warn them that to take such a resolution was easier than to implement it: had they really faced what it must mean to them? But if he gave such a warning, it might sound like condonation, and he could not believe that it was right for him to condone a relationship condemned by society and by the church as sin. Yet this, also, was love.

However impossible he found it to believe, it was love; constant, unselfish, enduring. What fault was it of theirs if they could find no other sort?

He said, 'Tell me about it.'

'Well,' said Peter, 'it's about the sidesmen.'

'The *sidesmen*?' Maurice felt he could not have heard correctly.

'We've talked it over, we haven't been hasty. Only — well, you know that we should like office in the church, no matter how humble, we want to take part in the corporate life. So we thought — well, the difficulty may be the two of us. That is, that there might only be a vacancy for one. So Lou and I agreed that if you should want only me to officiate — or, come to that, only Lou —' Peter added, without much pretence of believing that such could be the case — 'neither of us would stand in the other's way. He'd be quite happy if it was me, he'd understand perfectly: and so should I if it were the other way round.'

He beamed above his kneecaps. He was assured, content, the decision was taken.

Maurice was too stupefied to say anything at all.

'We've always tried not to be selfish or possessive,' Peter went on. 'If a problem does crop up, we thresh it out together. I won't pretend this wouldn't be a sort of wrench, as we do love to do things together; but we're quite firm. We're in complete agreement.'

'There aren't any vacancies,' said Maurice.

'Oh, but there were! I mean, there's dear old Mr. Garrett, but he's only temporary, isn't he? And so very slow.'

Maurice said he was afraid old Garrett could not be set aside. He was sorry, but he didn't think any sort of office would be free for a very long time.

Peter looked, for a moment, bitterly disappointed. He wrinkled his forehead, so that the grey cap moved with his scalp. The firelight shone on his knuckles, his agate ring, the toes of his shoes. Then, boyishly, he sprang up; he was bright again. 'Well, anyway, you do know the situation, don't you?

And you'll bear it in mind? Please don't take the fact that there are two of us into consideration — Lou and I simply want you to forget about that.'

He took his leave cheerfully, holding Maurice's hand a second longer than usual, as if to seal an understanding. 'Bless you, Vicar, you're always so nice.'

Well, Maurice thought, when he had gone, Peter had come in time to save him; one of the more mysterious of mortal instruments. The nagging impulse had gone. He no longer wanted to write letters. He intended to go on enduring, by himself, preserving the hope that one morning he would wake to find the prospect of the coming day an easier one. He went about the room clearing it up, picking Foxe's *Book of Martyrs* from the floor where Dick had left it, open at one of the more grisly illustrations, emptying ashtrays, probing out from behind a picture a forgotten, dusty sprig of holly. He heard Kate go out, the sound of a car starting up.

Chapter Twenty-two

WHEN she left her flat behind she believed, almost honestly, that she had no idea where she was going. This was simply a walk in the promising dusk of a March evening: the air was mild, the bushes in the park greening over under the grape bloom of soot. She might have turned right or left, it would not have mattered. In fact she turned left and went westward in an easy, undestined stroll. In the sky ahead there was a faint glaze of sunset, not an added colour, but a spring-like shine.

She was trying not to liberate the destructive fantasy. So far as it was possible not to think, she believed she was not thinking. She was halted by some brief desire for a dress in the window of a beautiful lighted shop: well, that was all right, that was fine. It proved that she was still surfacing, concerned with things that could not matter in the least to him.

She turned left into the weighty Victorian streets, the residential squares now springing into lozenges of light. Right in front of her, in the window of a small house squatting between two high ones, a lamp flashed up; and the dusk between it and herself was like the snow-dusk over the fields. She knew now where she was going and nothing could stop her. She *must* go, not to see him, but to sidle humiliated, like a private detective, round the streets where he was, to know that she was near him. For seven weeks she had held the longing down; had held it down by not thinking, or by thinking herself into the stimulating fantasies of anger. He had started it, hadn't he? (She scraped at his image with the oyster shell of vulgarity, of termagant contempt.) He had started it all by saying (and no, she was not going to cry, he was not worth it) 'Will you be there?' If he had loved her at all he could not have let her go, no matter what he was, no matter whether or not it tumbled his life down, and the lives of everyone else. She raged at him, she made him answer back, she put into his mouth words for which she could despise him.

Now, as she looked at the window, she stood still, feeling the awful, masochistic submergence into active love. It made her giddy, it made her ill, the blood rushed to her head.

You are forty-two, she said, forty-two, not a girl, you must not do this, you must not do it. But the voice sounded tinny. Without realising it, she had closed her eyes. Now, opening them, she found them gummy with tears. She walked rapidly on, full of determination.

It was a quiet time of the evening in these backwaters. Office workers had come home to tea. Children were being bathed and put to bed. Girls were dressing to go out.

It was just dark enough for her to slide by unrecognised, if she sheered away from the street lamps. In Vernon Square no one was about. St. Lawrence's loomed up like an accusing presence, a catcher-out. She approached it, almost on tiptoe, as if she were playing Tom Tiddler's ground. Now she was within touching distance of the privets. On one of the bushes somebody had hung a child's red woollen glove, hoping the loser would claim it; in the dusk it burned like a lamp.

She went softly up the path and opened the door. From behind the baize inner doors came the rumble of the organ. She looked in. Only Plym having a choir practice, lights only in the choir, and the rest of the church in darkness. She slipped into a back pew. She could hear her own heart, reverberating with the organ.

Plym shouted, 'Stop it!' and raised his right hand like a traffic policeman.

The meagre lights sparkled on his corduroy shoulders, sallowed the faces of the singers.

'Now look here——'

She could hear him well, the acoustics at the back were

good, and Plym had the penetrating, parade-ground voice not uncommon in very small men:

'—we are going to have some *decent* hymn-singing, which, so help me, we have never had in this choir. Lord knows I don't blame you for breaking down on some of the old muck — no need to look pie-faced, by any literary or musical standards it is old muck — but we're doing one of the only three that can stand up in their own right. So this is gorgeous, see? This is worth singing. This needs both men-tal and mor-al beef behind it.' He broke the words for emphasis, as if reading from an infant's primer. 'Men-tal and mor-al *beef*. Hi, Joan!'

He called up to Mrs. Johnson-Black in the organ loft. 'All over again. Now then: basses. I want the sort of boom one gets in the *Dies Irae* which, I am pleased to say, I do not have to train you to sing. But that sort of boom: and not flat, N-O-T F-L-A-T. If you feel you're going flat, try to go sharp. With luck, you may hit it somewhere in the middle.'

There was a titter. There were people who wondered how the choir endured Plym's rudeness, not realising that for some of the singers he was a prized comedian, whose turn could be enjoyed for nothing.

Normally, Alice would have wanted to laugh also: but now she could not. She was still too shaken by the assault of desire and loss, too conscious that what she was doing was dangerous, degrading and silly.

> 'Pavilioned in splendour
> And girded with praise.'

'Oh, listen,' said Plym, stopping them again, 'even *I* can feel it! It's rich. It's gorgeous purple. You're singing it spinster's mauve.'

Suppose Maurice came in? What should she do? Could she crouch down in the pew so that nobody might see her? And if she did, and stayed, what would happen? She could be locked in the church, she could be made utterly ridiculous. There are times when people in the depths of love hate love, when they

155

bitterly resent it. Alice felt this hatred, this resentment now. It was like being at the mercy of drink or drugs, it changed and it degraded. Yet she could not get up and go, now, when it would be safe, not even now that the singing had begun again and Plym was letting it continue, for the moment, without interruption. She tried to steady herself by looking at the lectern, which had gathered to itself a tissue of golden light, as if preparing an annunciation.

Plym stopped them again to rehearse the treble descant for the penultimate verse. He abused the sopranos, pleaded with them, gave them up. 'All right! Last verse. And we're going to take it slower than the others, all stops out, slow and swinging, St. Michael and all angels singing this, please — if you can stretch your imagination so far — wingtip to wingtip, all spread, angelic basses rumbling like the Bakerloo line. Good. Got it? Then off you go.'

They did grasp a little of his meaning, for the singing rose in something like grandeur, the church shuddered with it, from the flagstones to the dank and vaulted dark—

> 'O measureless Might,
> Ineffable Love——'

— rolling like the sea, with a deep ground-swell.

> 'While angels delight
> To hymn thee above,
> Thy humbler creation,
> Though feeble their lays,
> With true adoration
> Shall sing to thy praise!'

Plym was silent for a few thunderous moments when the organ had died away. ' "Humbler creation" is about right,' he said, 'just about right. But I've heard worse. Miss Laycock, if you can't get up to "lays", just mouth it. Nobody will know. All right, whole shoot again, once more.'

Alice rested her head on her arms. Very well: in a weakened

state one cried at things. A good hymn, like this one. Soldiers with drum and fife band. 'O God our help in ages past' sung around the Cenotaph, in meaningless memory of too many dead. Bad sentimental films, good sentimental films. She meant to leave before the hymn came to an end: there were still three verses to go.

Half-way through the second, Plym shouted, 'That's quite enough of it! All go home.' He dispersed them with flapping gestures as if they were fowls, drove them out through the vestry door. Joan Johnson-Black came down, and he spoke to her for a moment. Then she left, past Alice, not seeing her.

But when everyone had gone, Plym came straight down the aisle and peered into the pew at the back.

'Oh, it's you. I was wondering who it was.'

She tried to smile. 'Now how *did* you know?'

'I could feel you there. I can always sense a visitor. Did you ever know a good producer who couldn't tell when someone had sneaked into the back of the pit during rehearsal? Come round to Golo's and have a coffee.'

She said she ought to be getting home. She had been passing by the church on her way back from a party, had just looked in for a moment. This seemed quite reasonable to her, and appeared reasonable to Plymmer, for he made no comment, except to say that it must have been a damned dreary teetotal fiesta because she didn't smell of drink. He persuaded her, however, to accept his invitation. If anyone did see her, she thought, it would seem natural enough for her to be in his company. Everyone knew that they were old friends.

They walked along towards Gloucester Road. Golo's was a large, garish café which had become a meeting-place for students of all races, living lonely on meagre grants: Indians, Swedes, Sinhalese, Chinese, Turks, Germans, Italians, they all came there, to sit for hours over coffee. Bubbles of light ran along the green and orange neon tubes: one could see the place a mile off.

Plym took Alice upstairs into the restaurant where, because the proprietor knew him, he was able to sit in relative quiet without necessarily buying a meal. 'Not that you don't deserve a meal, ducky,' he said to her, 'after all that lurking.'

She looked at him.

He put his hand over hers. 'I know lurking when I see it. Now I will tell you how he is, so you don't have to get round, by some elephantine route, to asking me. He is dreary. He preaches awful sermons based on absurd *minutiae*: why did St. Somebody go somewhere by one route rather than another? Complicated geographical matter thrown in. Or why some temple or other had a certain number of bricks and not half a dozen more. He is bored, so is the congregation. Nobody cares. Both expect to be. Our Lib sparkles rather too brightly and continues to be admired for her good works. What good works, you may ask me? God knows. But it is said that she is always "on the go".'

He was talking to steady her. He told her Kate Morley was running around with a seedy journalist, and that tongues were wagging. 'However, that is her affair. She's always been resolutely unchurchy.'

'And David?'

'Also a little down. He and Maurice aren't quite so close. But if you should ask me why, I can't give you an answer. Search me. It's just so.'

In the deforming light the coffee looked yellow; all faces, whether white or black, took on a violet tinge. The plate-glass windows were blotted with steam. Out of the bright nightmare she said, 'Plym, what shall I do?'

'What can you?' His expression was oddly detached: he looked at her as if she were giving a performance of some kind.

She turned away.

He patted her knee. 'Well, ducky,' he repeated, 'what can you? As my old mother used to say, What can't be cured must be endured. You just have to behave yourself and stick it out.'

She said, in a stifled voice, that this was not what she had expected, from him.

Someone had turned on the wireless. A female voice, tearful, genteel-American, was singing about a little white cloud that cried.

158

He turned on her in a small rage.

'What did you expect? I have to put up with my life, I've had to stick it out for years. Why should I encourage you to make the sort of filthy mess I have always restrained myself from making? Good Plym. Brave Plym. Catch me giving you any blessing.'

She said she had not known he was unhappy.

'No, you didn't, did you? Clever Plym. I haven't got on with Jenny for years. Ha, ha! I fall in love with other women, too. Luckily, in large numbers. That helps. Have some more coffee?'

She refused.

'Oh, do. Or I shall think I've offended you. But I tell you, I can't cheer you on, not even to fix our Libby, the Belle of Saint Ell's.'

'All right, Plym. Let it go.'

He told her she was his poor old Alice, nobody could feel for her more than he did. He had been in love with her, for about a couple of months, in the old days at Cambridge.

She had to smile. 'No, you weren't.'

'Yes, I was, but not for longer than I said.'

His eyes, cold and large in the delicate, gnome-like face, examined hers. She realised, with a shock of irrational surprise, that he was a middle-aged man; she had always thought of him as an eccentric boy in his twenties, never taking himself quite seriously because he believed no one else would. Life had left him high and dry with none of the things he wanted; even as a musician he had failed.

'Like what you see?' he said. 'I never do.'

He walked with her to a bus stop. As they waited there, he asked what she wanted to take buses for. He reminded her how she had said, not so long ago, 'I am rather rich.' 'What made you say it? It sounded extremely odd.'

'I felt out of things. And I can't bear false pretences.'

'Good. Then keep up the good work.'

He was gone. Peering through the window, she saw him making off again in the direction of Golo's.

He could scarcely have done her more harm. He had disappointed her, made her angry. If he had given her sympathy, had urged her to the kind of free, all's-fair-in-love behaviour to which they had paid enthusiastic lip-service when they were young, he might have given her the spirit to stay still. He had always made her counter-suggestible: it was one of the reasons why she liked him, yet had never wanted to see too much of him.

Back in the flat, she turned on all the lights, then went to the telephone. If he didn't answer she could hang up again.

He did.

'Maurice?'

There was a long pause.

'Are you alone?'

'Yes.'

'Come and see me!'

Another pause. Then: 'It would do no good.'

'You don't want to.'

He answered quietly, roughly, 'You know that's not true.'

'Just for a moment.'

'No. And don't ring me again.'

Incredibly, he had hung up the receiver. She sat staring at it, completely demoralised, distraught. How long she sat there she did not know, holding her hands down between her knees, trying to keep calm. She said to herself, Oh no, oh no, oh no. No. No. No. This could not have happened, she could not believe it. What was there to prove it had happened, that it was not just some horrible hallucination born out of the silent squares, the organ rolling in the half-lit church, the sickly blaze of Golo's? The telephone was quiet in its bed. Her coat lay over the chair where she had flung it. The clock said ten past ten: when she first came in it had said the same. There was *no time* in which it could have happened.

She got up, her legs trembling under her, picked up the coat and hung it in the wardrobe. She started to tidy the room, putting everything precisely four-square. When the telephone rang, she was so shocked she almost screamed.

'Will you be in to-morrow night at half-past ten? I'll come for a quarter of an hour, and that's all.'

She said, 'Oh, dear God.'

Now the room was transformed, the hands of the clock had moved on. She was shuddering with relief and joy: yet not joy altogether. Beneath it she felt the drag and race of shame, of self-condemnation. It had been like this on the night her father died. It had been like this on a night she would not even think about. It had been like this on a night, two years ago or more, when, on the mountain above Montreal, above the flashing sea of the city, she had told Miles that she had stopped loving him: had seen him step back like a comic who has received a slap, open his mouth wide like a comic, and move his tongue thickly around in it as if it had been turned into fur. She had repaired this later, had sworn she had not meant it, that it had only been the last unvomited bitterness of an old disaster. He had had to believe her; he could not have done otherwise. And somehow she had grown fond enough of him once more to make the rest of their short married life something she herself could look back upon with tenderness.

But she knew it was easy for her to do wrong, and because doing wrong made her suffer she longed to have a faith, like Maurice's, that would keep her in leading-strings. She did not want to be alone. She dreaded herself. She had always done so. There was only one face she feared, and it was her own.

Chapter Twenty-three

WESTLAKE took her arm as they emerged at street-level from the club.

'That is partly affection and partly because you need support,' Kate said.

He laughed at her, pulling her hand into his ribs.

This part of Pimlico was black and quiet, the wall of warehouses blocking away the dazzle of the river. As they walked along to his car, they caught sight of the power-station, sending out floodlit plumage of brown and copper smoke.

'You're in no fit state to drive.'

'Don't you talk to me like that, young woman, or I'll turn you upside down.'

'I'll drive.'

'When did you last handle a car? And where's your licence?'

Five years ago, she told him, and her licence was long out of date and long lost: nevertheless, she thought she would be safer than he. Because she went on arguing he stopped, pushed her face up and kissed her long and thoughtfully, as if he were an expert tasting a fruit for its commercial possibilities. As always, she was melted by him, drugged by the cleanly smell of his flesh, the heathery smell of his coat, by the experienced affection in his hands. She had long ceased to hope he would start drinking less: this was the way he was made, or the way he had made himself. When she did not struggle with him, she was almost happy. She was surprised to find how little she thought of a future for either of them. There was no point in thinking about it, so she simply did not. She was enjoying the physical release he gave her, and the vaguely raffish life of which he was able to show her a little; though she knew it was not to his older haunts that he took her, and she met none of his friends. It was not out of prudery that he kept them from her. He had simply cut himself away from everything likely to remind him of failure.

'Not in the street,' she said.

'Why not? Nicest in the street — or no, not nicest. But nice.'

He stumbled at a kerb, and she caught him round the waist.

'No,' he said, stately at once, 'that was a perfectly ordinary trip, such as a little child might have made over the lace of his gym-shoe.'

She dissolved into laughter, leaning her head on his shoulder.

'Katey, Katey, Katey, we have lovely times together. Do we not?'

'We have lovely times.'

They sat in the car.

'You can't start it if you forget the damned engine,' said Kate.

He looked at her with an air of revelation. His eyes, in the light from the dashboard, shone like gooseberries, protuberant, a little hazed over not with prickles but with a film of water. 'No more I can! Really, you are clever: didn't I know from the first moment I saw you, that you were a woman of capacity?'

As they moved off, he said carefully, 'I wonder whether it has ever struck you, Katey, that the illuminated "Keep Lefts" on road islands are the colour of dead persons in ice-boxes?'

'Keep your eyes on the road.'

'Darling, if you want me to do that you should put a sack over your head. Must I take you straight back?'

She told him that to-night he must: Maurice was going out at a quarter-past ten, and she had promised to be home by that time. Libby was in bed with a cold, there was nobody else to answer the telephone.

'Does it ring incessantly? I find that hard to believe.'

'You find so much hard.'

'For instance?'

He swung the car in a wide sweep round St. George's Square. 'The Giant Racer! Walk up, walk up!'

'Oh, hold your tongue, and be careful.'

For a little while he obeyed her. He persisted, 'But for instance?'

'That I love you, for one thing,' said Kate, 'and that I can't be at your beck and call whenever you want me.'

'If you did, you could.' He put his arm round her shoulder. She threw it off.

'No, Tom.'

But her action had been so abrupt that for a moment he lost control of the wheel: the car swung out on to the crown of the road, skidded back again.

'Look here, I'm getting out.'

'Not a bit of it, you're not.'

She looked at him and saw that whereas, five minutes ago, he had had too much to drink, he was now drunk.

'Steady, then,' she said, as quietly as she could.

He did his best. They moved slowly, cautiously, into Grosvenor Place and round Belgrave Square. 'If my wife were gathered to her fathers, of which I see no likelihood, I would marry you, Katey. Do you realise that?'

She was by no means sure that she wanted any such thing. She was living in a time of suspension, enjoying the pure astonishment of this love affair that had sprung out of nothing, at a time when she had not thought herself likely ever again to interest a man. To marry him would not be much fun for her. At present, she could leave him when she pleased, shutting the door upon his bouts and forgetting everything about him but the agreeable side until he was sufficiently recovered to see her again. She knew what the squalor of life with him would be. Like most drunkards, he was a poor drinker: he had no real stomach for alcohol, he could never acquire tolerance. At present it was up to him to clean up the mess he made, to groan himself into recovery. He did it decently alone. She did not want to be there. Nevertheless, she longed to know, once more, the lesser, cocooning intimacies of marriage: the talk in bed, the sharing of the morning papers, the dressing and undressing, the return at evening, the key in the lock. Though she could imagine how scratched that particular lock would be.

They had just returned into Brompton Road when he cried, 'Hah! A friend.' He stopped the car, pulled down the window. 'Hi! You there! Plym!'

'Oh don't,' Kate said. She felt her own safety was sufficiently at stake. She would be glad to be back home.

But he went on shouting. He had taken a fancy to Plymmer, whom he had met casually some years before.

'Hi! Want a lift?'

Plym peered in at them. 'Oh, it's you, Thersites, is it? And Mrs. M. Yes, give me a lift by all means. I've got a corn.'

He climbed into the back.

'I must take care of my doubly precious burden,' Westlake said solemnly, 'K-K-K-Katey and Saint Cecilia. Are you still giving musical education to the tribes of the Congo?'

'I am thinking of trying out the tribes on the Fauré Requiem,' Plym replied, 'and you have drink taken, dear boy, so if I were you I wouldn't talk.'

Westlake said he could always drive, drunk or sober; apart from a minor incident a long time ago, he had a clean sheet. As they shot off Brompton Road into the darker streets, he increased his pace. He began to sing:

> 'My old man's a fireman,
> Whaddaya think of that?
> He wears gorblimey trousers
> And a little gorblimey hat——'

'Why are you going this way?' Kate demanded. 'It's all round the earth.'

'Shush, it's a short cut.' He swung across the road again, making the car prance. ' "And all the trumpets sounded for them on the other side." Look out, you bleeding fool!' This was to a pedestrian, whom he had narrowly missed.

'That's just what they will do——' Kate began angrily as

they left the shout behind: and then it happened. Westlake had just skirted a road island, bumping his rear mudguard. In attempting to pull himself into the straight again, he had angled too sharply, and had shot the car off, right across the road, into a side street. Kate saw rearing up before her what seemed to be an enormous sheet of khaki cardboard. She put her hands to her eyes, held her breath. With a violent shock and a noise like a huge door slamming, they went slap into a stationary van. Plym gave a curious high scream. Westlake swore. The windscreen had cracked but had not shattered; the edges of the fracture winked and flashed in the light of a street lamp.

Not death, Kate thought, by the grace of God we are still alive; and probably — she touched herself cautiously — unhurt.

'That fixes it,' said Westlake, 'I'll lose my licence this time.'

'Oh, you silly damned fool,' Plym was wailing. 'Oh, you damned fool!'

Kate's brain began to work. Leaning across Westlake, she opened the door. 'Get in the back with Plym. Quick.'

The delayed reactions of the street began. Lights went up in windows.

'Quick, do you hear!'

She bundled him out, moved over herself into the driver's seat. 'I was driving, do you both understand? I've less to lose.'

Now people were looking down at them. She was just in time.

'If you think I'm going to commit bloody perjury——' Plym began.

'Oh, shut up! And *all* get out, now!'

They clambered on to the pavement. Westlake almost fell and Plym grabbed at him. Kate emerged more slowly, wanting to be seen. She was trembling, she could not control her lips.

'I will not perjure myself——'

'Look, you fool, Tom would get it for being drunk in charge of a car. It's happened to him before. Nothing much can happen to me, so please keep quiet.'

They saw what damage had been done. Their own car was worse off, the front mudguards buckled, the bonnet bashed in: the rear door of the van was broken, wood spouting from it in strips, but that seemed to be all.

Westlake went to a lamp-post, supported himself carefully by one arm, leaned forward and was sick in the gutter.

People were gathering now in ones and twos. Kate, hearing herself addressed, looked into the innocent face of a young police constable.

'Now what's happened?' he said coaxingly. 'What's happened here?'

For a moment she could not answer him. She did not even know where they all were. She looked around in bewilderment, then saw lamplight on a street name. It was a mews, wide, cobbled, a dead end; little flats in paintbox colours over the garages; windowboxes; fancy lanterns and wrought ironwork over the doors.

Was this her car, he asked her?

No, she told him, but she had been driving it.

He took out his notebook and looked thoughtful. He wrote down her name and address, and Plym's. He asked Westlake for his, but without result, so Kate gave it.

He asked to see her licence.

She said she was sorry: she had not got it. She explained the circumstances.

'Afraid that's going to get you into a bit of trouble,' he said, as if he were really sorry.

And that is all the trouble, she thought, with any luck. I don't know about insurance. Tom may have to pay, but that won't kill him. The trembling in her legs had lessened, she was beginning to feel better.

He asked her why she had been driving.

'Because we'd been to a club, and I thought Mr. Westlake wasn't in a fit condition to drive himself.'

He was standing stonily on the edge of the pavement, swaying only a little. His mouth was tight, his eyes protruded.

'No,' said the policeman, 'I see what you mean.'

Someone said, 'That's him! I took his number. I thought it was him!'

A small man was standing there, a small, upset man in a mackintosh, who had been running.

'That's who?'

'That's the car that nearly ran me down back there, talk about dangerous driving, it was all over the road, I had to jump for my life. You!' he apostrophised Westlake, 'you're not fit to push a pram——'

'The lady says she was driving,' said the constable.

'Lady? I thought it was him.'

'Well, it wasn't,' said Kate. 'It was me. Wasn't it, Plym?'

He nodded. She saw that he was furious: words were on the tip of his tongue.

'Women drivers ought to be chucked off the roads. Here, you take my name and address.'

The constable said he would prefer to take a statement at the police-station, if they wouldn't mind accompanying him.

The small man, whose name was Hathaway, said he would mind very much indeed. His wife was waiting for him. He was late already.

So am I, Kate thought. 'Shall I be able to telephone my brother-in-law?' she asked.

The policeman said yes, told Hathaway he might be needed later as a witness, and escorted Kate, Westlake and Plym out of the mews like a young man of social accomplishment leading his elders to the supper-room.

Kate was glad to be out of the mews, out of the yellowish ring of detached faces. She had counted the cost to herself pretty carefully: now it was a matter of whether Plym and Westlake kept their heads.

The police-station was modern and bright, a handsome, cleanly building with a welcoming air, a cross between the best municipal flats and the latest primary school. Here there was light and warmth. She entered it with something like a feeling of relief.

On their way Westlake had whispered to her, 'Damn your eyes. Can you leave me nothing?'

He was walking fairly steadily. He did not touch her.

She had expected that they would now be brought before some senior official: but it seemed that they were still the concern of the young constable, who took them into a small room, gave them chairs, and with a business-like, pleasured air sat down behind a table.

Kate said again that she wanted to make a telephone call, and gave him Maurice's name.

'Mr. Fisher? He's a fine chap. He does a lot of good.' He regarded her with favour. 'We'll get him for you.'

Kate spoke to Maurice. There was a silence at his end of the wire.

'I'd better come down,' he said at last.

'No need.'

'I think I'd better.' He hung up.

He had sounded angry: and though Westlake's anger had not touched her, the two reactions, together, did. She felt an outcast, everyone's hand against her. She was bitterly resentful.

The constable began to take a statement. He wrote slowly and neatly.

'Let's hear your account of this, Mrs. Morley. You say you thought Mr. Westlake was not in a fit state to drive?'

'No.'

'Did you take the wheel immediately you left this club, or let him start off and then change over?'

'I drove all the time.'

'Mr. Hathaway alleges that you were driving dangerously. Will you tell me exactly what happened?'

'I don't remember exactly. I made a turn at the island and skidded.'

'Why were you going into the mews? Were you visiting there?'

'No. In fact, I don't quite know how I got there. I turned too sharply, I think, and then it seemed best to go straight ahead. I don't think I was driving dangerously, that is, not all the way. But I was rusty. I admit that.'

He looked at her in a puzzled way. He is thinking, Kate said to herself, that I am obviously not drunk. Therefore: how did I come to do anything so mad?

'What do you think happened, Mr. Westlake?'

Westlake stirred. He had slumped in his seat, had taken out handkerchief and pencil, and was making a doll with them.

'I don't know. You heard Mrs. Morley. I was the worse for wear.'

'Mr. Plymmer?'

Plym had flushed up to the edges of his hair. His face was scarlet and tapering like a radish.

'I don't know.'

'You must have been aware of something?'

'It was all too quick. I did hear a shout as we went round the island.'

'—and then?'

'I told you, it was all too quick. We did a bit of a skid, turned right out of the main road and hit the van.'

'Was it your opinion that Mr. Westlake wasn't fit to drive?'

'How would he know?' Kate broke in. 'I picked up Mr. Plymmer on the way. We were just giving him a lift.'

The policeman continued to look at Plym.

'I should have said he wasn't fit,' Plym said at last.

'You've heard the lady and gent,' said Westlake, 'and now you can hear me: *I* say I wasn't fit. Which makes a consensus of opinion.'

'Don't I know your face, sir?'

'I shouldn't be surprised.' He mentioned his paper.

'Oh!' Again the social, almost partyfied air. 'That would be it, then. I've seen you in court.'

'Be seeing me there again, I dare say. Well? What happens next?'

'I'll have to make my report, sir. You'll be hearing from us later on.' He turned to Kate. 'You'll receive a summons within fourteen days.'

'About the licence?'

'There may be another charge. We shall have to see the gentleman who complained.'

'What now?' Plym asked.

The policeman rose and glanced at the clock. It was a quarter-past eleven. 'No need to detain you.'

He held the door for them politely. 'I'll see to your car, sir,' he said to Westlake.

Outside on the pavement they met Maurice. He was breathless; he had been running. 'What is it? What's happened?'

'Over,' said Kate, 'at least, for the time being.' She gave him her account. 'Let's get home. We'll make beasts of ourselves and have a taxi.'

'Not for me,' said Westlake, 'I'll go along with the *flic* and see about the car.' He looked almost sober, and very haggard in the glare of the sodium lamps. 'Goodnight, all.' He turned without another look at her, and went back into the station.

Plym said in a stifled voice that he didn't want any taxi; after all that tomfoolery he wanted some fresh air.

'Don't be silly,' Kate began, 'it's a long walk and you're late——'

'If I want some air, I'll have some air. It's up to me whether I have air or not.'

She saw Maurice look at him, saw him taken out of his own mysterious rage by curiosity.

'Plym,' she said, 'do come with us——'

'I've had enough. It's a wonder I'm not dead. We'll see plenty of each other when all this comes up. Sorry, Vicar, but I'm off.'

Maurice said nothing to her while they were in the cab; but when they entered the house, pushed her before him, as if she were a child, into the study.

'Now, then.'

'Did I stop you going out? Did it matter?'

He flicked his hand impatiently. His eyes were pebbly with anger. For the first time she was afraid of him, she did not know him at all. 'Never mind that. What is this cock-and-bull story?'

'I told you.'

'You were driving that car?'

'Yes.'

'I am sure you were not.'

She started to protest, to talk as rapidly as she could, as if she were shaken and offended. He simply listened to her till she ran dry.

'And Westlake will let you do this?' he asked. 'He and Plym are proposing to lie under oath?'

She blustered at him: nobody was lying. He must be out of his mind to accuse her. What a fantasy! It was so absurd she didn't know what to say, she couldn't argue with sheer unreason.

'If they find you out, you'll all be on a perjury charge.'

'But there isn't any question——'

'Be quiet, Kate.'

Sitting down, he took two cigarettes out of a packet, and threw one to her.

'Just be quiet. Don't talk now, because I can't stand it.'

She told him she was going up to bed. She had had a bad enough shock, without listening to nonsense from him. He got up.

'So that drunk is going to let you take the blame for him, is he?'

'You told me,' she said tightly, 'not to talk.'

Raising his hand, he slapped the cigarette out of her mouth.

She burst into a storm of tears. She was terrified. She leaned against the wall and covered her face. She dared not look at him. In place of the brother who had always looked after her, whom she in her turn had cared for, this furious stranger stood. She wanted to run right out of the house, go anywhere, it would not matter.

She felt him tug her hands gently down. He was wiping her eyes with his handkerchief, trying to put the cigarette back between her lips. 'Kate, Kate, what am I going to say? Oh Kate, oh Kate.'

He led her back to a chair. It was as though they had both been ill. They stared at each other, helpless.

She said, 'It's all right. Don't think about it.'

'Forgive me when you feel like it, but for God's sake don't pretend to now. It's too soon.'

She said, 'Tom was driving, of course.'

It was peaceable to say it, an infinite relief. She lay back like a convalescent, comforted by the small pleasures, the flavour of the restored cigarette, the warmth of the fire on her legs.

'Will you tell me why you're doing it?'

Two years ago, she said, Westlake had been convicted of being drunk in charge of a car. If it happened again he would lose his licence for good; and such work as he did do, which was all the work he could do now, depended upon it.

'I see. All the same, I can't let you do this.'

'But I shall never admit it, except to you.'

He did not reply.

'I spoiled something for you, didn't I?'

'Oh, no.'

'I thought there was something.'

'You think too much,' he said, with a kind of ghastly lightness. 'Come on, it's time we both got some sleep.'

As they rose again — 'Poor old boy,' said Kate.

She would have to learn him again, even his face: he did not look the same to her as before.

She added, 'It is an impropriety for us to have scenes. We won't have any more. But don't try to change my mind.' Her throat was aching with strain.

'Not yours,' he replied.

Chapter Twenty-four

K NOWING he could not go to Alice, he tried to telephone her before he left for the police-station: but had got no answer. It was then twenty minutes past ten.

He could imagine her waiting for him. It was as though he had an iron band across his chest, restricting his breathing, suffocating him with the fear of no-escape. He had been so angry with Kate, with her dangerous, lying quixotry, that he had not known how to speak to her. It was bad enough that she should have ruined for him the joy which had been rising in him all day, drawing him so much within it that he had been insulated from the world outside, unable even to see other people except, as it were, through a shell of thick glass. He had been deafened by it, even his own voice had sounded from far away, as over a wireless set at low volume. It was worse that she should have thrust upon him this problem of her own, making him think about her: he did not want to think about her, he could not bear to. His thoughts had been so glued to the idea of Alice that it was an agony to have them torn away; it was like the rip of plaster from a wound.

When he had sent her up to bed, he went back into the study and dialled again. It was now five minutes past twelve. Again there was no answer. He dialled O. After an interminable wait — 'This number seems to be out of order.'

'It can't be,' he said.

'If you'll wait, I will check with the engineers.'

He waited. Libby opened the door, plaits hanging over her green dressing-gown. She was swollen with cold, and fretful. 'What *are* you doing? Aren't you ever coming up?'

'Somebody seemed to want me.'

'Well, let them. I can't get to sleep until you come.'

The telephone rang.

'Oh, do go up, Libby! You'll only catch a worse cold, hanging around the passages.'

She lingered.

He lifted the receiver. He was sickened by the beating of his heart.

'Your number is out of order. The engineers are trying to correct the fault.'

'Let it go,' he said, 'it doesn't matter.' He made himself smile at her. 'You are in a bad way!'

'I am a miserable old thing. I am an awful mess. You went out earlier on, didn't you?'

'I'll tell you about all that to-morrow.'

They went upstairs together, in step, his arm about her waist, as they had walked when they were first in love.

He tried to tell himself that this was meant, that this had been intended.

At the turn of the landing she went ahead of him: and he saw that she was no longer a girl, that she had, in the bowed line of her back, that tension of the middle years which must one day turn into the awful meekness of old age. As the tape of a tape-recorder flicks suddenly away from the spool bringing, in a particle of a second, termination and silence, so he saw the last of youth wind away for them both; a whirr, a flicker, and death stood there.

He held her for a moment, as if she could save him. 'What's the matter with you?' she asked him in surprise. 'So affectionate all at once.' It sounded, because she was tired, because she was not well, like the raillery of an old woman.

Chapter Twenty-five

ALICE got back to her flat at twenty-five past ten. She had been to her neighbour across the hallway to borrow some coffee, and had been kept talking. She was afraid Maurice would be there before her, but it was all right. She sat down to wait.

It was odd, she thought, even through her daze of excitement, how final in itself was the precise minute of a proposed meeting. When it arrived (as it had now, the time being precisely ten-thirty) something happened: the hour that was promised had come. It was in itself a finality. But people did not keep appointments on exact moments of time; they were a little early or a little late, and if there was no particular importance attached to their coming one did not notice which way the pointer lay. She shook off the momentary descent of unquiet, just because her door-bell had not rung at exactly half-past ten. Probably he was coming along the street now, he had turned the corner, was passing the pillar-box, soon she would hear his step. She would not look out of the window.

But at five-and-twenty to eleven she did look out and the road was empty. There was lamplight inside the trees and moonlight on the upper branches. A cat slipped along the gutter and ran between railings.

Five minutes meant nothing. She took out a cigarette, then put it back again. There would not be time to smoke. Her darker mind took fright before she did, because her heart began to beat disagreeably. 'This is silly,' she said to the room prepared for him, soft and bright, but with no flowers; coffee tray, if he wanted coffee, glasses, if he wanted a drink. Getting up without conscious volition, she looked in the glass and saw a staring face.

Twenty to. But now there were steps on the pavement, a man's, rapid, rather heavy.

She went quickly into the little hall and waited. She would not open the door immediately, or he would think she had been standing close behind it. But neither would she delay, deliberately to make him wait, to punish him because he had made her ever so slightly anxious, for so short a time. She listened for the lift: no. For feet on the stairs? She heard them, through the noise of her heart: she felt the heat wash over her head, it was like drowning. He must wait, then, just for a second, just while she pulled herself together. She dreaded the sound of the bell as she would have dreaded a pistol shot on the stage: she wanted to put her fingers in her ears.

It came, but not loudly. It was faint and far away. Not the bell of her own door. Unable to bear it, she switched the door open upon voices raised in greeting. Her neighbour was welcoming a guest.

Quiet then, quiet then, quiet, she thought. It will be his ring next time. This is stupid, it is still early. Seventeen minutes to eleven: only three minutes have gone by since I thought I heard him coming.

She lit the cigarette, and walked up and down the room. She could not sit still. Now there was something wrong with her hair at the back, there was a spot of grease at the corner of her nose. She would just put it right, and if he came she would come slowly from the bedroom and open to him without haste, not even saying 'Why are you late?'

When she came back the heat had left her, and she was very cold. Squatting on her ankles before the electric fire, she held out her hands to it. No point in looking at the clock, watched clocks never boiled. That was a joke: she heard her own panicked laugh. A quarter to: by which time he should have come and gone.

She did not care now whether he saw her looking for him. She pushed the curtains back, pressed her face to the pane

Still quietness in the street and the cat on the run again, a grey thread running through the needle-eye of moon and lamplight.

It was not possible to look steadily for long because the cold of the glass made her shiver; she began a series of journeys back and forth, from window to fire, from fire to window, making time, taking in time. First she was afraid: he had met with an accident, nothing else could have kept him from her. Then she was giddy with anger: he had never meant to come, he had only meant to put her off.

A car ripped up the street, whining as it skidded into Knightsbridge. A passing policeman flashed his torch into a basement. A girl in evening dress ran along shouting for a taxi, stiff white skirts swept up like a sail over her arm. Where was she going, and to whom? Or simply home, to no one? Home in happiness, home in grief?

Eleven o'clock.

She knew quite well that he was not coming, but she could not bring herself to stir for a while. At last she sat down on the sofa, her head in her hands.

She could not ring him, not at such an hour. But why not? If he did not reply at once, or if somebody else answered, she could hang up, as she had meant to do before. Why not?

She seized the telephone and listened: it was dead. She banged and banged at the chromium knobs, as if she were sending some desperate message in Morse code. If she could not ring him, how could he ring her? Perhaps she could go across the way, ask them to call the exchange and have her telephone put right.

As she opened the front door noise sprang at her, the grind of music, the parrot-house din of party voices. While she had been waiting alone other guests had come. It was no use: she could not enter into *that*, she would not be able to bear it. Better any misery in solitude than the shock of being where people were not unhappy, where the world was just as usual.

There was a sort of luxury in being alone to despair. There was nobody for whom she need 'put a face on it'; she could sit, lie, walk about, cry herself ugly or control the tears till her teeth chattered. It was not unpleasurable now to look at her staring face.

Let go, she thought, let go, relax, you are alone, quite alone, no one to see you. Think simply of that, of being alone. There is one face of love that many people know, but few admit to; the funny face it puts on grief, the one young girls suddenly perceive at the cinema when grief is shown, and giggle at because it has scared them silly.

For a while she counted the ticks of the clock. Then, all of a sudden, as if a current had been snapped off, she was tired: tired, and nothing else. She was greedy for sleep as old people with nothing else to look forward to are greedy for food.

Chapter Twenty-six

No, he wasn't at the newspaper office, he wouldn't be in till the afternoon; they could give his home address.

Maurice wrote it down, half his attention on the door. Kate had been in the kitchen when he had last seen her, but he did not know when she might come to the study. He was feeling shaken after a bad night, and self-contempt was not helping him. He had never really known before what it meant to be surreptitious: and here he was seeking out Westlake without Kate's knowledge, planning to ring Alice from a call-box as soon as he could get away from the house. During the long, ticking, tumbled night he had told himself that he was not meant to see her again: the warnings had been perfectly clear. He had always believed in the direct finger of God, moving not so much mysteriously as with the sort of impatient plainness by which a parent has dealings with a child. But it was one thing to see the signs, another to obey them. That morning, he knew he could not.

There had been an unpleasant scene at breakfast, when Kate had given the family her version of the trouble she was in. For some seconds, nobody had said anything. Then Dick had burst out, 'A *stationary* van! Good Lord, only a fool would do that!'

She had shut him up sharply. Simon had said, 'Well, I hope they let you off,' and whipped out of the room.

Libby had said, bitterly, slowly, dramatically, 'Have you thought what this is going to mean to Maurice?'

'It wouldn't make the least difference, at this stage, what I thought.'

'I knew there would be trouble through that man,' Mrs. Marsden said, in a voice so minute but so penetrating that it might have proceeded from an ant in some anthropomorphic fairy story.

'For God's sake, Mother, what does he have to do with it? He was only a passenger.'

'I don't know, dear. I don't know *what* he has to do with it. I am merely saying——'

'I shall be glad if people will not "merely say".'

Libby, rising to her feet, had made a strange denunciatory gesture. 'It will be spread all over the papers!'

'I dare say so.'

'Suppose you get a magistrate who wants to make an example? Could you get sent to prison?'

'No, Lib, I shall not get sent to prison. No harm was done. And there is no need to be hysterical.'

'I am not being hysterical! I want to know if they *can* send you to prison!'

Maurice had intervened to say that no, they could not; but did not manage to bring to an end the stream of denunciation, sadistic foresight, and wounded feelings. It had, in fact, ended when Dick was found to have forgotten his manhood and to have lapsed into quiet, childish tears. This had been such a shock to Libby, Kate and his grandmother that they had been forced to unite in comforting him. Whereupon Maurice had escaped.

Now, as he walked towards the crumbling street where West-lake had his lodgings, he wondered what could happen next. It lay just off Earls Court Road, and behind it the bulk of the Empress Hall towered like a Welsh slag-heap. The house was one of a dingy row that must, at one time, have been held by one owner, since all had the same beetroot-coloured doors and railings. As he stood looking at it the door opened. A young Negro ran out whistling, negotiated the steps with the easy, boneless air of a puppet on strings, and went off towards the station, his movements primitive and joyful in the stiff greyness of the morning.

Maurice inspected the names above the row of bell-pushes. Westlake's was at the top: a calling-card, stuck with a rusted drawing-pin, over the metal name-strip of a previous tenant. He waited impatiently. He wanted to get this over, so that he could try Alice's number again. There had been no answer from her flat.

At last he heard feet on uncarpeted stairs. Westlake himself opened the door. He looked dragged and puffy, he smelled of drink: but he was neatly dressed, his linen white and glossy.

'Why, Vicar! Come in. To what do I owe——? No, turn that up. I can guess what I owe it to. Will you go upstairs? I warn you, it's a bit of a climb.'

But he was not really certain why Maurice had come, and his eyes were watchful.

'You just go on up and up till you can't get any further,' Westlake panted behind him, 'and then, considering the general state of this house, I hope you may have a reasonably pleasant surprise.'

It was a fine room, airy, freshly painted and curtained, the room of a man who liked comfort and was prepared to be a little old-maidish about it. There were good rugs, some beautiful pieces of furniture — 'My mother's,' he said, waving a hand, 'the little that was left.' He motioned Maurice to the low divan, before which was a long, rectangular table of Swedish manufacture, standing about eighteen inches from the floor. On it, laid out as if for sale, were a row of ashtrays, Venetian, cloisonné and English glass, a silver cigarette-box, a table-lighter of chromium and soapstone, and a box of Turkish delight. 'I don't do myself badly. I leave all the bad treatment to life in general. Oh God, what a soapy thing to say! — as Kate would put it. Will you smoke?'

Maurice refused.

'Oh dear,' said Westlake, 'that looks extremely bad.' He made a show of throwing off the facetious rôle, and instead regarded Maurice with an air of great frankness. 'Look, I couldn't be more sorry about last night. I should never have let Kate drive. I can't forgive myself. Mind you,' he went on, as there was no reply, 'it will be something of a storm in a teacup. Even if they do charge her with dangerous driving, it will only be a fine of fifty quid or so, and I'll see to that part of it, naturally.'

'Kate wasn't driving,' Maurice said.

'What do you mean, Kate wasn't——'

'Oh, come! I know she wasn't.'

Westlake sat down. 'Did she say so?' He was still cautious. 'Yes.'

'But what did she say such a thing for? I mean, why?' The smile was absurd and doll-like; it could have convinced nobody, and it enraged Maurice.

'Will you stop that? I guessed at once what had happened and I got the truth out of her.'

'All right,' said Westlake after a pause, 'I was driving. Between ourselves, that is.'

'You'll have to tell the police so.'

'Is Kate prepared to tell them the same thing?'

Maurice hesitated, and lost the advantage.

'So she's not. Well, neither am I.'

'I will not let my sister and any friend of hers perjure themselves in a witness-box.'

Westlake felt his handsome, pulpy nose as if afraid it had received some injury. He lay back on the divan, crossed his legs, hitched his trousers in a finicking fashion to display an inch of sock. 'On moral grounds?'

'Of course.'

Westlake seemed to consider this, as if it were an entirely new conception to him, and one that he could not brush aside without at least a degree of respectful examination. Then he began to explain, as to a child, what his own position was. No harm could possibly come to Kate, but he would be ruined. He would certainly lose his licence for life, which would make his work impossible: and as he would also be charged with drunkenness, it was not beyond the bounds of possibility that he might get a jail sentence. For Kate it would be a brief unpleasantness, without stigma attached: for himself, ruin. 'Do you think I like putting it on to her?' he asked, and raised his head.

Maurice looked into the veiled green eyes and saw in them something he could use as a weapon. He knew that Westlake was ashamed, that shame was eating him.

'I know you don't like it. I know you hate it. That's what makes it disgusting: that you should hate it, and go on doing it. Especially as I suppose you are in love with Kate.'

The lips stiffened in a stony face. 'You suppose right.'

'And you can do this?'

No answer.

Maurice said she was buoyed up now by the excitement of her own quixotic action, by the idea of making a sacrifice, but that when it was all over she would wonder what sort of a man she had made it for.

Westlake relaxed a little, and tried to smile. 'She has no illusions. But we're fond of each other, and to tell you the truth, I am madder about Katey than I ever expected to be about any woman. I wish I could marry her. I've told her so.'

'It seems strange,' Maurice said, 'to have to tell a grown man that he must not lie on oath before God or encourage other people to do so. But obviously I have to tell you this.'

His tone was wrong, his words were wrong, and he knew it: his momentary advantage was sliding rapidly away.

'Obviously you have to,' Westlake replied with heavy courtesy; 'it is your professional duty.' He looked vaguely at the far wall, and addressed it. ' "It was his duty, and he did." No, seriously, Vicar, I appreciate your point. I like lying as little as you do . . . well, possibly it moves me rather less, but I still dislike it. I can't pretend, though, that an oath as such has the same importance with me as it must have with you. Whether I swore by God or the elephant at the Zoo, it would all be the same — forgive me: I shouldn't talk to you like this. But I have to be honest. Yes, it is certainly your duty to tell me what you think, and I respect you for doing so. Only I can't let it make any difference.'

'Suppose *I* gave evidence——' This was foolish, and Maurice knew it.

'My dear, what the soldier said! You can't. You weren't there. And what a hubbub you'd cause! Far worse for Kate than if you'd pipe down and let them get it all over with in ten minutes.'

Maurice asked if he thought Plymmer would lie for him.

'Well, you know, I've been thinking about that. Plym's story will be that he wasn't paying attention when the crash happened, and that therefore he can't help. I don't imagine it will occur to anyone to ask him who was driving — why should it? Kate was. The *flic* didn't even query it.'

'If you love Kate, you'll let her off this.'

Westlake was looking ghastly. His flesh, in the sharp sunless light of the morning, seemed damp and coarse and old. His hands were shaking.

'I can't, and that's that.'

Maurice got up. 'You expect me to condone it?'

'What else can you do?'

'I shall work on Kate.'

Westlake rose too, stumbling as he did so. 'I'm sure you will. And you'll have a clear field, I expect, because I rather think I shan't be seeing her till all this is over. Anyway, not much.' He looked at the clock. 'Quarter to eleven, not an unreasonable hour. It would astonish me if you'd have a drink, but I'm asking you.' He went to a handsome wine-cooler, took out a bottle of whiskey. 'The hair of the dog's not a legend, it is a cold fact. But once it is an empiric fact to you, you're finished. I don't suppose you know much about drinking, do you? There is a point at which it ought to cease to be reprehensible, since it isn't a thing one does: it is a thing that happens to one.'

He did not look up from his glass. Maurice left him and made his way down, past shabby doors, past other voices, past a gramophone, past a quarrel. Then he heard Westlake shouting down the echoing well of the stair in the hilariously despairing voice of a demon, 'It's no good, old boy, it's no good, it's no good!'

He stood in the street, considering what he should do. He could, of course, go to the police himself and make a statement: they would listen to him. But that would mean God knew what to Kate. Anyway, he needed more time to think (though he knew what the result of thinking would be). He might tell David.

The thought of this was a comfort. At least he had a confidence here that did not touch his own person, he could share that. He was lonely for the friendship they had once had, now that they could not speak to each other without the slight, cautious halting of breath before words carefully picked. Yes, he could tell David. But then: what help could David give? Only the hard advice Maurice could not take. He believed that for his curate morality was extremely simple. There was a right thing and a wrong. If the right one caused pain and the wrong healed a wound, it was nevertheless the right thing that must be done. 'It hurts me more than it hurts you. . . .' David was one of the very few human beings who could have said such a thing and meant it. He was entirely unsadistic and the cheerfulness of his life seemed, to Maurice, to arise from his confidence in the simple codification of moral laws, to be followed as precisely as a good book of kitchen recipes.

He could tell Alice. At the idea of this, he was swept by longing: of longing not for sensual joy, but for a quiet place behind the lighted window, far out, where he would talk to her and she would listen, her hand in his, ready to help him.

He came to himself with a jolt. He was late for his religious instruction period at the school; ten minutes late already, and it would take him another five to get there. He arrived breathless and ran along to the classroom, only to see, through the glass panel of the door, David bobbing, beaming, and merrily gesticulating as if he were telling the children a series of racy stories.

Maurice thought: then where ought I to be? If this is David's job, what is mine? He found he had left his pocket diary at home.

'Why, Vicar!' The young Cockney headmaster stared at him in surprise. 'What can we do for you?'

It seemed important not to be thought a fool, to give away to no one that he was losing grip on his work. He said he thought he had mislaid a book, had looked in to see if David had it, and had then remembered lending it to one of the churchwardens.

It was a lie the size of a grain of mustard seed, of no importance except in its capacity for germination.

'All's well that ends well, then.' The headmaster was jolly. 'I tell you, I pretty well forget my own head these days. Forms, forms, forms, I bet one kicks off in hell by filling up a forty-page form in triplicate.'

The greyness had cleared and a cold sun was out. Some of the bigger girls were playing netball on the asphalt, red or green ribbons passed over a shoulder and under an arm. They looked lumpish and plain.

'When you think, Vicar, that within two or three years quite half that lot will have found chaps to marry them, it restores your faith in the bounty of nature. But as for teaching them anything — no. Pure waste of time. Their boy friends are too well off these days.'

The whistle shrilled over the playground.

'Off-side,' said the headmaster, with professional interest, 'there they go again. Too much bumping and boring. They aren't much good, those girls. Not a flier in the batch.'

He pointed.

'You see that fat one, in goal? Young Fraser tried to make her once. We had him here, you know. We had to hush it up. But he'd be better off dead, that lad would, better off dead.'

Home again, Maurice asked Libby if she had seen his diary. She had found it on the floor, she replied, he had left the study in a pig-muddle. 'You really are a mess these days, darling. I don't know what I'm going to do with you.'

'I should have been at the church. Fawcett was bringing his people down for another look at the roof.'

She rested against him. She was better again, she had powdered her face, her beauty was restored. 'Funny old thing,' she murmured, forcing him into quite a new rôle, the foolish, muddled parson of a drawing-room comedy. 'If it wasn't for me looking after you, I don't know where you'd be. Old rattle-pate! I'm sorry I got so upset about Kate, though I must say I'm furious with her — she's been abysmally stupid. We'll see this thing through together, you and me.' She paused. 'Can you imagine, driving a car into a *stationary* vehicle, not even on a skiddy road? Dick was quite right: "Out of the mouths of babes and sucklings——" Oh dear, why won't people let us alone, just us, so we can enjoy ourselves in peace?'

Chapter Twenty-seven

H E went straight to her after compline, not thinking any more, giving himself over to a kind of restlessness that was not his but a stranger's. It did not matter if she were out, or even if she were not alone. Words would come to him when he needed to speak them. At one of the houses in her street a party was going on. There was a striped awning from door to kerb, though it was not raining. Cars streamed up and festive people got out, men in their formal blotches of black and white, girls in dresses that rustled and flashed. A small crowd of lookers-on blocked the pavement, and Maurice had to push past them. He found the flats in which she lived, went, still without thinking, into a little hallway, dimly lit, soft-carpeted, smelling of soap, polish and scent. There was a very small, old-fashioned lift, big enough only for two or three people. Someone rang for it, and it creaked up out of sight. She would be on the second floor: two flats to each, hers was number five. He went up the stairs as in a climbing dream, giddy but calm, up and up.

When she opened the door to him, neither could speak to the other. Behind her was a bright empty room, all the lamps blazing away as in the electrical department of a shop. She was wearing a black dress, and there was a cigarette in her hand. She stubbed it out. She said at last, sociably, in a high, cracking voice, 'Hullo!'

She moved back, and he came into her flat, shutting the door behind him.

'I have got to come and be with you sometimes,' he said. 'It won't be more than that. It can't be. But now and then, even if it's only for half an hour, I shall have to be with you.'

He held out his arms and she came into them, gripping him around his neck, pressing her lips into his cheek.

Later there would be difficulty and much pain. But for the moment he was utterly happy, as he had never been in his life before, and he knew she was too. He drew back a little to look at her, at her shining eyes, then pulled her to him again. There was nothing here but joy.

'What a lot of lamps you have. I never saw so many.'

Her muffled voice: 'Yes, haven't I? I'm very fond of light.'

Chapter Twenty-eight

LUCY and David, walking home together after the Parochial Church Council, heard running feet; and Jeremy Fawcett, looking angry, caught up with them.

'Beattie! I want you a minute.'

They all stopped under a lamp, now entangled in the maze of chestnut boughs sticky with bud.

'Was I the last to hear about Kate Morley?' Fawcett demanded. He would, he said, have known nothing about it had it not been for the Pelhams. 'After all, you can't utterly dissociate this sort of thing from the life of the church. We're members one of another — even if I do sound stuffy — in a pretty real sense, and if Fisher has lost confidence even in his own wardens——'

David broke in to say that he himself had heard about it only the night before. He added, with unusual irritability, that he couldn't see what all the fuss was about. It had nothing to do with anyone but Kate herself.

'But it's not just a licence offence! It will be in the Press. It's serious. I really did feel, when I'd talked to Humphrey, that I'd hand in my resignation.'

'Oh, but Mr. Fawcett, you can't!' Lucy could not contain herself. 'Not without the consent of those who appointed you.' She continued, with a detached, schoolmistressy air, 'In any case, a churchwarden can't leave before they've appointed a successor. It seems awfully unfair, but——'

'Look here, Miss Simnett, if you'll forgive me, I was talking church business.'

She blushed, and set her feet apart. She flashed at him

unexpectedly, 'I didn't know. I thought you were talking about Mrs. Morley.'

David smiled; he could not help it. She was his dear comrade, perhaps a bit silly, but there was no one like her.

'I see it *is* common property,' said Fawcett. He went off, face set, into the dusk.

'Pompous beast,' said Lucy.

'How did you come to know, by the way?' David asked her curiously. 'It seems to have been very much hushed up. She got the summons yesterday morning.' Though he did not wish her to see it, he was very hurt indeed. There were a lot of things he and Maurice could no longer talk about; but surely he might have been told this? He felt desolate. For the first time he wondered whether he would not, in fact, try to make a move. Something else, too, was worrying him, shaking what confidence he had; that night the door had closed a little further against him.

Plymmer, she said, had told her. Her brow puckered; she was worried. When she ran into him just before the meeting, he had spoken to her so shortly that she had teased him about it. Instead of brightening up, he had informed her furiously that he could see nothing to laugh about, he didn't want to be involved in any damned police-court cases, and he was just about fed up with everyone and everything.

'So I asked him straight out what it was: and he told me. He really is an odd little man! I don't think it's nice of him to be angry with Kate just because he has to give evidence. After all, *he* won't be in the dock! It isn't charitable,' Lucy added, in the explosive, half-tearful fashion with which she contemplated the shortcomings of mankind.

David suggested, in an attempt to shake off his depression, that they should brave scandal and have supper at a café. 'After all, we are engaged.'

As they walked through to Gloucester Road, they met Simon and Dick Morley, pushing each other about in the casual unloving, unhating manner of brothers with a gulf of years between them. David had to shout at them so that Lucy could get by.

'Oh, sorry,' said Simon. He hooked Dick slyly round the ankle but did not succeed in tripping him. 'Sorry, Mr. Beattie. It's this lout here. I do my best to make him behave, but it's no good.'

'You do your best! Well, I'm damned! Who started it?'

'Now, now, naughty language! I really must apologize for my young brother, heaven only knows where he gets his manners.'

'You'd better mend yours,' said Lucy, in the clear voice she used to her Guides. 'You're out late, aren't you?'

'Pictures,' said Dick. 'Only time we're let out in the evenings is when you have a church do.'

'I'm let out when I please,' said Simon, 'because I am a responsible person—— Got you!' He caught Dick's arm and pinned it behind his back.

'You let go, or I'll bust right in and tell Uncle Maurice you're an atheist!'

'Huh! Listen to old big-mouth. *He* will bust in, *he* will dash the hopes of his kind uncle, *he*—— Sorry, Mr. Beattie.'

'If I had those two boys in the Youth Club,' said David, as he walked on with Lucy, 'I should resign.'

But he was not thinking of them or of the club; not even of her. He was remembering how, once or twice, as he sat there listening to Hannaway's report, Kitson's balance-sheet, the confirmation of old Garrett as sidesman which had finally dashed the unrealistic hopes of Peter and Lou, Maurice had smiled *at* the speakers but *to* himself, out of some inward satisfaction too strong to be utterly concealed. Why should he be happy? There seemed at this moment little cause for joy. How many people had noticed that smile, or, having noticed it, had been made curious by it?

Chapter Twenty-nine

U P to now Kate had succeeded in concealing from the household that she was frightened and ashamed. Despite her own fierce temperament, her life had been a quiet one: she had never had to stand up before many eyes to give an account of herself. She dreaded the hearing in court, did not know how she was to keep the panic down in the weeks that lay before it. She kept telling herself that what she was supposed to have done was not a crime but a misdemeanour, that it would all be over quickly, and that everyone would forget about it. There wouldn't be much of a public present: only the policeman, court officials, reporters, all used to that kind of thing, all bored by it. Yet she could not have felt much worse if she had been waiting to stand in the pillory.

Westlake was frightening her, too: it was a week since the collision and she had not seen him. She had telephoned him: he had put her off. They would meet soon, he said, they had things to say to each other. But at the moment he couldn't manage it. Of course, she told herself, there was no reason for him to suppose she needed him more than she usually did, through the ordinary needs of love: she had made her gesture airily enough, had not given anyone the least idea that it was a strain to her to stand by it. And of course she would stand by it. But she was repressing, in her mind, a germ of hope, crude, stark-naked, that at the last moment he would not allow her to do this thing.

Though she was not a religious woman, she had been too much with Maurice, too much in contact with the life of a church, to take lightly the fact that she must lie on oath. She would have said, with Westlake, that it was all one to her whether she swore by God or an elephant: but this was not so. She would do it in a good cause, she knew that: and it would still be wickedness.

The only real comfort she had, at this moment, came from an odd source: from Simon. He had been so friendly to her, so casually sympathetic, that she was tempted to tell him the truth. Wasn't he nearly a young man? Wasn't he old enough to give her help, if only the help of his moral support, when she demanded it? The answer was, and she knew it, No, he was not. So she did not speak. Dick thought the whole thing a huge joke, which was no comfort at all.

As for Libby and her mother, they did not actually reproach her: they merely mused at her. *How* had she done it? It seemed so odd. Was she dazzled by the lights, or something like that? She hadn't, perhaps, been trying to avoid an animal?

'No, I was not trying to avoid any damned animal!' she had shouted at them.

And again: what did she see in Mr. Westlake? As everyone knew, you couldn't hope to reform a man who drank. Of course, if they had known him better, if she had brought him home in a natural, open way, they would perhaps have been able to see for themselves what she saw in him.

She would not talk about it at all to Maurice now. He had tried once again to persuade her to put the blame back where it belonged. 'It belongs with me,' she had said. 'If you think I told you anything else, you were dreaming.' She looked between his eyes, not into them. 'I said, you were dreaming.'

He did not press her further: which gave her a wrench of loneliness. She had noticed his new happiness and had a good idea of the cause. A year or so ago she had been afraid she might fall in love with him. The dangerous impulse had been conquered: but the period of near-loving had left her with the habit of watching for his thoughts. She knew him better than anyone. She could not help it.

She did not know what was likely to happen to him, and at the moment could not make herself care. Even when she least wanted him to concern himself with her, she knew the touch of resentment that he did not: well, he could sink or swim. She was locked in her own trouble, it took her all her time to seem careless of it before the rest of them.

She thought grimly that it had done one thing for her: it had, for the moment at least, shifted her headaches. When it was all over, they would come again in full force, taking their revenge because her practical anxieties had driven them out. For the first time in her life she had taken to reading in bed. She retired early with a paper-backed detective story, took a sedative, and then read till she could no longer see the print. It was the only way of getting to sleep.

Libby knocked and came in. 'Are you still up? Can I come and talk to you?'

Her hair was loose on her shoulders. She was like a faded fairy-tale princess.

'You do look comfortable,' she said, and it sounded grudging. She sat at the foot of the bed. The light from Kate's lamp threw a frieze of gold along the line of her nose, her lips, her long, rounded chin.

'If you are going to start wondering about me again, and why I have got myself into a mess, then no: you can't come and talk to me.'

'It wasn't about you.'

Libby raised her foot in one of her curious, graceful gestures. The skirts of her dressing-gown slipped away from her leg: she looked at it, as if in abstract admiration.

'Thank God for that.'

Kate waited. They had not exchanged many confidences since girlhood: they had always wanted different things. It occurred to her that she was passionately eager to get on with her story. She had come to an exciting turn in it, soon she would know who the murderer was. Irritation rose in her like thirst.

'I think,' said Libby, 'that Maurice is turning away from me.'

This was so unexpected that Kate forgot the book and stiffened with caution. Her mind raced in an effort to keep ahead. Did Libby know anything? Probably not: but what was there to say if, by any chance, she did?

So she pretended to suppress a yawn. 'What makes you think that?'

'We've never been close to each other,' Libby said. She sounded forlorn. 'I mean, you and me.'

Kate said she thought Maurice was in pretty good form, far more cheerful than he had been for some time, far more energetic in his work.

'Yes. He's nice to me, too. But he isn't thinking about me.'

Kate suggested that it was unreasonable, after twenty years of marriage, to expect a husband to be in a state of constant thought about oneself; or indeed, in many cases, to think about one at all. Marriage, for better or for worse — she would say, unquestionably for worse — was a state of mindless acceptance. It wasn't a bad state. It was, at least, a lasting one.

'Oh, don't be cynical,' said Libby, 'that's so easy.'

'Not at all easy. I had to make the effort myself.' She was beginning to relax: instinct might be here, but not knowledge. 'What is the matter with your foot?'

'My foot?'

'You've got it stuck up in the air.'

'Oh.' Libby put it down again. 'Do be serious. Listen: you and Robert. Did you ever find yourself saying just the things you knew would drive him mad, without being able to help it?'

This was not within Kate's experience. She had that violence of temperament which is sometimes given the mutation of an almost easy self-control: she knew that life had often been more difficult for Libby than for herself, but had never been able to understand why.

'I mean — well, this: I tell myself that I won't touch a certain topic, because I know it maddens him. And I have only to make the resolution to hear myself doing just what I said I wouldn't do, and worse. It's my voice, but I didn't tell it to speak. I keep on doing it. I can't stop.'

Kate felt the gulf of misunderstanding that lay between them, but because she was so different from Libby, she could not bridge it. Indeed, she didn't try. She was hating these confidences, that were like an exposure of the flesh. With men she had always been easy; modesty had seemed to her merely a word for sexual politeness. Yet she had always shrunk from the slightest intimacy, mental or physical, with other women, even with her sister, with her mother. As a child she had locked the bathroom against them both, had turned her head if she had to be with them when they undressed for the night. Any warmth of family affection, within her own sex, had seemed to her a kind of incest. She had once had a dream of walking naked down Piccadilly, happy and at ease, even with a sense of superiority to other human beings, until she realised that it was women who were watching her.

'It is, I know,' said Libby, 'my time of life.'

This was surer ground. 'Tell Maurice that, if you like. Not me. It is rubbish, and you know it.'

'I am losing him.'

It was said almost affectedly, as by a passable amateur actress of decent elocution and over-riding confidence: yet it was a plain statement of fear.

'Do you sleep with him?'

Libby started. 'I do think that *is* something between husband and wife!'

'All right, then you don't.' Kate picked up her book and pretended to go on reading. The sedative was taking its effect: the print blurred and melted.

'Don't be so hard. You're always so hard.'

'Maurice can't live like a monk. No man of his kind can.'

'I prefer not to talk about it.'

'Lose him, then.'

Libby got up. She went drearily towards the door, twitching the dressing-gown around her. Kate was touched by compunction. She could not understand the way in which people like her sister loved: yet presumably they did love. One could not simply deny them the faculty.

'Oh don't!' she cried out. 'I'd help you if I could, but I'm worried stiff myself.'

She had offered Libby an extreme confidence: that she was scared. Not for the world would she have offered it had she not been sorry for her own indifference. It was a tremendous offering, it was the half of all she had.

It went unnoticed.

'Never mind,' Libby said coldly, 'I expect I shall get on all right.'

The door closed behind her. Kate put the book down, turned out the light and made herself ready for sleep, but the sounds of the house, hatching in darkness, disturbed her. Libby had left a tap dripping again: she was always doing it. The bed creaked in her mother's room. Maurice was on his way upstairs, walking softly, trying not to disturb the sleepers.

So many of them. She had always realised what it had meant to him to be surrounded by people, in his work, in his home, to have nothing for himself. He had never been free from the demands of others, they had all weighed upon him. I may have weighed a bit less, Kate thought, because I earn my keep: but Mother, Libby, the boys with their tempers and their carpentry and their gramophone records, God knows how he has managed to stick it.

She had been torn between her desire to make things easier for him and her desire not to repress her sons. There was little freedom for them, really, in such a house: she could not constantly be telling them to keep quiet just because they owed Maurice so much. She had always believed it was not good for children to have to owe things: recently, it had struck her that it did them no harm. Sooner or later they would have to acquire a sense of obligation, and the sooner, perhaps, the better. When she could get a grip upon herself, she would deal harder with the boys.

Someone knocked at the door, opened it a little way. 'Are you still awake?'

She put the light on again. Simon came in. He said casually, 'I say, I've got an awful pain.'

'Where?'

'Stomach.' He indicated the spot and groaned.

Getting out of bed, she made him lie down. 'Keep still.' She undid his pyjama jacket. He gripped his trousers, and glared.

'All right, all right,' Kate said, 'I'm not interested in your silly anatomy. I want your appendix.' She prodded him, gently at first, then with a firmer pressure. He did not move. 'I can't find anything. How are your bowels?'

'Thank you,' he said, turning his head away with an air of affronted dignity, 'quite all right.' He sat up. 'Actually, I feel better now.'

She asked him what he had had to eat. Well, he replied, she ought to know; she had cooked it.

'I mean, anything else? Anything to upset you?'

She was beginning to suspect that he had not been in pain at all.

'It might have been those dates. They were a bit on the hard side.'

'You shouldn't be such a pig.' She watched him as he swung himself off the bed, and retied his dressing-gown. 'What did you come in for?' she asked him curiously.

'I told you, I had a hell of a pain.' He went very slowly to the door, as if he were playing the game of Grandmother's Footsteps. He paused, with his hand on the knob. 'If I were you, I shouldn't worry about all this old bosh.'

She was deeply touched, feeling love for him not as a maternal routine emotion, but as something which sprang like a hot jet. 'But, my dear boy, I don't!'

'Oh no,' he said readily, 'of course you don't, really. But just in case you did — well, I wouldn't. All those old hens, they don't count.'

'Sim,' she said, after a pause, 'you are dead right: I don't like it at all. I hate it. But that's a secret between you and me.'

He gave her an open and beautiful smile, his face clear. It startled her to see him like this: it was a precious moment, but she must not let him think so.

'Do you think I'm going to talk?' He added dramatically, 'Your secret is safe with me.'

She told him he had no idea how much better it made her feel to tell the truth to somebody.

'The truth?'

For a second she was scared, fancying that somehow he had found out the whole of it. 'I mean, that I am not quite so care-free as I look.'

'Oh, I see. Well, don't get in a state. Actually, nobody of my generation would give a rap.'

He was gone.

She smiled at the thought of him, at the hope he had suddenly shown her of the man he might become. She had never taken much comfort from Simon; she had loved him, would always love him, but had never really expected to like him. He had been too moody, too withdrawn, too cold a child for liking, and she had often turned with relief from him to Dick's undistinguished stolidity. It was Simon whom she had longed to like: for liking, she thought, was rarer than loving between parents and children. In the middle of her fear, her sense of disgrace and desertion, the nucleus of happiness glowed like a coal.

Chapter Thirty

MAURICE knew that, in the evenings, Alice had almost ceased to go out. She kept herself in readiness for him. Usually he could come for no more than half an hour — sometimes for less than that, occasionally for a full hour. They sat in her dazzling room, held hands and talked. He kissed her when he came and when he left: that was all. But they were behind the lighted window together, the secret window high in the night, and it was enough.

It was extraordinary to him that with Libby, whom he did not love, it had been hard to control the drive of his body: with Alice, whom he did love, it was far easier. Neither of them hoped for more than they had: at least, he did not, and he believed she, too, was keeping herself from any thought of the future. They were in a fullness of love: it seemed to him God-given, though he supposed it could not be.

In this suspension of life, a globe of gold hanging, like earth in the Shakespearean cosmos, between the height and the depth, he felt innocent. She did not believe: but he could talk to her of belief, and feel the ardent flow of her imaginative sympathy. Here he did not have to leave God on the doorstep. He knew perfectly well that they were doing wrong, since they were depriving Libby of her place at the centre of his life. She had been blown out of it like a shadow, she was wandering between stars where he could not follow her. It was wrong: and it had a rightness satisfying as the completion of a perfect circle.

Being able to talk with absolute freedom was a release so delightful that it seemed like a newly-created joy, never so much as imagined before. Alice was not, by temperament, an adviser: she was a suggester of advice. She put in a question here and there, so that when he answered it he was answering his own doubts. She left him more fully a man than he had ever felt himself; he had no sense, when he was with her, of being directed, guided, in any way 'handled'. She placed decision like a tribute between his hands, offering him as much of her strength as he chose to take and casting away the rest of it as if it were of no value at all.

She had spoken only one directing word, and it was on the night he had come to her.

'We've all the time in the world now. Let's not hurry about anything. Let's never hurry.'

One evening, just as he was about to go, a friend of hers called unexpectedly, a man. He had taken Alice about a good deal after her father's death: he had thought about marrying her. She introduced Maurice clearly and simply, and when he left went out with him as usual into the hall. She told him later: 'You see, it doesn't matter. There would be nothing strange about your calling on me once. It would seem strange if he knew how often you called; but he doesn't.'

They smiled at each other a little awkwardly, embarrassed by the intruding edge of deceit. They did not mention the man again.

It struck him as he sat with her, moving his hand along the line of her neck and shoulder and down her arm, how much less sheer beauty mattered than any woman thought. Alice was comely, but not beautiful at all: and it was she who woke delight and admiration in him where Libby failed. He spoke to her of his disbelief in beauty, choosing his words carefully; she had the normal human vanity, she would not have chosen to be the beautiless example in a comparison.

She shook her head. 'Oh no. A woman is noticed for it first.'

Suppose, he said, that this were true? — which he doubted. The whole charm of it lay in newness; it might last perhaps for a year, until its lines were familiar and accepted. It was like hearing a fine and unusual Christian name. You married its owner and you spoke it until it lost its unique flavour on the tongue; it became, like all names, simply a designation.

'Or the other way about,' she said. 'Alice is a very ordinary name. But does it sound new to you because——?'

'Because it's yours? Of course. I hear it as if you were the first person ever to bear it.' He slipped his fingers on to her pulse and shared the life racing through her.

'We talk of small things,' she said, 'in the very little time we have. I keep on feeling that what we say should have tremendous importance.'

He told her it was she who had insisted that they had all the time in the world. 'So we have,' he said. 'And anyway, it isn't so much with words that we speak to each other.'

Once he found her in a dark mood; she had not been like this with him before. She spoke shortly, moved restlessly under his touch.

He asked her what was the matter.

'I was thinking: it's all rather rarefied, isn't it? I suppose it has to be. But God, how I wish, sometimes, that it wasn't!'

'Do you suppose I don't? Is that all you know of me?' He was angry that she had brought him to a danger point. It was only by the exercise of both their strengths that they could go on living as they did, without thought for the morrow, for the flesh, or even for the bliss of lying side by side in a bed, murmuring the time away.

'It's such a lyric love, half angel, half damned bird,' Alice said, her voice thickening. 'Is it good enough?'

'If it isn't, then I must stay away from you.'

'Don't try to blackmail me!'

He dropped his hand from her shoulder and walked away. He was filled with bitterness and fear. They had so much happiness, and of course it was not enough. But there was no more to come, and it was vital that both, not merely one of them, should accept it for what it was.

She came to stand beside him. Lifting his arm, she drew it around her waist, and he tightened it.

She said, 'I am very sorry.'

Nothing else was necessary; it had not even been necessary for her to say it. He had felt the blackness lift from her, like a relaxing of air pressure in the room.

He said he had something for her. It was the first present he had ever given her. He was poor; and if he could have saved a fair sum of money, would have felt that this, at least, was by right Libby's. But his father had left him an agate seal ring, which he had kept for years in a drawer. He had had the stone put on a brooch-pin for Alice.

Holding it in the palm of her hand, she looked at it as if it were the most priceless jewel she had ever seen. Then she looked up at him, shining, at first unable to speak.

'It isn't——' he began.

'Don't.'

'What?'

'Don't tell me it isn't much. Or that I have so much already. I have never had anything like this.' She pinned it on to her dress. Taking his hand, she kissed the palm of it.

She said: 'This is love.'

As the spring progressed, it irked them that they could not go out together in the soft evenings: sometimes this seemed like their only deprivation. They wanted to walk side by side. All they could do was to open the windows wide on to the London night, where the rush of traffic was like the sea, and some of the freshness of the flowery park penetrated the petrol fumes. Often they turned out the lights and leaned together on the sill, craning their necks to see, at the corner of the square, a tree thickened over with blossom, the colour of oatmeal in the lamplight.

As the day of Kate's appearance in court drew near, he told her about the substitution. She was a little offended that he had not done so before, that he had kept so much from her.

'I think I didn't want the real world to touch us,' he said.

She replied, 'Oh, do let it! It gives me the illusion that it exists.'

But afterwards she turned her careful thoughtfulness upon the problem, with as much concentration as if it had been her own. She tended to brush off the moral aspect Maurice found in it: there was, she said, no step he could take that would not cause practical harm. 'You aren't your sister's keeper, not in this.'

What worried her was Westlake's desertion of Kate. This concerned love: and love absorbed her so completely that she could only think within the radius of its light. 'He'll come back when it's over. Shouldn't one think well of him because he's too ashamed to see her now?'

Maurice said he saw nothing praiseworthy in the indulgence of a sense of shame at the expense of another person's happiness. 'I always suspect people who put conscience before kindness, though of course I should not.'

'Isn't that what you would do, if you made poor Kate confess?'

He could not help grinning.

'Now what have I said?'

'It is the bare idea of poor Kate confessing. She is iron, solid iron.'

'You admire iron,' Alice said pensively, carefully separating the two words, 'I must see what I can do about myself.'

'I shouldn't admire it in you.'

'If Kate won't confess, then, and Westlake won't, what on earth can you do?'

'I should work on Plym. I should have done it before if it hadn't been for you.'

'Leave Plym alone,' Alice said, on a hard note. 'You can do nothing with him. He is very odd. And he does not like other human beings.'

Chapter Thirty-one

PLYMMER said he could stand so much and no more. Kate, he insisted, waylaying her on her morning round of the shops, must take him to what he called 'The man Westlake'; and in his voice there was all the trembling contempt of the artist of small build for the journalist of large. 'I am not putting up with this, not for you or anyone else, certainly not for that soak.'

She tried to pass. In the middle of Earls Court Road, in the cosmopolitan weaving of the pavements, the bumping and boring, the perambulators pushing into obstructive legs, he barred her way, dancing in front of her like a little demon.

'He won't see me, if you want to know,' she said; 'he certainly won't see you.'

'Then you listen to this. If he won't see me now, he is going to see a lot of me at the bloody police court, because I am going to deny this tomfoolery thrust upon me, I am going into the witness-box to state that the car was driven by a drunken oaf, and not by a woman.'

She urged him to be quiet. She would see what she could do, if only he would not impede her now.

'Look, I know where he lives. He lives down there' — Plym shot out his arm, a finger quivering at the end of it like the loop of leather on a hunting crop — 'I got it from his stinking paper.'

She told him quietly that he would make nothing but misery for herself, for Maurice, for Libby. She was, of course, going to plead guilty. She did not even expect Plym to be called as a witness.

'But I might be!'

She said pacifically, 'I'll find out what's likely to happen.'

'You understand, I am not going to perjure myself.'

'Moral grounds?' She could not resist asking him, or keep the edge from her voice.

'No,' said Plym, 'fright': but he was bluffing. She saw that, deep down, he loathed the idea of the bare lie, as he might have loathed getting some smear of filth on his hand. His standards were mysterious, probably even he did not comprehend them; but they laced him up, he was corseted within them.

'There's no need for fright, I promise you.'

'I'm going round there.'

'That's no use. He'll be out. He always is at this time of day.' She told him she must go: she had all her work to do, the midday meal to cook.

He stared at her, still standing in her way. 'What makes me sick,' he said, 'is love.'

She said angrily, 'Plym, let me get past.'

Then he stepped aside. 'I'll be at Westlake's to-night at seven. You'd better be there, too.'

'I shan't!'

'You'd better. Love!' he said again. 'You make a fool of yourself, you mess everyone up just because you're in an abnormal state, it's as if you were drunk or dotty. And while you're like that, everyone else has to suffer.' He went off into the crowds at a smart pace, dodging among them, his corduroy shoulders hunched Quasimodo-like, his hands deep in his pockets.

That night at a quarter to seven he telephoned her. 'I'm just going along to number sixteen. I thought you'd better know.'

He could not have chosen a worse time. She had not finished laying supper, Libby was out at a meeting, and Mrs. Marsden was tearfully demanding justice because, she said, the boys had been rude to her.

'I insist that they apologise.' She set her chin, a structure of iron beneath the softening droop of old flesh. 'You must make them. I will not have them laughing at me. Look!' she cried hysterically, 'they're laughing now, both of them!'

'Oh, hell, I'm not laughing,' Simon shouted, but Dick, the idea of mirth suggested to him, was struggling to keep a straight face.

'That's what it's like all the time, rudeness and bad language! I should have thought their mother——'

'Get upstairs and stay there till supper,' Kate told them sharply. 'I've got to go out for an hour.'

'I must insist——' the old woman began.

'It is no use insisting, Mother, because I have no time for a fight. Tell Libby I'll be back by eight-fifteen at latest. The pie's in the oven.'

'I know,' said Mrs. Marsden very gently, 'that the *weakling tears* of old age must seem very funny to these boys, but——'

It was too much for Dick. He gave an involuntary yelp of painful, undesired laughter. Kate lost her head and swung a slap at him.

'Hi!' He squared up to her, outraged, himself on the verge of weeping. 'Just don't you *dare*!'

'Simon, take him away! Go on, both of you. Do you want to drive me mad?'

'Sometimes,' said Mrs. Marsden, 'I think it's me they want to drive mad. Well, boys, are you satisfied with your work?'

Simon said, 'Look here, Grannie, Mother's got enough on her plate,' took Dick by the arm and marched him away.

'Oh, how can you let them talk to me like that, Kate? It's made me feel quite ill and trembly. Feel my hands, they're trembly.'

'I can't. I've got to go.'

Leaving this strewn battlefield behind her, Kate slammed out of the house. She felt unbearably strained. It was enough to have so much trouble ahead of her, to be torn by Westlake's withdrawal, to be forced to humiliate herself in this manner — for wouldn't he think she was merely making an excuse to hunt him down, even suspect Plym was her accomplice? — it was all of it enough, without her mother's caprices. Mrs. Marsden was docile as a rule, a creaking door with so gentle and rhythmic a swing that everyone was used to the noise: but recently, troubled, perhaps, by uncomprehended tension about her, she had taken to stirring up little scenes of which she could take the centre.

Kate ran nearly all the way to the street where Westlake lived. His landlady, who was just putting her key in the lock, let her in. Kate raced up the stairs, stopped outside his door to get her breath. She had expected to hear voices, but there was silence.

She knocked.

He called, 'What is it?'

As she did not reply he flung the door open, staring at her as if he were a monarch broken in upon by some menial who had slipped past the guards. She had never seen him look like this. He was in shirt sleeves and braces, collarless. He must have been asleep or lying down, for his hair fanned out in spikes at the crown of his head like the plumes of a demoiselle crane. He did not look as though he had washed that day.

'Where's Plymmer?'

'Who?'

She repeated it.

'That squirt? Why should he be here?'

'He said he was coming round at once.'

'Well, the hell, he's not here.'

'I am, however,' Kate said steadily, 'and I don't much like it on the mat.'

He shrugged. 'All right, come in at your own risk. The room hasn't been done. It's in a filthy mess.'

The landlady, whose room was on the floor below, heard this. She cried up the stairs, 'It would have been done, Mr. Westlake, if you'd given anyone half a chance to get in!'

'Oh, all right, all right! I wasn't criticizing you!'

She banged her door.

The evening light came full through the staircase window, which was stuck over with coloured paper representing stained glass. Lozenges of red, green and blue light, bright and clear as the symbolic flasks in the chemist's window, spread themselves over the worn linoleum. 'Well, *come* in,' Westlake said in a fury of impatience, 'and don't stand there looking like fair Madeline.'

He pulled her through the doorway and into the sour heat of a kiss; he rubbed his fingers through her hair, put a hand to the back of her neck and held her against his mouth.

'You would come,' he said at last.

She twitched herself away from him. 'Listen, Tom, Plym said he was coming up here to threaten you.'

'What about? Go on, sit down, take a cigarette, there's some whiskey left. Why should he threaten me?'

'He says he's going to tell the police you were driving.'

He smashed his fist into a sofa cushion. 'Is everyone going mad? I think I am. What is all the raving on and on about a tinpot matter like this? If he does, we'll deny it. We'll say he's got a screw loose.'

'If he does, I shan't talk at all,' Kate said sharply. 'I shall have had enough of lying.'

She felt herself existing on two levels: the level of anger, and the level of driving, unstemmable desire. He looked dirty and repulsive, a caricature of himself at his worst: she had hated him to touch her, and she longed for him to touch her again.

He lifted the cushion gingerly between his thumb and forefinger, elevated it to his own height, and daintily dropped it. He sat down with a heaviness that made the sofa creak. 'All right,' he said, in a voice drained of interest, 'do as you please. I don't care. I expect you have had enough of it, at that.'

He let his hands hang ape-like between his knees. Discovering, on the carpet, a spot of something like sealing-wax, he began to pick away at it, as if his whole attention were involved.

'Oh, Tom!' she cried out, and heard the plea in her own voice, 'what's gone so wrong with us?'

'Oh, I don't know. One thing and another.'

'Can't you see, I don't mind what I do if only you don't' — she hardly knew how to put it — 'shut the door?'

'Any door with me behind it is better shut. Hasn't that struck you by now, my girl?'

She caught sight of herself in the Venetian mirror opposite, and her own image reassured her. She was miles from being composed: yet she looked composed, in her neat, dark dress, hair neat, lipstick unsmudged. It was odd to see herself looking so, since she had rushed out without a glance in her own glass, had not renewed her make-up, combed her hair, so much as washed her hands. She spoke less to him than to her calm white mirror-face, wedge-shaped, like Libby's, but not so young, and not beautiful. She thought, she said, that he had stopped loving her: if that were so, she could only make a fool of herself by talking of love to him. Yet the hard fact was that she could not fall out of love in half an hour, nor pretend she had done so.

'Where is all this leading?' Getting up the last gram of wax, he ran his tooth under a fingernail to loosen it. He turned his attention to another spot.

'Simply,' she replied, feeling herself go cold, 'that nothing I'm doing for you, and God knows it's not much, mattered a rap so long as you wanted to see me.'

'Oh, I want to. But somehow, it doesn't help. I think I'll get along to the *flics* and tell them the grisly truth.'

'You know I won't let you do that.'

'Then, my dear old Katey, what *do* you want?'

She said: 'It doesn't matter to me. It does matter to you.'

'Of course: that's obvious. Still, if you're going around like a cripple with your conscience for a hump, you'd better put yourself straight again.'

'You know it's not that!'

He looked up at her, not raising his head, only turning up his flaring eyes. 'Oh? Then you might tell me what it is. If it's your idea that I have to thank you every half-hour, I'm quite willing to thank you — will you have it by phone or post?'

Beside herself, she chopped her hand down, catching him on the side of the head. He swayed, nearly fell on to the rug.

212

Righting himself, he resumed his hanging posture, head lowered, eyes raised to her.

'Oh, God help us, God help us,' she said.

She could not move, and he did not budge.

Outside in the street a barrel organ began to play. The jangling, jocular tune filled up the room like an incoming tide, inch by inch, to the skirting board, to table level, mouth level, nose level.

The bell rang.

'That, I expect,' said Westlake, 'is your chum Plymmer. Perhaps you'd let him in. I don't feel like the walk myself.'

She ran downstairs.

'Sorry I'm late,' Plym said, 'one of the girls cut herself on a tin, bled like a pig.'

'You can't come in. Tom's not well.'

He considered this. 'Have you called the doctor? No? Well, then he can't be too ill to talk. He's drunk, is that it?' Then he looked at her. 'You are in a state.'

'I am in a state. And I beg you to go home.'

'Look here,' said Plym, 'I tell you what I am going to do: I'm going to talk to Maurice.'

'You'll tell him nothing he doesn't know already.'

He opened his eyes wide. Pale green, the iris cloudy, the whites very clear, they regarded her. 'You mean that Mother Church is going to stand meekly by while you——'

'He can do nothing else because I won't let him. And he wouldn't, I don't think, if I did let him, because of the hideous silly mess it would make.'

'I see, I see.' He tapped his foot against the step, carelessly at first, then with an assumption of scientific interest. 'Hollow. Odd. I never stopped to think whether steps were or weren't.' He backed gently down to the pavement, gave the last step a gentle kick. 'All right. I won't impose myself on Westlake, or on Maurice. But when the time comes I may have to go my own way.'

She began to sweat with terror. 'Oh, Plym, you can't! Do you want to get me into serious trouble?'

'Tut, I'm not thinking about you. I'm thinking about myself. If I don't nobody else will. The point is, what risk do *I* run? *I, I, I!*' he shouted suddenly on a high and dangerous note. 'Yes! That's important to me, odd as it may seem.' Then he gave a small, sideways smile as if he were ashamed of himself. 'Well — we'll have to see. We'll have to see.'

He left her standing there; walked off at first very quickly and then fell into an idle stroll, running his finger tips along a railing as he went.

She did not go back to Westlake; she was afraid. She had the vision of a city crumbling, as after a giant flash and wave of heat, first the plaster curling away from the stone, and the loosening of brickwork: a concrete wall bellying out slowly as in a fabulous pregnancy, then the crack appearing like a flesh wound: the trembling of the ground, the first soft, almost comfortable subsidence, and then the swallowing abyss: and into the hole houses and shops and schools and churches, men, women and children tumbling like toys, under a sky that was like fire roaring away red and yellow under a copper-lid of smoke that fitted itself tighter and tighter down upon the final liquefaction.

I shall have to be careful, she said to herself, or I shall be ill. It would surprise everyone if I were to be really ill, not only lying in the dark with the old boring trouble, like death to me, and a yawn for everyone else. At that moment a little black thread appeared on the screen of the sunset, lifted a little and beautifully descended, rose up once more like the jet of a fountain.

Oh, not ill. Just the same thing again. It has been so long that I had forgotten to recognise the signs.

Chapter Thirty-two

'**B**UT poor Mrs. Morley,' Georgina said, 'I am so sorry! It must be hard on her.'

She was entertaining Libby and the Fawcetts to tea.

'Well, yes,' said Libby. She gave a rueful smile. 'And a tiny bit hard on me, though I know that should be the least of it. But she did give me quite a lot of help, really, and of course I miss it.'

'Of course you do!' Humphrey looked at her as if she were a gallant child. He gave her an avuncular pat on the knee. 'We all know how hard you have to work, and shameless persons like Georgina and myself can be no use to you at all. Too old. Perhaps too lazy.'

'You help by being a comfort,' Libby said simply, 'and that is a very big thing.'

'What actually *is* a nervous breakdown?' Fawcett enquired. 'I thought it was a term without medical meaning.'

'Well, precisely, so it is.' Libby was grave. 'In her case, it seems to be the result of' — she was going to say 'overwork', but decided not to give a wrong impression — 'over-strain. All the worry about that frightful police-court business.'

'She needn't appear, need she,' said Fawcett, 'if her doc. writes a letter?'

'Well, we hope not. Maurice has got on to her solicitor. Kate wouldn't have one at first, she said that as she was going to admit everything it was an unnecessary expense.'

'But how,' he persisted, 'is her "over-strain" taking her? You understand, it's of purely scientific interest, so far as I'm concerned.'

Libby explained that Kate was said to have a 'tired heart'.

'Forgive me, but I don't even know exactly what that means!'

'Oh, nor do I!' Libby retorted. They broke into abashed laughter. She grew serious again. 'The trouble is, Kate can't bring herself to make an effort. We feel she'd be so much better if she did. After all, one just has to rouse people from some states, doesn't one?'

Georgina said thoughtfully that she was by no means sure. She had once been ill for quite a long while herself, and the one thing she had resented, during her convalescence, was persons of rousing temperament.

She had, perhaps, phrased this opinion with a little too much edge: for Libby gave her a quick, smiling look and made no comment.

'When does the case come up?' Humphrey asked.

In a week, she told him: it had been pending for months, or so it felt. In fact, it had been six weeks. Libby burst out, 'I can't praise Kate enough! She's been a wonderful sister. When I haven't been able to cope with household chores she's always lent a hand. You know, a little cooking, or cleaning, or washing-up — I miss her dreadfully. It's been brought home to me now how much all those small things meant.'

They were silent in tribute to this generosity, that is, all except Georgina who, having constantly met Kate bowed under loads of shopping with never a moment to spare, doubted whether her assistance had been quite so auxiliary as Libby implied. It was a new idea to her, the idea that Libby Fisher could be touched by human jealousies. She brooded upon it as she collected teacups for refilling.

'I don't care what anyone says,' said Louisa Fawcett, who had not spoken before, 'but when people have to let one down, it's horribly hard not to tell oneself that they *needn't*, if only they'd pull themselves together.'

'Darling, what a horror you are!' Jeremy said lovingly. 'You will have to go in the corner when you get home.'

They looked at each other, their eyes sparkling.

'I don't mean it nastily,' she said, 'it's just ghastly human nature, feeling nobody ought to be ill but oneself.'

'In the corner,' said Fawcett, with a parade-ground rasp, 'no jokes!'

They made Georgina a little uneasy by their playfulness. She suspected that they took pleasure in publicly exposing their real bedroom fantasies, under the pretence of comedy. She and Humphrey had not been without their fantasies too, when they were young, but these were only for the fever of the mood: they had never referred to them except at the moment of enjoyment. She said to Libby, 'It must be hard on your husband, too. I know she was a great help to him.'

'She certainly enabled *me* to be!' Libby replied, with a full, fresh vigour. 'We both miss her dreadfully, of course.'

Another guest arrived, a doctor called Massingham, fiftyish, good-looking; he had been one of Humphrey's pupils at Cambridge, and they had only just caught up with him again. He gave Libby a look of open admiration; she was most handsome that afternoon, in a cotton dress she had made for herself.

When he was settled, the talk went on.

'Maurice is tremendously good about it,' Libby continued. 'He knows I do all I can to keep the house running just as it would be if Kate were up and about, and he never makes the least complaint.'

'He is quite an exceptional man,' said Georgina, 'and people are so fond of him. Our charwoman' — she never used the nervous contemporary circumlocutions, such as 'daily woman' or 'daily help' — 'says that when she was in hospital, he never missed visiting her for a single day. I gather he used to make her laugh, which I do think is the most astonishing thing to be able to do for people in hospital.'

'Is that Mrs. Mason?' Libby enquired. 'Well, it's quite true: he always went whenever I couldn't manage it, no matter how busy he was. She is such a dear old thing.'

Georgina, knowing that Libby had visited the charwoman once, was silent.

'We are talking,' Fawcett said chattily to Massingham, with an air of repairing the negligence of his hostess, 'of our vicar, always a topic of intense interest, as you can imagine.'

'Is that Maurice Fisher?' the doctor asked. 'I met him once.'

'You met my husband?'

'I think it must have been. A rather big man.'

'Maurice *is* big,' Libby agreed, smiling a little, 'and his waistline is a gathering torment to him. Where did you meet him?'

'At Alice Imber's, I think. Yes, it must have been.'

Libby did not hesitate. 'Oh yes, she's a dear. I believe her new flat's extremely nice. Not that I've seen much of her since she left our immediate environs. A church,' she explained, 'somehow tethers you, like those goats in France, at the end of a long chain.'

Everybody laughed. Fawcett caught his wife's gaze, and seemed to be pinned by it.

'Maurice said it was a lovely flat,' said Libby. 'Actually, he knows Alice better than I do. She was a great help in the church, the entertainments and so forth. I used to say to her, "Why you bother, when we all know you're a heathen——"'

Everybody laughed again.

'The children's play she did for us was quite delightful,' Fawcett said smoothly. 'We're still talking about it.'

They began to discuss the charm of children's performances, how they could never, in the last analysis, fail entirely. Massingham was very interested in the subject: he had a niece who had wanted to act ever since she was five, and was now at a ballet school.

Libby did not join in. Her face was glowing, rose-red, like the face of a woman in love, or a woman brutally shocked.

Georgina cast a glance at Humphrey: he did not return it. Fawcett and his wife were devoting themselves to the discussion with the straight-staring absorption of players at a casino.

Libby said, 'I hate to break up this nice party, but I've been lazy long enough. I'm so grateful for the interlude, Mrs. Pelham, guilty though I am at having taken it!'

They rose. She shook hands all round, pressing each, bowing a little over each, like appreciative royalty.

When she had gone, Massingham said, 'What a very pretty woman!'

'For a vicar's wife,' said Louisa, 'it is a bit disconcerting.'

'Mew-mew, pussy,' said her husband.

'No, I mean it! She is! But I think the vicar's rather attractive too, in a battered sort of way.'

Fawcett said smoothly that he thought he had better take his wife away before her enthusiasm for another man overstepped the bounds of propriety. 'It is no business of vicars to be attractive,' he said. 'In fact, it is their plain duty to be the opposite.'

'Was his nose broken at some time or another?' the doctor enquired.

When they had all gone, Georgina turned upon Humphrey. 'I don't believe you spotted a thing!'

She bore her hands down upon his shoulders as he sat in his chair.

'My dear,' he said mildly, 'you must take me for a clod. Poor Brian Massingham dropped a brick, as they say.'

She regarded him in wonderment. 'Humph, you are really very clever! I have never thought people appreciated you properly.' She added unhopefully, 'Perhaps she knew about it, in any case.'

Humphrey replied that obviously she had not. Yet, he supposed, there was no reason for anyone to be surprised. Clergymen had to visit people, and much of their visiting was confidential. Alice Imber might well have had spiritual problems for him to tackle.

'I should have assumed,' said Georgina, not without heat, 'that it probably was a spiritual matter, if it hadn't been for all that talk, not so long ago.'

'Brian was always a silly boy,' he said reflectively, 'a slow boy, really. I used to be astonished that he got through his examinations.'

'Does that mean that nobody can ever admit to meeting anyone anywhere?'

'At our age anyone can,' said Humphrey, 'more's the pity.'

Georgina said that, on second thoughts, she saw no reason to assume that Maurice's visit to Alice Imber was anything but innocent: indeed, it would be absurd to imagine that it was not.

'How I hate vicarage scandals!' Humphrey exclaimed. 'I infinitely prefer college ones. They, at least, were carried on by persons who had to make a pretence of objectivity and to disguise their moral indignation as something else.'

She sat on the arm of his chair; cinder-haired, fresh-faced, the aged girl as interested in all things as she had been in her youth, she smoothed her hand over the top of his head.

'Humph, it occurs to me that I do not much like Libby Fisher.'

'My dear darling, I never did.'

'You never said so!'

'Why should I?'

'You should say all things to me.'

'But in this case the question did not arise.'

'I'm sure it must have arisen. I'm quite sure it must.'

'In any case, we should keep right out of this.'

'Oh, indeed keep out!' she agreed. 'No one else to tea. No more invitations.'

It sounded like one of the delightful excluding phrases of their first love: it left them alone in their pleasant, ragged comfort, the sky lime-green beyond windows too high for adequate screening, too broad to stop draughts, alone in this house which, when people like them were dead, would have no fellow. The reinforced concrete would rise, the curtain walls stretch up against the air, there would be no more shabbiness: which, Humphrey thought to himself, would be so much the worse.

'If you don't like Libby Fisher,' said Georgina, 'why did you pat her on the knee?'

'You have never,' he replied, 'realised the social value of our pretences. You're too forthright, my dear girl. Take it from me, and don't be.'

Chapter Thirty-three

KATE lay in the peering light of the eight-watt lamp, her hands clasped behind her head. She allowed herself to enjoy the sensual exercise of relaxation; from the top of her head to her feet all muscles were relaxed, her bones like jelly. This was peace as she had never known it; she adored her refuge. In a sense, she knew, she was malingering, hiding away in illness from things she could no longer bear: and in another sense the illness was real. It was true that she felt no desire to get up: and also true that she could not, that her will refused to screw itself to such a spring. It seemed to her very odd and very satisfying that the urgencies of the house had no longer any power over her. Her mother was stumbling about next door: she had no impulse to go and find out what she was doing. Libby was clattering dishes below: well, she could clatter them. Outside in the passage the boys were giggling together; God only knew what they were up to, and she did not care.

She had been lying like this for nearly ten days. She could not remember much about her collapse, except that she had gone to bed in preparation for the migraine which had not happened and had found herself unwilling or unable (it was the same thing) to get out of it. She had cried a great deal, steadily, noisily, interminably: and that had alarmed everyone. They had called the doctor because she would not stop. What she now knew about those tears, and they did not, the doctor did not, was that they had been delightful: she had wanted them to go on. She did remember the boys being pushed out of the way, Libby turning the pillow over because it was sodden.

Strong Kate, she thought, sturdy Kate, take a look at her now. Here she was safe, provided only that she did not budge.

She fancied they were waiting for her to make a movement a little too sharp, speak in a voice a little too awakened. She was not going to do it. Here even the thought of Westlake could not hurt her much: or if it did hurt her, she could cry it off in peace. Maurice had written to him about her illness, and he had not replied. For all she knew, he was not even at his lodgings.

Raising herself gingerly on an elbow, she blinked through the gloom at the sick-room clutter. On the table by her bed were two medicine bottles and a couple of pill-boxes, a furry spoon in a tumbler, a jug of lime juice and water, a thermometer, a jar of flowers. Pushed to the end of the bed were a crumpled newspaper, a detective story, her bedjacket. The room smelled fusty: she liked the smell. The wires between this room and the outside world had been cut. Outside there might have been a waste of waters, quiet, without light, without shores.

Maurice had been sitting with her for some time, and had been called away to the telephone. She could just hear the rumble of his voice from the study below.

She looked at the little lamp, the only light she felt she could bear. Inside it was a red coil in the shape of a pine-cone. It would not go out, the bulb should last for a year or more. Whatever happened to her, she would not forget this, she would always remember the peace of the glowing cone, the symbol of her life's blessed dislocation.

Libby looked in to ask how she was feeling. The query was high and brisk.

'Much the same. Did you enjoy your tea-party?'

If it had not been for the half-dark, Kate might not have heard the change in the voice. 'It was all right.'

'Who was there?'

'The Fawcetts. Some doctor or other. Do you want any tea?' She seemed to imply that only a glutton would.

Kate said she would have just a cup.

Maurice came up with it after a while. 'That was the police station. No, it's all right, it wasn't about you. The Fraser child's run away, and they thought I ought to know.'

She asked what they were going to do.

He replied that it seemed rather pathetic. The police would not do much looking for him: they would simply wait till he got home. 'They all go home,' the inspector had said, 'where else have they got to go to?'

'I can't see,' Kate said, 'that it's your bother.' Indeed, she found it quite hard to see that anything was anybody's bother. She looked back, with a kind of wonderment, to her own days as prop, as factotum.

'Oh, it's my bother, all right.' He sounded depressed. 'Somehow, it would have to be.'

Libby walked in and switched up the light.

'Oh, don't!' Kate could not bear it.

'I'm sorry. I can't stumble around here in the dark. I've got to tidy you up.'

'I don't want to be tidied.'

Libby said she must not let herself go. She went smartly about the room, flicking and straightening. There was a firm line to her lips; yet, Kate thought, she isn't angry with me, it is something quite different.

Once she caught her staring at Maurice, an open-eyed look, half scorn, half incredulity: but when he glanced in her direction she looked away again. She had intended, however, that the look should be seen: not by Maurice, but by Kate.

Then she will be back, Kate thought, when he has gone.

Alone again, with her lamp, she waited. She had thought of pretending to be asleep, but had decided this would be no good. In her twilight halfway between illness and malingering, it was a torment to her to make up her mind about anything. Did she want, out of pure detached curiosity, to know what was wrong with Libby, or did she want to be left alone?

She fell, in the half-light, into the half of a dream. Westlake was there, he was leaning down to take her, the warmth of his body comforting hers. She felt his mouth, like a hundred mouths seeking; they sought over the downy cheek of the dark like bees seeking through clover. She made herself rigid, stretched her feet down till they touched the footboard. He was there but not there: if only it could be like that, neither the knowing nor the unknowing! When the door opened she sprang up in bed, sweating, her heart thundering.

'Kate, Kate! Are you awake? You were wrong about Maurice, Kate; he has been seeing Alice Imber, I found out, I'm quite sure. You were wrong, do you see?'

Libby blundered forward, her eyes unused to the dimness, plumped heavily down on the edge of the bed.

'You're well enough to listen, aren't you? I can't talk to anybody else. There's nothing to stop you listening.'

She told Kate what she had learned at the party. She did not seem particularly distressed: her attitude was more like one of pleasurable horror at some gossip about an acquaintance.

Kate said, 'How silly. He may have seen her. Does he tell you everything about his pastoral work? A lot of it comes to him in confidence.'

'How can you be such a fool?'

'If I were you, I'd talk to him. It's no use talking to me, is it?'

There was a silence. The light made extraordinary shadows in Libby's face. She was like the Virgin in a picture Kate had liked, a night-picture of the Nativity, a candle-lit doll in a manger, another candle-lit doll above it.

'I can't,' Libby said at last. 'If I did it might make it come true.'

'I expect I believe in him more than you do.' Kate was really fighting against sleep now; if you simulated sleep, she thought, it would take its revenge by overcoming you, by bearing down upon you like a feather pillow, when least you wanted it.

'What anyone can see in her. . . .' Libby spoke sadly, with real wonderment.

'Talk to him.'

'No. That would be a lack of faith.'

'Oh, heaven help you,' said Kate, 'I can't follow all this!'

Then again she was alone, having failed her sister, and she did not care at all. The wires were cut, the waters stretched out; there was not even the guessed-at shine of a star, the momentary shiver of a reed. Just black.

Chapter Thirty-four

MAURICE heard the voice of someone unaccustomed to the use of the telephone asking for him repeatedly, not waiting for a reply. Then, after he had patiently demanded again and again the name of the caller — 'It's Mrs. Fraser. F — R — A — S — E — R.'

A long pause.

'Yes?'

'He's here.'

He called up to Libby, who was still with Kate, that he was going out: there was no reply.

When he came to the bungalow he found the door on the latch. There was a dead silence everywhere, in which fear was breathing.

They were in the prim sitting-room together, she on the sofa like a woman of marble, facing straight ahead, hands locked between her knees, he erect in the big chair. He wore anonymous grey flannels; if it had not been for his perfunctory haircut, he would have looked like any child from a decent preparatory school. His eyes were staring and blind, his mouth twitched. He was undersized; he might have been eleven or twelve. He did not stir when Maurice came in, not even from fright. His gaze was upon his mother, who now drew herself into the corner of the couch and tucked her legs up beneath her, as if there were some insect or rat scuttling about the floor.

'Mum,' he said, 'it's only me, Mum. It's *only* me!' He jumped out of the chair and ran at her, burying his face in her thigh. 'I wanted to see you, that's all it is.'

'Filth,' she said, stretching her mouth to the word, so that her small upper teeth showed, 'you're filth. Get away from me, Filth.' She looked at Maurice. 'Well? Didn't you bring them?'

'Bring them?'

'The police.'

'Did you want me to?'

She looked at him in sick scorn. 'Let them take him away, that's all I want. When I think what he's done, what he's always been like — I tell you! When he was quite a little one he had a filthy, old-fashioned face, he used to scare me. Let them get on with curing him, who pays for them but us? What do they think they're doing, letting him get away, spreading his s— all over decent people?'

Maurice told her to stop it. Derek was her child, and he needed her. They would not leave him with her long.

'What he used to do when he was a kiddie, it made me ashamed; if you knew how ashamed I was! It made me creep to see him.' She pushed at the boy so that he fell away from her on to the carpet. He stayed on all fours, staring down.

Maurice asked if he had had anything to eat. He did not move at first. Then he shook his head.

'Then, for God's sake,' Maurice said to the woman, 'get him some food! At least you can do that!'

No man can deal with the appalling images that come unbidden. They come with their leathery, dirtied wings out of the muck of the mind, heaving themselves out down-weighted by mud, scrambling one on the back of another. At the last moment his conscious thought was a rescuing paraphrase: Woman, look at your son. And at that moment, as if she were gifted with extra-sensory perception, Mrs. Fraser gave a groan that turned his heart over.

He took hold of her shoulder and shook it, not roughly, but with the gentleness of extreme anger. 'Get up and find him something. Then I'll take him to the station myself.'

When she had left them, the boy got up and stood patiently at his side. 'It was only to see Mum,' he said. He blinked, leaving a shine like a snail's track on the whitish flesh around his eyes.

'How are they treating you?'

'All right. The grub's not bad, we have sausages Fridays. They haven't sent no mind-doctor, though, not like they said they would.'

Maurice asked if he thought he needed one.

'Well,' said Derek with a touch of resentment, 'it's not my fault, see? It means I've got something wrong. So they ought to get me right.' He asked rather doubtfully if he could have a cigarette.

Maurice hesitated. 'All right. But if you haven't eaten you'll feel sick.'

'Not me. I used to smoke fifty a day,' he said, 'when I could get them.'

He sat down and smoked in silence. The apple moved in his throat. He put his chin in his hands and looked down.

Mrs. Fraser came back with a plate of bacon and eggs, banging it down on the table with such force that one of the yolks split under the impact and ran over the meat. 'Here you are. Put that inside you.'

Derek stubbed out his cigarette carefully and preserved what was left. He came with a sidling movement towards the food, like an animal fearful of being teased. Then he started on it, not ravenously, but with an absorbed steadiness.

Mrs. Fraser sat on the couch. She murmured to Maurice, 'Don't think too bad of me, Vicar. It's not that I'm hard. But it's all got on top of me. After all, if you had a kid and he'd turned out like that, you wouldn't be exactly pleased, would you?' There was a genteel note in her voice. She got up to see if one of the plants had gone dry, sat down again. 'It's only human nature to be disappointed, see? — what with all the neighbours passing remarks behind their hands every time I go out. But I'm not a hard woman.'

He reminded her of her grief on the night of Derek's arrest. 'You were so upset, wondering what they would do to him.'

She answered, rather sharply, 'Well, now I do know, and what's more I've lost the habit of him, him being away. He

227

doesn't seem like mine any more, and if that's what they wanted him to seem, they shouldn't have taken him.'

Derek turned round. Munching still, he looked at her.

'I wasn't talking to you!'

He turned away again.

Maurice told her the child needed her very much, and begged her to be kind.

'I haven't hit him,' said Mrs. Fraser. She took off her shoe, which seemed to be hurting her, flexed it and put it on again. It was a red bedroom slipper on to which she had sewn an artificial rosebud.

Derek pushed his plate back. 'Can I have an orange, our Mum?'

'Please yourself.'

Maurice asked her about the other two children.

'They're staying with their auntie. That's a piece of luck for me, isn't it? Otherwise they'd have seen him.'

When the boy had eaten his orange he went out of the room. In five minutes he was back again. He had washed himself, combed his hair. 'I'm ready,' he said to Maurice, and stood waiting.

Mrs. Fraser looked at him. She rose and said doubtfully, like an uncertain hostess to a guest who has stayed long enough, 'Well!'

'Cheero,' said Derek.

She seemed to nerve herself. Stepping quickly forward, she gave him a peck on the cheek. 'And don't go running off again. You'll only get into more trouble.'

In the street, he lit up the last half of the cigarette Maurice had given him. He would not walk by him, but a little behind. All the stars were out: it was a warm night. They walked slowly in single file, not speaking. Then Derek threw the butt into the gutter and caught up. 'Better step on it,' he said, 'get it over with.'

When they came into the police station, the desk sergeant looked up. 'Oh, it's you, is it, my lad? Thanks, Vicar. Where was he? At home?'

'I thought I'd bring him myself.'

'I say,' Derek spoke to Maurice. 'They did ought to get me a mind-doctor. You tell them!'

'I'll try. Good luck.'

'Oh, *luck*,' said the child. A constable was waiting for him. He turned docilely and went away.

When he was out in the street again, Maurice looked at his watch. None of this had taken as long as he had expected. He wanted to talk to Alice, to tell her about it. He ought to be able to manage half an hour.

As usual, standing outside her door, he dreaded to find her out, and his heart sank in anticipation. As usual, she was there, hoping for him. They had not met for over a week.

'My darling,' she said, putting her arm through his.

'I've had a wretched evening.'

In the bright secret cell of comfort, he told her about it.

She said, 'Poor little boy.'

'You once asked me if I wasn't glad I had no children, and I said no, I was not. But now I'm not quite so sure.'

'I was implying a lie.'

He asked her what she meant.

'Miles and I had a son, our first year in Canada. It was still-born. Nobody over here knew, not even my father-in-law. I couldn't bring myself to tell you before.'

'Not even me?' He felt the hurt strike him. 'Why not?'

Because, she said, it was her fault that the child had not lived.

It was an afternoon in the brief, brilliant Canadian spring. She and Miles were at their week-end cottage on the shore of Lake Ontario. She was seven months pregnant, and feeling extremely well. She was proud of this sense of well-being: it had become a dominating vanity. They had a long garden leading down to the water, divided by a stone path, neat and straight as the parting in a head. Half-way down was a plinth, and on it a stone vase filled with aubrietias. They were having tea with their neighbours, who had a wild and noisy son of ten. While nobody was looking, he had deliberately managed to

229

topple the jar over onto the flags, and was pushing it up and down like a roller. Earth and flowers had spilled out all round it; it was a horrible mess.

Shouting to him to stop, she ran across the lawn to him. His parents did not move; they were lethargic, easy-going people, immune to noise, to mischief, to the major and minor irritations of life. His mother called out, 'Oh, Johnny, you *are* a fiend!' — and laughed.

Alice was seized by an irritation so violent and so unfamiliar that she lost her head. Pushing the child away, she seized hold of the jar.

Miles called, 'Don't touch it! It's too heavy!'

She shouted back furiously, 'I can do any damn thing——' and with a jerk that strained every muscle of her arms, her back and her stomach, heaved the heavy vase back onto the plinth, grubbed up as much as she could of the earth and the fallen flowers and stuffed them back into place. As she straightened up again, she felt sick. She saw brightness everywhere, golden and emerald leaves sifting the blue air, the dazzling blue shine of the lake. She was panting, she could not speak.

They all scolded her. Feeling rather better, she sat down and went on with her tea.

'Honestly, Johnny,' said his mother, 'we shall not take you out any more if you're going to behave like that. What will Mrs. Imber think of you?'

'All right?' Miles whispered.

The irritation persisted. 'Of course I am. I'm as strong as a horse. For God's sake don't make an invalid of me.'

At two o'clock next morning the pains began, and at six, in the light of a roaring dawn, she expelled the dead child.

Maurice said after a moment or so, 'I love you. And now you've told me, it's all over.'

She put her face to his breast. 'It is so odd. I don't think I am a wicked woman. I never wanted to be. But all I do is bad.'

'I wish,' he said, 'that you had a more generous idea of God. Do you think he is such a pettifogger that he would punish you for a minor vanity by killing your child?'

230

'I don't think he is anybody at all. That is just it.'

'It makes no difference to his existence whether you think so or not. Forgive yourself, will you? Because it is probably asking too much to suggest that you should be sensible, and stop believing you have any guilt at all.'

'I am guilty in just leaning on you, as I'm doing now. But that is worth the guilt.'

She was still shaken by having achieved the confession she had never meant to make.

'It is an extraordinary thing,' Maurice said, 'that you have no beliefs of your own. I could be more sure in mine, and far happier in them than I am now, if you were my wife and I could love you honestly. I wouldn't have to confine God to specified hours, as I find myself doing now — I could feel him in every hour of my day.'

It was getting late. He told her he must go.

'I am going to sleep so peacefully to-night,' she said to him. Her face was rapt and tender. 'Do you know what? I wish I could give the same sort of peace to you.'

He said, 'It is something we can share, I think, as we would share money.'

Chapter Thirty-five

JOHNSON-BLACK walked up and down the room, swishing round at the corners as if he brought a tail with him. He was conscious that he must show no change in his face which might give Fawcett any sense of achievement; he was not aware that his face seldom showed much change, whatever the circumstances. So long as he continued to prowl, he felt, he need make no comment, but the moment he stopped he would have to.

Fawcett sat there patiently, smoking with his usual neatness, a draw at the cigarette, an immediate tap at the rim of the ashtray.

It was foggy outside and in the room. The reading lamp sprayed out not so much light as slats of darkness. Johnson-Black noticed that one of his sleeve-buttons was hanging from a thread, and he snapped it off. The action halted him. He had to speak.

'Look here, I know Fisher.'

Fawcett stirred and sighed. 'Well, my dear chap, yes: but what does one mean by "know"? I don't think anyone can really hope to know another human being.'

This was irritating. Johnson-Black observed that one knew people well enough for practical purposes, and that if one didn't, everything would come to a stop. Anyway, this was an assumption he had always made in the army. 'I can't see for the life of me that there's anything odd in a priest paying a call on an ex-parishioner, or anything odd about him failing to tell his wife where he is every moment of the day.'

Fawcett said regretfully that he would have thought the

same, if it had not been for the outbreak of scandal on the same subject early in the year.

'I never thought there was anything in that.'

'If I said "no smoke without fire", you would be quite sick, Colonel, and properly so. But you know — well, let's say there's nothing in the whole thing and *yet* it gets around. Wouldn't you say that, for the sake of the church, Fisher ought to be asked to put a stop to it?'

The Colonel sat down and touched his bluish chin gingerly as if someone had hit him there. He said, 'I'm the vicar's warden; I am on his side. But that doesn't mean that I feel myself in a position to suggest courses of conduct to him.'

He was, he thought vaguely, Maurice's man: and the word suggested some idea of feudal loyalty that was not unpleasant. It gave him heart: he could, he thought, cope with Fawcett, send him to rightabouts.

'Well, no,' Fawcett said gently, 'that is hardly what one could do. But I think one could, or should, drop a word.'

The Colonel had met subalterns like this, sleek men who spoke softly of responsibilities. 'If, for the sake of argument, Fisher was having an affair with Mrs. Imber——'

The other flinched, as if the suggestion were in the worst of taste.

'—he could hardly be expected not to know that he was. Therefore, to tell him so would be superfluous. If he wasn't having an affair, there'd be no point in it.'

This seemed to him so conclusive that he hardly expected Fawcett to put his head back and give a boyish peal of laughter.

'My dear Johnson, that really won't do! The point is that behaviour must be *seen* to be good. "Avoid the very——" One doesn't need the old tags. And after all, if our Libby gets upset it will be frightful all the way round. Personally, being selfish, merely from a selfish point of view, I don't want her upset. She does far too much good in the parish. Her sister's absurd business has shaken her quite enough.'

233

'Jeremy,' said the Colonel, 'why do you like to meddle?'
He had spoken as to a boy in his charge; if Fawcett chose to
peal like a boy, then he must be treated like one.

There was a long silence.

'Look, Johnson, that's uncalled-for. Am I right in thinking
— one' — he ticked it off on his forefinger — 'that you are
concerned not only with the administration of the church but
for its reputation? Two, that it is better for you and me to have
a quiet talk together, which can do no harm, rather than to take
the matter further? Three——'

'Please do not count at me. And there is no question of
"taking further" something that had better be forgotten as
quickly as possible.'

The other man got up and walked into the atomising rays of
the lamp. He was all lights and shadows now, part of the foggy
air.

Johnson-Black went on steadily, without expression, his eye
steady and dull. 'Have you any reason whatsoever to suppose
that Fisher is keeping Mrs. Imber?'

This brought another uninhibited laugh. 'My dear chap, he
couldn't keep a mouse! Poor old vicar — like all poor old vicars,
he can hardly keep his own household going.'

'Very well, let me put it in a way that may seem clearer to
you. Have you any reason whatsoever to suppose that Mrs.
Imber is his mistress?'

'Oh yes. Quite a bit. I'd hardly come to you with pure
tattle.'

'How?'

'Louisa's seen him up that way several times. Her sister
lives in Wilton Crescent.'

To Johnson-Black, this new, if frail, piece of circumstantial
evidence was a shock. He had honestly believed, up to this
point, that there could be no truth in the story at all, had
not really thought that it was credited even by Fawcett, that
sleek subaltern, that barrack-room lawyer. But he was a
judge of men: and he knew that the other was pretty sure of
himself.

He said steadily, 'All this sounds very trivial to me. But let us suppose for the sake of argument that Fisher goes to see Mrs. Imber now and then. Is there anything essentially wrong in that?'

Fawcett came back to his chair. 'Oh yes, of course. Let's not be blue-nosed, but of course there is, if he's doing it under the rose.' He paused. 'Oh yes, Johnson. Another thing. You and I may not have seen eye to eye over a few minor matters, but I haven't known you discourteous before.' He was angry: he had been thinking something over. 'You tell me that I "meddle". I'd rather like you to withdraw that.'

'I will put it,' said Johnson-Black heavily, 'in another way. I will say that you're tending to make trouble where none is necessary.'

Locking his long fingers behind his head, raising his face, Fawcett whistled soundlessly to himself for a moment or two. Then he said very lightly, 'You know, I never like to make a parade of religion. As a modern man, perhaps one has to practise it a bit more, but also a bit more quietly. One can't, as I said, look blue-nosed. But if the church — forgive me if I sound portentous — is to look other than immaculate, one simply has to put one's oar in.'

'Parades and oars,' the Colonel muttered, letting rudeness have its way for once.

'I'm not watching my prose style, Johnson. I am simply asking: do you or do you not care if there is a scandal in this parish?'

'If we mind our own businesses there will not be.'

'Well, you wait and see. Good Lord, when I think what the Archdeacon would have to say——'

'I have no respect for anything Sandeman says.'

'Oh, have you not?' Fawcett cocked his head as if this were an interesting point of view.

'No. And this nonsense must not get to Sandeman.'

'Oh, for Pete's sake! You don't suppose I'm going to tell him?'

The Colonel said he did not know what to suppose. He admitted, in his most even manner, a manner which, in the army and in the boardroom of a modest company or two, had quietened even if it had not conciliated, that if any sort of talk should arise in the parish, he would be prepared to bring it to Maurice's attention. On the other hand, he would never, himself, believe that talk. 'You and I are laymen. Because we are, we can be more easily tempted to misbehave ourselves. We can outrage our own consciences without having to outrage our public commitments. We're not like priests: we aren't committed to behave well.'

Fawcett, smiling, asked if there were no turbulent priests, no adulterous ones.

'But not Fisher,' Johnson-Black said simply. He got up.

'Then I may have your promise?'

'What promise?'

'To take it up with him.'

'Not until I am assured there is anything to take up.'

'Others might take it up.'

'I shall have something to say to others who do,' said the Colonel, edging his guest towards the door. 'Oh, and by the way.' He stopped.

'Yes?'

'Let us imagine that Fisher has, in any way, however slight, fallen from . . .' he sought for a word, hesitated between two or three and then said, with an air of apology, 'well, grace. For nearly twenty years that man has been the best priest a parish could have had: and in circumstances which have not been easy. Never mind what or how. I know they haven't been. Aren't we to take those twenty years into account?'

'Oh, we are!' Fawcett said with a bright, awakening air. 'And, of course, we should. But most people won't. It's only human nature.'

'The more I see of human nature the less I like it.'

When he was alone, Johnson-Black sat down to think. He did so deliberately, making careful choice of a chair; thinking was, for him, an activity that could only be carried out in a seated position. He was profoundly disturbed. That there was something between his vicar and Alice Imber he had little doubt; but he was not, unlike Fawcett, prepared to jump to conclusions as to what that something was. It struck him how very little the layman knew about the priest. The latter, by his initial choice, was set apart: there was a factor which made him different from ordinary men. To Johnson-Black, Maurice had been a priest first and a man second; yet because he felt he was a whole man, he had given him not only respect and admiration but a deep personal affection. He thought him, in a way, a freer man than himself; and could never quite understand why he should do so. It was something like this: though he could not conceive him behaving other than conventionally, he had fancied that, were it suddenly a matter of overthrowing convention in a good cause, Maurice would have done so with rather greater ease than he would.

What he did not know, and could not guess, was how far a priest, violently tugged by some strong sexual emotion, would, by the very force of his faith and his moral intention, be more resistant than other men. Johnson-Black, by no means sophisticated, found it hard to conceive that a man and a woman drawn together by love could refrain from its expression: it might not be a 'right true end', but it did seem to him the obvious one. If Maurice had not been a priest, he would at once have assumed that he and Alice Imber were lovers. There was quite enough smoke for that sort of fire.

Nevertheless, he did not believe it was true. Maurice might well have been tempted: his life, as the Colonel had told Fawcett, had been hard enough. Johnson-Black had been long enough in the army to recognise a skrimshanker when he saw one, and he had long mused with something like admiration upon Libby's expertness in that direction. She had succeeded in fooling nearly all the people all of the time: a feat he had only seen equalled by a lance-corporal called Combermere at Aldershot between the wars. Combermere had been such a bright, active-looking man, always on his toes, always seeming so brisk in transit from one job to another, that for months he had deceived not only his officers but his mates. When it became obvious that he could not work his confidence trick much longer, he had applied, with every appearance of justification, for posting to another unit, where, so far as Johnson-Black knew, he had continued in his old and successful ways.

An odd thing, he thought, Combermere and Libby Fisher had not been at all dissimilar to look at. Eager faces, hazel eyes, full round chins and the lips never quite closed, except in anger. Yes. Libby and Combermere.

The clock struck and Joan came in. It was dinner-time.

Over the meal he told her everything.

In one particular, perhaps the only one, Johnson-Black had been unconventional all his life: most people might say that he had been thoroughly unprincipled. He had kept nothing from Joan, even of the most secret order. At the beginning of the war, before it was decided that men of his age should be quietly retired, he had worked at the War Office, and had come to know a good many highly confidential matters. He had told every one of them to Joan: and she had told nobody. She had been his safety-valve. Once she was told, any desire for further telling left him: his excitement was spent. He did not know what he would have done without her or what, if his superiors had known, they would have done to him. His real safety, as he was well aware, lay in her almost total lack of interest in anything but himself and music. (Her only longing was for a hand-made gramophone: he had given up one of his clubs in the hope of squeezing the gift out of the money saved, but it was no use. They simply could not afford it. As it was, she no longer smoked, and they bought wine only at Christmas.)

He went on talking. She looked at him with her wise owl's eyes that were so steady and incurious. She said at last, 'Well, dear, the only thing is to pooh-pooh it, don't you think?'

'One hopes that that will serve.'

'It will have to,' said Joan, 'because that is what we shall do, and the only thing we shall do.' After a decent interval of appearing to reflect a little further on the problem, she began to tell him the latest of Plymmer, how he was proposing to usher the congregation out, next Sunday, with Hindemith's Organ Sonata, Number One.

'Well, I shall not recognise it,' said Johnson-Black, 'so at least it won't worry me.'

Chapter Thirty-six

MAURICE was back from the police court by mid-day. Libby was with him. She had insisted on going — to stand by him, she said, though he had tried to tell her that he was in no trouble himself. All the way home she held his arm, which ordinarily she never did, and walked with her back stiff, her chin jutting in the air. She did not speak much.

When they came in she started up the stairs, but he held her back. 'I'll tell Kate.'

'Surely it's my place as her sister——'

'No, dear,' he said, 'please let me.'

He had a shock. The curtains were undrawn, the sun was pouring in and Kate, fully dressed, was sitting on the edge of the bed. She had lost a good deal of weight. Her eyes seemed to rest on the bony crescents below them, and between her rouge and her cheeks there was a transparency, as if two glass slides separated colour from flesh. She asked no question, but her eyes enquired.

He sat down at her side. 'It took exactly fifteen minutes. You were fined fifty pounds, as you thought, and you would have lost your licence for a year if you'd had one. It's all over.'

Her hand moved over his. 'I'm up.'

'So I see.'

'Who was there?'

'Westlake. Plymmer. The independent witness, whatsisname. They didn't call Plym.'

'Well?'

He told her as briefly as he could what had happened. Her solicitor had entered her plea of guilty, and her sworn statement had been read. The constable had given his evidence in a brisk, genteel voice, reporting all statements without apostrophes so that the effect was like a reading from a Victorian children's book — (Kate smiled faintly) — and then Westlake and the other witness were called. That was all.

For a little while she was silent. Then, with a sly and casual air she said, 'Did they ask Tom if he knew I hadn't a licence?'

He hesitated.

'Not that it matters,' said Kate.

'Yes, I think they did.'

'What did he say?'

'He said no.'

'He said no,' she repeated. 'He said no.' She added in a curiously harsh, bronchitic voice dragged up from her chest, 'You'd have thought he'd have told the truth about *that*, wouldn't you? It's not much to tell the truth about!'

Her cheeks were burning red. Her hand was hot upon his own. 'It wouldn't have been much,' she said, 'it wouldn't have been much,' and she wept.

'You're not strong enough to be up,' said Maurice.

'I must be. I can't lie here alone any more. All this morning I've been telling myself that they would ask him that, and he'd say, "Yes, I knew." It couldn't have made any difference to him, could it?'

Libby knocked and put her head in. 'It's all over, darling! Nothing more to worry about.'

Kate told her to go away.

'But, darling——'

'Go away, go away!'

Libby crashed the door shut, so that the house sang.

'Now listen,' Kate said very softly, when the tremor of the crash had died along her nerves, 'that would have made all the difference to me. He could have given me that.' She asked then if he had talked to Westlake. Maurice said no: the moment the decision was given he had left the court.

'Tell him I want to see him. If he won't come here, I'll go round. Telephone him. Tell him that.'

He did as she asked. The landlady answered: Mr. Westlake had gone away. So far as she knew, he had gone up north. She did not know when he would be back.

When Kate heard this, she turned upon Maurice a look of such desolation that she might have been mad. 'Just help me through the next few days,' she said, 'as best you can.'

They were not easy. First, there were the local papers: 'Vicar's sister-in-law convicted.'

'It looks a bit ridiculous,' Maurice said, and managed to grin.

'I am *sure* it is libellous,' said Libby. 'They have no right to bring us into it!'

Then there were notes of condolence, displays of loyalty, flowers from the Pelhams. Then a cheque from Westlake for fifty pounds. He wrote a few lines with it, but gave no address. The envelope bore a Liverpool postmark.

Every day Kate got up and dressed, but did not come downstairs. She was ravenously hungry. Libby, or Maurice, or the boys took trays to her; she sent them down scraped to the patterns on the plates.

Maurice said one morning at breakfast, to a silent family, 'I think it is high time we got a sense of proportion. From the way we are all behaving, one would think the whole of this nation was concentrated upon the doings of the Church. One wishes it were. But it isn't.'

It was a relief to hear the didactic flow of his own voice, to see the puzzlement on their faces; he did not often (if ever) speak to them like this, and it gave him a secret satisfaction to do so. It was speech out of character: book-speech: head-of-the-family-vicar-speech; he found he could achieve it very nicely.

The boys stole glances at each other and made a noise with their knives and forks.

'Interest in the Church is at such a low ebb in England,' he went on, 'that one is always trying to avert one's eyes from the facts. The number of people in this district even dimly interested in it, let alone showing an active interest, is minute. So

do let us stop pretending that the eyes of half London are concentrated upon us and poor old Kate.'

Nobody answered him. Simon gave him a quick, direct look
which he interpreted as approval.

'But isn't that,' said Libby, 'an ostrich-like approach?
People are concerned. They must be. We are still the leaders.'

'Oh no,' said Maurice impatiently, 'we're not. We ought to
be, because we are the only people with any answers. But
partly because we are inconceivably bad at giving those answers,
we are not leaders at all.'

'If you feel like that, Maurice,' Mrs. Marsden said, using his
name to emphasize the weight of her disapprobation, 'I wonder
you can carry on at all.'

'I can carry on because the answers still seem clear enough
to me. But I am no good at making them acceptable to very
many people. Few of the clergy are.'

Libby locked her hands under her chin and rested her beauty
upon them. She looked at him steadily. 'Isn't it a failure in
the clergy if they're not listened to?'

'I sometimes think it is, so far as the men at the top are
concerned. If they're good enough to get to the top, they should
be good enough to give a lead. But one can't expect great oratory
and a great message from the run-of-the-mill parson. If he had
it they'd give him a better job.'

'But if,' said Libby, 'his life is an example?' He caught a
fanatic gleam and his heart sank. 'His whole life?'

He answered sharply that they were straying away from his
original point. He had simply wanted to remind them that,
important as St. Lawrence's might seem to them, the vast
majority of the neighbourhood merely regarded it as another
lump of stone. That was regrettable in all respects save one:
and that one, in respect of their present trouble. The whole
world was not concerned about Kate. Or about himself.

'We,' said Simon to Dick, 'are going to be late for our place
of education, which might seem desirable to a half-wit like
yourself but is not so to me.'

'You're a half-wit!' his brother retorted.

'Prove it! Who's still in a B-form, you or me?'

Dick threw a crust.

'There are starving people who would be glad of that,' Mrs. Marsden said.

'And I'd be glad if they had it,' Dick retorted. He looked at the clock. 'Snakes, we are late, too!'

In a moment the room was swept of them.

The two women looked down at their cups.

'More tea, dear,' said Libby with horrible gentleness.

Kate came in with the tray. It was the first time since her illness that she had been downstairs, and she tottered a little. When they protested, she shook her head. 'Can I use the study for twenty minutes?' she asked Maurice, 'I want to telephone. I'll make a note of what the calls cost.'

'You can't hope to trace that man——' Libby began.

'Mind your own business.'

She went out and Maurice followed her into the study.

'And I don't want you either, old boy,' she said.

'Come on, come on. What are you going to do?'

She lit a cigarette. Sitting at his desk, she drew the telephone to her and clasped her hands before it. 'I had a note this morning: Simon brought it up. He is getting such a tactful boy, he knows I don't want the family turning my letters over and peering at the stamps. There is great good in Simon.'

Westlake, she told him, had still given no address: but had mentioned that he might try to get work in the north of England. This, she had decided, meant that he was going the rounds of the Liverpool papers. If she rang up the newspaper offices she might have a chance of getting his address out of one of them. 'A long shot,' she said. She paused, then added, 'Would you like to see what he says?'

'If you want me to.'

'Oh, I think I do: I have to share with somebody.'

It was a short note.

'"Dearest Kate, Whatever I said now wouldn't make sense. I think I might find something to do up here, and if I have luck will of course let you know. You have made me a nasty mess in my own eyes — perhaps not your fault, but there it is. Don't try to help me again if there is an 'again'. Other people will have to, but it mustn't be you. Love." '

'At least,' she said sadly, 'I am someone special.'

He thought about Westlake angrily, as he crossed the square on his way to see David. It struck him that there were few things he liked less than the kind of exaggerated sensibility which was driven to victimise others. There might be something praiseworthy in Westlake having scruples; there was nothing praiseworthy in his using them to make Kate suffer. Maurice knew he loved her, and was realistic enough to know that when he was over his burst of wounded vanity he would be back again. People in love were separated only by practical factors and not by barriers of elaborate high-mindedness. What Kate could not realise was that her lover was in a temper. It was a slow-burning, lachrymose temper, the temper of the alcoholic. Westlake was quite willing to accept all the benefits which accrue automatically to a man who has lost his self-respect, but not willing to accept them with grace. He had to point out that he knew they were charities, despised them as charities, and had still teeth enough to bite the hand that fed him. He would not be able to offer Kate love again until he had made her beg his pardon for having saved his skin. Maurice's stomach turned at the thought of it. It was to be a nice, delicate, sickening business, protracted, pleasing to one side alone. Kate was to be made to act a part: Westlake would dress her up for it and make her go through all her ridiculous lines; and then, when she had made sufficient fool of herself to restore his own feeling of superiority, he would let her wipe the make-up off, get back into her own clothes and give him a kiss.

He found David in shirt-sleeves, standing on a box, clipping his landlady's hedge. This seemed such a summery thing to do, David such a neat, cheerful bird of a man, that Maurice was jolted out of the tunnel of his thoughts; and found himself smiling with the relief that the majority of minutes, for the majority of people, were ordinary ones.

'Improving the shining hour,' David said, hopping down.

245

'Is it cockeyed? Oh Lord, it is! I'm not much use at this sort of thing.'

His hands were sooty from the leaves.

'Wait till I've cleaned up the mess and washed myself and I'll be with you.'

He swept up the clippings into a box, and put the shears with them. 'She's a good old girl, she does what she can for me.'

When he was ready they went along to the church to discuss services for the month, how often David should preach, whether they ought to approach Kitson now about new hassocks or leave it till later on. They inspected the old ones, found more than a dozen beyond hope of repair.

'One wonders,' said David, 'whether he is as mean in his own house as he is with us. One does have to go cap in hand.'

'My cap,' Maurice said, 'has been in my hand so long that Kitson must take it for part of my anatomy. Stingy he is: but I doubt whether we should have been better off if we'd had a treasurer open-handed with money the church simply hasn't got. He is saving up for a rainy day.'

Just to be with David on these bits of formal business, to talk with him in the old easy way of matters of small account, was a lightening and a relief. The smell of the church was comforting: it smelled of damp, yes; but of flowers too, of carbolic soap, and of sunshine. Sun flashed from the lectern and turned it into a burning bush. The worn carpet was a beautiful red, crimson with a golden underglow, like raspberries ripening on the cane.

My church, Maurice thought, and was peaceful.

Plym had begun to practise. He was playing something broad and calm and acceptant, the sound flowing through the building not like a tide but like a lake overspilling its shores, a solemn inundation at an appointed time. David sat down to listen.

'What is it?' Maurice asked him.

'Bach, *Komm, Süsser Tod*. It's not bad, Plym is improving.'

The sun had shifted and was spilling down upon the altar, sparking the small cross, the scribbled edges of Mrs. Hathaway's clove pinks.

'Plym is coming on,' David murmured, his lips folding sweetly.

As a rule Maurice had to make a conscious effort to get anything out of music, had to follow it anxiously, holding firm to the thread which would lead him about and out again: but that morning it invaded him, taking away from him consciousness of all things but a deep happiness and the fact of being tired to death. He had never felt so tired. He did not really see how he was going to get up again and do all the things he had to do

Plym stopped in the middle of a phrase.

'He would,' said David. He got up. 'Well, well, this isn't going to buy the baby a new bonnet.'

The church trembled under them as they went to inspect the hymn books, flicking them through in search of tatters, of pages missing. They worked on together, Maurice wondering why they did so: it was a job for the verger, not for them. But his curate seemed determined to prolong the morning, passing from one thing to another with snail-like deliberation.

'Whole index missing here, and there's some sticky stuff on the cover. You remember all that talk, some time ago.'

'About the books?' Maurice was puzzled. Then he noticed that David's neck had reddened, his ears were rosily transparent like autumn leaves.

'No. All that gossip; you know. It's started up again, I think. I thought you ought to know, sir. That is, from somebody.'

David looked up, his blue eyes pleading. He did not want to be forced to say any more.

'About me?'

He nodded.

'I see.' Maurice smacked the books into their piles again. 'David. Do you think I'm doing something wrong?'

'No.' It was hesitant. Then, firmly, 'No, I don't.'

'Where's all this coming from?'

'I've no idea, but my louts have got it.' David looked wretched. His gaze fell, his shoulders drooped. He tried to find something to do with his hands, but failed.

247

'I'm glad you've told me.'

'Someone ought.'

'Yes. And I'd rather it came from you.'

'It is all a lot of bosh,' David said, bursting out with sudden fiery energy, 'I know that all right. Don't you think I don't.' He added, after a moment, in a quick, frenzied rush, 'Well! This won't buy the baby a new bonnet.' But he had said it before, and the consciousness of repetition deepened his flush.

'No,' said Maurice, 'it won't.' He touched David's shoulder and left him. He could not think of anything to say, though there were questions he needed to ask. He went out into the bright sunshine, where the square shone in its everyday torpor as if nothing ever happened in it.

Chapter Thirty-seven

HE could not sleep. About two o'clock he slipped out of bed, not waking Libby, and went down to the study. The air was warm, the windows were open on the field of stars. Across the street a sick-room light burned dimly in a red shade. He turned on his reading lamp, lit a cigarette and tried to read, but that was no good. His thoughts were ordered, ready for examination, and he could no longer shy away from thinking. He knew now that the happiness he had must come to a stop. He did not think he was ready to end it at once; but he must tell her soon. That morning he had known, before David had spoken, that he could no longer make God a matter of geography. He could not walk out of his church, as he had done for so long, and bar the door; and if he could feel the reality of God in his own house only through suffering, then he would have to suffer. It was not that love had seemed to him suddenly a lighter thing; if anything it seemed to him heavier, an equal weight in the balance, something good in itself (it would have been easier, could he have felt that it was evil) to stand against something which was better. What did amaze him, when he thought about it, was that most people would expect him to give up love without question, in obedience to the rules. A moral stringency was merely expected from a priest, not admired in him. He was more than a man; or had agreed, when he was ordained priest, to behave for the rest of his life as if he were. And the choice was made young.

It occurred to him that his decision must be harder on Alice than himself. She was bound by no rules: she had not even a belief to cling to. She had partially deceived herself that they were doing no wrong, were harming nobody, since they were not lovers in the flesh: she would be the last to give him credit for the agony of a decision, she would attribute it to a love less than her own. And this would be the hardest thing of all.

A late car went by the study windows, sweeping its lighthouse beam over the square. Across the road, the sick-room lamp went dark. A cat, shut out, started to mew with a tongueless but human note.

Maurice heard footsteps, and he felt his flesh shrink. He could not talk to Libby now, not at this moment; for she knew about him, he had guessed that. She had been strung to the limit by her resolve not to speak.

It was not Libby, it was Kate. 'I couldn't sleep either. Mind if I join you?'

He asked her how she knew he was up. She had been restless, she replied, she had looked out of the window for diversion and had seen the study light shining out across the pavement. She sat down opposite him, relaxing into the chair as if her bones had softened.

'I shall be up and about my work soon,' she said. 'I may as well get hardened. Shall I make tea? This seems to me rather like a midnight feast.'

He found enough sherry left in a bottle for a glass apiece. 'This will do instead.'

'And somehow it seems more wicked,' said Kate. 'By the by, I traced him. He is working in Liverpool. But he hasn't sent for his things yet.'

Maurice said nothing.

'I shall wait a bit. Meanwhile, get on with my chores.'

There seemed, for a while, nothing to say. He felt an odd charm in this hour of mutual unhappiness; it was snatched, as everything treasured by him had been snatched. She was as neat as ever, it was not like Kate to be dishevelled or slovenly, even in the small hours. Her red woollen gown was put on neatly, her hair was combed.

'I was thinking,' she said at last, 'that our sort of trouble, yours and mine, must be very piffling in the light of all that is happening in the world. Just before I was ill, I had an idea — it was a highly visual one — of everything falling into destruction. I suppose it must happen some day, though nobody really believes it. If you give a child a penknife, he has to stick it into something—— I say, you've no conception of what it was like — my idea, I mean. I had it in the middle of Penywern Road. I never knew my imagination could be so graphic. Maurice' — she leaned forward to touch his knee, and her eyes shone as if in pride of one of her sons who had been clever — 'it was quite extraordinary! But if men have the means to destroy each other in bulk, they must obviously do so, don't you think? Before which fact,' she added with a light air, 'our own problems are negligible. I wish, anyhow, that I could believe they were.'

'We are all in the hands of God,' he said. 'We must hope that he will restrain us from doing the obvious thing.'

'You honestly believe — it is absurd for me to ask you this, but I have to — that he could?'

'I know he could. I only hope he will.'

Kate thought about this for a little while, then suggested that man was perhaps not the happiest of inventions.

'Not the happiest, perhaps. But not bad. When I see what we have already invented and domesticated, I don't think so poorly of us. Having made an infinite number of motor cars, we still manage to get about the streets. I am struck by that sometimes.'

'What sort of hope have you? — For my ears, not for Libby's, or Mother's, or for the congregation's.'

'Much hope,' said Maurice. 'There are far more sensible men around than one thinks.'

'And for yourself?'

He looked at her. Her face had changed.

'For me personally?'

'Yes.'

'Not a lot.'

'You're in love with Alice Imber, aren't you?'

'Yes.'

'And you see her.'

'Yes,' said Maurice. 'And that is all.'

She threw her cigarette away. The butt stood upright on the bars of the grate for a moment before toppling. 'Now if I had tried to do that, I couldn't have done it in a thousand years. What shall you do?'

'I shall have to stop seeing her.'

She broke out bitterly, 'Is that easy? I don't find that it is.'

'It's the hardest thing on earth.'

'It can't be, or you *could not* do it!' She added, 'But you haven't done it, yet.'

He shivered, and said nothing.

'Upstairs, just now,' she continued, in an almost conversational tone, 'I had the horrors. When the wind is blowing this way you can hear a very faint hum of machinery. I don't know what it is, but it goes on all night. I got it into my head that it was a cranking up for something that was to happen to us all, that it was right outside the world, that nothing would stop it. I found myself cowering in the bed as if I didn't want to be seen. And when I tried to think about the people near me, to tell myself that they were peacefully asleep, that no horrors had occurred to them at all, I couldn't believe it. They were all cowering like me: so was everyone in the street outside: so were millions of people shut in their houses all over the world, with their heads under the blankets. Do you know that there are moments when the truth cracks open and we see right inside? Thank God there aren't many moments like it.'

He told her she had been ill; it had been a dream of illness.

'Maurice, we could not dream it if it weren't true. How could we possibly make it up?'

The desk-light went out. At that moment another car went by, sweeping the room with its brilliant lamps. Kate cried out.

'Wait.'

He went to the door and turned the top light on.

'That's better, isn't it?'

'Oh, that's better,' she said, trembling, 'it just shows one mustn't sit in the half-dark. That's always a very tricky thing to do.'

After that she talked a little longer, ramblingly, about household affairs, slating Libby's ineptitude with a freedom she seldom allowed herself. He let her go on, until at last she said, 'Thank you, I feel all right now. I'm going up. Are you?'

'Soon.'

Before she left him, she moved her fingers along his face. 'I know what it must be like. I couldn't be sorrier. Believe me, I am *for* you.'

Chapter Thirty-eight

A WORD too quick or too slow; a gaze a little too steady; too great a start to attention, too sympathetic an eye, too prompt a change of subject. By all these things he could sense the rumours surrounding him. He was an island in a river of talk. When he went into the pulpit there was a little rustle, not of whispering, but of a slight shifting of bodies on well-rubbed wood. The air seemed to rise and then to settle; a change of pressure had been achieved.

Libby said nothing, but sat in her pew with a special smile on her face, bright and unblinking. At home she treated him with great politeness. She wore a strange air that was somehow a little merry. They did not talk in bed any more. The moment she had said her prayers, she sighed 'Oh, I'm tired!' and, jumping into bed, lay down and screwed her eyes up tight. Every night he waited for it: 'Oh, I'm tired!' Every night it came.

Even the hospital visits were tainted; the sick had relations in the parish. Only his churchwardens, his treasurer and his secretary seemed to know nothing, their manner towards him unchanged. How much of it was real and how much was his imagination he could not tell, but he knew imagination was the least of it. In the late spring of that year he went around like a cat on hot bricks, trying not to placate by a smile or a word. He did not tell Alice about it. His time with her was short, and too precious for soiling; it was always easy to pretend, when he was with her behind the high soft flower of their window, that there was no world elsewhere.

A week had gone by since he had talked with Kate in the

study. She was furiously at work again, elbowing Libby out of the way, refusing to let her mother do so much as a little silver-cleaning. She now worked through her headaches, going blindly about, her eyes half shut, her lips screwed together. She would not rest. So far as Maurice knew, she had not heard from Westlake, and she did not mention him.

She was regular at early service, releasing Libby, as she put it, 'for higher things', and afterwards she brought David home to breakfast. 'We have a house full,' she said, 'we might as well make it fuller.' David, who got a good enough breakfast in his own lodgings, was uneasy, and Maurice was uneasy when he was near. A broken friendship, he felt, was not half so worrying as one in suspension. The emotion was there still, the drag of affection and anxiety; but words had dried up and there were no more straight glances. He was trying to think of nothing but the immediate moment (at eight o'clock, on a coldish morning, half his mind was on the dusty window-sills, and on the church cleaners who would never think of touching them), the immediate job in hand. It was an effort. He began to have the illusion that he was wearing a hat and that it was too tight. He found himself putting a hand surreptitiously to his scalp, trying to loosen it.

One morning Kate said at breakfast, 'I daresay you can all get along without me for a couple of days. I'm going to Liverpool. I'll be back some time to-morrow night.'

'Oh, Kate!' Libby burst out. 'You were going to take the Mothers' Union for Mrs. Walkeley!'

'Well, I can't. You'll have to.'

'You're not going to run after that man?'

'Yes, I am. And it's my business.'

'It's degrading.'

'I dare say so. I've told the boys, by the way.'

'Told them what?'

'That I want to see him. Naturally they are not enthusiastic.'

Libby said the boys must think she was mad.

'I do not care what they think. The company of children isn't enough for me.'

255

Mrs. Marsden rose and came round the table. She rested her hand on Kate's neck, and Kate shied away from it. 'Now I want you to promise me you'll do no such thing. I know I'm old, but I have seen life — as I say to Libby, "It's the experience that counts, even in silly old women", and I'm going to stop you doing something you'll regret.' She smiled like a fairy godmother, bursting out of a dim disguise to do good undreamed of. The smile quilted the corners of her mouth, made her eyes sparkle.

Kate shot up from her chair. 'Mother! Do you seriously think that, at my age, anything you say could have the slightest effect on me?'

'You have not,' Mrs. Marsden said firmly, 'been well.'

'Maurice! Stop them! Make them stop. They're treating me as if I were off my head!'

He began to speak, but Libby cut across him. She addressed Kate. 'Have any of us got the *money* to spare for fares to Liverpool?'

Kate breathed hard. 'Good God, I'm not asking you to go!'

Maurice said, 'That's enough. She has a right to do as she pleases. And I am sick of scenes.'

Libby protested: it was not her fault, nor her mother's. They had a duty to Kate.

'You have to me,' he said, 'to keep my house quiet.'

And indeed he was carried away by the longing for quietness: it seemed to him that his grievance against them all was unanswerable, it had been growing for years, it was now crying like blood from the ground.

'Oh?' said Libby. 'And haven't you any duty to me?'

She walked out. He followed her into the study.

'What is it?' he asked her.

He knew, she said, he knew. There wasn't any need for her to tell him. Well then, if he insisted, she would: she knew what everyone else did, that he was unfaithful to her. She repeated, 'Unfaithful', in a loud flat voice, and she clenched her hands at her sides. 'A priest,' she said, so softly that he could scarcely hear her.

'It is utterly untrue,' Maurice said.

She told him that she had been loyal to him always: a vicar's drudge, content to drudge, so long as she had his love and his gratitude. The trouble with him was, he had no imagination. He was conceited! That was what it was, conceited. There were always women after a parson, that was a commonplace — sly, frustrated women, lurking like alleycats. The parson's wife was supposed to look on and smile. But *she* was different. Didn't he know she was different? She didn't want to boast, but she was not bad-looking, some people even thought she was beautiful. Was he so blind as not to see that *she* had resisted temptation, time and time again? 'Do you think I haven't been admired?'

He was so taken aback by all this, so shocked by the bitterness of her imaginings, that he found himself saying, 'Who by?'

She brought up her head. Her face blazed at him, the colour mottling her forehead and lying down the vee of her dress. 'Do you think I'd tell you? I'm loyal. To me that sort of thing just doesn't *matter*. George Kitson's always looked at me, if you must know: I could have had him by lifting my little finger. And even Fawcett—yes, Fawcett!'

He could think of nothing to say to her.

'But you,' she went on, 'you've betrayed me, and your vows, and everything, with that beastly woman who was always throwing her money about. You go and sneak off and visit her——'

'Libby!'

She stopped, biting her lip till her chin shook.

'It's untrue,' Maurice said. 'I wouldn't lie to you. At least, the worst is untrue. But I do see her sometimes and talk to her. That is all.'

'Oh, what a thing to ask anyone to believe!' Her tone was light, a tone almost of raillery. She took a dancing step.

'But you have to believe it, don't you?' Taking her hands, he made her sit down. 'I shall tell you what there is to it, if you will listen.'

She drew her hands away and wiped them carefully on her handkerchief. 'Of course I shall listen. I should like to.' She

257

looked at the butcher's calendar on the wall, a view of the Lake District, with what appeared to be an awakened interest. She might have been an art dealer who had suddenly suspected Giorgione.

He told her, then, about everything except the meeting at Trumpington. He did go and talk to Alice, sometimes only for a few minutes, never for more than an hour. It meant a great deal to him to do so; he felt he could not bear to have so little taken away from him.

'You are in love with her.'

'All things pass,' he said, 'even that.'

'Oh, so I can see! Do you think *I* wouldn't realise it?'

'There has been nothing more. There never will be.'

She said, as if idly, 'I hope you don't discuss me.'

'No.'

'You left me right out of it, I suppose, as if I didn't exist!'

'Libby,' he said, 'you can't have it both ways.'

'I don't know how you could.'

'I've done you no harm.'

'Oh yes, you have!' She was quick with this. 'You've given her everything I care about. If you had slept with her, what would that be to me?'

In a sense it was true enough, and he knew it. She had not wanted physical love from him, but she had wanted all love besides it. And it was this he had taken away from her and given to Alice.

'It's silly,' he said, 'to pretend that the physical has no importance. Of course it is important. It is the absolute intimacy. And I haven't given that.'

Now she gave him a steady, earnest look: she was an enquiring pupil. 'What I can't imagine,' she said, 'is what you *do* find to talk about.' She put her head on one side.

He did not answer.

'Of course, I realise I'm not much good to you in that way. I'm too tired. At the end of the day I can't stop my mind racing over all the household and parish worries. Probably they have made me narrow, but that isn't my fault. Women like Mrs.

Imber, who have nothing else to do, are usually wonderful talkers.' She paused. 'But,' she added, 'though I am trying to believe you, though I can almost sympathise with you, wanting to get out of this zoo of a house, you will have to stop it, won't you? You must see that I can scarcely be humiliated in public. In private, I shall have to put up with it.'

She was emboldened by his silence, excited by it. 'So,' she said, 'I want you to ring her up and tell her *now* that it is to stop. I'll go out of the room while you do it.'

He had truly meant to bring things to an end: now he felt that he could not. He said, 'In my own time.'

She answered him sarcastically, her eyes flashing, hand sprayed at the nape of her neck. She was parading the one quality she could be sure of, that Alice could never match. Maurice struggled against rage, raced his thoughts towards Libby's essential rightness: for she was in the right, she was betrayed, he had humiliated her.

He told her he could not talk about it any more, not now. They would talk again later. He knew that if only she would go out of the room he might be able to keep his temper.

She dropped her hands to her side. She said solemnly, 'Wouldn't it be a good idea if we both prayed?'

He went by her, opened the door. 'I'll try.'

'After all,' said Libby, her lips quivering, 'we aren't ordinary people. We have special resources. I think we ought to pray *together.*'

He left the house and walked around for a while, to steady himself. Rage and shame struggled for the upper hand. Everything she claimed was right, everything she said was wrong. Yet they were together, they must always be. Somehow he had to come back to the realisation of that, to look at it squarely and to accept what it must mean to him, not over days, weeks, months, years, but for the rest of his life. He thought of the music Plym had played in the church, last time he and David had been there alone together. *Komm, Süsser Tod.* It had told him that death could be beautiful, a soft lying down and a grateful closing of the eyes. It need not be like old Imber's dying, the frantic, terrified clutch at the lips of a black and crumbling hole, with a fire burning below: or else nothing at all. He felt very cold, walking along the streets on that grey, moist morning. All was vanity, since love decayed with the body, and beyond love only the empty years stretched out, rheumaticky and food-loving, fretted with the silly resentments of old age. Men had died and worms had eaten them, but *not for love*: curious words for a comedy. Millions had died by fire, by bombing, by torture, by starvation, had died in the past twenty years of his own time: but not for love. Four hundred years ago they had died at the stake, curling into the flames in agony or in ecstasy, according to what sort of men they were; but not for love. The ring of iron was too short for the girth of John Hooper so he pressed his hand to his belly and obligingly pushed it in, saying he would be all right. Maurice stood still for a moment, made giddy by the downward glance.

'Mucky day,' said Mrs. Fraser, 'it doesn't look like we're going to get any summer.'

Her gaze explored him. Then she turned away and went into a shop.

Chapter Thirty-nine

'EXCELLENT,' Kitson said, and seemed to count all heads. 'All here.'

There were not many heads to count, only three besides his own.

He said he hoped not to keep them long. There was a matter that must be discussed, and he felt it better that for the moment it should remain among the four of them. 'Unorthodox, I know, but I think you may agree that unorthodoxy's best in this case.'

He had summoned them by telephone. They had gathered after dinner in his brusque-looking flat, decorated with crossed spears, cowrie shells, and some matter-of-fact water-colours of reefs and seas. When they first came, his wife and son had been there, giving a social air to the gathering; but after ten minutes they had withdrawn.

'Nice-looking lad, yours,' Hannaway said, 'got a fine brow. Getting on all right?'

'No,' said Kitson, 'he's bone-idle. But he may take a turn yet. Whiskey?'

'No, thank you, dear boy. Just a little of that orange-squash, if I may. Never drink after dinner.'

'I do,' said Fawcett, 'the only time it does no harm. I suppose it has a basis to rest on. Now Louisa is precisely the reverse: she's quite obsessive about having a drink or two at six o'clock, and then she stops.'

Johnson-Black said he did not imagine Kitson had called them together for a symposium upon their drinking habits. 'If it's about Fisher,' he said, 'which I hope it isn't, I shall have to withdraw.'

'It is about Fisher, and you can't. None of us can blink what's going on.' Kitson leaned up against the wall. Without taking his eyes from his guests, he drank half a tumbler of whiskey and water, then shoved the glass back on to the tray, with no apparent intention of refilling it.

'Now look, my dear man,' Hannaway said eagerly, 'you know I'm the last to be a stickler for the conventions. But so far as I'm able to judge, the person concerned should be present when this sort of thing comes up. We can't go behind his back.'

'I am trying to save the person concerned a damned disagreeable meeting.' Kitson's look remained steady. 'This is unofficial and preliminary.'

'If I had known——' Johnson-Black began, and half rose.

'You did know. Of course you did. I said it was urgent, and there's only one thing of the slightest urgency going on in this parish at the moment.'

Hannaway said, 'As we are all here, we might as well have it out. We'd look foolish if we didn't, don't you think?' He settled himself comfortably, tasted his orange-drink and remarked that it was delicious, far better than the stuff his wife got from her grocer.

Kitson said, 'Let me state the case.' He did so, calmly, fairly, with no appearance of passing judgment. He himself, he added, was concerned for one thing only: that no stigma of any kind should touch the Church. He was not, he had never pretended to be, much of a moralist. He believed a man's morals were his own affair, just so long as they did not become a matter for public concern.

The Church did its job in keeping people on the rails, but could only do so if its leaders were seen to be on the rails themselves. He was not — he preferred straight speaking — accusing Fisher of an adulterous relationship——

'I hope you're not,' said Johnson-Black.

'—I said I was not. But I am suggesting that his behaviour is causing wide concern and giving rise to open scandal.'

Nobody spoke for several minutes after this.

262

Then Hannaway said gently, 'I still think this is a little improper, my dear George. I still think Fisher should be here to answer all this.'

'Surely George is only trying to save everyone a certain amount of embarrassment?' Fawcett locked his fingers behind his head. 'After all, we're not a court of morals. I take it his idea is that we should get the vicar's warden to make an approach to him *with* our backing.'

'I shall not make such an approach,' said Johnson-Black, 'I won't insult him by it. And by the way, Fawcett, how did you know what George's idea was? Had you two been in consultation before calling in Melvyn and myself?'

Fawcett flushed, and asked if this were important.

'I think it is. I have a feeling that there is a certain amount of ganging-up going on against Fisher.' It was a measure of the Colonel's anger that he used the slang-term: had he been less upset, he would have been cool enough to find another.

'Oh no,' Kitson said easily, 'oh no. I've talked about it with Jeremy, of course. Everyone has been talking about it: that's the trouble. If I thought we could handle the whole matter by behaving like clams, I should make precisely that suggestion.'

Johnson-Black knew him well enough to believe him. Kitson was something of a bigot, but not a sexual one. He was not in the least excited, and because of this might be the hardest to move; but Jeremy Fawcett was titillated, he smelled blood, he fancied a chase. As for Hannaway, he was an earnest and a simple enquirer, the one to be swayed.

'If we seem to be untouched by all this,' the Colonel said, with just that degree of weight which, if he could achieve it, might drop matters into place as neatly as the holing of a long putt, 'I think the talk will die down. Fisher is popular, and people trust him.'

'It's a regrettable fact,' said Kitson, 'but twenty years of popularity and trust won't stand for a moment against the impulse to kick the parson once he's found out.'

Fawcett said earnestly, with a gleam in his eyes, 'Also, people are going to take up cudgels for Mrs. Fisher. We know the feeling about *her*. She's the presiding genius to a lot of the women, anyway.'

'Then they are in error, dear boy,' said Hannaway unexpectedly. He looked around with his fiery smile, swept back his hair from high brown forehead. 'A nice woman, a very nice woman. But the burden is Fisher's, and far too much of it. I support Johnson. I still think silence is best.'

Fawcett asked, with the smoothness of anger, how long a term he proposed to such a silence. Wasn't it a mere lack of moral courage, to stick one's head in the sand? It was all right for Hannaway, even for Kitson, whose offices were purely administrative; but Johnson-Black was responsible to the vicar, and he himself to the people. His, he felt, was the harder part.

'Lord bless my soul, Jeremy,' said Hannaway, 'you young men! You're too stern for us, you make us too aware of our weaknesses. But even if I am aware of mine, I shall have to stand by them. They are really all I have, dear boy, I have to act by their light. And there are worse lights, I sometimes think, far worse.'

He got up.

'Well, that was a very nice drink, George. I must tell Dolly. *Sunray*, *Sunray*, that's what I mustn't forget. And now, if you'll excuse me, I must run along. Let me know what you decide. But if I were you, I really wouldn't decide, I really wouldn't.'

Fawcett said, 'Look here, we can't leave it like that——'

'We'll have to,' said Kitson. 'That is, for the moment. If Johnson-Black and Hannaway won't give their support to a general approach, there's nothing further we can do to-night.'

He did not seem at all upset by the failure of his meeting, nor give any indication that there were other plans in his mind. He accepted Hannaway's withdrawal with no more emotion than the chairman of a meeting might accept the result of a vote which was of no possible interest to himself.

Johnson-Black caught up with Hannaway in the street. 'I was glad you felt as I did.'

'Oh, but mind you! Mind you!' Hannaway raised his forefinger. 'Kitson may well be right. But I cannot, I will not sit in moral judgment. If it must be done, let stronger vessels do it. I have little fibre, and I've always been happy without it.'

The Colonel said he was unable to understand the attitude of Fawcett.

'It's the young, dear boy, it's the young. Tortuous, they are. And poor Jeremy is so eaten up by jealousy of that silly girl Louisa that he wishes to scourge all betrayers of the marriage-bed. Not that poor Fisher is one, of course, and not that Louisa's glance ever strays, so far as I know: but that's what is wrong. So foolish. So disagreeable.'

The Colonel considered all this in silence, and was humbled by the thought that other people knew so much more than he did. He had known the young Fawcetts casually since their marriage; but had never had the slightest idea what it might be like. He said tentatively, 'I was glad you made the point about Fisher doing too much of the work.'

'Well, my boy,' said Hannaway, trotting busily along at his side, 'one has eyes, one has eyes. A beast of burden, one has always seen it.'

They came to the block of flats in which he lived. Comfort shone out from behind the windows, far up into the rusty sky. Outside a public house on the corner, a group of boys and girls made music with a guitar and two washboards. It was a dank summer, and the girls wore jackets over their cotton dresses.

'The young, the young! Strictly between you and me and the gate-post, Colonel, I don't care for them. People think I do — must never let them know the truth — but I don't.' He smiled benevolently across the street at the music-makers. 'No man's much good till he's fifty. Well, let's hope all goes well with poor Fisher. One wishes him well, notwithstanding.'

'Notwithstanding what?' the Colonel asked heavily.

'Perhaps a small irregularity,' Hannaway replied, with every appearance of light-hearted sympathy. 'We are all men.'

He waved his hand, so close as to flick the Colonel's nose, and went indoors.

Johnson-Black went home to his wife, to whom, as usual, he told everything.

She turned upon him her large, wise eyes, their expression sympathetic but a long way away.

'Of course you must all keep quiet,' she said at last.

'Hannaway thinks there might be something in it.'

She said she would not blame the vicar if there were. Libby Fisher was one of those women who found one's raw edge and ran her finger-nail along it. 'If I can't bear her for fifteen minutes, how can he do so, day in, day out?'

Johnson-Black suggested that her attitude might be thought unsympathetic.

'Oh no,' she said positively, 'it is a statement of fact. But I am desperately sorry for dreadful people, because it isn't their fault that they are dreadful. They never know they are. I mightn't know if I was.'

'I would know,' said her husband, 'and you are not.'

Chapter Forty

THE birds on the Liver building soared against the cobalt sky, like portentous fowls of Rome. It should have been warm, but an east wind was battering the streets and giving people neuralgia. The moan of the shipping rose and fell over the city; there was the excitement of quick seas running to lands a long way away.

Kate believed she had never been so happy. She had been taught that a man should hook his hand beneath her arm; but instead she hung on Westlake's like a girl tripper, dragging him down to her, making him keep pace at her side. Her hair blew about and she thought that it became her. Here she was free and easy, triumphant, not a neat housewife, but a girl blown by the wind, assured of love, uncaring for her looks.

'If you miss your train,' he said, 'don't blame me——' but in the fond and teasing voice of one privileged to be blamed and to account for himself.

In fact, it was time they turned back towards Lime Street Station.

There may be a moment in the sexual life when, even after the years have seemed to offer experience of all possible pleasure, the body amazes. Joy touches a new peak with such ease and naturalness that all which has gone before is discredited, apprentice-work, no more than the possibility reflected. Kate had known it: and was filled with gratitude towards her lover because he had given her this release. She knew it was nothing to do with skill, or even with some additional force of love: it was arbitrary. He could neither have withheld nor offered it at his own will. Yet she could not escape the feeling that he had bestowed on her the highest gift within his power, had chosen her to receive it, had picked his time, and had given her absolute joy as a prince might have given her some absolute beauty in a pearl or a diamond.

The eye of her intellect was perfectly clear; with it she could see him as a man of fifty, worn by years and disappointments, his hair thinning, his flesh pulpy, wariness at the extremes of his eyes. It was true, and it did not matter. With the eye of love she saw him whole, touched only by the grace of time, not a flake of colour in his flesh that was not precious to her, remarkable, unique. That, also, was true.

They were on the platform, waiting for the time of parting.

'Now, you *are* coming back,' said Kate.

He said confidentially, 'My dear, if it were any good in this city, I shouldn't. But it isn't. I am at your disposal.'

'Would you be, if it were any good in this city?'

He slapped her bottom sharply, and jerked her against him. 'Would I, wouldn't I—— Oh, mind your own business! What are you going to say at home?'

'I don't know.' She did not, but was untroubled. She would find words. It would all work out for her somehow.

'Get in,' he said, 'and behave yourself. Don't pick up strangers on the way. I'll know if you do.'

She was both repelled and delighted by his new tone of confidential vulgarity. He was not vulgar; but by pretending to be so he established his triumph over her, he put her firmly in her place. Last night, before giving her pleasure, he had made her cry, had taken his time about it, had slowly, methodically reduced her determination to stand straight at his side, his equal at least. He was not having that. He had taken too much at her hands to allow her equality in private, whatever their public relations might be.

'That's enough from you, my lad,' she said in a hearty voice that sounded feeble in her own ears. She could not look at him without catching her breath; the memory of the night stood firm between them.

268

She leaned down from the carriage window and they kissed.
'Promise you'll be back next week,' she said.
'I dare say I shall.'
'Say you will.'
'Going, going, gone,' said Westlake, stepping back. The whistle blew.

It was curious that he should have made the joke about not picking up strangers, because it was just what Kate, normally the most reserved of women, felt impelled to do. She was so full of happiness that she needed to communicate it. Within half an hour she had struck up an acquaintance with a leather salesman; within an hour had brought him to a generalised discussion of the proper relationship between men and women, and had accepted his offer of lunch. Afterwards she had to snub him and move to another carriage, but even this she had carried off with grace.

The world through the window seemed extraordinary to her in its beauty, the brilliance of the fields of corn and mustard, the dazzle of the rivers, the race of the cloud shadows, brown and violet, over the roundness of the land. Children waving were strong and lovely, the ugliest towns were beautified by the sun and by the love that she imagined beneath their roofs. Nothing tired her. She had forgotten to buy papers, but she did not need them. When she came to London it seemed to her that the crowds along the streets were participating in some slow, mysterious ritual dance, each gesture symbolic of an aspect of love.

She could not find her key. While she was fumbling for it, Maurice opened the door to her. 'All right?' he asked her doubtfully.

She put her hand on his arm as if to steady herself, as a dancer might when the music came to an end. 'Quite all right, dear.'

'Is he going to stay there?'
'No.'

He asked her if she were tired. She shook her head. 'But I'm dirty, I must have a wash. Are the boys all right?'

He told her they were out with friends.

'Good. Bless you.'

She went on upstairs, moving as quietly as she could, hoping not to disturb Libby. She knew there would be questions, that everyone would make trouble for her, including the boys. Well, she was not going to provoke more of it than she needed. Looking at herself in the glass, she saw her eyes still feverish and sparkling, the colour still in her cheeks. The sight fascinated her. She soaped her hands slowly, cleaned her nails, not withdrawing her gaze from her own eyes.

When she went downstairs supper was ready and Libby was on the sofa. 'I'm dead to the world,' she said. 'I'll eat here, if you don't mind.'

Westlake was not mentioned during the meal but Simon, when he came in, followed Kate up to her bedroom.

'Well,' he said, 'did you track him down?'

She told him not to stand there looking like Hamlet. He did not budge from the door. 'Well, did you?'

'Yes. He's coming back to London.'

'That'll be nice for you, I suppose.'

Yes, she said firmly, it would be: it meant that she had one friend; which was reasonable, scarcely a social whirl.

He smiled then, and came to sit on the stool before her dressing-table, where he puddled around with a display of interest among her few cosmetics. 'Phew!' he said, as he opened a bottle of setting lotion, 'what a stink!'

'Put that down, will you?'

'A boy at school knows him, or his father knows him. He says he drinks.'

'A bit, yes. He's not a drunkard.'

'I think drink tastes beastly,' said Simon.

'Good. I'm pleased to hear it.'

He got up. 'Oh, all right. Glad everything was O.K.' It was an effort to him to say it, and her heart went out to him. She decided she could tell him nothing yet awhile; he would have to get used to Westlake by degrees.

He was given his first chance on the following Saturday,

when Westlake returned, earlier than she had expected, and telephoned her. He said in a bright, forced voice that he proposed to take the boys to the Zoo next morning, if they could get out of church. 'Do they like the Zoo, or are they either too old or too young for it?'

'They will have to like it,' she answered.

It was a dank day with a grey wind blowing. He had Fellows' tickets. There were few people about. Both boys began by trailing their feet.

Westlake was determinedly good with them, treating them neither as children nor, a lesser mistake but still a mistake, as men. He did not ask Simon how he was getting on at school, but having heard from Kate what his interests were, talked round and about them as if for his own benefit. For Dick's pleasure, he made slightly broad, simple jokes. The atmosphere began to thaw a little. They went into the rodent house, which, he assured them, was the most attractive of the lot; and persuaded the keeper, who knew him slightly, to let him take the galago out of its cage. It squatted between his gloved hands, looking at him with scared, toffee-coloured eyes. 'Stroke him,' Westlake said to Dick.

Dick touched the layered fur, gingerly, then lovingly.

'Can I hold him?'

'If you do it the way I show you. Otherwise, he'll bite you. He won't mean it, but he'll get frightened.'

The galago, escaping in transit from one pair of hands to another, sprang on top of the row of cages, bounding along them upright like a kangaroo. Simon, who had been pretending perversely that he was more interested in the Indian fruit bats, gave a shout of joyful laughter.

Westlake flushed with triumph. He caught the animal and gave him to Simon, who held him expertly and put his cheek to the fur, for a moment absorbed and unselfconscious.

It might be possible, Kate thought, for the four of us to be together.

They had lunch in the Fellows' Restaurant, overlooking the camels' clocktower. The gardens were filling up a little now, mothers pushing along the yellow pushchairs hired out to the smaller children.

Westlake had taken care to treat Kate on the same acquaintanceship level as the boys, but once, emphasising something which had amused him, he laid his hand for a second on hers: and she saw Simon flush and look away.

Idiot, she thought: it may have spoiled everything.

He, too, had seen the boy's withdrawal, for he said to her easily — 'Sorry', and began to talk to Dick of zoological rarities; he appeared to know a great deal about animals, and Simon, despite himself, was drawn to listen.

After lunch the rain fell so heavily that they had to stay in the roaring vaults of the lion house until it had lessened enough for them to run for their bus. Oddly enough, this dash through the wet seemed to do more for their unity than anything else. Westlake was short-breathed and ran heavily: Kate and the boys beat him to the gates and the boys triumphed.

'I say,' said Dick, 'you haven't got much speed, have you?'

Simon shrugged in his meaningless way, but he smiled.

Westlake went home with them but would not come in to tea. Kate, in an agony of impatience, waited to hear what they thought of him, hoping some stray word would give her the clue: but the moment they were indoors they appeared to forget about their day altogether, and went tumbling in to play the gramophone.

'How did it go?' Maurice asked her. As always, when he spoke of Westlake, he looked away from her.

'All right, I think. Yes, quite all right.'

He asked her if she were coming to church that night. Libby felt too tired, her mother had an attack of sciatica.

'Are you preaching?'

'David is.'

'Well,' said Kate, 'there's always a strange charm in that.'

He did not laugh. She looked at him and saw how strained he was, but took it for his customary weariness. She was still strung up by the anxious elation of the past few days and could think of nothing but herself and the new problem which had come to her. Alone upstairs, she relived the more violent moments of joy: the memory was still strong enough to give her a bodily reaction, spreading out like rings in a pond or the deep reverberations of a bell.

Chapter Forty-one

MAURICE repeated the Collect for the day, and heard them all listening, their listening breaths poured out upon the tense air of the evening.

'. . . and because through the weakness of our mortal nature we can do no good thing without Thee, grant us the help of Thy grace, that in keeping Thy commandments we may please Thee, both in will and deed. . . .'

He knew what they were thinking: Weakness of his mortal nature is just about right.

Johnson-Black and his wife sat bolt upright in their pew, their eyes tight shut, their hands brought down in prayer. He did not kneel because of his stomach-trouble, and she sat up to keep him company. The Kitsons slid half-off their seats, knees almost, but not quite, to the hassock. The Hannaways knelt properly and comfortably, as if they were taking a little nap. The Fawcetts rejected hassocks, and knelt rigidly on stone. In the front pew, Kate made her slight formal genuflection, but had forced the boys to thump down by pushing at their shoulders.

There was a larger congregation than was usual at Evensong, and Maurice fancied some of them had come for the kill. The moment that he finished the Collect he wished he could repeat it to them, for he had spoken mechanically, without thought except for himself.

He did manage, later, to make the prayer for the Clergy and People in a firm and minatory voice. He and the people, he felt, needed help, they no less than he. During the hymn preceding the sermon he saw that David was pale, singing out straight ahead of him without his customary quick glance of love at Lucy Simnett, who had been waiting for it. Throughout the whole church there was a feeling of wrongness. As he settled in his stall, he thought to himself that he would fight it by the defiance of silence, the defiance of his refusal to take action of any kind.

The sermon did not begin at once. Maurice looked up sharply, with a sense of disturbance.

David moved over to the right of the reading desk, as he always did, but did not lean in his usual confidential manner over the rail, pushing himself up on his toes to make himself look taller. Little, tense, he stood back an inch or so. He opened his lips, but no sound came out. He cleared his throat. The congregation rustled like dry leaves, and Maurice saw Kate crane her neck round.

Maurice thought, What is he up to?

When David did speak his voice was pitched too high; he had to jerk it down again after the first two or three words. '"Through the weakness of our mortal nature",' he said. 'Yes, indeed. And to-day we are going to try to face up to that weakness and know ourselves for what we are.'

The Pelhams shot scared glances at each other; they were quick off the mark.

Dear God, don't let him do it, Maurice prayed. This is not the kind of help I want. Let him change his mind.

'You all of you know,' David continued on a chatty and more familiar note, 'how easy it is not only to speak evil of our neighbour but to believe what we are saying. We don't so often speak because we believe, but start to believe because we have spoken. To take away a reputation is easier than picking a pocket, and, except in the rare cases brought before the courts of law, carries no penalty.'

Maurice felt the sweat break out, first on his neck and fore-head, then on his cheeks. He wanted to wipe it away, but dared not. He believed it must be glistening in the sallow light for all to see. This was appalling: he had never expected this, this blow innocently dealt out of loyalty, lovingkindness, and the desire to please.

David was making it clear now, to gossip-mongers, slanderers, self-appointed judges, that if they were to look into their own hearts they would find little cause for self-congratulation. He was feeling better now, getting into his stride. Possibly, Maurice thought with a flicker of humour summoned to give himself courage, he had that bishopric in mind again.

'When we speak evil of a neighbour, condemning him for his apparent guilt upon a single occasion, do we try to balance it against all the good we have known of him? The charity, the selflessness, the untiring endeavour on our behalf?' He made a dramatic pause. 'No, we do not.'

It was perhaps a mistake for Maurice to have allowed humour in. It was turning against him into a kind of hysteria; never, he thought, had he heard anything so funny in his life.

The congregation by now appeared to have settled into the placid enjoyment of something quite out of the way.

'*No, we do not,*' David repeated, and at that moment was interrupted by a clatter: Mrs. Fraser's umbrella had rolled off the seat on to the flags. Maurice saw her bend to pick it up.

'We do not, because we seldom manage to think of more than one thing at a time. That is one of our mortal weaknesses. But do we take this into account, when our tongues are hasty, when we are eager to believe the devil himself because he often seems a more exciting counsellor than God?'

Maurice was gripping the edge of his stall. David's rhetorical questions and answers were more than he could bear, as he sat there with their eyes upon him; if the answer this time was, 'No, we do not,' he believed he would laugh aloud, and go on laughing till he had no more breath, till they were all on their feet, all asking one another to run for a doctor.

'We do not take it into account,' said David mercifully.

He went on for another fifteen minutes without rhetoric but with extreme clarity. No one in his senses could have imagined that his sermon was general in application, nor that it could have applied to any other person but his vicar. It was true, Maurice told himself, that the number of persons present who could make anything of it at all, since the range of gossip was necessarily limited, might be no more than twenty-five per cent: anyway, he hoped it was no more.

David's little face glowed pink as he rose, literally rose, since he had heaved himself onto his toes and had at last hung himself over the edge of the pulpit, to his peroration. Lucy Simnett had ceased to look worried, and was beatific, intensely proud of him and sure of his future.

'So let me leave with you the words: "Judge not, that ye be not judged." Familiar words, aren't they? One might almost say hackneyed. But at our peril we forget them, and at our peril we forget the charity we owe our fellow man, not only the least of our fellows, but also the most prominent among them.'

He skipped down, casting at Maurice one brave, exalted glance. The congregation reared up with its after-sermon uncoiling movement and attacked the hymn vigorously, books held at breast-level, backs brought in sharply to the waist-line. It had been a stimulating evening. Now that the rain had ceased, the sun was pouring orange and rose and gold through the clerestory windows, and the congregation seemed to soar upwards through the torrent of light as in some mass apotheosis.

As Maurice spoke the Benediction, he heard the tiredness in his own voice. He knelt in prayer, half wishing that he might never rise again, but pass from this sleepiness into nothing at all.

He raised his head, put out a hand and levered himself up. They rose at varying rates to varying heights, looking, for the fraction of a second, like skyscrapers in the evening glare of Manhattan island.

Plym burst into the voluntary. It was all over now, that was, the event: only the consequences were to come.

It seemed at first as if there would be none. Maurice could not speak to David or meet his eyes. He made his usual race to the doors and was at hand to greet the exiting crowd. The greetings were as usual. Nobody stared, nobody who normally greeted him made any attempt to slip past. The leaves of the square, still surfaced with rain, were scarlet with the falling sun. The road surfaces were red and wet as the flesh of figs.

Kate sent the boys on ahead and waited to walk home with him.

'Well,' she said, 'that should have put the cat among the pigeons. Has he gone mad?'

'He expects me to be pleased. It's extraordinary that he should.'

'I shouldn't ask you this: but I must know. How much is there in it?'

'Of what they're thinking, nothing.'

'No, I didn't really suppose so. Poor old boy.'

He said sharply, before he could stop himself, 'I will not give up a friend, and that's that.'

'We are sad people, we do everything wrong.' She opened her lips as if she meant to say something else, but closed them again.

Next morning, after early service, he said he would not return to breakfast: he wanted to speak to David.

'Well,' David said uncertainly, 'come and have breakfast with me. My Martha can manage an egg.'

They went down to his basement room; they had not spoken on the way.

'I've put my foot in it,' David said at last.

Maurice told him that how he could do such a thing was beyond his comprehension. His voice was bitter; he could feel nothing of the old affection.

David sat on the shabby club-fender and looked forlorn, almost as if he might cry. 'I thought they deserved it.'

'Did you also think I did?'

The landlady came in with the tray, which she set on the table. They managed some sort of chat about church affairs, knowing she would have smelled quarrels in a silence. Luckily for them, she was not a churchgoer; she was unlikely to know anything about yesterday's sermon.

When she had gone, David said, 'I wanted to walk into them. You couldn't possibly have believed that I meant you any harm.'

'I couldn't have believed you would have been so damned stupid.'

'It might,' David mumbled, 'have passed most of them by.'

'It wasn't meant to pass them by. — Yes, I'll have some tea. I can do with it.'

Maurice drew his chair up to the table. He had the hunger of acute anxiety.

'You know I'm sorry; I don't have to tell you. I don't have to tell you how much I've admired you, how grateful I've always been. I wish I could cut my tongue out.'

Maurice said impatiently, 'A pity you didn't do it this time yesterday. Now you've brought everything crashing down on me, through your idiocy.'

David pushed his plate away. He was red with distress, his hands were trembling: but when he spoke it was not without dignity. 'I don't suppose you'll want me much, after this. I'll go as soon as I can find something. I'd rather.'

'You'd rather go than what? I don't feel like offering you an alternative. Yet,' Maurice added, his anger suddenly and mysteriously subsiding, 'it seems incongruous to say that to a man whose breakfast you happen to be eating.'

David gave a high, hysterical laugh, then fell silent, the beginnings of a smile upon his face which he could either encourage or quell, according to what happened next.

Nothing happened, except that Maurice poured another cup of tea and reached for toast. David, who had eaten nothing, tentatively drew his egg towards him and cracked the shell. They both went on eating. When they had finished, Maurice offered his cigarettes.

'I feel rather better now.'

'I wish I did,' said David.

'There's no question of your going, that is, unless you really want to and can get something a good deal better than this.'

'There's no question of me wanting to. I mean, of course I don't.'

Maurice smiled and felt almost happy. For some reason, the old comfort lying between them was restored; he hoped

David felt it too, though it would be something like thought-transference if he did.

'If there's anything I can do——' David began.

'For God's sake don't do anything. We must weather things somehow, even if Sandeman appears on the scene. Of course, there may just possibly be nothing to weather, though I'm not optimistic.'

He wondered why he should have this impulse of happiness, realised that it was because of the thing he had been jolted into telling Kate: that he would not give Alice up. He couldn't and wouldn't, no matter what happened. She was his whole life and there was nothing besides her.

'Dare I confess,' said David, with a touch of the old, arch gleam, 'that I detest Sandeman?'

'I detest Sandeman, too. In my less regenerate moments I even think he is a bad man.'

They went together up the area steps and stood in the sun.

'Look, Maurice,' David said, doing penance by forcing himself to the name, 'I know it was a bad idea now. But it did seem a good one at the time.'

'I think we won't worry about it any more. Let others worry for us, which others assuredly will.'

Chapter Forty-two

THE idea had been with her all the week, not as a practical one on which she could possibly act, but as a thick and angry fantasy. She had carried it with her through her waking hours and, once, into a dream, elaborating it as she went, arranging precisely the way it should begin and the way, through questions and answers all pat, it should continue. The ending was beyond her; she could not conceive it, frame the correct words of peroration, the other's words of cession. In a curious way, this gave her the first happiness she had known for some time. The idea itself was bad, made out of heat and darkness, dangerous to approach; but once the threshold was passed there was comfort and stillness inside of it, an echo-chamber, where the words flowed back and forth, perpetually soothing and far away.

She was insulated by it from the normal and abnormal life of her household; from her mother complaining of palpitations, from Kate going about silent and glowing, from Simon's retreat into one of his black phases, from Maurice's shuttlecock routine activities and from his anxious courtesies. None of it mattered. She began to snatch ten minutes extra time each day at her dressing-table, to make herself look even more beautiful for the impossible event. She examined her face and neck minutely for any new signs of age. The skin of her throat seemed to her a little crepey, so she massaged it with cold cream. She pulled out a few grey hairs at her temples, she fancied some slight discoloration in her cheeks, a flick too purplish or too pale, and she bought a heavy foundation lotion to cover it up. She was in training like a soldier: but there would not be a battle.

She would not have believed that in her mind any real purpose was hatching; yet one evening, when she had come back from a brief appearance at the Young Wives, she went straight into the study and, still in her hat and mackintosh, dialled a number.

'Mrs. Imber? This is Elizabeth Fisher.'

It was done. She felt no shock of surprise, except a faint jolt of wonderment that all this time she should have borne within her the powerful intention she had quite failed to recognise except in the context of fantasy. She smiled as Alice replied, taken obviously off her stride, finding nothing to say but (in a breathless, high voice rising to something that was almost a squeak) — 'Oh, hullo. How are you?'

'I'm very well,' said Libby. 'And you?'

'Thank you.' Libby did not speak: so Alice went on, 'I haven't seen you for a long time.'

'That's just it. I'd like to have a word with you. May I look in?'

'Well . . .' A long pause. Then, 'Well, yes, of course. When would you like it to be?'

Libby suggested about nine o'clock that evening. She was delighted to hear equivocation at the other end; she had not really expected (in the dream had not expected) to have her enemy so completely on the run.

'I was going out,' Alice said, 'but I could put it off.'

Libby said the last thing she wanted to do was to cause the slightest inconvenience.

'I will put it off, it doesn't matter. All right, I'll look forward to seeing you at nine.' Another pause. 'How is everybody?'

'Maurice is worked to death as usual, poor dear,' Libby replied, rejoicing in ownership, 'it is really far too much. And he has anxieties on top of that.'

When she had hung up exhilaration deserted her, and she was terrified. She was committed now, by something not outside herself, but inside, a creature she could neither control nor expel. For a moment she felt she could not move, not even to go into the hall, to take her coat off. She sat there, holding her breath.

Then she heard her mother calling, and she went up.

'What is it?'

Mrs. Marsden marvelled that Libby could speak in so sharp a tone. She had had, she said, a bad day. She would have been in bed, if it had not been necessary to give the boys their tea. Kate ordered her work badly, she could well have got through it in the morning and not left others to carry the burden at teatime. The boys were too much of a strain, Simon was insolent and Dick noisy. And she did not like her palpitations: she could not describe just how they differed from the others, but differ they did.

'But what did you want?' Libby asked.

'Only to be sure you were in. I thought I heard you.'

'Well, you can go to bed now.' She saw that the old woman had a high flush, but saw it with detachment; it seemed no affair of hers.

'Perhaps you could help me.'

'Can't you wait ten minutes? I've had no tea myself.'

Libby went downstairs, and a few minutes afterwards heard a heavy fall. She ran up again. Mrs. Marsden was lying against the fender. Her armchair had skidded half-way across the room and had rammed itself up against the wardrobe.

'I was just sitting down to take my stockings off,' she said, 'and the castors slipped, or something, and I fell.'

'Oh, couldn't you have waited?'

'I was only taking my stockings off.'

Libby tried to help her up.

'No! I can't. I daren't move. I may have broken something.'

'No, you haven't. Come on.'

She put her hands under her mother's armpits and tugged, but the old woman was heavy. Libby shouted for Simon.

He came slowly upstairs, loafed whistling into the room. His face changed. 'What's happened?'

'Help me to get her on to the bed.'

Between them they managed it. She did not seem to be much hurt, but she was badly shocked. She stared from one to the other of them with pale eyes, and the flesh below her chin trembled.

Simon was walking round the room muttering to himself, 'Oh dear', and 'Tsk, tsk'.

Libby told him to be quiet and put the kettle on. When Mrs. Marsden had had tea she seemed better, but nevertheless rooted to the bed. Libby could have screamed. A long spell of invalidism and trays upstairs was more than she felt that she could bear, and the moment she heard the key in the lock she went racing down. It was Maurice and Kate, who had coincided on the doorstep.

'Oh, damn,' Kate said, dumping her basket on the floor, 'Oh, damn it all!'

'If she'd waited for me! She had *only* to wait. But no, she would try to undress herself, and now look what she's done! I was perfectly willing, perfectly——'

Maurice went up. When he returned, he said the doctor ought to see her, if only as a precaution. She was old, a fall was a dangerous thing.

Libby could think of nothing but how she was to get away if anything serious had happened. Kate would be at the Mothers' Union, since Mrs. Walkeley was ill. She could not leave Maurice to nurse her mother. What possible excuse could she make? She felt as if she were in a high fever, all faces ballooning and remote, all shapes distorted into something quite different.

The telephone rang and she answered it.

'It's the Archdeacon,' she told Maurice.

While he was still talking, the doctor came. He did not think the old woman had broken anything, but the ribs of her left side seemed tender. They had better keep her quiet, and he would come in again next day.

'He says he doesn't think it's *anything*, Mother, not anything, do you hear?'

Mrs. Marsden said nothing, but turned with a groan on to her right side.

Libby met Maurice coming out of the study and made her report. He seemed hardly to listen.

'Are you in or out to-night?' she asked him.

He said he would be in by eight-thirty. 'Why?'

Nothing, she said, she just wanted to know. He walked past her.

'What did the Archdeacon want?' she called after him, but he did not reply.

Mrs. Marsden slept under sedatives. Kate got supper, instructed the boys upon their proper bedtimes, and went out. Maurice had gone out already.

Libby looked in at her mother, who was wailing a little in her sleep, tidied the sheets and went to her own room, where she worked on her beauty with thought for it alone, frenzied, racing thought, wonderfully concentrated on this point, on that, on this, on that. If she thought about a person at all, it was about her mother; and she did so with such exasperation that it brought the tears to her eyes.

She could have waited just five minutes. Who had asked her to undress herself? It was not *fair*.

When Maurice came back, Libby was ready. She was wearing her best coat, and was hatless.

He asked her, with some surprise but little interest, where she was going.

'I am going out for a walk,' she said, 'quite a long walk. Mother's asleep, and if I don't get some fresh air I shall go *mad*.' Aware of the unusual emphasis in her voice, the exaggerated down-beat, she tried to pull herself together, to speak more easily: but he seemed to notice nothing out-of-the-way. 'Can you give an eye to her now and then? Simon's in the bath, Dick's in bed reading.'

'You look very nice, Lib,' said Maurice. He put a hand on her shoulder, touched his lips to her cheek. His mouth felt cold.

Then, for a space of time too brief for thinking, she felt an impulse to cling to him, to tell him she was not going out at all, to beg him to love her: but it passed, and she was in the street, walking briskly towards the buses.

285

She thought, when Alice opened the door, We are like two cats: and she nearly laughed.

'Did you have any difficulty in finding me?'

Libby did not reply. She had in fact had no difficulty: every day for a week she had looked up the street in Maurice's London guide, had put her forefinger to it as if, by obliterating the little parallels on the map, she could have obliterated the buildings themselves.

'Well, do come in,' Alice said awkwardly, 'and sit down.'

Libby was dazzled by the brightness. She even knew a momentary twitch of disapproval at this waste of electricity.

So this was where he came, into this smart, bright place, into this room of light colours only the childless rich could afford, into this snugness, this hidey-hole. Hidey-hole, she repeated to herself. She did not remember ever having used such an expression before. It seemed to her *le mot juste*, incomparable, a gift of encouragement and favour from God.

'This is a very nice little hidey-hole,' she heard herself saying aloud, 'how lucky you are!'

Accepting an invitation to sit, she kept her gaze on Alice's startled face. She crossed her legs to display their beauty, ran her hand along her calf. 'I don't smoke.'

'No, I remember, of course you don't.'

She thought Alice rather ugly, though her figure was good, and was able to despise her because she tried so self-consciously to make the best of what looks she had. The grey in her hair had been used by a good hairdresser to make a smart effect; and it was not the honest grey of a middle-aged woman, it had been rinsed to an ashy-blue. Not much lipstick: that was inverted ostentation. Perhaps she did not want to emphasize her little muzzle. Stuff on the eyelashes, yes, and on the lids too. Rather an old-looking dress, dark and straight, which once cost the earth. A good neck, long, very small arms, a bit monkeyfied.

Libby looked at Alice and hated her flesh: if for some reason she had been forced to touch it, she would have been sick.

'I usually do remember when people don't smoke. This is an uncommon lapse on my part.'

Libby went on smiling. For the moment she could think of nothing else to do, and it seemed to baffle her enemy.

Alice said, 'What did you come to say? I'm afraid there was something.'

Libby knew the first wave of fear: she conquered it, or seemed to.

She said, politely, almost cosily, as she had planned, 'Well, I do think it's miles better to be straightforward about things, and to talk them out rather than to have misunderstandings.'

Alice then gave quite the wrong cue. 'I suppose it is about Maurice.'

Libby's throat closed. Her mind was a wilderness, with no path clear.

'Maurice does come to see me sometimes. But we are not lovers and we never shall be.'

Libby heard a farcical voice proceeding out of her own mouth, uttering a speech from some bad play.

'I should hope you wouldn't.'

She saw that her enemy had recovered from the initial paralysis, that she was sitting easily, her hands clasped between her knees, her face sad, calm, with no ray of triumph.

'Well, that is the case. But I am in love with him, and I must tell you so. There's no hope for me at all, I should say. I can't take anything away from you. I am the one who will be left alone.'

Libby said tightly but conversationally that it would be rather too much to expect her to feel sorry, though she did see that Alice was in a difficult position. 'I have never doubted Maurice,' she added in a firm, full voice. 'But there is very grave scandal going about, and I can't have him exposed to that. You see, people know.'

'Are you sure of that?'

'Perfectly.'

Alice beat her hands quietly together three times, then clasped them.

'Well?' Libby asked.

'I can't say anything. I should have to talk to him first.'

'There must be no more talking,' said Libby, blessedly finding herself back in the play as she had written it. At that point she expected Alice to give way, to admit realisation of what she had done. Instead she got up, smoothed her skirt down and suggested that Libby should go. There was nothing more she could say without consulting him, and she could make no promises for herself.

'It's contemptible,' Libby told her softly, 'you're contemptible. Trying to break up a marriage is a sort of vulgarity, but putting a man like Maurice in danger is worse. I don't see where the "love" comes in.'

'It comes in. But otherwise you're right. I'm ashamed before you,' Alice said steadily, 'as I should be. And if only for that reason, I should like you to go now.'

'You are "ashamed before me"?'

'I said so.'

'Oh, how can you!' Libby burst out. 'This is all words, words, words! You don't mean a word you're saying. You're so sure of yourself, you can just talk.'

She was lost in the wilderness again: it was tossing around her, the sprigs flying back in her face. She was burning hot, freezing cold.

'You beastly woman!' she cried out, as if this were a culmination, with peace to follow it. She swung her body round so she should not see Alice any more.

'Oh, Libby!'

'Don't dare to call me that.'

'You're right, do you see? I admit it. But I can't say to you, "I'll never see Maurice again", I just cannot say it.'

'You, with all your clothes——'

'Please stop.'

'—and your blue hair.'

Alice opened the door. 'Please.'

'What have you got to give him but this sort of thing? It is a sort of snobbish thing.'

'I can only assure you that there was no harm.'

Libby rose, finding it an effort to do so, having to put both hands to the edge of the chair and push herself upwards. She straightened her coat, touched her hair and went past Alice into the hall. The outer door was open for her now. She went through it on to the landing.

'I'll call the lift,' she heard Alice say.

It would have been better to walk down the stairs, to go away at once, but she lacked the impetus even for that. Out of the corner of her eye she could see Alice's long arm, pale brown, with a very faint bloom along it, bluish almost in the diffused light, and her sickness returned. The lift rose up. 'I don't know how to work it,' she had to admit.

So they went down together, Alice carefully explaining the buttons, the precautions to be taken in closing the doors, as if it were her job to sell the machine. She walked with Libby to the outer door.

'It's raining. You'll get wet. Shall I lend you an umbrella?'

'I don't mind rain.'

Alice said, 'I expect it will come all right for you.' Her voice was so clear in its desperation that it rang along the street. She turned and went in.

Libby walked home. She could not take a bus because people would see the state she was in. Outside the vicarage, she stopped to blow her nose on a handkerchief already sodden with mucus and tears, dabbed powder over her swollen face. She meant to go in quickly, say she had a headache and be in bed, in the dark, before Maurice came up: but when he met her in the hall he did not notice her face at all.

He told her that her mother had woken in great pain, that the doctor had come and would get her into hospital next day. He now thought that there was a fracture: and that after an operation, healing might be very slow, weeks in bed, perhaps months. So Libby was able to cry at that, tears of pity, frustration and pure irritability obliterating the tears she had been so hard put to it to conceal.

Chapter Forty-three

'PERHAPS you don't know,' said Plym, 'but beau Sandeman has had him up and given him a talking to.'

He had summoned Alice to Golo's: he would not come to her flat, could not have her to his since his family were all over the place.

'Kitson told Sandeman because his heart was pure. And the vicar was in such a rage he told David, without the slightest regard for the fact that I was in the vestry. Which is how I know. And if you don't, you ought to.'

Alice simply stared at him, while the jazz thumped round and round them, and the dung-coloured coffee cooled under the neon lights.

'So you get out,' said Plym, 'or you should get out.'

She managed to speak, and when she did so the words came in a rush. She was glad to talk to someone, even if it were someone hostile: which Plym, in his tight-shut way, certainly was. Telling him of Libby's visit, she found herself doing so with vicious detail, alert, painful, sub-comic. She was too much hurt to spare anybody. She had, she felt, behaved well for long enough, but when she put this point of view to Plym he gave her a disagreeable smile.

'You've behaved well? You're rolling in it, you've got the world to choose from. What do you want with a wretched, overburdened parson with a cartload of relations and a hopeless end to it all?'

'You and I used to get on well. Why are you attacking me now?'

'I hate adultery,' Plym answered, 'old-fashioned tripe-hound that I am, I hate the grease of it, and the sneak of it, and I hate people who commit it — whether it's physical or emotional — because I have had the guts to prevent myself from doing just that. Also, I like it here. I like the church, I like my job, though I ought to have a better one, and I like Maurice Fisher, even if I can't stick the Queen of Love. That's what she is, you know, one of those medieval pussies who kept sending chaps out on tomfool neckbreaking errands and giving them a heavenly smile and a mucky old sleeve when they got back. Off the point. What I meant to say was, I don't want you breaking up *my* life for me, or Fisher's. And everyone's talking about you now, you're the Scarlet Woman, the little home-breaker. Strip and tar you, they would, if someone made the suggestion and collected the materials.'

Leaning back as if exhausted, he swallowed his coffee in a gulp and pushed a cigarette at her between fingers browned and wrinkled with nicotine.

She paid no attention. She was hating him, because she knew his cruelty. He was humiliating her with delight, picking his smearing, tarring words as surely as he would pick out a tune on a piano. He hated her, too, as he would always hate anyone who bore elation in themselves; his own black humour made him appear high-spirited, but underneath it all was only disappointment. Yet she knew that, whereas normally she stopped seeing people she had come to dislike, she would always see Plym. He was a life-giver. It might be an ugly life that he gave, but it was life nevertheless. He teased, he stimulated, he put an edge on the nerves and made thought run quicker.

'Did you suppose I was committing adultery?' she asked him.

'Oh, don't try to fool your Uncle Reginald,' he said, with sudden savage vulgarity, '*I* believe it's all bee-ewtiful, all up in the head. But you're committing it all right, and the mess you're making is nobody's business. Why do you think I'm bothering about it?'

'Oh, to jab at me. Even at Cambridge, you liked to jab at people.'

Whatever lip-service Plym paid to the desirability of frankness, he was annoyed by this. That was damned nonsense, he told her in an airy voice, and only a tinpot mind could think it. He had admitted his own desire not to have a rumpus in the church. Couldn't she also credit him with having Fisher's good at heart?

'You've nothing good at heart.'

'How well we get on! Considering all the things we say to each other, how very well we do.' He called out, showing off, '*Cameriere! Il conto, per favore.* Sure you won't have another coffee?' he asked Alice.

She shook her head, and got up.

'You are a damned attractive woman,' Plym said, appraising her, 'which makes it all the more deplorable that you're after such miserable fish. "Thank Heaven for a human, or humble, whichever it is, heart, and let the foolish vicar go."'

She turned on him. 'Shut up, Plym! I can't stand any more.'

Courteously he settled her coat on her shoulders. They went downstairs together and through the cosmopolitan hubbub of the café. 'Why Kitson?' she asked him as they went out into Gloucester Road.

Kitson, he replied, was something nobody like herself (probably no woman) could ever understand. For him, the Institution was sacred, the established order more tenderly, more shyly adored than a boy's first love. A crack in it, and the whole might crumble: leaving for men such as Kitson only a desert of broken bottles, soiled newspapers and bones picked by carrion. 'It makes him tremble, the mere thought of it. He feels naked already, he feels the cold wind. Already his trousers are falling down.'

It was the first time she had been out in the evening for the past fortnight, and during that time Maurice had not come to her. But in the course of it she had received the first letter he had ever written her: and to protect him absolutely, though he had asked for no such protection, she had burned it. It was one of the hardest things she had ever done in her life. She had not even kept it long enough to know it entirely by heart; but a few phrases remained to lift her into a state of amazed happiness whenever she thought of them.

That night, however, he was waiting for her. Careless of whoever might see him, he had been standing for nearly a quarter of an hour outside her door.

'I did so hope for you.'

When they were inside the flat, he lifted her right off her feet and kissed her till she felt bruised; he carried her to the sofa and dumped her down there, afterwards sitting beside her and holding her as closely as if she might be torn away from him.

'I cannot and I will not let you go. I don't care what happens to me, I don't know what will happen, but I am so in love with you that I would rather die than be without you.'

Yet half his mind was not on her.

She said, 'You have been seeing beau Sandeman . . .'

'Who?' He nearly laughed.

'Plym's phrase.'

'How did you know?'

'He got me to meet him, so he could tell me about that, and other things. He says I must stop all this.'

'All this.'

'Yes.'

'Well, you are not going to. Nor am I.'

'Was it bad? I mean, the Archdeacon.'

'He considers it his duty to pass my misdemeanours on to the Bishop. He was suave. There was an all-men-together air about him that I found peculiarly nauseating. Yes, it was very bad.'

'And——?'

'And what?'

'Were you tactful?'

'Not particularly,' Maurice said. 'No. I did myself no good.'

'Word for word,' she said, 'I want all of it.' She did: it would be a relief to hear what had passed between him and the

Archdeacon, a lightening of tension, since it would seem like a play rather than something which had really happened. But he replied almost angrily that he couldn't go through it all again, it was more than he could bear.

He began talking rapidly, as if to himself, and as she listened, she felt she could hardly breathe; she strained to listen, the noise of her own pulses drumming across his words.

Somehow, they would have to be free, no matter who suffered; even that did not matter any more; there must be a way of finding money, though God knew how, as he would be ruined — though between a parson's income and total indigence there had always seemed a very small space.

'You're mad,' Alice said, 'none of it could come true.'

'I am so in love with you. I thought I could break things off, but I can't.'

'There is Libby.'

'I don't know about Libby. She hates church work. At least, she wouldn't have that to worry about any more.'

'She came to see me.'

'What?' He was so startled that he let go of her.

Alice repeated it.

'When?'

'Monday. Shall I tell you about it?'

'No.'

'She made me ashamed of myself.'

'She would be no poor hand at that,' he said.

She protested, filled with shame for them both. They were the injurers, he and she: they had no right to injure her further, even by so much as a word she would never hear. Alice was still hot with excitement; yet under it she felt the squirm of every old guiltiness, like the breakneck twisting of water into a subsidence. It seemed impossible for her to reach him, at this moment when they should have been so close. Love and anger were tearing at him; he looked unlike himself, as though he were drunk. 'I must have you,' he said, 'there's nothing else at all.'

'I suppose everybody is peering at us now.'

'We have got to be together. We ought to have known it when this thing began.'

She said she hated to be peered at; he paid no attention.

'We could live somehow.' He looked at the clock. 'I must go.'

'Don't say anything yet, promise me.'

'Why? So you can run away? Do you want time for that?' His eyes shone with suspicion. He looked at her steadily.

'I won't do that.'

'I shan't come up here one night and find you've gone?'

'No. If I promise you I won't, will you promise me not to tell Libby or anyone?'

He said he had no time to promise, or to think about promising.

Now it was as though he could not leave her quickly enough: she actually felt him pull away from her, jerk his hands free from hers.

When he had gone, she walked quickly up and down the room, her hands to her cheeks. Movement was releasing, the mere sensation of the rapid step, the swing round, helping to distract her thoughts. She did not know now what she wanted, or what would happen to them both.

Chapter Forty-four

BEHIND Vernon Square there was another square, with houses and communal garden of quite a different order, and it was to this garden that several of the Vernon Square residents had keys. The bombs had fallen heavily here, completely destroying the north side and severely damaging the west: so that after the demolition work had taken place new, quite small and very expensive houses had been built, to fetch prices of six or seven thousand pounds apiece. The garden was tidy, the right of entry jealously guarded by a committee which had, by operation of mysterious skills, contrived to deny keys to residents in the old and dingy houses on the south and east sides. Here there were cut lawns, trimmed laurels, serpentine paths, standard roses and rhododendrons.

Here, on Saturday afternoon, the Pelhams encountered Louisa Fawcett, who was exercising her son and her Bedlington dog.

Louisa, in a very smart linen suit, greeted them emotionally; if she could have brought tears to her eyes, she would have done so: she was really upset.

'Oh, it is awful, it goes from bad to worse! Do you know Kitson went to that beastly Archdeacon? Jeremy is livid.'

The Pelhams were taken aback. They found it hard, for the moment, to reply, since their own feeling was not so much one of sympathy for Maurice or indignation against Kitson, as of stupefaction at the reaction of Jeremy Fawcett.

'Yes, it is dreadful,' Georgina began, 'but——'

Humphrey, more direct, asked why Fawcett should be so angry. 'It was he who seemed shocked, Louisa, I remember that he seemed shocked.'

The little boy fell down, had to be picked up and dusted. 'You be more careful,' Louisa told him, 'I don't want to wash and wash for you till all my fingers drop off. — Isn't that a sordid picture?' she enquired of Georgina, 'I don't know where I get my imagination. — Oh, *Jeremy*! People never understand him. He loves a horror story, he gets awfully up in arms, but my dear, he would never actually *act*.'

They all sat down together on a rustic seat before a screen of laurels. The afternoon sun shed an ochreous light over the grass. The little Fawcett attached himself to a group of children playing in charge of a nannie; here there were nannies still, the last of their kind, though only two wore any sort of uniform.

'Jeremy did his best to stop all this,' said Louisa. 'He went to Colonel J-B and asked him to talk to the vicar; he felt that if someone dropped a word, it might save trouble later on.'

Georgina was convinced by now that Louisa was trying to protect her husband. She knew Fawcett well: even as a child he had combined moral indignation with that kind of devilment which stirs up trouble just to see what will happen next. She believed he had, in fact, added his quota to Maurice's present troubles, was scared of what he had done and was eager now to withdraw.

Louisa went on, 'Of course it was that dotty sermon from that silly little David which really did the trick. Kitson would have felt bound to take notice, being what he is.'

'I should like to tell him what he is!' Georgina said warmly. She pushed her hat back from her brow, giving herself an embattled look.

'Yes, dear heart,' said Humphrey, patting her arm, 'but you know you must not. Remember Madingley Road?'

She blushed and laughed. 'Well, she did deserve it.'

'But you should have found out she was related to the Stephens.'

'How could I have found out? She was so vulgar!'

Louisa said they must certainly tell her what all this was about, she was wild with curiosity. It would be too mean of them to keep a good story from her.

'But I shall keep it from you,' Georgina said, with a little stately smile, 'because I was very young at the time, and Humphrey was a young don, and I nearly got him into very bad odour by speaking my mind. Nevertheless, Humph, she was a most displeasing woman, you're obliged to admit that!'

The Bedlington was bounding like a lamb before them, his fleece violet in the strong light: he wanted sticks thrown, and Humphrey obliged him.

'Look, dears,' said Louisa, 'poor Fisher has to go and be ticked off by the Bishop.'

Georgina asked her how she knew.

'He told Jeremy. He's telling everyone. He just doesn't seem to care any more. Oh, isn't it awful when one likes all parties in this sort of thing! I do like the vicar, and of course one adores Libby. They will simply have to make a go of it together, won't they?'

'Also,' said Humphrey, 'one very much liked what one saw of Alice Imber.'

But this Louisa would not admit. Marriage had got to be made to work. She and Jeremy had made up their minds years ago that if ever there was the least trouble between them, they would talk it all over and throw it out. And if anyone tried to come between them, they would throw him or her out. 'One doesn't want to be stuffy,' she added, 'but marriage is the whole foundation of society.' She stretched out her pretty legs in front of her and clicked her heels. 'Adrian!' she called. 'Don't grab that little girl's train! It is *her* train!'

Humphrey, who had had no difficulties in his own marriage and in gratitude was always tolerant of the difficulties of others, since these seemed to him to bring the worst kind of misery, said nothing. He had always found Louisa smug: he did not wonder that she and Jeremy got on so well together. There were a good many young people like them to-day, Conservative in politics, middling to high Anglicans, or even Roman Catholics, who lived elegant, comfortable lives based on a set of moral precepts old enough to seem new, even to seem *chic*. They did not wish, like many older persons of their type, to hang murderers or to restore the birch: but their views on sexual morality were as hard as nails, in an age when magnanimity was at a discount, and hardness fashionable almost to the point of being smart.

Both Georgina and Humphrey, who liked to behave well, to take pleasure in their fellows, and to please rather than to displease, found the Fawcetts a little tiresome and were worried because they did so. (It was obvious to everyone that the Fawcetts were good.) They were also (to their own surprise) just a little afraid of them: neither, for instance, would have admitted to Louisa or to Jeremy that their sympathies were still Radical, that they voted for the Labour Party, and that they had never taken a holiday in Spain since the Civil War, nor ever would, so long as General Franco lived.

'What I mean,' Louisa explained, 'is that though I think Fisher is behaving desperately badly, I do loathe the idea of Kitson making it all public, more or less. I am *not* absolving Alice Imber.'

Georgina, stung, said she thought no one of the laity should arrogate to himself the right to absolve anyone from anything. 'The best thing we can do for our neighbours, and certainly for the poor Fishers, is to mind our own business.'

'Ticked off,' said Louisa cheerfully. She got up. 'But you do know what I mean, dear Pelhams. Well, bless you both: I must go home and give this monster his beastly sticky tea.'

Georgina looked after her. 'What I did in Madingley Road, Humph, would have been quite all right if I'd put it a little differently, don't you think?'

Alarmed, he asked her what she was up to. She meant, she explained, that it had been right to rebuke the horrible woman: somebody had to. It was the choice of words which had been wrong, and perhaps the self-election of the rebuker. 'I was too young for it. It seemed worse because I was.'

'It is a curious and interesting fact,' said Humphrey, 'that if, in your younger days, you had been able to fight upon the barricades you would actually have done so, without the least self-consciousness. You would also have made a very good showing at the stake——'

'How can one possibly tell?'

'Oh, I know. But none of these things would be within the range of the young Fawcetts and their friends. Their beliefs are like rock, my dear, but are not passionate. And if they had to defend them, they would somehow contrive to do so by a sultry sort of private parliamentarianism. A more mature attitude, perhaps; but, my love, I confess that the thought of you attacking with a broken bottle is somehow more pleasing to me — more emotionally pleasing, which I can explain, and more morally pleasing, which I cannot.'

She glowed. It was by such odd compliments that he offered her the whole of his love. They were both too old for anything but the intellectual compliment to be real, and since they both knew this, they had kept their marriage not only stable and comfortable, but alight. They were together. They were one. The yellow sunlight, filtered through a thickening mist, was for their delight and they offered it the tribute of their dedicated admiration.

'But,' Humphrey went on, 'what was in your mind?'

'To tell Kitson what I told Mrs. —— just about forty-five years ago, but with the weight of experience behind it.'

'We scarcely know Kitson,' Humphrey said, 'and not socially.'

'That may be a drawback,' Georgina replied grandly, 'but is not necessarily a decisive one.'

What, he asked her, just to amuse himself, would she say to him when the obstacle of meeting had been overcome? She lowered her head, stuck her hands into her pockets and gave herself up to full, flowing, imaginative thought. This was one of their old games, this elaborate envisaging of situation and outcome. 'We haven't played this for a long time,' she said, still thinking.

'Do you remember when we did last?'

'Torquay?'

'No, no, no! St. Tropez.'

'So we did.'

'I never cared for it, St. Tropez.'

'Nor did I. Why on earth did we go?'

'I haven't the least idea.'

'I know!' Georgina stopped and raised her face, rosy now, with a stipple of tiny red lines that was still, at a distance, like the milkmaid flush of youth. 'I should say, "Mr. Kitson, I think it better to be direct with you."'

'Good,' said Humphrey. 'And next?'

She had a natural talent for mimicry, when she was not attempting a performance. Her eyes narrowed, her upper lip lengthened, she was Kitson. 'Then he will say, "Excellent. Go ahead, Mrs. Pelham, go ahead." I shall take my time: I shall give him a long look, then say——'

'Wait a minute,' said Humphrey. 'Where *are* you?'

'Oh, at the Fawcetts'. We have just looked in for a moment, and he happens to be there.'

'Which room?'

'Drawing-room — no, hall. We are standing in the hall. Louisa and Jeremy draw back a bit, they know there is going to be a rumpus. I say, "Why did you do this thing, Mr. Kitson?"'

'Stagey, a bit,' Humphrey murmured.

Georgina retorted that stageyness was the essence of all 'scenes', and hers was to be no exception. She continued her embroidery as they walked home through a mist that was now melon-coloured; she was enjoying herself so much that she had forgotten the inspiration of the game. It was only as Humphrey put his key in the door that she said, 'How callous we are! I am truly ashamed of us both.'

He stood back, bending a little as she went by him in acknowledgement of her mistress-ship of his home. Then he followed her in, and put his hand on her shoulder. 'We are both sorry for Fisher, he is a good fellow. But are we personally touched by all this?'

'I suppose not.'

'Well, then, let us stop our game if you feel we are being harsh, but let's not forget that we enjoyed playing it.'

As he hung up his hat it slipped from the peg. He bent down to retrieve it, righted himself with some difficulty, groaned and smiled at once at the stiffness in his legs. He is getting old, Georgina thought, with a pang. So am I. Oh God, I hope I go first. I do so hope I go first.

Chapter Forty-five

LUXURIATING after pleasure Kate lay on her back, her head on Westlake's shoulder, ready to talk about all manner of things. She was always talkative after love, and knew that he liked to hear her.

'I have realised recently,' she said, 'that I do not like my sister. If she were not my sister, I would be quite unable to stand her. But blood ought to be thicker than water, don't you think? It makes me feel guilty.'

It was true enough: but at that particular moment she did not feel guilt at all, not even the rather enjoyable guiltiness of remembering the totems of her youth. She was simply happy.

'I was fond of my brother,' Westlake said, 'though we never had anything to say to each other. Yes, I do think blood ought to be thicker than water, whatever that may mean. Were you in love with Fisher?'

Enjoying the pleasure of confession, she told him she had been in danger of falling in love with him, but had willed herself out of it.

'Did you will yourself into love with me?'

'Of course,' she said. 'Maurice always insists that it is an act of will, and I'm sure he's right. If it weren't, where would all the moral obloquy come from? The censorious know, all right. They've got the secret. They know we say, not "I am in love", but "I now propose to be in love". There's the sparking point. Once it has sparked, we can't help ourselves: but we have the decision to make, and that's a free choice.'

The room was dark except for the glow from the electric

fire, shedding its flushes of flamingo light over the floor. She jerked herself up to look at it, fell back again in contentment.

'We shall have a drink soon,' he said, 'when I can heave myself out of this agreeable stupor.'

She asked him if he did not detect some slight improvement in his condition, inasmuch as a stupor of any kind could keep him from drink.

'No. You mustn't be unrealistic.'

Slipping his arm from beneath her head he sat up and reached for his dressing-gown. She saw him moving across to the wine-cooler, select a bottle and glasses. She heard the suck of a cork.

'Stay there,' he said. 'This is good stuff. We shall drink it at ease.'

They sat up together, pyramidal in the sheets, and drank.

'To us.'

'Certainly.'

'When will you tell them?'

'All in good time,' Kate answered. 'I will not be rushed.'

He lit a cigarette and put it into her mouth. 'It will spoil what you're drinking, but you wouldn't know. Also, the smoke will spoil the taste for me; but not so much as not smoking would spoil this moment for you.'

'I don't believe you can taste any more,' said Kate.

'Perhaps not. But I like to preserve the illusion that I can.'

Sometimes, at the moment of the greatest happiness, the most bitter thought intrudes. Kate felt herself thinking, with disgust, We are pretending this is beautiful, but it is all quite sordid. We are planning something that will bring a bit of pleasure to ourselves and misery to everyone else. That is the truth of it all.

But it was a thought she could not face; and she switched it for another, which was: Why does one try to spoil joy for oneself?

Because we are punishers, and must punish ourselves.

Oh yes: the usual talk, quack, quack, quack. But why should

I punish myself? I have had all things but this one taken from me. It is the takers who should be punished, Death himself who should be punished. She saw Death, in a long grey gown, being whipped with bits of string.

'Go on,' said Westlake, 'talk. I love it. Do you dislike your mother or the boys?'

She shook her head.

'Drink up. You're shivering.'

'I'm not cold.'

'*Do* you dislike them?' he repeated, with a journalist's persistence.

'If I did not know any of them I should still quite like my mother, even though she is now running me off my feet all day. When I go to the hospital, she sends me out a dozen times for little errands and it will be worse when she comes home. I should quite like Dick. I should not like Simon. But as it is, I love Simon.'

The bad moment had passed; she could not even remember what had distressed her. Laying her hand upon his heart, she made the room beat with it, the light of the fire throb up and down with it, rose to purple, purple to rose.

'I'm still alive,' he said, and laughed.

He often managed to jar her out of a mood; it was one of the things she disliked about him, for, though she loved him utterly, she had never liked him very much.

She said, 'I can see you are; and now, however little I want to, I must go.'

She switched on the bedside lamp as if this were the determining action of a lifetime, and they blinked at each other in the glare.

'Ruthless,' said Westlake.

The skin below his eyes was very delicate above the puffy flesh, delicate as the skim on milk, as delicately veined as skim when the heat increases below it. She touched his fine nose, the deeply vaulted sockets under his brows.

'Oh yes, I was once a fine figure of a man.'

'You are now.'

'No.' He closed his eyes, and the muscles of his face relaxed. He appeared to be thinking of nothing at all, or to be asleep. Kate touched his lips: he kissed her fingers.

She sprang out of bed and got dressed. He did not watch her, he never did. Rolling on to his face, he folded his arms under his forehead and lay still.

When she was ready, he said, 'I should escort you, I know, do something decent. But you are used to me.'

'I may be. Of course, it might be gentlemanly if you just made the effort to sit up. You make me feel like a trollop.'

His voice was muffled. 'That's the way I like you to feel, "lineaments of gratified desire", and all that. Don't get too big for your boots, my girl, because I won't stand for it.'

She did not answer. She knew he was weak as water, and that she would always have to pretend he was stronger than she. It was boring and humiliating to have to do so: but worth doing, because he would switch love off like a light if she did not.

She walked quickly home through the chilly summer night, making her usual mental effort to put Westlake behind her before she entered the house.

Simon glanced up from his homework as she went into the sitting-room. 'Oh, hullo. I've had my supper.' He looked down again. 'Aunt Libby is going round looking most peculiar. I thought you ought to know.'

Kate asked him what he meant. He shrugged. Just peculiar. He didn't know why, and he didn't care.

'Where's Maurice?'

'Just gone out. He left his supper in the oven, so I shared it out with Dick.'

Her heart sinking, she went to look for Libby whom she found going about the kitchen with a silent, floating movement and a quiet smile.

'Don't wash up,' Kate said, 'I'll do all that. Did you go to see Mother?'

'I don't think I could wash up,' said Libby, and floated away. She called out in a vague faraway voice from halfway down the

306

stairs, 'Mother is fractious, but all right. I'm going to bed now.'

Kate looked at the clock: it was twenty-five past eight. She followed her sister up into the bedroom. 'What is it?'

Libby was undressing with extreme rapidity and neatness. Her fingertips poked like pearls through her plaits as she undid them. She slipped her nightdress over her head and finished unclothing herself as in a tent. Then she put on dressing-gown and slippers and sat down to brush her hair. She was still smiling, on her face a look of that absolute calm indicative of a dangerous degree of self-control.

Kate repeated her question.

'It is quite all right,' Libby said softly, 'I shall be brave, I am honestly going to behave myself.'

'Maurice?'

'We talked quite quietly. He is determined that he will not give up that woman, he is behaving as if he were mad, but I am *not* going to lose my head. Katey, dear, you are in my light.'

An awful tiredness fell on Kate, like a heavy coat from a peg. 'Then what does he propose to do?'

'He seems mad enough to think he can leave me. I pointed out just what a silly idea that was, I tried to laugh at him a little, even.'

'And how successful was that?' Kate sat down on the edge of the bed, feeling an ache across the base of her spine. She lit a cigarette.

'Don't smoke in the bedroom, there's a dear. I do so dislike it, as you know quite well, and there are other rooms in the house.' Libby replaited her hair, carefully chose two strips of baby-ribbon from a Cellophane box, and tied up the ends with perfect X-shaped bows.

'What does he think he is going to do?' Kate persisted. 'Because this is my affair also.'

'I think mine, mine *only*.' Libby bit her lips hard, tossed her head back and gave the new airy smile.

Kate said perhaps it would be better not to debate just whose affair it was. What she wanted to know was whether Maurice

307

had practical plans for them all, in the event of his resigning the living and running away.

'I think he thinks, I think he thinks' — Libby's face worked: she just managed to control it — 'that he could make me an allowance. Where do you suppose he would find an allowance?' The smile reasserted itself. 'Perhaps Mrs. Imber would pay. That would be laughable, wouldn't it?'

'None of this is laughable,' Kate said, 'but I cannot believe he means it.'

Libby rose and touched her shoulder. 'I want to get into bed. I am going to turn my face to the wall. And, Kate,' she burst out in a sudden, whipping fury, a strum of the nerves, 'will you *kindly* put out that cigarette? This is my room, my room!'

'Oh, dear, waste not, want not.' Kate went into the passage and stubbed it out carefully in an ashtray. She returned to find Libby lying, still in her dressing-gown, outside the covers, her face, as she had announced, to the wall. She looked as if she might still be smiling.

Kate leaned over and touched her hair, though it was, as always, an effort of will to make the physical contact. 'Don't worry. He cannot do it.'

'He will. He can't see reason any more. He can't see the horrible disgrace for us all. The poverty, you and me left alone with Mother and the boys living God knows how, with everyone pitying us. He can't see that she's only a grabber, man-mad, the kind of cheap pest you get in every parish——'

'Did you tell him that?'

'I tried to make him see it,' said Libby. 'I wanted him to pray with me, but he wouldn't. After all, he *is* a priest. He could have done that much.'

Kate said unsteadily, 'Don't sound as if you were laughing. I know you're not, but it is a strain on you and I hate to hear it.'

Libby spoke very softly and clearly, her lips almost touching the wall. 'One is very primitive, really. I should like to get hold of her and slap her till her head rocked from side to side and then slap her again, I should like to slap her till she bled——'

'Stop it.'

'That is what I should like to do.'

Up she came from her quiet recumbency, rearing up with a violence that made the bed tremble. She shot out her arms and grasped Kate by the shoulders, thrust out her grief-stricken face, the eyeballs meshed with blood. 'Katey, Katey, help me, help me, I want to die!'

'No, not again. These uproars never do any good. We are not the right people for them; or I am not. It will all look just as silly as it really is, when to-morrow comes. Where is he now?'

'At the confirmation class,' Libby replied, and gave a bawl of laughter. 'That's where he is!'

Kate picked her hands away. 'I wish you'd cut your hair.'

'Why?' Her sister was halted in mid-hysteria. Her eyes seemed to dry as in a hot wind, her mouth opened.

'Oh, I don't know. But I wish you would.'

At that moment they heard the front door open.

'He's back!'

'Go on lying down,' Kate said. 'I'll talk to him.'

He was hanging his hat up.

'You're back early.'

'I only had two couples, and both cancelled.'

'You didn't eat your supper.'

'I didn't want it.'

She told him what she had heard from Libby, and half-expected him to ridicule it as a piece of hysterical misunder-standing. Looking at her, he slightly shrugged his shoulders.

'You can't mean this,' she said.

'I have had enough of my miserable life,' said Maurice.

She opened the study door, and almost pushed him inside. Indeed, he stumbled as he went in, and shooting out his hand, brought himself up short against the desk. 'I am not going over all this with you.'

'I know it's not easy.'

'Easy!' He rubbed his fist hard up and down the bridge of his nose as if to wake himself up.

'An understatement, I know,' Kate said, not without impatience, 'but I am doing my best.'

'This kind of love,' Maurice said suddenly after a silence, speaking as clearly and slowly as if he were addressing a class of students, 'is the only thing that really stands up against all the decencies. Everything one has learned goes by the board. Kindness. Ordinary good behaviour. God. Because they all become abstractions. I can't see you, Kate, except through the plate glass that encloses me. I know you're there, I know your name, I know your history, and I know what your rights are. You have laid up a store of endless rights by now, and I ought to honour them. But I want one thing for myself now, and nothing else seems real to me in the slightest degree.'

'I might want something, too,' she said; and left him.

There were times, she thought, when the conflict of two wantings became too great for discussion. If one of the wanters were to lose everything, then it would not be herself. She would cause enough destruction: but far less than he would. And so he would have to yield. Like him, she was in the plate-glass shell of love; she could see him outside, she knew his name, his history, his 'rights'; and he was less real to her than West-lake's name on a strip of dirty cardboard over a bell-push. Though it would be impossible for her to tell Maurice to-night, she could not keep her secret much longer. She was going to be married.

Chapter Forty-six

SCENE I, a room in the Palace, Maurice said to himself as he walked up and down it, waiting. He looked about with detached interest: he was cool enough for that. He hardly knew what he had expected a bishop's house to be like: but at any rate, not like this. All was cosy, cared-for, on the shabby side, central heating the only apparent luxury: for there was a radiator at each end of the room, gold-painted, properly dusted. There were plum-coloured curtains worn in places to a thin, purplish rose, and deep plush chairs that did not quite match them. On the walls were Victorian portraits of men, women and children, none of them good, and one, of a little boy in skirts stiffly carrying a hoop, downright bad. The bishop's desk was big, and littered with photographs; there was a telephone on one side, an anglepoise lamp crooked over like a drinking stork on the other. In the grate, as a luxurious concession to the cold summer's day, a tiny fire sparkled rubies and gold. The air smelled of tobacco, the curtains were full of it. In the middle of an irrelevant sideboard was an épergne, struggled all over by cupids, in which was a pile of apples beginning to spot with black and bronze.

Maurice had been offered a chair, not by a housekeeper or secretary, but by the bishop's tall, vague, gentle wife, who had plumped on to his knees a dozen copies of the *National Geographical Magazine* and said, 'Do smoke, we do.' He had smoked, he had tried to read: but after waiting for ten minutes had found himself unable (calm though he was) to sit still. He was trying to suspend all thought about himself, to pass time by taking a mental inventory of everything he saw about him. The fire, which had seemed so pleasant, was now making the room far too hot. The windows were all tight shut: the bishop did not seem to like fresh air. Outside in the untrimmed garden, standard roses were wagging in the wind and the branch of a cedar, dangerously rotted, creaked as it swung. A child's swing hung by a single chain, the other chain trailing in the long grass. There was a sand-pit, and in it a toy wheelbarrow, red and yellow. Immediately outside, stuck in a flower bed, was something which appeared to be a surrealist object, a cane with a bow of ribbon on top and a cardboard box attached with wire about half way down.

Only the ribbon and the wheelbarrow were bright. Everything else was made monochrome by the dull light, even the few roses, the lupins in half-mourning by the wall. The gilt clock had a loud, aggressive tick that seemed to find an echo from the sideboard; investigating this, Maurice found, behind the épergne, a travelling clock in a leather case with quite a powerful tick of its own.

The little bishop came bouncing in, his hand outstretched. A swathe of plaster covering the right side of his jaw made him look like the subject of some botched piece of plastic surgery.

'My dear Fisher, I wouldn't have kept you waiting for anything! But I had a little accident shaving, nothing deep, but so very effusive, if I may use the word. Aren't you smoking? I am. My first, the best and sweetest of the day. Do sit down.'

He drew up a chair for himself, so that they sat on either side of the fire. It might have been mid-winter, they were so snug.

'Well, well, we don't see much of each other, do we? I wish we did. And I wish we weren't seeing each other now over something troublesome, I really do.'

He had very tiny, Pickwickian feet on which he wore curious black pumps with small, flat bows of corded ribbon. He punted a stool towards himself, and put them up. 'Let me say at once that I have never once, over all these years, heard anything about you that was not good, or was to your discredit.'

Maurice thanked him. He saw, in the little round face, the mature and steady eyes.

'Except, perhaps——' the bishop looked vaguely round. 'Ah yes! There it is. The tray just behind you, if you will, it may be a little early for sherry, but I don't think a glass would hurt us. What was I saying? Oh, except for that matter of marrying the divorced couple, what was the chap's name? — it's escaped me. But that is old history, and between you and me, I could not feel so strongly as I should have done, taking the particular case into account—— Put the tray on this table, if you will be so kind — that's right. Oloroso: too sweet for you? I am retreating from this absurd snobbery about the highest excellence residing in the greatest sourness. I have come really to detest Tio Pepe.'

Maurice thought, with what he knew to be an unworthy spurt of bitterness, that the bishop should know better than to discuss the merits of wine with his underpaid clergy. He accepted a glass, however, and managed to smile.

'Not,' the bishop continued, 'that you can have had much chance for comparative drinking since you came down from the university. I know what your problems are, and I'm enraged whenever I think of them. Indeed, there are moments when I wonder how much longer we're going to get young fellows of the slightest quality whatsoever coming into the Church, when they know it means living on a beggarly stipend. In fact, we are not getting quality: heaven forgive me, but I sometimes think we only get the fellows who wouldn't be smart enough either to teach or to go into industry.' As he sipped the sherry he observed that a compromise would have to be made; this was a bit too much on the sweet side. 'But I am talking my head off; do forgive me. I am probably light-headed after carving my face up with a razor.'

Maurice said he had nothing to say as yet, he could have nothing, until he knew what the bishop was going to say to him.

The bishop put his glass down carefully. He said, in quite a different voice, that he was sorry: he had wanted to get to the point, but it had seemed to him better to arrive there by degrees. His face was open as a daisy; he was a nice man, and an honest one. 'To tell you the truth, Fisher, I hate having to intrude myself into the personal lives of others. If it were a question of heresy now. . . . I wonder when we last had a heretic around? . . . That would be an abstract sort of thing, even intellectually pleasing. We are not "by schisms rent asunder . . .", that is to say, not to speak of—— My dear Fisher,' — he bounced forward in his chair, illuminated by memory — 'have you ever heard a crowd of *children* sing that hymn, and found it hard to keep your countenance? What do they suppose it means? What can it possibly mean to them?'

He stopped, as if he had lost himself: but he had not, and Maurice knew he had not. He was a clever man, he had gone far in the Church and there were those who thought that despite his apparent liberalism, he might go further. It was sometimes said that if he had been four inches taller he might have had a hope of Canterbury.

'Look, Fisher,' said the bishop, his face calm but not particularly grave (it was a face not meant to terrify, and he had never tried to terrify anybody with it), 'your name is being coupled with a woman's. Let me say at once that I am ready to believe whatever you tell me, but all the same, I have to take official cognizance of my information.'

Maurice found that he could not speak much beyond yesses and noes. He said Yes.

'Try to tell me about it,' said the bishop.

'I expect the Archdeacon has given you his version.'

'Of course he has. But I have not heard yours.'

The two clocks ticked away, not synchronizing.

'There is nothing much to tell. I knew Mrs. Imber years ago. I am deeply in love with her, but we have not become lovers. I see her and talk to her sometimes. You have my word that there is nothing more to it than what I have said.'

The bishop put the toes of his little shoes together, contemplated them and sighed. '"Man looketh on the outward appearance", you know that. The Lord looks into the heart. But we have to consider man, and the public example we set him.'

'Yes,' said Maurice.

'Don't think I am not sorry for you. It is the hardest thing, to give up earthly love when it's real.'

'I can't give up the little I have of this.'

The bishop's eyes sharpened. He hitched himself up in his chair. 'It must be obvious to you that the last thing I want to do is to threaten you with a Consistory Court. That does the Church so much harm we hate to face it. But things can't go on as they are.'

Maurice did not speak.

'I accept your word, that is, concerning the actual circumstances.'

'Thank you.'

'But you realise the unhappiness this must be causing your wife?'

'Yes.'

'I am afraid,' the bishop said, 'that you will have to put an end to this association.'

'I have no sort of life. I've had none for years.'

He came to a halt. There seemed, at that moment, nothing more for either of them to say. And then:

'God bless my soul, that *cannot* be snow! It really can't.' Jumping up, the bishop went to the window. 'But there are flakes—— Oh no, it's Mary's doing, she's throwing something out from the nursery. I believe it's soap-flakes! Oh, children, children, one can never get upsides with them——'

He banged on the pane, and after a moment or so the fall of silver ceased. He turned away smiling. 'It really looked rather pretty.' He paused. 'Fisher: one of the things we may be asked to do when we enter the ministry is to put up with having no sort of life. I hate to say this to you, because my own life has been pretty satisfactory. But it is the truth. We are often called upon to make appallingly hard sacrifices, which I suspect yours will be.' He paused. 'I knew old Mr. Imber quite well. And the son, the one who died in Canada.'

'I am not going to make a sacrifice,' Maurice said, 'I can't. Whatever happens to me, I can't.'

315

Without remembering how he had risen from his chair, had crossed the room, he found himself at the bishop's side, and both were looking out into the garden, now sallowed over by a pale gleam of sunlight.

'Now what,' said the bishop, 'is that extraordinary object with the bow on it? It looks like some contrivance of Stephen's. I should think it was meant to be a pastoral crook if it were not for the box. No, I really can't think what it is, can you?'

Maurice said he had not expected anything like the kindness he was now receiving: he wished to say that, if he could say nothing else.

'Why, it is rather like the eleven-plus exam, you know. In some areas only the written papers count, but in others they weigh the headmaster's report. I have weighed all I've heard of you.' The bishop bounced round with a peculiar energetic lightness. 'Now what can I do that might make things easier?'

Maurice said there was nothing.

'What shall you do?'

'Nothing.'

'You realise what may be forced upon me?'

'Yes.'

'Think about it. Go away now. Think about it. Pray about it.'

He talked for a little while longer, drawing, with something of a novelist's imaginative detail, a picture of what life would be like for Maurice if he resigned his living and went away with Alice Imber. He left nothing out. He meant to warn, to sting, and he also meant to convey that no whit of the pain of any of it was lost upon himself. 'Go away now,' he said again. 'Then get in touch with me again. I will give you two days. But now, let's go into the chapel.'

It was grey there, and cold. On the altar was a bunch of moss-roses, compact as enamelled flowers in a gilded cup.

The two men knelt together and prayed in silence: or the bishop prayed, and Maurice tried to. There was a tumult in his head, as if rocks were falling down a cliff side, bouncing and crumbling as they went. He followed the slipping pebbles with his mind's eye, the shower of sand. He could not think. He wanted it to be over, that was all, he wanted to be alone again. He heard the bishop rise, felt the hand upon his head.

'The Blessing of God Almighty, Father, Son and Holy Spirit, be upon you and remain with you always. Amen.'

Maurice opened his eyes.

He felt a passionate impulse, so sudden that it was like the impulse of a dream, to cry out, 'Help me!' — as if, in the little man now gazing at him, God himself had been made flesh: but he said nothing, for he knew there was no help anywhere, that the bishop was a man like himself, that he, too, was locked in bewilderment.

He found nothing to say but goodbye.

He stood outside the bishop's house, in the grey street, went over to the bus stop and waited. It had all seemed quite unreal to him, the kind little bishop, the surrealist object, the sherry, the fall of soap-flakes. It had done no good at all, because he had stayed so far outside it. It was now twenty-five minutes to eleven.

He went straight to the hospital to visit his mother-in-law, whom he found propped up on pillows, reading the *Daily Mirror*.

'Well,' she greeted him, 'and what have you been doing with yourself this fine morning?' — for the sun was out again, striping the carbolic air of the ward.

He made a noncommittal reply.

She tugged his sleeve, looked covertly around to make sure nobody was listening. 'Maurice, I wish you could put in a word with Sister. I can't see what use it is your being a clergyman if you can't.'

He asked her what the matter was.

She rattled off a string of complaints. The nurses were callous, especially the younger ones: that Irish one with the red face was actually rude. There was no need to wash one in the small hours, and certainly no need to make one wait for a bedpan. One was at the mercy of these people and they knew it, they rejoiced in it: one could see them laughing when they brought along the horrible stuff that passed for food. Also, they kept no proper restraint over the people who needed restraint. That woman in the next bed, she was almost well, she was going out that week: but they let her moan and groan all night, waking everybody up.

'Well,' Maurice said, 'you will be home the week after next, so can't you grin and bear it?'

She gave a remote, all-knowing, all-pitying smile, remarkably like Libby's. Yes, she observed, it was really strange the power these nurses had managed to achieve over everyone: it was quite plain to her that even Maurice was afraid to raise his voice.

The Irish nurse came over. 'We're getting on famously, Vicar, healing up like a girl of seventeen. I tell you, we're proud of this patient.'

'*We* are getting on famously?' Mrs. Marsden delicately enquired. 'I didn't know you'd hurt yourself. Have you had an accident?'

'Oh, get along with you,' said the nurse cheerfully, 'you're full of jokes; we know you.' She passed along to another bed, tweaking so helpfully at the patient's tulips that they all fell out of the vase.

'They do not treat one with respect,' Mrs. Marsden whispered indignantly.

Libby came down the ward, her arms full of white daisies, the sun scintillating on her beautiful hair, strewing it with minuscule, multi-coloured florets of light. Heads turned towards her. Seeing Maurice, she stopped short, then came on more slowly.

'Why,' said Mrs. Marsden, 'a bevy of visitors! Are those for me?'

Libby dumped them on the foot of the bed. She said to Maurice, her face stony, 'How did it go?'

He mouthed at her, 'Later.'

'How did what go?' Mrs. Marsden cried. 'Come along, I don't get much news mewed up in here.'

'He had to see the bishop,' Libby enunciated clearly through a cracked, malicious smile.

'The bishop? What? That does sound exciting! Does this mean promotion?'

'Nurse,' Libby cried in a ringing voice, 'would you please empty this water away and bring me some fresh? It should have been emptied before, it smells.'

'No,' said Maurice, 'it does not mean promotion. It was just church business.'

The Irish nurse, not charmed by Libby, snatched up the vase and bore it off. 'Doesn't smell,' he heard her mutter.

Libby said to him, 'Are you going straight home?'

'No. I've got to see Plym about this afternoon's wedding, and there are a couple of dozen other things, too.'

'Well, come home as soon as you can.'

'But the bishop,' said Mrs. Marsden, 'you don't set eyes on him very often. It sounds most exciting.'

'I shan't be back before one,' he said to Libby.

'I'll leave you something in the oven, then. I can't wait about for you.'

Mrs. Marsden interrupted them to say she had understood that this was *her* visit: they had enough time to themselves, they could at least spare her a little attention.

Libby crammed daisies into the vase, which the nurse had restored to the locker.

Maurice hesitated. 'I could go back with you and telephone Plym from there.'

The old woman gripped her daughter's sleeve. 'Listen, I was telling him about some of these nurses. The offhandedness, the sheer rudeness is really intolerable. After all, we are Some-body around here——'

'Who are we?' Libby retorted, turning a flaming and furious face. '*I* don't know. And if we are anybody at all, it's a sure thing we won't be for much longer.'

'We shall always be somebody! I'm glad you talked to that girl as you did, she's the worst——'

'Oh, go ahead, Mother. I'm listening. What now?'

'Look here,' said Maurice, 'I'll get along, drop in on Plym on my way and wait for you.' He said goodbye to Mrs. Marsden and left the women alone.

Outside, he spoke to the ward-sister, asked her how long it would be till his mother-in-law could walk again.

She said, with her remote, worried smile, that it was hard to tell. Weeks perhaps, or months. It depended, in this case, on the patient. Her ribs had healed well enough, but she was hotly resisting any sort of physical therapy and showed no desire to help herself. 'You will have her on your hands for some time, I'm afraid. She's no longer young and she actually likes bed. It's far more difficult to cope with elderly people when they do.'

Maurice had a word with Plym, which took him a little longer than he had expected; when he got home he found Libby there before him, in the study, facing the open door, so that she could speak to him at once.

Chapter Forty-seven

'I'M waiting,' she said, and clasped her hands tightly before her so that the stone of her engagement ring dug into the flesh.

She had expected to feel calm and cool-headed at that moment, so closely had she prepared for it: but the floor sloped under her feet and he was a long way off.

He told her he could not and would not repeat what had been said. None of it had been unexpected: for the moment, anyway, no action was to be taken. He was looking at her in an odd way as if asking her to help him, not in a crisis but in some ordinary domestic thing such as moving a piece of furniture or holding a ladder steady; it was less an appeal for help than that she should 'lend a hand' — as if they were on the same side, as if they were together. He could not control his mouth, he could not have intended there to be a half-smile upon it.

'Is it going to mean utter disgrace?' she cried. It was not what she had meant to say. She hardly cared at all now for the disgrace, the humiliation; she could not imagine it. It was the horror of total loss which was making her so sick and faint; yet somehow she could not quite bear to show him what had become the truth, even if it would have helped her.

He did not answer.

She said, 'I am going to stand by you.' This was better, this was what she had planned to say.

'Stand by me?' Still the half-smile that was a rictus of misery and of sheer embarrassment. It was horrible that they should be talking like this, in that worst kind of reality which is like the worst kind of play-acting.

She told him in a loud clear voice that yesterday at a meeting Mrs. Walkeley had made a reference to Alice Imber. 'I walked straight up to her. I came right out with it. I said I'd heard the gossip, of course, and that it was without foundation of any kind. Everyone heard me. I said Mrs. Imber was a friend of us both. That's what I said.'

He took her hand. At his touch, she felt a violent repulsion; she was soiled by his kindness. 'I'm desperately sorry, Libby.'

'I can forgive you. I thought I couldn't, but I can and I will.' She hardly knew him. She was as awkward with him as with a stranger. 'The moment you've told her that you won't see her any more, I shall stop talking about it. I shall never talk of it again.'

And then she found herself wanting to tell him something else, something she had not thought about before. 'I don't know how to put it, but I know it will be dreadful for you too.'

He asked her drearily what would be dreadful for him.

'If you really do think you love her.' It was wrong: at the word 'think', he flinched. She should have said 'If you love her', but had not quite brought herself to do it. 'I mean, if you do, it will be dreadful for you. It would be for me, if I didn't love you — which I do — having to stay with you always. Oh, Maurice, do try to understand me! It isn't easy, and I'm trying so very hard!'

'Libby,' he said, 'I wish——'

She was terrified. Whatever happened, he must not make a decision in words, for if he did so it would be against her. Naturally unperceptive, dedicated to the idea that each man was as simple as the next one and that nobody but a fool could fail to choose between wrong and right when the time came, she had been brought by jealousy and unhappiness to the realisation that he himself did not really know what his decision was to be. He would not know, unless he spoke it: and at all costs she must stop him doing so.

She tossed her head back. She meant to look exultant, was frightened that she might look a little mad. She had to carry him with her, bear him up, hypnotise him by her own faith.

'It's going to be all right! I prayed for strength and it's been given me. Whatever you say, I *know* that we're going to make a new start. We're going to be happy again, we're not going to let all those years go for nothing.'

'I don't know what is going to happen to us at all,' said Maurice. 'But I think——'

'Don't say anything now. Please.' She dragged her hand from him, took a backward step and dropped heavily into a chair. Something moved over her cheek like an insect. She struck at it violently, hurting herself, fumbled, discovered a straying hair. She pulled it out of her head. 'Not now, don't say anything now. I thought I could bear it, but I can't.'

He was standing in front of her. She could not raise her eyes. His long legs, like pillars, blocked out the rest of the room.

Suddenly she clasped her arms around him, leaned her head against his thighs and wept. Not entirely for herself this time but also for him, because he could not love her and because his loneliness was something she could feel in the rigidity of his body. She thought confusedly that he must surely know what it meant to her to surrender all pride at a time like this, to force him to bear her touch because she was too weak not to seek his own. He ought to think the better of her for it, he ought to know how destroying to her pride it was that she should have to cling to him like this. She did not want to ask for his pity: she had to. And she had to try, however feebly, to offer him hers.

'All right,' he said at last, lifting her as gently as if she were crippled. 'We'll let it go for now. We're neither of us in a fit state to talk.'

The boys came in from school, bumping and boring along the passage, shouting at each other in their usual tone of insult.

'And I haven't got their dinner ready,' she said. She had to ask him if she looked dreadful, she could not stop herself. Even now, she could not believe her beauty valueless. She wiped her face, blew her nose, said, 'Don't tell me, I'm sure I do.'

Then, because he did not answer, she could not endure it, and went off into the kitchen where she found herself making

323

a termagant's noise, banging about, turning on taps, clattering dishes. The boys had put on the gramophone and the searing wire of the trumpet was cutting through the walls as if they were made of cheese.

But he hasn't said anything, she told herself desperately, it hasn't happened yet.

Somehow they all got through the meal. Kate was out; the boys were in the thick of a squabble and paid attention to nothing but their food. In the afternoon Maurice had to take a wedding service, and Libby had to go to it, because both parties were rich and St. Lawrence's was not.

Afterwards she was amazed to find how little she could remember of what she had done, what she had worn, what had been said to her, what she had said to others. She had only one idea, at the heart of this nightmare, which was to give her husband no time to speak to her alone. She prayed for time. With every hour that passed, she believed something had been gained.

When they returned he went off by himself to the study, and did not appear till supper was on the table. As luck would have it, the boys were out: Libby looked across at him in dread. She made a remark about the bride, how she had looked, commented upon the reception. He answered her shortly, and she was afraid that he was framing words. He is growing steadier, she thought, and I'm not. I must keep a grip on myself.

Kate came in.

Libby jumped up in a near-hysteria of relief. 'So here you are! If I weren't a good sister to you, you'd starve to death, but I can find you something. We didn't expect you back so early.'

Kate said, 'Don't bother about me, I've eaten out.'

She sat down with them at the table, took out her cigarettes and pushed them across to Maurice. 'I ought to get this over,' she said, 'but I imagine you've guessed, anyhow.'

Libby was bewildered, so jolted out of her own preoccupation that she felt she had been made a fool of: it was as though someone had come up and pushed her. 'Guessed what?'

'Oh, come. I am going to marry Tom.'

It seemed like a joke, but an incomprehensible one. She had to say something. 'But you can't.'

She saw that Maurice was staring at Kate quite blankly, as if he did not know her.

'It's my life, after all. I am the one who is free to do as I choose.' She sat like a sibyl, expressionless, the corners of her mouth deeply indented.

Now, when Libby tried to speak, no sound would come at first. Then she managed to say, though she did not know why she was impelled to say it because some uncomprehended instinct was trying to tell her that this was good news, not bad, 'That drunk.'

'Yes,' said Kate. 'That drunk.' She smiled, and seemed cruel.

'But he's already married.'

'Well, no.' Kate had a bizarrely reasonable air, as if pointing out to them some misconception which had existed all the way along. 'Because his wife, R.C. or not, is now proposing to divorce him. He knew that before he ran away to Liverpool. She wants to marry again, God be praised.'

Libby heard Maurice say, in a flat voice, 'What about the boys?'

'They must lump it.' She cleared her throat. 'Simon's growing up and will soon be off my hands. I will not wreck my life just to pamper him for a year or so, and Dick won't much care what happens to him anyway, so long as he gets his creature comforts. For you two, as I think you'll agree, I have done quite enough.' Her voice broke.

'More than enough.' Maurice was speaking slowly, as if each word had to be separately formed, each letter drawn on his mind. 'As you say, you are the one who is free.'

She got up and walked out of the room.

Libby saw Maurice looking after her as if he could see her through the closed door. She saw the shock standing out on his face, and for a second could not understand it. But it was never true, what some people hinted, that Kate was once keen on him;

and he was never keen on her, she would have known if that had been so. It could not, it simply could not be that. What was he so shocked about — except, of course, that Kate had no right to take her sons to such a man, to be so selfish, so uncaring for everyone but herself? If anyone suffers, I shall, Libby thought, everything will devolve on me, I don't know how I shall stand it.

Then she did understand; and the triumph that filled her was so like disaster that she said aloud, and in her panic meant it, 'I am going to be ill.'

He said on a note of furious irritation, as if he were going to break from all control, 'No, you're not! You're never ill!' He stood up, he was shaking all over. 'Oh, Lib.' He came round the table and put his arm round her shoulders. She neither acknowledged it nor moved away from it. She found herself running her hands up and down the buttons of her cardigan as if she were playing an accordion: she might go on doing that, it would show him how really bad she felt, it would scare him, it would gain time for her. They were a pretty colour, pale blue with a purplish tinge, she remembered buying the set in a little dark shop where there was a cat sitting on the counter.

He stood quite still at her back, touching her, now, for comfort.

So it was all right. Nothing would be said. There was no longer anything to say.

Chapter Forty-eight

N EXT day was the day of the annual garden fête, to which
Maurice had given no thought because he was never
asked to do so. His duty was simply to attend: the work
was done by the women of the parish, Mrs. Walkeley, Mrs.
Hannaway, Lucy Simnett, Mrs. Johnson-Black and Louisa
Fawcett, in whose garden (she was one of the few parishioners
who owned such a luxury) it had been held for the past five
years. It usually brought in about a hundred pounds.

The Fawcetts owned a long, white, smart house which had
been erected on a bombed site. There had been a private hotel
on this site once, and since the Fawcetts' house was smaller
than the original building, they had been able to add their
surplus land to the garden already in existence. When the day
was wet, the sale had to be held in Louisa's drawing-room, a
thing she hated: but that day was quite dry, if on the chilly side.

Neither of the Fawcetts enjoyed organisation themselves so
were glad to hand over a considerable sum of money to Peter
and Lou; with the result that the garden presented an appearance of somewhat specialised elegance admired by more sophisticated members of the congregation and giggled at by the less.

'I can't see myself,' David said nervously to Maurice, trying
to make conversation, 'why most of the decorations should be
based on molecular structure, as I know it from the Science
Museum.'

Lucy, shivering, but dressed determinedly for a garden party
in pink cotton, said she thought it represented the spirit of the
age and was very nice.

Maurice was wondering how he was to get through the day
at all. His feet, as in a nightmare, seemed weighted with lead:

it was an eternity to walk from one stall to another. Also, he was sick with the sense of crisis, both in his own home, and as it existed in the minds of his parishioners. For they all knew: they must all know. He half-expected people to turn their backs.

The only discourtesy he did in fact receive was from Plymmer who, strolling by with his big wife and daughters, greeted him with a sort of rowdy camaraderie, as if he were an unfrocked priest due for reception into the world of the *louche* and the lost. He raised his hand, gave Maurice a half-smile, a smile of complicity, and said, 'Hullo, having a good time?' Among his family he looked a different man, neither a better nor a worse man, but a domesticated stranger. Even allowing for the width the corduroy coat gave to his shoulders, both his girls looked broader than he: tails of pale hair swished across their backs as they walked, and as they fell into line with their mother, letting him precede them towards the tea-tent, they swallowed him up like water.

'What on earth is the matter with Plym?' Lucy enquired, fastening comfortably with both hands on David's arm. 'It may be his stomach again. I thought he was awfully odd after the wedding yesterday.'

Maurice did not know how he had got through that wedding. There had been a long reception afterwards, Libby in a new hat, and heavily powdered over red eyes. The sore was open now for everyone to pity.

He did not know, also, how he was to get through the afternoon.

Last night, the whole night through, he had seen it all; that he was to be deprived of Kate, who had held his material life together, was to be left with Libby and a helpless old woman, that without Kate he could never leave them.

He did not know how he was to get through the afternoon, or through the rest of his life.

He strolled over the grass with a word for everybody; he had to have a word for everybody, it was expected of him, particularly now.

Because the day was one of the few sunny ones in a poor

summer, the sky cobalt-blue, the white clouds flickering across it to the lash of the east wind, the fête was crowded. There were the usual stalls, not many of them, but well arranged: the usual amusements. Peter and Lou had set up a candy-striped booth for a kind of Aunt Sally game. There were paper balls to throw at sixpence for four; and Lou crouched on his haunches behind, jerking up and down an arrangement of three Nuraghic-looking dolls on sticks, labelled respectively Mollie, Katie and Connie. Simon, with manic concentration, was taking shies at them, paying out coin after coin. He was growing again, Maurice noticed, the turn-ups of his trousers were at his ankle bones.

'Poor Lou,' Peter said to Maurice, 'he is going to get so tired of doing that. It was his own idea entirely, and he gets so cross when he doesn't get his own way, but he is going to suffer. I shall be nursing him for a week,' he added tenderly. 'You must think of me, Vicar, smoothing the sheets.'

Johnson-Black was running a game of bowling through croquet hoops; he did not look as though he thought it a good game or considered that any person of sense ought to be playing it. His wife and Hannaway's had the hoop-la.

'I ought to be doing my stint with the tea,' Lucy said fondly to David, 'not idling around with you. And I must tackle those Guides again, or they'll mess up their display.'

She went away.

David said, 'You know how I feel.' He swallowed, as if his throat were sore. The light had gone from his face, and so had the redeeming boyishness which made his physical oddness less apparent.

'All right,' Maurice said, 'all right.' He wandered away to buy a raffle ticket, and was greeted with nervous jocosity by some of the women. Their eyes were steady and curious, no amusement in them at all.

'Aren't you going to guess the weight of the cake?' asked Mrs. Walkeley. 'Come on, be a sport.'

He saw out of the corner of his eye that Libby had just come in. She went straight into the tea-tent.

'They ought to guess the weight of the vicar,' Maurice joked feebly, 'I am putting it on.'

'No bread and potatoes is my New Year's resolution,' said Louisa, coming up behind him. She looked expensive and comfortable: she was wearing a fur cape. 'But that is a long way off, I thank Heaven. I adore carbohydrates. Do forgive Jeremy, he couldn't get away.'

The nightmare went on. The Archdeacon appeared, unaccompanied, but managing to give the impression that others passing through the gate at the same time as himself were in attendance upon him, like the clients of a distinguished Roman. 'Flying visit,' he said to Maurice in such a loud voice that he appeared surprised by its volume himself, 'then I must be off. All going well, eh? Where's Mrs. Vicar, turning all heads as usual? Ah, James,' he greeted the Colonel, passing from Maurice with obvious relief, 'I must have a whack at that, yes, I really must chance my arm.'

A soiled-looking cloud was rising over the trees.

'Oh, blast,' Maurice heard Louisa whisper to someone, 'if it comes on to rain I shall have those Guides gathering their damned peascods all over my drawing-room.'

But it did not rain. The weather held up, and grew colder. The garden began to empty a full hour before the time of official closing; and when the last visitor had gone, Louisa invited Maurice to come into the house for a drink. He felt that she, at least, was really sorry for him; she was young, she was still in the comparative earliness of love, she felt his unhappiness rather than his disgrace.

He saw Libby leave the tent with Mrs. Hannaway and go off towards home. She had not spoken a word to him.

'I won't,' he said, 'thank you. I shall have to go and cast an eye over the takings.'

Yet he lingered when she had gone into the house, exchanging desultory words with departing helpers. Kitson would be in the tent, and he dreaded the moment of facing him.

The garden was empty, the sun had darkened. There was litter over the grass and flower beds, boards and trestles stood bare in the biting wind. To-morrow the Scouts would come in and clean everything up.

He walked slowly over to the tent and was comforted by the wave of warmth that came from it; to be warm, at least, would be something. He lifted the flap and went in. Kitson was sitting at a table, counting money. No one else was there but David who, with the rigor and stare of a tin soldier, was standing in front of him, waiting to get a word in. Maurice came forward, noiseless on grass. David, seeing him, shot out a hand as if to push him back.

He said to Kitson in a strangulated, yet almost social voice, 'It beats me how you could have done what you have done.'

Kitson looked up. 'Oh, hullo, Beattie. Half a tick, I must check these sixpences or I'll be all at sea.'

He went on counting.

'That can wait,' said David.

'No, it can't! Nineteen, twenty, twenty-one, twenty-two and six.' He wrote it down. 'Now then. What's the matter?'

'I said, it beats me how you could have done what you did.'

'About the vicar?' Kitson said heavily. 'I hadn't any choice.' He saw Maurice, and stopped.

David went straight on. 'It's uncharitable and immoral. Do you think everyone's on your side?'

'Now listen,' Maurice said, 'the least said from now on the better. I have said rather too much myself.'

'I am talking to Kitson.' David's legs were trembling; his flannel trousers rippled like a stage back-cloth in a draught. 'I have a right to talk to him, and I'm going to. For sheer lack of charity and common fellowship, for sheer underhandedness and priggishness, I have never come across anything like this. You know all the vicar's done for this church. You know he hasn't spared himself a brass farthing. He's used himself up for us and we've all used him. What have you got against him that you couldn't even leave him to sort out his personal life in decent privacy?'

The wind was rising strongly, the canvas straining at the tent pegs, flapping with a noise like sails at sea. The poles creaked; a gust, running and low, stirred the warm grass.

Kitson folded his hands before him. His forehead wrinkled. He looked honest and thoughtful, a little troubled, but not deeply so.

'That's all very fine, Beattie,' he said without heat, 'but you must realise that your own spirited sermon — not well-timed, if I may say so, though excellent in intention — forced me to take action. And I think it fair to say that, though they might have denied it, the other church officers wished to see it taken. I'm well aware that I haven't made myself popular, but I think I can bear that. You're a young chap: you ought to fight, at your age. But you are not being particularly sensible.'

To Maurice, it was as though they had both clean forgotten him. He stood outside all this, it was not he whom they were discussing, but some other man whose name he had not managed to catch.

'I am not going to put up with your condescension,' David retorted, the muscles pulling in his neck. He was red in the face, his blue eyes were moist. 'My age has nothing to do with it. To put not too fine a point on it, Kitson, you make me sick, and you'd be surprised how many other people you've made sick, as well.'

Kitson took a pencil from his breast pocket, put one finger to the point, another to the unsharpened end, and moved it slowly up and down as if measuring space. 'Yes, I think that isn't too fine a point. I think we might say it isn't.'

Maurice had a sudden sharp desire to disassociate himself from them both; or, more honestly, to move farther from David and nearer to Kitson. He was ashamed of the impulse. He was being defended out of a hot, deep affection powerful enough to conquer natural timidity; he should have been grateful for it. He was not. He wished David would shut up.

Kitson rose. Strolling round the table, he balanced himself on the edge of it and surveyed David up and down with a detached judicial stare.

'Now look here,' he said, and it was as if he had come to a decision, 'do you believe a word of what you're doing in your job? Have you ever really thought about what it means?'

'My job?' David repeated blankly.

'If you haven't thought about it, I have. You have talked to me and I've listened to you. And one thing has struck me throughout: that the whole meaning of what the Church stands for to-day and what we must expect of it has utterly escaped you.'

'I don't think——' Maurice began.

'Excuse me, but I need to talk to Beattie. I don't particularly mind being abused if I think I've done the right thing, but I prefer to be abused by people who have given some thought to what the right thing is.'

'From a layman——' David burst out.

'Now, come,' Kitson said gently, 'we are not going to argue on the basis of a *mystique*. This is not a question of theology.'

The whole tent reared with the wind, as if it would fall on their heads. Through the flap, Maurice could see grey flowers tossing, grey ghosts of paper trundling above the ground.

'The Church is having the deuce of a time to keep its end up,' Kitson said, as if beginning a lecture. 'It gets all the chances, the broadcasts, the last minutes of the old year on TV, the support of the royal family and what have you. But it is staggering along in neglect — and that is the real truth — without twopence to rub together and with about a handful of people really prepared to work for it. Lip-service — plenty of it. It's respectable again, people have to say they believe in God. But it is staggering on its feet. And it has got to stagger on till it can stand up properly, because nothing else except the Church has got any rules for promoting decent social behaviour.'

'Is that all it is to you?' David said. 'Is it just a discipline to keep the natives in their place?'

This was so violent, coming from him, that even Kitson blinked. Maurice started to speak, but was overborne.

'And if,' said Kitson, 'it did just that, wouldn't it be of inestimable value? I think it would. It has got the rules: no better rules have ever been formulated and they never will be. And if those rules are going to be put over by an organisation so rocky financially and intellectually that if it were an industrial concern it wouldn't have a hundred shareholders, that organisation has got to have absolutely clean hands. Not only have they got to be clean, they've got to look clean. So the bosses, if I may put it that way, have got to be beyond reproach.' He said, on an unfamiliar note, angry and emotional, 'Do you suppose you're the only one who likes the vicar and admires him? Well, you aren't. I do, and I don't mind saying as much to his face. But of all his admirers I am the only one who has put the Church first.'

He walked round behind the table, swept up the cash into a box, and pocketed the papers on which he had been making his jottings.

'Quite a speech,' he said drily, 'and the last of its kind. Excellent.' He gave them his kind, cold smile, and held out his hand to Maurice. 'Someone,' he said, 'had to act.'

He nodded impartially to them both, and left the tent.

For a few minutes they said nothing at all.

'You did all you could, David,' Maurice said at last.

'God, the smugness of it! I tell you, I tell you——' He did not know what to tell anybody.

They walked out on to the lawn. Louisa called to them as they passed, festively waving a bottle. Fawcett had come back from his office and was beside her, waving also. Maurice raised his hand in acknowledgment, shook his head and went on.

'To have to stand there listening to that——' David began.

'Oh no,' said Maurice, 'let's not go on about it. Anyhow, do you suppose he's really happy?'

He felt that, in this grey, tossing, littered garden where there had been such din and was now such silence, he had come to a finality. He had left behind him the last hope that perhaps, after all, he had been in the right. Kitson's disciplinary religion had little appeal for him; but at the core of it there was a hard truth. The Church held the only set of rules for most men to live by;

334

and it was vital that the hand which held them should be a trusted one.

Do you suppose, he had said to David, he's really happy?

Yet he knew that Kitson, happy or not, would sleep the sleep of the just, his clothes neatly folded, his watch laid out upon the bedside table. Some people simply did not object to doing things that would make them unhappy if they felt those things were right. There was joy and there was justification: and there were those who could make the choice between them, when it arose, without any groaning of the spirit, feeling, indeed, that if happiness were not to be their portion something just as agreeable would turn up in its stead.

'I don't know,' said David, 'and I'm damned if I care.'

Chapter Forty-nine

WESTLAKE had taken the three of them out to lunch at the most expensive restaurant the boys had ever known. They had eaten with wolfish greed in almost total silence, Dick scarcely pausing in the process, Simon occasionally flashing just beyond his mother's head a secret, wild smile. Kate was in misery. This was no good, this would never do. However hard he tried, Westlake would never bring them round.

He looked uncommonly spruce in a new navy-blue suit, bright white linen, a blue tie with a silver spot in it. His face was still puffy, but his eyes clear; he had something of the ruddy look of a countryman. He asked them if they would have coffee. Kate said yes, Simon shook his head violently and the smile went out: he might have been offered some unique and distasteful food, such as the sheep's eye at an oriental feast. Dick said, 'No, thanks. I suppose I couldn't have another Coke?'

'Of course you may. Will you have another, Simon?'

No answer.

Westlake waited till Dick's Coca-Cola had been brought, dressed up with ice, orange-peel and mint, until Kate had poured the coffee. Then he shot his cuffs and leaned forward on the table, clasping his big hands. They were very pink, the nails manicured.

He said with the appearance of ease and mastery, 'You know, Simon, old boy, there is really no point in your continuing to sulk. I am going to marry your mother: and as you can scarcely go on sulking for a lifetime, it would be sheer commonsense to stop doing so now. Don't you agree? We can all have a very decent time together, I think.'

No answer. Dick inspected a plate of *friandises* and cracked a toffee-covered cherry with a loud noise.

'Actually,' Westlake went on, 'I'd like to see you cheered up a bit before we look at the house. It is quite a nice house, and I'd hate you not to inspect it in the proper spirit.'

He thinks he is being matey, Kate said to herself despairingly, but he only sounds sarcastic, and that will get him nowhere with Simon who at a tender age is quite a master of sarcasm himself. She framed this sentence in her mind and it stood there, whole and stiff.

She said aloud, 'It honestly is a nice house. It was a surprise to me, too. I didn't know Tom owned such a thing.'

'Who used to live there?' Dick asked, showing some faint interest. He had drained his glass in a gulp.

'It's let at the moment. But I can get the people out.'

'Fun for them,' said Simon. It was almost his total contribution to the conversation up to that moment.

'Your mother's had a roughish time. I want to take care of her. You don't object to her marrying again? Because if you did——'

'It's her business.'

Westlake agreed, still with an air of cordiality, that this was so. 'You see,' he went on, 'it won't be all these years before you go out into the great world yourself and leave her standing; so it would be a pity to spoil things for her now, when she might have an easier life, wouldn't it?'

Simon said, 'It is nothing to do with me,' and this time glanced about him with such sudden forlornness that Kate thought, I can't do it. I must not do it.

'But it is. Because you will have to put up with me as a stepfather. I assure you I shan't get in the way, I'll be too busy. Well!' he signalled the waiter. 'Time's getting on.'

Dick was finishing up the *friandises*: he must have eaten a dozen.

'Isn't it your birthday soon, Simon?' This was a pretence of changing the subject.

337

No answer.

'Sixteen. Is that right?'—To Kate: 'Good God, how the years go by! You know, Simon, I could just about run to a decent gramophone, if you'd like that. I heard yours going when I looked in the other night, and, if you'll forgive me, it does make rather a bloody noise.'

Dick grinned at this, flattered at hearing bad language spoken in front of him.

'The sound-box is pretty well worn out,' Westlake said. He smiled at Kate. 'A new gramophone would be a present for you as well, wouldn't it? Or is it a case of better the devil you know——?'

Simon had flushed such a dark red that he looked wet. 'If my mother wants to marry you it's her affair. Good luck!' The flush paled to a dead whiteness. He repeated harshly, 'Good luck!'

'Oh, come on,' Dick said, 'I want to see the house. I say, I am full up!' He tapped his Adam's apple.

Kate half rose. Westlake touched her sleeve and urged her down again. 'In a moment.' He paid the bill, left a large tip. His voice changed. He said to Simon, without irony, without any touch of the *faux bonhomme*, 'Have you got something against me, or would you feel the same if I were someone quite different?'

No answer.

'Simon,' Kate murmured, 'Tom's talking to you.'

The boy raised his head. He had fine eyes, greenish, darker than Kate's or Libby's, rimmed with mossy gold. 'You both keep on wanting me to say something. I've said good luck. What more do you want?'

'I used to drink a good bit,' said Westlake, very steadily. 'I believe you heard something about that. It is all over and done with now.'

But it's not, she thought, it will never be: and she knew what life would be for her, keeping as much as she could of his drinking from the boys.

'Oh, that,' Simon muttered, as if drunkenness were a

338

peccadillo that could not possibly concern him and to which he had given no thought.

'All right.' Westlake got up now, and the others with him. 'Let's go.'

They got a taxi and drove towards Bayswater, the boys perched silent on the bucket-seats.

'*Strapontins*, a nice name.'

'What is?' said Simon.

They stopped before a neo-Georgian house in a square. Westlake marshalled them on to the pavement and they stared up.

'Shall we have *all* this?' Dick asked.

Simon scuffled his feet while the rest of them talked. So Dick was won, Kate thought, and could have wept.

Feeling the tears rise up, she shook her head violently to dispel them. Simon had wandered off and, hands in his pockets, was staring down into someone's area. 'Come here,' she called to him, her voice shaking, 'don't desert the party like that!'

He came slowly back, the smile tight and small.

'I wish I could show you over,' Westlake said, 'but I didn't tell them we were coming and they might feel it was a bit of an invasion.'

There seemed nothing more to say, either about the house or anything else, so he drove them home again. Outside the vicarage, both boys thanked him stiltedly for taking them out. Simon added, 'Very decent of you to think about the gramophone. But the one I've got's all right, and it would only be a waste of your money.'

Chapter Fifty

HE was there for the last time in the bright room; by Libby's permission, Libby's wish. For once there was no particular need for hurry. He did not have to get up and go, not yet awhile.

He sat in an armchair, Alice on the floor beside him, resting back on her heels, her back stiff, her hands clasped in front of her. They had talked it all out; there was nothing more to be said, or nothing of any importance.

Someone in the street outside might be looking up at that glowing window, envying the happiness he fancied lay behind it.

'What will you do?' Maurice asked her.

There was the usual resource of the well-to-do, she replied: she would most likely go abroad for a while. She could go to friends in Canada, or to some cousins in New Jersey.

She added later, 'It isn't really true, of course, any of it. It can't be happening.'

He said, 'I ought to go. We are only making it worse for ourselves.'

She put up her hand and laid it on his knee. He circled her wrist with his thumb and forefinger. 'You're getting thinner.'

'Don't go just yet. You shall, soon, but not just now. I have to be able to bear it, and if you went just at this moment I might break down. I don't intend to do that.'

Catching sight of himself in the glass, he thought he looked old, ugly, drained, even de-classed. In this room he was like a run-down salesman who had been asked to sit down for ten minutes to rest his feet. Even now, he was passing away from her life: the voyage had already begun.

'In a way,' Alice said lightly, 'I shan't mind. It will mean that I am not doing wrong for once. And if I can face this decently, I may be forgiven some of the other things. It is curious that though I cannot believe in God, I am continually aware of the presence of some spiritual book-keeper with a profit-and-loss account.'

He smoothed her hair, fine, short, silky, slipping beneath his fingers, and was seized by a sexual impulse more frightening than any he had ever known in her company. It was like a hot shooting pain; he felt his face blazing. He needed to make love to her, just once, for the first and last time: what could that matter to anyone but themselves? They would have it in memory always, one thing, one violent joy.

His hand stopped moving: she realised the cessation and knew what was in his mind. She stayed rigid, her eyes closed. 'No,' he heard her say as if she were a long way off, as if she were so ill that it was an effort to speak at all. 'We have done so well, so far. Let's make the last effort of all.'

He got up and left her. In the bathroom he rinsed his face with cold water, ran it over his wrists. They had done so well, so far. Even this would have to be borne.

When he came back she got up, springing easily like a girl from her crossed ankles, and kissed him. He put his arm about her waist and they stood side by side.

It was the most dense suffering he had ever known in his life, and he knew that greater lay ahead in his dark house, among the dark familiarities with which he must live from now on, all curtains drawn against some lamp that might one day spring up between the branches of the night.

'I shall always love you.'

'I shall always love you.' She paused. 'It will become bearable in time.'

'I suppose so.'

She broke out, trembling in his grasp, that she did not want him to agree: she wanted him to say, at least, that it would never be bearable, that the anguish would never pass away.

'Lord knows I shall have plenty of work to do,' Maurice said.

She quietened. 'I know. And at first we mustn't try too hard not to think about each other. That would be too much of a strain. We must think, if it comforts us.'

She was wearing an old dress of some dark striped material. She had not had the heart to do much about her appearance, this last time. She touched the brooch he had given her. 'This is mine.'

He said he had something else for her, and took out of his pocket a thin silver bracelet, old-fashioned, rather like a child's, which he had seen in a jeweller's window and had been able to afford. The thinness of her wrist had always fascinated him; he wanted to see it emphasized. He stripped off the tissue paper and clasped the bracelet upon her. She kissed it. 'Thank you.'

How long they stood together, silent and unseeing, he did not know. It seemed impossible that they should ever break silence, should ever move apart.

Then Alice drew away from him, her small round face set, no tears in her eyes. 'You'll have to go now.'

'Yes. . . .

'I can't kiss you,' said Maurice, 'even for the last time.' He meant, on her mouth: he bent and kissed her cheek, and the inside of her wrist.

She cried out, then, and struck herself on the breast.

He could give her no consolation; he had none for himself. He turned and left her, went out of her room, down the stairs, out into the road and broke into a run. He did not stop till he was out of sight of the window, and he never knew whether or not she had looked after him.

He came at last, after walking without conscious volition for an hour or more about the streets, into Vernon Square. His church stood out against such a cramming together of stars that the sky itself was silver. The chopped spire was ugly in its mutilation, it looked defeated. He found himself thinking, They will have to restore it. Kitson will have to get on to them about it.

He unlocked the church doors and went in, turning up only the chancel lights. Kneeling in his stall, he began to struggle

342

with God. Thou knowest, O Lord, I have done my best. Lord, I can think of nothing to say, I do not know how I can endure this without Thee. O God, help me.

No response. He listened hard to his own imagination, but the room was empty.

O God, help me to be kind, help Libby to make me kind. Let me be able to touch her, make my hands tender.

No answer at all.

He looked up. The sour light fell without kindliness upon the ugly choir-stalls, picked out a film of dust along the altar-rail. The flowers needed changing, they were strewing their petals.

He tried again, speaking to God in anger, trying to explain how much he had done that night, the sacrifice he had wrenched out of himself. And it won't only be for to-night, it will go on and on: there is nothing left for me of human happiness. Why is it given for us to know such a hope of joy, if it is so little in Thy sight?

No answer, no presence in the church or in himself. So after a while, exhausted, he stopped struggling, stopped think-ing, simply went on kneeling with his face in his hands, his whole being open to invasion by God, but without hope of it or even any conscious desire for it. He was aware of nothing but the hardness of the wood under his hands. He moved their position, so that he could rest more comfortably. He stayed upon his knees for an unreckonable time.

He was told that it was time for him to rise. He got up, staggering a little since he was cramped with kneeling so long, and smoothed down his clothes. Peace was upon him, he was inhabited, even as the church was now inhabited, the master at home at last.

The trees smelled sweet. There was a smell in the air that was lovely and strange, as if it might be the scent of the stars.

As he neared his own gate he thought he saw a woman standing on the corner, then fancied it was a trick of the shadows: but it was a woman after all. Mrs. Fraser in her decent black.

She greeted him, said she was glad to have run across him. She thought he might like to know that she was moving, her sister's husband had died, there would be room in her house now, and it would be better than being lonely. 'So I'll be in Fulham,' she said, 'just off the Lillie Road. I expect I'll be going to her church, it's nearer.' She thanked him perfunctorily for all he had done for her. 'Yes, it was a bit of luck meeting you, I thought it was you but I couldn't be sure. Well, cheer-oh. I'll remember you to Derek.'

She melted away, walking south.

Maurice let himself into the house. Libby came out to greet him. She had made herself very beautiful, she was trying to smile, but her eyes were haggard with anxiety. For a moment he saw her as a complete stranger, and knew the spurt of almost social panic with which one might encounter a stranger in one's own house.

'It's all over,' he said. He put his arm round her shoulders. 'Nothing like it will ever happen again, Lib, I promise you. I am sorry I have made you so miserable.'

Jerking her head round, she pressed her lips hard upon his hand. She said brightly, 'That's all right. I always had faith in you. I knew that nothing could really harm *us*. Whenever I prayed for you, I knew it would be all right. I never had the slightest doubt, not for one second.'

She stepped back. She seemed about to propose some light-hearted celebration, perhaps to dance. 'Are you coming up?'

'In a while,' he said. 'You go. I shan't be long.'

He went into the study. The boys had been using it in his absence, and Libby had not cleared up after them. Simon's trigonometry book lay on his desk, with a piece of half-gnawed chocolate weighing the page down. Dick had left Foxe's *Book of Martyrs* open in the armchair. The silence was like singing: it was that absolute of silence which is never empty, never without sound.

Maurice took up Foxe and sat down. He looked for a story he vaguely remembered, and after a while he found it: it was about Thomas Hawkes of Essex, a gentleman who had been at court, now condemned to be burned, with five others, on the 9th day of February, 1555.

'A little before his death, there were some of his familiar acquaintance and friends, who seemed not a little to be confirmed both by the example of his constancy and by his talk; yet being frightened with the sharpness of the punishment, they desired that, in the midst of the flames, he would show them some token, if he could, by which they might be more certain whether the pain of burning were so great that a man might not therein keep his mind quiet and patient. Which thing he promised them to do; and so it was agreed secretly between them that, if the rage of the pain were tolerable and might be suffered, that he should lift up his hand above his head towards heaven, before he gave up the ghost.

'Not long after, when the hour was come, Hawkes was led away to the place appointed for the slaughter, by the Lord Rich and his assistants; at the stake, he mildly and patiently addressed himself to the fire, having a chain cast about his middle, amid a great multitude of people assembled; to whom, after he had spoken many things, especially to the Lord Rich, reasoning with him about the innocent blood of saints; at length, after he had made fervent prayers and poured out his soul unto God, the fire was set to him.

'When he had continued a long while in the fire, and when his speech was taken away by the violence of the flame, his skin also drawn together, and his fingers consumed, so that all thought certainly he had been gone, suddenly, and contrary to all expectation, this blessed servant of God, being mindful of his promise before made, reached up his burning hands over his head to the living God, and with great rejoicing, as it seemed, struck or clapped them three times together; at the sight of which, there followed such applause and outcry of the people, and especially those who understood the matter, that the like hath not commonly been heard.'

Maurice thought that a man like himself, so much more obviously of the humbler creation, was a small creature to a man like this; and that what he had to offer was little enough. (It

345

seemed to him, for a second, that he ought to stop thinking while the room cleared of blown smoke and the last spark blackened.)

He had at least done what he could, had made a beginning: yet the beginning was the easiest part, with the strongest impulse behind it; the human sense of drama, perhaps, had been of no small assistance. Almost anyone could achieve the first moment. But ahead of it lay the regrets, the drag of desire to undo what had been done, the wrench of desire to swing round and go pelting down the road back. The hardest part was what had to be done alone, and in silence.

He got up, and put the book back on to the shelf. He could not keep Libby waiting any longer, he had to lie down beside her, to turn out the light and offer himself hopefully to sleep.

Well, he thought, I have just about managed to heave one hand out of the fire.

The smell of the smoke had not quite gone, it lingered in the corners of the room and in the creases of his palms.

And I can only hope, God being with me, to keep it there.

THE END